Sailing Dream Maker -
The Taino Amulets

By J.J. Reich

Published by Dream Maker Publishing, USA

First Edition, August 2025

ISBN: 979-8-9932824-0-4 (paperback)

ISBN: 979-8-9932824-9-7 (eBook)

Printed in the United States of America
For more information, visit www.sailingdreammaker.com

This book is dedicated to my parents.

To my late father, Karl, who taught me so many things. We learned to sail together. Thanks, Dad.

To my mom, Patricia, you always told me I could do anything I set my mind to. With those words, you opened the door to limitless possibilities in my life. Thanks, Mom.

INTRODUCTION

In February 2023, I became the steward of *Dream Maker*, a 1981 Ta Chaio CT-54. When I found her, she had been out of the water for nearly fourteen years, weary from neglect and on the edge of being lost forever. Her hull was sound, and her interior woodwork still carried the warmth of craftsmanship, but her systems had failed, her decks were soft, and time had stripped away her strength. To most, she was a relic too far gone. To me, she was possibility.

Even in her tired state, *Dream Maker* held a beauty that could not be erased. Her lines were elegant, her presence commanding. People who walked past often stopped to admire her. I knew then that she deserved not just repair, but rebirth. I resolved to bring her back to life—stronger, modernized, and ready to carry stories across the sea once again.

Restoration is a slow and humbling journey. Thousands of hours have been invested in sanding wood and fiberglass, replacing tanks and systems, and breathing new life into every space aboard. All the while, I imagined her under sail: how she would move through the ocean, how she would respond to the wind, how it would feel to stand at her helm as the horizon opened. In my mind's eye, I was already sailing her, even as she remained on land.

This book is the beginning of those imagined journeys. It is the first in a series of tales spun from the hours of work and dreaming that have gone into restoring *Dream Maker*. While she is not yet finished—her bottom awaits paint, her engine and helm await installation—she is close. Close to being ready to write new stories upon the waves.

1

There are many books about sailing, but most are nonfiction, including memoirs of voyages, logs of adventure, and chronicles of hardship and triumph. They are wonderful, but I found something missing—a modern voice telling fictional stories of the sea, alive with the adventure, folklore, and mystery that have called sailors to the water for centuries.

Sailing is not just a way to move from one place to another. It is a way of life, an immersion in the present moment. At sea, the destination is uncertain. The wind, the weather, and your own spirit decide the course. To sail is to accept the ocean as a companion, to let the stars and waves speak to you, to feel the same freedom sailors have known for generations.

That is the spirit of *Sailing Dream Maker*. This story will carry you to real places—Puerto Rico, its neighboring islands, and the Virgin Islands, both U.S. and British. My partner and I explored them as part of this journey, and their beauty is woven into these pages. I hope that one day you will have the opportunity to see them for yourself. Until then, may you experience them here, aboard *Dream Maker*, and let the sea invite you into its timeless adventure.

CHAPTER 1

THE PASSAGE

The sudden roar of the storm enveloped Junior Wright, drenching him in salt spray as he gripped the rails of his newly refurbished CT-54, Dream Maker. The skies had been deceptive, clear when he left Luperon in the Dominican Republic, but now a fierce squall tore across the Mona Passage. Waves crashed against the bow with a force that shook the entire vessel. Junior's instincts took over, honed by years in the Navy, as he faced the unraveling night ahead. What was supposed to be a calm solo crossing had turned into a trial of endurance and reflex, every sailor's nightmare scenario brought to life.

James Wright, Jr., callsign "Junior," retired from the Navy ten years ago, having served for twenty years. He didn't leave because he stopped loving the Navy or the lifelong friendships he developed; he had simply achieved all of his goals and decided it was time to start his next adventure—buying an old sailboat, restoring it, and exploring the world. During his time in the Navy, Junior logged over four years at sea, ironically, none of which involved driving or navigating ships. Instead, he spent all his time on aircraft carriers—Junior was a retired naval aviator. Rather than steering ships, he landed on them, day and night. Remarkably, his time flying in and around the carrier, as well as planning and executing combat missions, provided him with an exceptional understanding of rapidly changing weather conditions, tremendous situational awareness, and a calmness even in the most hectic and dangerous environments.

The Mona Passage lies between Hispaniola and Puerto Rico, a stretch of water as treacherous as it is beautiful. It's a wide, restless channel—eighty miles of deep blue where the Atlantic meets the Caribbean and currents churn like a drunkard's thoughts: unpredictable, strong, pulling you where you don't want to go. The trade winds blow steadily from the east but can trick you, shifting when you least expect, gusting up to thirty knots even at night. Squalls come fast in the Mona Passage, black clouds piling on the horizon, dumping rain and wind before many sailors have time or foresight to reef their sails. The sea can turn from calm to a boiling mess in an hour, waves short and steep, five to eight feet, sometimes more, slapping the hull like a boxer's jab.

Most sailors prefer crossing the Mona Passage at night to avoid the worst of the wind, but darkness brings its own troubles. Reefs lurk off Mona and Monito Islands, sharp as a bull's horns, and the charts don't always tell the whole truth. Currents run north or south, sometimes both in the same hour, setting even the best navigators off course if they don't watch the stars or their GPS. The passage is a test not just of skill but of nerve. Trim the sails, check the rigging, and keep one eye on the horizon for freighters that cut through like blind giants. Ships groan, the wind hums in the stays, and anyone daring to cross the pass will feel the weight of the sea beneath them, vast and indifferent.

Old sailors talk of the passage as if it were a living thing. They say it decides who crosses and who doesn't. Some make it in twelve hours with a fair wind; others fight twenty hours or more, battered and tired, cursing the day they left port. The key is preparation—a strong hull, tight lines, and a crew that knows the difference between fear and respect. It's said that there is no conquering the Mona Passage. You meet it, shake its hand, and hope it lets you pass.

When things go well, at dawn, lucky sailors see Puerto Rico's green hills rising with the sun like a promise. The air smells of salt and earth, and the sea flattens as land approaches again. It means you've made it, not because you're better than the water, but because you moved with it, listened to it, rolling with the wind and waves as much as harnessing them. The passage doesn't care about your name or your story. It only cares that you sail true.

Squalls gathered on the horizon, intent on testing both Junior and Dream Maker. The CT-54, drawn by Bob Perry's hand, is more than a handsome vessel; she is Junior's shelter on the open water, his refuge from the storm. Dream Maker is not just a boat, but a story still unfolding, her hull marked by the sweat and vision poured into her over four long years of restoration. She is a floating heirloom, a vessel that asks for care and respect, much like the wooden boats of another age. Every repair is a promise to the sea, a quiet agreement to keep her whole. She carries the weight of Junior's labor and affection, shaped by his hands and the lessons of the ocean. Built for endurance, not for speed, she moves with the slow, patient rhythm of the deep. In her, Junior seeks something elemental, the old struggle to shape a dream from fiberglass and steel, to chase the sunrise where sea and sky become one.

The gale was coming. Junior felt it in the air, sharp and heavy, and saw it in the sea, the waves building, foam streaking white. Dream Maker moved steadily under full mainsail and mizzen, her twin masts tall against the darkening sky. But the pending winds would be too much, and he was alone on the vessel. The wind was rising, and it was time to reef.

Leaving the helm, Junior relied on the autopilot to hold her course. First things first: making sure all of his safety equipment was ready and secure. Being out on the open ocean by yourself can be scary, even in calm seas, let alone with the rising seas and winds of a coming squall. He stood alone on the deck, wind beginning to gust, salt spray stinging his face. Here, every decision was a silent dialogue with the sea. Trust or adjust: that was the mantra. The harness was his first choice to trust, its webbing tight against his chest, buckles cold and firm, showing no fray, no give. What if he'd skipped testing it? The tempest could toss him over like driftwood. Then the tether, its clip he tugged sharply, the snap was reassuring in the gale, locked to the jackline that ran fore to aft, taut as truth. An unexpected slip would no longer mean a plunge into the abyss. Lastly, the life jacket, bulky but sure, hugged him like an old friend, its whistle tucked, its strobe light ready to scream in the dark, promising a lifeline if all else failed. The consequences of skipping any of these steps hung in the air, unseen but substantial, adding a new weight to each beat of the safety check.

He knelt, inspecting the jackline, fingers tracing its length, seeking weakness, finding none. The deck pitched, slick with spray, but his boots gripped like they knew the stakes—the SeaDek under his feet providing a firm and reliable base. He checked the knife in its sheath, blade keen, strapped to his thigh—ready to cut free if the sea turned cruel. The reefing lines, coiled and clear, waited for the mainsail's fight. He eyed the winch handles, secured.

Each piece of gear was a promise, a silent understanding between sailor and sea. Clipped in, Junior moved forward, the storm's voice rising around him. The mainsail stood tall, straining, but he was ready—tethered to the boat, focused on the work, alone and steady. He advanced with care, one hand for the boat, one for himself, as every old sailor knows. The mainsail pulled hard, tight as a drum. At the boom, he eased the halyard, letting the sail fall just enough. The canvas fought back, snapping and booming like thunder, but he hauled the reefing lines, drawing the sail down to the first reef. His hands burned as the lines whipped through his grip, but he tied them off, the knots holding fast. He secured the clew, lashed the loose sail, and checked the boom. Everything was set.

Dream Maker started heaving as the seas swelled—making Junior's passage back to the cockpit as slow and methodical as his move forward.

The mizzen was next. He moved aft, the boat rolling beneath him. The smaller sail was easier, but the wind was stronger now, gusting fiercely. Junior lowered the mizzen, again tying the reef points, and secured it fast. The CT-54 settled, her motion smoother, the strain gone from her rigging. She wasn't heeling as much now that both her main and mizzen were reefed, but she was still carrying too much sail forward and was out of balance.

As a cutter-rigged ketch, Dream Maker often runs with two forward staysails. Tonight, though, even with just the genoa pulling and guiding the ship through the night, it was too much. The genoa was full and straining on the forestay, pulling hard—too big for the coming gale. So Junior decided to furl some of the genoa in, rolling it up like a giant window shade, hoping to balance Dream Maker out and help her weather the conditions just a little bit easier.

Clearly, the winds were picking up, and the sea was churning, waves spitting foam, tossing Dream Maker around like a cork in a whirlpool. Junior read wind gusts on his gauges now topping 35–40 knots. Luckily, during his refit of Dream Maker, Junior rerouted all of the genoa sheets and furling lines into the cockpit. This meant he could furl the genoa without the risk of having to leave the cockpit again. Unfortunately, even in the cockpit, the wind made things difficult. Junior's skin was cold and raw—cutting from the wind and spray off the port bow as he continued on a southerly heading. He gripped the furling line, heavy in his hands, and began to pull. The Genoa fought, its canvas snapping like a whip. The process was slow at first, but with a steady haul, Junior rolled the sail in —the roller furling system grinding under the strain. When the genoa was about fifty percent furled, he stopped furling, the genoa taut but smaller, balanced for the gale. The furling line was secured, and the free line was coiled to minimize the risk of tripping hazards. It held.

Taking the helm from the autopilot, Junior felt the boat's balance. Dream Maker moved lighter now, her bow cutting the waves clean, no longer pulling to leeward. The mainsail and mizzen, reefed tight, worked with the half-furled genoa. The sea roared, the sky was black, and the boat was ready. The captain's hands were raw, shoulders heavy, but as he looked at the sails, trimmed and right, he knew they were good. The gale could come, and they would safely sail on.

Dream Maker cut through the Mona Passage, her wake trailing a ribbon of starlit water. Each ripple shimmered with bioluminescence, tiny lanterns of green and blue flickering in the darkness, as if the sea itself breathed light into the night. The glow moved with the waves, following the boat like a comet's tail, fading where the horizon vanished and sea met sky. Junior glanced back and smiled, knowing that without the storm's shadow overhead, he might have missed this quiet beauty.

Unfortunately, although she was gliding smoothly across the seas as could be expected given the conditions, the winds were directly out of the east. While Dream Maker was making excellent progress, nearly eight knots over the ground, it wasn't in the direction Junior hoped: east toward Puerto Rico. Instead of a general 100-degree course, the best easterly heading Junior could get out of Dream Maker was only about 135 degrees. This course was taking him and Dream Maker toward the Isles of Monita and Mona.

As he assessed his course, Junior's mind ran through a silent calculation. The tactical checklist was now more than just routine; it was a necessity. The winds weren't cooperating, and he felt the weight of the decision pressing. Should he adjust course now or wait for the winds to turn? Regret briefly passed through him as he acknowledged how weathered his plans were becoming. Yet, in that same instant, a deep-seated confidence surfaced, a resolute commitment to adapt, acknowledging the unpredictable nature of sailing. With the islands looming closer, his experience guided him to stay vigilant, ready to alter his strategy in a heartbeat, knowing all too well that the sea demands such adaptability. His resolve steeled, Junior kept his course steady, prepared to face whatever challenges lay ahead.

Monita, the more northern of the two islands, sat small and defiant, a mere speck of 36 acres, its shoreline cliffs thrusting up over fifteen stories, barring the sea's advance—and giving no chance for anyone to reach the island by sea. It was barren, a place of brown boobies and sparse shrubs, where the wind sang low and the world felt older than it should. No man trod there; the island kept its own counsel, untouched, unreachable, a hard truth in a soft sea.

Mona Island, bigger and more approachable by sea, still lay heavy in the Mona Passage, a slab of limestone carved by wind and waves. Its cliffs rose 200 feet above the shores, sheer and ominous, like the face of a man who had seen too much. The island was broad—twenty-two square miles of scrub and cactus, caves hollowed out like secrets in the rock. A few beaches clung to its edges, white sand soft as regret, but the heart of Mona was harsh—a plateau baked under the sun, where iguanas scuttled and the Taíno's ghosts whispered in the ruins. No man lived here, save the rangers who watched the land, their eyes sharp for the rare hawksbill turtle or the Monito gecko, small and fleeting as hope. Visitors were welcome, often with a guide. Still, it wasn't by any stretch of the imagination a hospitable site, as visitors needed to bring everything with them to survive, including not only food, but also any fresh water needed during their stay.

The water around the two islands, alive with coral and fish, marlin and sharks, was clear, deep, and cruel, hiding reefs that could tear a hull apart. Men came to dive, to hunt, to chase the wild pigs on Mona, but the islands cared nothing for them. They stood as they had for centuries—solid, silent, waiting for the next storm to break.

As the night wore on and the winds subsided, Junior made the swift decision to stop at Mona Island to anchor and rest. The unexpected gale-force winds had altered his plans, but his naval experience meant being adaptable was second nature. He saw this as an opportunity for some recovery and possibly exploring the island. With this change of course, a new phase of the journey began.

The sun cracked the horizon, spilling gold across the sea, and the air was cool, sharp with dawn's edge, just as Monita Island came into view. The island's western cliffs loomed over the horizon like the shoulders of an old giant, shrugging off the sea's whispers as the boat crept closer to the island's limestone walls. Just a couple of hours now until he would be able to drop anchor and take a break from the activities that kept him up all night.

To make things easier on the approach into the waters off Mona, Junior decided it would be best to do so under power rather than sail. This marked a strategic change from his reliance on wind throughout the night. He reached down, turned the key to the motor, and moved the throttle forward. The silence was deafening as Dream Maker's electric motor began assisting the sails. The batteries were fully charged because the propeller spun all night long, transferring the energy of movement through the seas into power in the batteries. Each turn of the propeller was smooth, unforced, the blades slicing through the current, driven by the boat's silent speed. And now she would leverage the energy harnessed overnight—still running silent.

With power now through the prop, Junior began the process of lowering the sails. First, the Genoa. Full and bold, it strained against the dawn's breath. He freed the sheet, let it snap free, then furled it slowly, the roller grinding as the sail coiled tight. The bow settled, cutting clean through the swell. Silence returned, broken only by the sea's quiet pulse. Next, the mainsail.

Junior eased the halyard, steady, the canvas shuddering as it fell, heavy with morning dew. Hands worked fast, folding it tight to the boom, ties cinched firm against the waking breeze. And finally, the mizzen. It stood stubborn, catching the young light. He slackened the sheet, lowered the halyard, and gathered the sail, working quickly and precisely, stowing it neatly as the boat swayed softly beneath him. The deck felt lighter, the hull eager.

Dream Maker stood ready, bathed in the new day's glow, free from the shade of her sails.

Now, under power, Junior turned his ship back toward Mona Island and the cove just west of Playa Sardinera.

The CT-54 hummed forward under electric power, her motor whispering steadily. The cove drew near, its waters calm, the depth sounder ticking down—twenty fathoms, then fifteen, then ten, and finally eight. Based on his preparation, that was as good as Junior would get today. Anything less would bring him too close to the reefs and rocks protecting the beach. He eased the throttle, feeling the boat slow, her bow cutting clean through the glassy swell.

Once the motor stopped, Junior stepped to the foredeck, sure-footed as the boat rolled very slowly on the morning swell, the electric windlass waiting like a faithful hand. The anchor, a plow heavy with purpose, hung poised. He hit the switch, and the windlass growled, chain rattling out, spilling into the sea's embrace. The anchor struck bottom, bit hard, and held. He returned to the helm, nudged the motor into reverse, the prop spinning soft as the chain pulled taut, testing the hold.

The scope was proper—six to one, fit for the cove's quiet. He turned the motor's switch off, and silence fell, broken only by the water's murmur against the hull. Dream Maker rested, anchored firm, the morning still, the work done. Junior stood alone, the day open before him.

CHAPTER 2

THE DISCOVERY

Junior woke from a short nap, mind clear, body ready. The cliffs of Mona Island waited off his bow, close enough to taste the salt in the air. He knew the rules—no one set foot on Mona without a permit, not with its beaches and caves guarded by law and time. Most people planned months ahead, but Junior figured he'd try his luck, see if he could get a day pass, even if it were just for a few hours or the next morning.

He settled into the cockpit, sun warming his shoulders, and pulled up the number for the agency that watched over Mona Island. Starlink had paid for itself a hundred times— no matter how far he sailed, the world was always within reach. He punched in the number for the DRNA, the keepers of Mona, and waited. The line was clear, but the voice that answered was a rush of Spanish, quick and sharp, words tumbling over each other. Junior tried English, speaking slowly and carefully, asking if they spoke his language, then explaining what he needed. The reply came faster, more clipped; the only words he caught were "permiso" and "Mona." His Spanish was a handful of old phrases, worn thin by time, and he knew better than to try them now. That only made people talk faster, and he'd end up more lost than before.

He tried again, his voice steady but tight. "No entiendo," he said, then repeated "permit" and "island," hoping something would click. The woman on the other end grew sharper, her words clipped and final. He caught "solicitud previa" before the line went dead, the silence sudden and heavy. Disappointment hit hard. Mona's cliffs loomed off his starboard side, close enough to reach, but out of bounds without the right words. The island waited, caves hidden in shadow, and Junior knew he would not wait for permission that would never come.

He set the phone down, its silence a taunt. Walking forward, he let the sea's hush fill his ears, Mona's cliffs rising sharp and bright from the water. Junior had always kept to the rules and respected the boundaries others set. But this island was more than just a forbidden beauty to him. Its tales are centuries old, stories of pirates, secret caves, and hidden treasures passed down through generations of sailors. To Junior, Mona was not just a speck on the map; it was a part of history, a link to something larger than himself. This island was older than any law, its iguanas and turtles outlasting men and their paper permits. To land without permission was to trespass, to risk harm to a place that asked only to be left in peace. He gripped the rail, knuckles white, weighing what was right against what he wanted, and also what he felt he needed to reclaim.

Still, the island called to him, its quiet louder than the wind. Junior lived for places like this, for the chance to see what others missed. To turn back now would be to lose something he might never find again. The caves could hold secrets or nothing at all, but he would never know unless he set foot on shore. He thought of the rangers, the risk, the shame if caught. But the dinghy rocked at the stern, ready, and the tide was kind. He could be quick, careful, and leave nothing behind but footprints. The cliffs seemed to watch, and the pull grew stronger—a man balanced between what was right and what he needed to know.

The sun was high now, a bright yellow sphere beating down on the sea's edge at Playa Sardinera, the sailboat swaying gently at anchor. The dinghy hung from davits, its hull slightly scarred from other adventures, swinging just above the water. He checked the outboard's fuel, the oars stowed neatly, the painter coiled tight, and slung a life jacket over his shoulder, worn as an old coat. He worked the davit lines, slow and sure, lowering the dinghy until it kissed the swells, soft as a whisper. Climbing down, he kept low, feeling the sea's pulse under him, and untied the painter from the sailboat's cleat. The motor coughed to life, a low growl, and he turned east, eyes on the pale beach, Mona's cliffs standing hard against the dusk.

The island waited, silent but for the waves' slap and the sharp cry of gulls. He sat at the helm, steering wheel in hand, the dinghy slicing the water, current pulling like a quiet grudge. The shore drew close, sand white, rocks dark where the tide gnawed them. Near the beach, he cut the motor, tilted it clear, and let the swells carry him. He rowed once, twice, the oars biting deep, until the bow scraped shore. Stepping into cold shallows, he tugged the dinghy up, tying it to a gnarled root. Mona stood wild, empty, the air thick with salt. He paused, breathing the silence, the sea patient behind him.

Junior stepped ashore on the western end of the island at Playa Sardinera, his Tevas crunching coral sand. He

16

barely had time to tie off his dinghy before he was greeted by two young rangers in a UTV. Neither could have been much older than twenty-five, but there was no doubt they were in charge. It must have been evident to the rangers that he wasn't Puerto Rican—possibly his more relaxed attire of cargo pants and an Omaha Soccer T-shirt screamed 'Mainlander,' or it was simply the Home Port of St. Augustine, FL, splayed across the back of Dream Maker. Their eyes held a mix of pride in their role and an underlying frustration that often accompanies dealing with unprepared outsiders. Junior wondered if they felt a sense of duty to protect the island's fragile beauty from those who might not appreciate it. Despite his intentions, he realized the island was in their care, and it wasn't his to claim without respect.

"Buen día, Señor. Soy Junior."

"Good day, sir. Do you have a permit for the island?" the taller ranger asked.

"Oh, great, you speak English. I was hoping you did, because I just used all the Spanish I know," Junior admitted sheepishly. Then he answered, "No, I do not." He continued, "I hadn't planned to stop, but the storm last night caused me to steer further south than I had originally planned, and I need a rest before finishing my crossing to Puerto Real. I did try to call the Mayagüez DRNA office this morning, but the woman on the other end didn't speak English. And well..." He sagged his head. "It was a pretty quick call, to say the least." As he spoke, a thought flickered: what could he offer the island in return for its beauty and peace? The idea of giving something back, a gesture of gratitude rather than just slipping cash, echoed in his mind, casting a new

17

light on his presence here. But he quickly pushed it aside, focusing instead on the immediate conversation.

At that, the rangers exchanged glances, then burst out laughing. The first one—who'd asked about the permit—grinned and said, "You must have been lucky enough to get Carmen on the phone. She doesn't speak English, and she doesn't always hand the phone off to someone who does. That is, if she is in a bad mood." He nodded toward Junior. "Is it just you on your boat?"

"Yes, it is. If it's a problem, I'll turn right around, take my dinghy back to my sailboat, and sail off at first light tomorrow morning," Junior offered.

The other ranger, silent until now, finally spoke. "No need to do that. I'm sure we can work something out. We're allowed up to one hundred people on the island on any given day. And because it's still very early in the season, we only have a little over thirty people here."

That was his cue. Junior pulled out a couple of $100 bills from his pocket. He wasn't going to offer anything too quickly, but as he heard "We can work something out," the ranger's lips curled, a thin, knowing twist, like a cat with feathers still caught in its whiskers. Junior handed each of them a crisp new bill. "Will this work?" he asked.

Just like that, the first ranger responded, "Gracias, Junior. Que tengas un gran día en la isla de Mona." They turned and walked back to their vehicle, then drove away.

Junior thought to himself, the trail waits—better get going before it gets too late. The main trail on the island is a two-track scar cut by men long dead, running five miles

18

from west to east—from Playa Sardinera to the lighthouse on the eastern tip. No fresh water flows on the island, and no voices carry, so you live and die based on your own capabilities, knowledge, and equipment on Mona. Rangers watch from their post, but you're alone with the island's truth—they aren't here to rescue you, only to ensure you respect the island and all its natural inhabitants. Mona is home to over 150 endemic species, including the Mona ground iguana, the largest native terrestrial lizard in Puerto Rico, highlighting the island's rich biodiversity. So Junior carried his water, heavy, a gallon for the afternoon, and moved out, legs steady on the dolomite crust. To hike Mona is to meet something old and hard. The trails don't forgive the careless—men have died, lost in the caves or baked dry under the sun. Junior moved deliberately, a primitive map he had printed before leaving in his hand, feeling the weight of what he carried. It's not a place for talk or hurry. It's a place to walk, to see clearly, to know the earth's bare edge.

The land is dry, cacti clawing at the sky. It's hard to believe this island is in the middle of the Caribbean. Mona ground iguanas, old as stone, watch visitors pass, eyes unblinking. The trail climbs gently, then levels, and you walk through heat and humidity that presses like a hand. Caves gape in the earth, dark mouths with Taíno marks scratched deep—men who fished and prayed here before Spain came. Junior paused, sweat stinging, and peered into one. Cool air rose, smelling of salt and time.

The five-mile trek each way across the island was more than he wanted out of his day. Other trails called, shorter ones, leading to the caves on the western part of the island. He chose one that appeared to take him north toward

Cueva del Diamante. This path was shorter but much less trodden, as the vegetation sprawled low and stubborn across the trail. The plant life on the island is a dry tangle of xerophytic shrubs and cacti clawing into the limestone. Subtropical dry forest, thin and tough, clings to the plateau, its leaves hard, waxy, bitter to any beast that tries to graze. Higo chumbo cacti leaned heavily with fruit, their spines glinting like barbed wire in the sun. Sparse grasses whispered in the sea wind, and invasive pines, their needles choking the sand, fought the native scrub for root room. Whereas most vegetation Junior was familiar with was soft and lush, everything on Mona was a hard green—inflexible, shaped by salt and scarcity, with no soft edges, only survival. The problem wasn't the rainfall on the island; it rained enough on Mona for most tropical plants to thrive. The real issue was that the ground simply didn't hold the fresh water long enough for most plants to survive—just those capable of enduring long periods of dryness. Even a couple of days in the sun and heat would leave most plants wilting, or even dying, from drought stress.

The trail north was a test—sun and heat pressing down, sweat running in rivers. But the land opened up, cliffs rising two hundred feet above the Mona Passage, the water below a hard, bright turquoise. As he neared Cueva del Diamante, the old guano cave, the world widened—limestone and sea colliding, waves breaking against stone, the horizon stretching out forever. The cave's mouth was framed by tough island plants, the air thick with salt and the promise of old stories. Every step was hard, but the view was worth it—raw, wild, and untouched.

Junior reached the entrance of Cueva del Diamante and came to a stop. Beyond it, the sea pounded the cliffs, white foam rising, the sky clear and endless. It was a hard thing to see, this dark hole against the bright water, and it pulled him forward. He felt the weight and history of the island engulf him, old and quiet, like a man who has seen too much and says nothing.

Inside, the air was cool, wet, heavy with the smell of stone and old guano. Light faded fast, and his flashlight cut shadows on high walls, smooth and jagged, shaped by years he could not count. Stalactites hung like teeth, and water dripped slowly, somewhere deep. The floor was uneven, slick, and he moved carefully, Tevas scraping. It was silent but for the squeal of bats and the echo of waves, far off, and he stood small in the dark, alone, feeling the cave's age pressed against him, steady and immovable.

There were rail beds for mine carts, long gone, when the cave was tapped for bat guano, that traversed the cave. Junior followed the one that appeared to lead deeper into the cave. He followed the rail bed north a couple of hundred meters through winding tunnels. Occasionally, there was light shimmering in from his left as the path split with an opening toward the sea to the west. At every step, Junior was filled with an overwhelming sense of awe at the thought of the thousands of years it took to create such beauty through erosion.

After hiking through the cave for about fifteen minutes, dragging his feet slightly to keep his balance on the wet stone, the darkness began to feel like it was pressing down. Shadows shifted under his flashlight, and the drip of water marked time, slow and steady. Occasionally, the flashlight flickered, casting unexpected shapes on the walls. His mind played tricks, turning each distant drip into a footstep echoing in the cave's vastness. Junior felt it was almost like the cave was coming alive around him. Then, a faint glow off to the west, away from the trail. Junior chose to take a chance and moved toward it, legs tired, heart steady.

The opening was tremendous—the light hitting him hard, bright and sharp. The sea roared below, waves breaking on cliffs, white foam climbing. The sky was vast, blue, unbroken, standing at the edge of the island's raw heart. Warmth flooded his skin, and the breeze carried salt and green. Junior stood still, eyes burning, feeling the world open again, big and fierce, after the cave's tight hold. It was like waking, or coming up for air, and realizing how small you truly are.

As he climbed out of the entrance to the cave, Junior noticed the shadow of the island starting to stretch across the Caribbean Sea. It was time to start back south toward Playa Sardinera, but before he did, he wanted to trek just a bit further north to El Uvero.

The beach, El Uvero, is a thin crescent of white sand, carved sharply against the turquoise sea. Waves break steadily, low and relentless, their foam hissing on the shore. The sand lies smooth, untouched, save for the tracks of crabs and the driftwood scattered like bones. It's not that people haven't been here—it's supposedly a common stop for some island tours—but it doesn't take long for the wind and rain to clear any trace of them. Beyond, the water stretches wide, clear to the horizon, where sky and sea bleed into one. The sun burns hot, and the wind carries salt, stinging the face. It is a place clean of men, raw and quiet, holding only the sound of the waves and the weight of the island's silence.

The trail down to the beach is treacherous. It's a trail only in name, with only a couple of broken branches every five to ten feet to suggest someone has been here before. After some thought, it might not be a human path at all. Instead, perhaps a wild goat or even a Mona ground iguana made it; no self-respecting tour guide would bring clients down this path. But almost as soon as he had the thought, Junior's right ankle rolled on a loose rock hidden in the tangle, and he fell hard. The earth was sharp, limestone biting through vines and scrub, tearing at his palms as he hit. Thorny branches clawed his arms and legs, holding him like a trap. The air was hot, heavy with dust and the green smell of crushed leaves. Junior lay there, breath short, the island's silence pressing down, unbroken but for the faint hum of insects and the distant sea. Pain stung clean, and the sun glared, unforgiving, as he rose, blood on his skin, the island watching, indifferent. As he sat up, cradling his ankle, a thought pushed through the haze of pain: maybe it was time to question why he always had to defy the rules and test his own limits. The island's indifference served as a stark reminder of his own vulnerability and the thin line he tread between bravery and recklessness.

Junior looked down at his ankle to make sure it was okay. He could feel a dull throb, steady as a drum, pulsing as he tried to put weight on it. Relief mixed with resignation as he thought to himself, I'll be able to continue, but I'm definitely not going to push things by continuing down to El Uvero. The damage was done; a rolled ankle is quick, merciless, and will continue to irritate until it is properly rested and healed. Frustration simmered as he realized the pain would be a new companion on his journey back to Dream Maker, one that would be stubborn and whisper to him of his own fragility. Still, as he continued looking down, surprise overtook the pain when he saw that the rock he stepped on was more than a rock. There was a petroglyph on it. He picked it up; it wasn't much bigger than his palm, but it was big enough to move and cause his injury. Curiosity momentarily eclipsed discomfort as he examined the marks on the stone, simple, worn by wind and time, yet stubborn, holding their meaning tight. It looked like a turtle, cut clean, no waste, no flourish— something his son would have drawn in kindergarten, he thought. The sun beat down, and the petroglyph stared back, its story hard as the rock itself. And on the back, there was more. It looked like it could be letters. Possibly an 'R' and a 'C'. Standing there, holding this relic, Junior found himself wondering about the hands that carved it. Who were they, those carvers of history? What responsibility did he bear in moving this piece of their past? The ethical dilemma gnawed at him. Should he pocket the stone, carrying a piece of the island with him, or leave it, respecting the silent dialogue between the past and the present? The weight of these thoughts made the stone heavier in his grasp, his decision yet to be made.

CHAPTER 3

RETURN AND REFLECTION

The markings on the stone were old, carved deep and worn by time, possibly Taíno, their lines faded but still speaking. As Junior turned the stone in his hands, it was as if a thread connected him to forgotten history, whispering a past he was not allowed to let slip away again. He wondered how it had stayed hidden for so long. No guide would ever come this way, he realized, thinking back to the rough trail and his own fall. The stone felt like a bridge between him and the island's ancestors, a responsibility tugging at his soul. Should he leave the stone where it lay, letting it vanish into the earth for another hundred years, or carry it back to Playa Sardinera, risking the questions that would follow? He felt the weight of it, not just in his pack but in his mind. This was a piece of Taíno history, a story that belonged to their descendants, to a museum, and to anyone who could see its worth. But how could he make sure it would be cared for, not lost or forgotten? The question circled in his head, pulling him back to memories of Iwo Jima, the island he had explored during his Navy days.

During his time stationed in Japan, Junior spent more than a month on Iwo Jima, which was scattered over a period of two and a half years. The island was nothing like it had been during the war. Now, the black sand lay quiet, wind whistling through empty caves. Yet, as Junior walked those shores, he could almost hear the echo of artillery thunder and smell the acrid bite of gunpowder in the air, pulling him back to 1945 when the place had been fire and chaos, the ground torn by war, thousands of Americans and Japanese fighting and dying in a single month. The hills still held the scars: bunkers half-buried, rusted shell casings, broken gear, rifles left behind. Today, Iwo Jima stands as a monument, tightly guarded by Japan, visited only with special permission. The old airstrip remains, used mainly by the US Navy for carrier landing practice. The caves, deep and silent, keep their secrets.

Iwo Jima was the perfect place for pilots to train, to practice landings before heading back to the carrier after weeks on shore. There was no city glow here, none of the light that washed out the night around the Kanto Plain. The darkness was complete, the horizon gone, just like it would be on a carrier at sea. The isolation helped, too—no distractions, no families waiting nearby. Pilots could focus on what mattered: getting ready to land on a moving deck, day and night, the ship cutting through the ocean at twenty knots or more.

Most of Junior's days and nights on Iwo were spent either in the landing pattern or at the end of the runway, watching, grading, and training other pilots. Downtime was spent exploring the island: climbing Mount Suribachi, playing golf (a story for another time), or spelunking. Just like on Mona, the caves were filled with history, albeit from centuries later. Hundreds of WWII artifacts from both Japanese and American soldiers—bullet casings, survival equipment, tattered clothes, even old rifles and pistols—

were scattered throughout. As hosts, Japan allowed its Naval guests to explore, but requested that nothing be removed. Their superstitious nature and respect for the circumstances of the artifacts made them fearful of the spirits of dead soldiers should their belongings be removed without an appropriate ceremony. Unfortunately, most US sailors and pilots who came to the island ignored the simple request, taking with them some trinket—something to show their children and grandchildren. Junior remembered holding several items in his hands... and his thoughts always returned to the thousands of men who gave up their lives on the island. Each time, he put the item back where he found it—honoring both the Americans and Japanese who fought for a piece of land that happened to be big enough for a runway.

The stone in his hand felt different from the relics on Iwo Jima. It wasn't about which was more important, but about what would happen if he left it behind. He realized that if he left it where he found it, the stone would likely be lost forever in the surrounding terrain. And that settled it— he would take it with him. Decision made, he looked down the trail toward Playa Sardinera, knowing another hard choice waited for him at the end.

The walk back to Playa Sardinera was more challenging than the hike out. His ankle throbbed with every step, the sun burning down, sweat stinging his eyes. More than once, his foot threatened to roll, but he caught himself each time, feeling a sharp twinge and pushing on.

As the sun dropped lower, Junior caught sight of Dream Maker, anchored and small against the vast sea. Her white hull curved in the light, masts rising bare and tall. Gentle waves rocked her, the last sunlight turning her lines gold.

She waited, tethered to the island by her anchor, the sea stretching out in every direction.

All the way back, Junior kept turning over the same question: give the stone to the rangers, or take it to Puerto Rico and find a museum that would care for it. Near the end of the trail, he passed the mouth of Cueva Negra, the Cave of the Dead. It was marked on his map, but he'd skipped it earlier, too eager to reach Cueva del Diamante. Now, with a bit of daylight left, he paused, curiosity pulling him toward the dark opening.

Cueva Negra is a dark wound in the rock, its mouth wide and silent. Inside, the air was cool, heavy with the scent of damp stone and the passage of time. The walls, blackened by soot, bore scratches—ships and gallows etched by hands long gone, Taíno and Spanish, their marks a quiet argument in the dark. Waving his flashlight in the darkness, one engraving stood out: plura fecit deus, a sailor's faith from centuries past. He stood quietly, the world around him gone. He thought back to his lone Latin class in college. "God made many things," he believed.

Junior never put much stock in signs, but he trusted the quiet voice that surfaced when the world went still. The words on the wall settled the matter. He wouldn't leave the stone for the rangers. He would take it, learn what he could, and make sure it found its way to those who would value it. With that, he left the cave and made his way down the hill to the beach, where his dinghy waited.

By the time Junior got back to Dream Maker, darkness had surrounded them both. The long couple of days caught up with him, and all he wanted to do now was crawl into bed and get a good night's sleep. He tied off the dinghy, went below, and headed straight aft to the Captain's Cabin.

He remembered getting undressed, but not much after that —he was asleep within seconds of his head hitting the pillow.

The sea was black, and Dream Maker cut through the water, sails taut, the night clean and sharp with stars. The crew, two faceless individuals, moved easily, their voices low, the boat alive under their feet. Then the wind turned cruel, a thunderstorm breaking suddenly from the dark without warning. Fifty-knot gusts screamed. The boat heeled hard, the deck slanting wildly, water rushing over the rail. As chaos erupted around him, Junior caught sight of the lone lantern swaying gently in its bracket, casting a pool of calm, golden light amid the fury. They fought to reef the sails, but the storm was faster, knocking the boat down, spars groaning, canvas flapping madly. Junior felt a surge of fear and determination; this was what he missed: the challenge and the unity of facing danger with his crew. The crew held fast, their hands bleeding on the lines, the sea and sky one raging thing. No time to spill the wind, only to endure.

The storm was everything, the boat and its crew a small, brave thing against it. Each cursed and pulled, their faces wet with salt and rain, Dream Maker trembling but not broken. The night roared, and they worked in silence, knowing the sea cared nothing for their skill or fear. The sails hung tattered, the wind still howled, but the boat rose again, stubborn, cutting the waves. They stood on deck, soaked and cold, watching the storm move off; the stars were gone, the darkness complete.

"Junior!" One of the crew yelled out in a voice that sounded familiar.

Junior woke sharply, heart pounding like a fist against his ribs, the sheets damp with sweat. The room was still, too still, the silence heavy after the storm's roar in his mind. His breath came quick, eyes wide, searching the dark for the boat, the crew, the screaming wind—but there was only the ceiling, the wooden strakes he had memorized in the long nights in the berthing. Fear clung to him, cold as the sea's grip, mixed with a strange ache, a longing for the fight, the raw pull of the lines, the boat's stubborn rise. He lay there, chest tight, half in the dream, half in the quiet, knowing he'd face the sea again, real or not. The question wasn't if, but rather when. In the haze of early morning, out of nowhere, Junior suddenly thought he recognized the voice that called him in his dream. An old friend he hadn't seen for years, but what would she be doing in his dream? It was a voice he hadn't heard or even thought of in months, Faidh's teasing laughter mingling with the wind. The night faded, and the next morning slowly arrived, the dream lingering as he woke.

Not in a rush to get underway, Junior woke up around 8:00 a.m. the next morning, wiping the sleep from his eyes; the lingering effects of his dream still weighed heavily on his mind. His focus shifted to the practical: he had already checked the tides in Puerto Real. He knew a 10:00 a.m. departure would get him to the dock just as the afternoon winds died down and the tidal currents subsided—all he would have to do was average about 5.5 knots across the rest of the Mona Passage. That was a very leisurely pace for Dream Maker, if the forecast held: winds out of the northeast at 10–12 knots and seas at 3–6 feet (20-second interval)—long rolling swells that would rock the boat like a cradle.

So, at 10:00 a.m., Junior turned on the key of his electric motor, grabbed his remote, and headed to the bow. As a solo sailor, Junior needed all the help he could get, and the remote was a significant investment. With it, he could remotely and wirelessly control the windlass to pull up the anchor and move the boat forward with the engine—all from the palm of his hand.

Slowly, Junior motored Dream Maker forward, easing tension on the anchor chain. Once the anchor chain was slack, he engaged the electric windlass—a steady hum cutting the morning's quiet. When there was plenty of slack on the bridle, Junior unhooked it first from the anchor chain. Then he turned around, unhooked both bridle ends from the Samson posts that stood firm and tall on Dream Maker's deck, and fed the lines through the hawse pipes. Once the lines were clear, he motored again slightly to keep the anchor chain as close to vertical as possible. He then engaged the windlass and stood at the bow, hand on the switch, the chain taut and dripping with water. Finally, Junior could feel the anchor break free from the seabed, sand falling away, water slapping the hull. The motor whined, pulling hard; each link of the chain clanked as it coiled in the locker. The boat rocked gently, free now, drifting slowly with the current. The morning air warmed his face, sharp and clean. The windlass worked steadily, no rush—just the grind of metal and the pull of the sea. The anchor rose, scarred and heavy, home again.

As soon as the anchor was settled into the bow roller, Junior turned off the windlass and started the boat slowly forward. He remotely set a westerly heading in the autopilot to take Dream Maker out to sea, away from Mona, and the bow began swinging to port until the hot sun was at his back. He then finished his work at the bow, properly securing the anchor, the windlass, and all the lines that were used while at anchor, and headed back to the helm.

It was time to sail—set the main and the genoa, turn south, and finish crossing the Mona Passage.

Now well clear of the island with room to maneuver, Junior turned back to the northwest, directly into the wind, and began setting the sails. He knew he didn't need to turn into the wind to set the sails, but it made things easier— and anything that made life easier when sailing solo was fine by Junior. Once into the wind, he hauled the halyard, and the main rose slowly, the canvas snapping as it caught the breeze, taut and full against the mast. The genoa unfurled next; Junior turned right to a southerly heading to get around Mona before turning east to Puerto Rico. The genoa filled with air first, its sheet pulled tight, the sail blooming wide, white and clean, pulling the boat forward with a quiet surge. Then the mainsail snapped as it filled with the powerful winds, and Junior set the rigging for a port broad reach. The deck tilted, the sea hissed, and the rigging hummed low, a sound like a man breathing hard. The sails set, the boat leaned into the wind, cutting the water clean, moving steadily toward the open blue. Happy with the rigging, Junior reached down, turned the motor off, and looked up with a deep happiness. He was looking forward to a smooth ride all the way to Puerto Rico.

By the time he reached the coast, the sun hung low, painting the sea gold. Dream Maker moved steadily, her hull cutting clean through the swells. Alone, he stood at the helm, the wind sharp and salty on his face. He switched on the electric motor, its hum soft but sure, a quiet strength waking beneath the deck. The genoa came down first, heavy canvas flapping as he hauled the furling line, muscles tight, hands calloused on the lines. The sail wrapped tightly around the forward stay, neatly stowed to keep the bow clear. Then the mainsail. He turned into the wind to take the pressure off the sail. The main came down smoothly, despite the weight of the sail pulling hard against him as he lowered it, reefing ties snapping in the breeze. Dream Maker slowed, her sails gone, but the motor thrummed steadily, pushing her toward the inlet at Puerto Real, the shore faint and the buildings still a blur in the distance.

The channel reached for the harbor like a hand extended in welcome, the water flat and clear as glass. He gripped the wheel and turned off the autopilot. His eyes were sharp on the channel markers, red and green buoys showing him the way. The tide was slack, and Dream Maker cut through the water like butter, her keel deep and solid. Light ripples slapped the hull, and he held her course, feeling the sea's pulse through the rudder. The rocks loomed close, jagged and black, but he knew the path, had run it in his mind before the approach. The motor purred steadily, and the boat slipped through the inlet's jaws, passing harmlessly,

Puerto Real's harbor opening calm and wide before him as he slowed even more, taking in the beauty of the harbor.

The town of Puerto Real, a quiet bustle of tiny homes and sea-based businesses, hugged the shore. Mangroves stood thick, green, and low, their roots clawing into the muddy edge on both the north and south walls of the harbor. Small houses, faded pink, turquoise, and yellow, sat close to the water, their rusty tin roofs glinting from the setting sun. A lone pelican skimmed low, wings steady, slicing the still air. In the distance, the hills rose gently in all directions, green and soft, rolling into the haze. The air smelled of salt and wet earth. The boat moved steadily, the town growing closer, simple and waiting.

At the T-dock, handlers waited, their voices carrying sharply over the water, calling lines and distances. Junior eased Dream Maker in, the motor soft now, just enough to nudge her close. The handlers moved quickly, catching the midship line he tossed, their hands sure, pulling her tight against the dock's worn wood. He threw the stern line, and they secured it, the boat settling gently, no longer her own but held fast. He turned off the motor; the only sound was that of the key clicking to the off position. Then, only the squeak of fenders and the lap of water against the hull. The men nodded, their work done, and he stood on deck, alone again, the boat still, the sea behind him, Puerto Real quiet under the fading light.

That's when he saw her walking down the dock. He had to wipe his eyes once, because what he saw was the beautiful face of a woman he didn't expect to see here in Puerto Rico. In fact, it was a face he hadn't seen in years, and her appearance now triggered a rush of surprise and curiosity about why she had come to find him.

"Hey, Stranger, want a Stella?" yelled the woman.

"Why, of course, Faidh, I'd love one, as long as you're joining me!" Junior enthusiastically shouted back as he jumped off the boat, ran to the woman, and gave her a huge embrace. Ear-to-ear smiles filled both their faces.

CHAPTER 4

THE REUNION AND PIRATE TALES

Faidh Dragan was a second-generation Irish American, and Junior had known her for a little over five years. She was tall, long-legged, with a mane of strawberry blonde hair and a kind of restless energy that seemed to spill out of her wherever she went. There was always a big smile, a warm hello for everyone, as if she'd never met a stranger. Yet, there was a subtle moment, almost imperceptible, when her smile lingered just a second longer than expected, her gaze flicking to her phone before meeting anyone else's eyes. By trade, she was a yacht broker, but at her core, she was a traveler, an explorer, someone who belonged to the world more than any one place. Perhaps it was this nomadic spirit that kept a distance, something unspoken and unreachable, like a faint scar hiding under a sleeve. Junior first met her the day she showed him Dream Maker, and from that moment, friendship came as naturally as the tide.

They kept in touch over the years, exchanging the occasional text or a quick photo from wherever the wind had taken them, sometimes just a birthday wish or a holiday greeting. Since Junior bought Dream Maker, though, their paths had only crossed once. That was three years back, at the Annapolis Boat Show, after Junior had spent months gutting the old boat, stripping out tired systems, and making room for something new. The show was crowded with vendors and sailors, and of course, Faidh was there, right in the thick of it. They found time for lunch, a couple of drinks, and the easy conversation that always seemed to pick up right where it left off.

Finally, Junior ended their long reunion embrace and said, knowing he wanted to make the most of their time together, "Let me finish tying off Dream Maker, and then we'll sit at the bar, do drinks, dinner, and catch up."

Faidh leapt aboard, tossing him a line, her grin like a ray of sunshine breaking through the clouds. "Absolutely."

He caught it, chuckling. "Could use you out there, you know," pointing toward the open ocean. "It gets mighty lonesome sailing alone."

Faidh stopped and looked directly at him, her eyes dark and knowing, holding him fast. That smile could buckle a man's knees, leaving him dizzy, as if he'd drunk too deeply from a bottle of good whiskey. Wanting to see if he'd invite her on board, she slyly said, "Say the word, sailor. I'll run your deck."

Junior's legs went to jelly as he reached for a lifeline. Faidh's laughter burst out—wild, infectious, brightening everything between them.

Junior tied off the final line on a cleat. He stood up, finished the Stella that Faidh handed him when he hugged her, and said, "Come on, let's go have something to eat and tell sea stories all night long."

She vaulted off the boat, landing lightly, all legs and energy. As they walked the dock, boards groaned underfoot and the sea's breath filled the air, salt-heavy. Junior nodded toward a shack jutting over the water, its neon flickering. "Pizza suit you? 9 Barrios is right there. They say the sunset's worth seeing from the patio. Mojitos aren't bad either."

"As long as they're strong," she teased, her voice playful, as if she knew something he didn't.

At 9 Barrios, the wood oven glowed in the corner, its warmth drifting out to meet the cool breath of the sea. Behind the bar, a woman moved with the easy confidence of someone who knew every secret the island had to offer. Her smile was slow, sly, the kind that could soften your heart and make you wonder what she knew that you didn't. Rum drinks slid across the counter, strong and sweet, tasting of Puerto Rico and long nights. Junior and Faidh took a table out on the terrace, where the sea pressed close, waves lapping at the pilings, the sound as steady and quiet as a confession.

Out in the harbor, a shipwreck caught their eyes. The water's surface, smooth as glass, was broken by the hulk of a half-sunk vessel, leaning into the tide like a drunk who'd lost his way home. Its hull, rusted and thick with barnacles, jutted up jagged as a broken tooth. Overhead, gulls wheeled and cried, their voices sharp in the salt-heavy air. The ship's bones, once proud, now splintered and creaking with every wave, seemed to whisper stories of storms and the men who braved them. It was a grave, but not a quiet one, still clinging to the harbor's secrets, daring anyone to guess what it once carried before the sea took its due.

Junior's eyes left the wreck. He leaned across the table. "Ever hear of Pirate Roberto Cofresí?"

She could tell he was excited to ask and, of course, wanted to goad him. "No, what position does he play?" Faidh's lips curled.

He laughed, shaking his head. "No, smart ass. A real pirate. 'Argh, matey' and all."

Her brow arched. "Should I know him?"

"Not necessarily, but I thought I'd ask. I found this yesterday on Mona Island." He slid a stone across the table, its initials, R.C., etched deeply, face up. "I think this stone might have been his."

She snatched it, turning it in her hands. The turtle petroglyph on the back side of the stone caught the bar's dim light. "This? Looks like my daughter's art project from first grade," Faidh laughed, then continued, "Or Mayan, maybe. But not your pirate Robbie Contussi's."

"Cofresí," he corrected, voice low. "See the R.C. on the back? I searched it on the way in from Mona. This guy was pretty famous and marked everything he touched."

She tossed the stone back, smirking. "And you think this stone is going to lead you on an adventure? To some possible treasure? And I suppose the turtle represents the name of his ship, huh?"

He didn't answer, just held her gaze. It was a loaded pause, thickening the air with possibilities neither dared to name. Yet, beneath his calm exterior, Junior felt the weight of what he might be risking. There was a thrill to the adventure, a chance that the stone could lead somewhere unexpected, but also a worry—a concern about the time and effort he might waste, and the possibility his pursuit could risk his reputation as nothing more than a fool's errand.

"So, what's your play, treasure hunter?"

Junior looked over at the bartender and yelled, "Excuse me, have you ever heard of Pirate Roberto Cofresí?"

The bartender looked up at Junior, her earrings glinting. "¿Pirata Cofresí? Sí. Local outlaw and hero. He grew up around here."

Junior grinned, triumphant. "See? He's famous. This stone's his."

Faidh rolled her eyes, but her smile betrayed her. "Was, you mean? You're chasing ghosts now?"

He chuckled at her comment, then thanked the bartender and ordered a couple of mojitos. She started making the drinks, muddling the mint and lime in the glasses, but was clearly trying to eavesdrop.

"Yeah, I'm chasing pirate turtle ghosts—sounds like a damn kids' cartoon or something. Actually, I'm confused by the stone. The turtle appears to be a Taíno petroglyph, but that makes no sense if the R.C. does stand for Roberto Cofresí. Cofresí didn't live until 300 years after the supposed Taíno genocide by the Spanish in the early 1500s."

"You are just making this shit up, aren't you? You're just asking me to pick on you, right?" Faidh smiled.

The waitress brought their drinks to the table.

Faidh leaned back, mojito sweating in her hand. "Enough pirates. This is boring me. I'd like to hear about you— what's with Dream Maker? You go first. What's new with you?"

"Well, I certainly don't want to bore you. As you can see, Dream Maker is now my full-time home. My kids helped me launch her back in September. We shook her down off the Jacksonville coast and then sailed down to Fort Lauderdale, where they both abandoned me."

He smiled at the thought. The last thing they would do is abandon him. His daughter and son, though, both had to get home and back to work. Junior was grateful they made time to help him for two weeks. Out on the open ocean, just the three of them, sailing and living together on Dream Maker—it was the best belated birthday gift.

Junior continued, "Then I set off solo across the Gulf Stream. Sailing through the Bahamas and Turks was a journey I loved - the water seemed to get prettier with each passing island. One night, right at sunset, the wind began to pick up, and Dream Maker and I were starting to get tossed around like crazy. It was so cool, reefing her and watching her steady herself right out - like the wind hadn't changed a bit. There are times I'm bummed that I'm out there all by myself, but not because I need someone else, but rather, because I would love to have someone to share it all with."

Faidh smiled, eyes intent on Junior, "I can understand that."

"Then, about a week ago, I stopped in Luperon. It was supposed to be a short stop to refuel and re-provision. But it turned out to be four days before a weather window opened up to cross the Mona Passage. And as it turned out, waiting didn't help. The weather turned crappy within just a couple of hours. Dream Maker handled it like a champ. She is everything I had hoped she would be. And she is ready for anything."

"Like you," Faidh said, her grin softer now. "Built for it."

41

He met her eyes, said nothing. The waves lapped below, steady as a pulse. Then he asked, "So what's new with you?"

"Oh, you know me. I'm just here for a good time—finding fun in everything I do. I flew down for a survey on a 70s-era custom catamaran—a very cool boat that has survived half a dozen hurricanes here in Puerto Rico. It's a simple boat, but solid and well-maintained. That was yesterday in Fajardo—the only place with a marine lift capable of hauling out a cat that size. To be honest, it's serendipitous that I was even here when you arrived. I'm only out here on the west coast introducing myself to all the marinas, dropping off business cards and brochures, trying to drum up new business around the island.

It's actually my first time at this marina. I was chit-chatting in the office with the Marina Dock Master, and lo and behold, I heard you call in on the VHF. I didn't recognize your voice at first, but when I heard the name of the boat coming in . . . BOOM! Here we are!" She finished with a big smile, arms splayed out, palms up, with the bravado only Faidh could pull off.

"Lucky break for me," he said, and meant it.

Just then, the bartender walked up and asked Junior, "Do you want to learn more about Pirata Cofresí?"

"Sí," replied Junior, using all the Spanish he could muster.

The bartender leaned closer as she spoke with a hint of urgency. "There is an old man who lives in town who knows all about Pirata Cofresí. His name is Domingo Montoya. He's the local Cofresí expert and loves to tell pirate stories to anyone who will listen. But you'll want to meet him soon —he hasn't been well lately, and there's talk he might be moving to live with family in another town." Junior's interest piqued further at this bit of news. "Where do I find him? Do you have his address or a number?" he interjected.

"I don't know where he lives, but I do know where he is all day, every day—right down the street, sitting in a folding chair outside the Restaurant Brisas del Mar, usually with a cooler beside him and a Medalla in his hand. I guess he's an old friend of the owner. He's a local landmark," answered the bartender.

Before she walked away, Junior ordered a couple of wood-fired pizzas—one for each of them. For Faidh, a mushroom, olive, and green pepper pizza; for Junior, just a Margherita. And he asked her to bring another round when she brought out the pizzas.

"Those'll be right out," the bartender said as she headed to the kitchen.

Faidh had to get in one more dig. "Oh, you are such a simpleton, aren't you? A Margherita pizza." She laughed. "Just like a little boy—just cheese and sauce, huh? No wonder everyone calls you Junior."

He smiled sheepishly.

They ate and drank, swapping stories about their lives and grown children, the conversation easy and unhurried. There was a comfort between them, the kind that comes from old friendship and shared miles. It felt, in its own way, like coming home.

Just then, Junior yawned and cursed himself for it. He didn't want Faidh to think he was bored. It had been such a perfect evening.

"I guess it is getting late," Faidh said.

"Damn it," he muttered, smiling. "Not bored. Just the sea catching up."

At this point, they were the only two left in the restaurant. Earlier, there was a boisterous cruising family with two teenage daughters eating dinner, but they left over an hour ago.

Faidh laughed and stood.

Junior walked to the bar, paid cash for the bill, and tipped heavily.

"Where are you staying?" he asked.

"Thank you for tonight, Junior. You are always so nice to me. I'm staying in an Airbnb just down the road. Why do you ask?" Faidh replied, her voice sly, slightly buzzed.

"Just curious. I didn't know if you wanted to come back to Dream Maker. There are plenty of staterooms." Junior replied, wanting to show hospitality, but never exactly sure what Faidh was thinking, doing his best not to send the wrong signal—even though he was sure thoughts of Faidh Dragan would likely keep him up all night. Faidh hesitated, her eyes flickering with a hint of something unspoken. The air hung with possibility, leaving Junior unsure whether her reluctance was a boundary or a temptation masked behind her words.

"I'm good," she replied, smiling and giving him a long, deep stare.

"Can I at least walk you back to your Airbnb? I'd hate for anything to happen to you."

"Yes, that would be nice."

They walked along the waterfront, the town quiet around them, most of it asleep. Starlight spilled across the docks, broken here and there by the yellow glow from an open window. Their footsteps and the distant sigh of the sea were the only sounds. Junior slipped a hand into his pocket, feeling the stone's weight and its cool surface, which grounded him amidst the night's calm.

"Do you have any plans for tomorrow?" Junior asked.

"I was planning to visit another marina in Cabo Rojo. Then I was going to drive north toward Aguadilla. There's a lot of fun on the west side of the island, but not many marinas. Most are on the east and south sides, except those in San Juan. But I'm not in a hurry. My flight out of San Juan isn't for three days. What are you doing tomorrow, Sailor?" she asked, hinting she was open to changing her plans if something interesting came up.

"If you're up for it, I'd love for you to join me when I meet the 'pirate expert' in town. I want us to share this adventure—it might be an experience we'll both remember."

At her boutique hotel, a low building with a tiled walkway, they stopped. She said, "Here I am," as she started walking away from Junior, up the walkway, seemingly ignoring his proposition.

She abruptly stopped, turned back, stepped close again, and hugged Junior. Her warmth lingered. "You're amazing," she whispered, breath soft against his ear. "I'll text you."

They held the embrace longer than either meant to. When she finally stepped away, her hair caught the starlight, and he felt the loss like a chill. "Good night, Junior."

He lingered, watching her unlock the door, hope caught in his chest. "Don't make me wait years again to see you," he said, voice barely above the night's hush.

Her smile flashed over her shoulder, then she was gone.

CHAPTER 5

THE DOM

The next morning, Junior stirred in the dim cabin, not ready to get up, the gentle rock of Dream Maker lulling him back into a deeper sleep.

The calm was shattered as the sea around him turned violent, waves crashing over the deck like thunderous fists. The boat heaved and groaned, her hull straining against an unnatural storm that seemed to rise from the depths. Junior gripped the helm, his hands slick with salt and fear, scanning the horizon for land that never came. Shadows twisted in the spray, and from the chaos emerged a figure—tall, cloaked in tattered sails, eyes burning like coals under a tricorn hat. It was Cofresí, the pirate legend made flesh, his voice cutting through the gale like a cutlass.

"Turn back, fool," Cofresí snarled, his form flickering as if woven from mist and memory. "The amulet is mine, cursed to guard what the sea has claimed. Continue on this foolish adventure, and death will swallow you whole—your boat splintered, your dreams drowned in the abyss." Junior lunged forward at the pirate, shouting defiance. Still, the

pirate dissolved into the waves, leaving only echoing laughter and Junior falling into the sea, the taste of blood in the water. He looked up and watched the boat pitch wildly before it was pulled under by the waves. All that could be felt was the cold embrace of the ocean closing in.

Junior jolted awake, heart pounding, the cabin's quiet sunlight mocking the terror that clung to him like wet canvas.   As he sat up, Junior noticed a blood spot on his pillow, just then realizing there was a lingering metallic taste in his mouth. He put his hand up to his mouth and noticed he was still bleeding - apparently, he had bitten his lip during the nightmare.

That's when he noticed his phone with a notification on it - a missed message from Faidh - and quickly the nightmare faded into the depths of his mind.

"Heading north to visit another marina. I'll be back later this morning. Let's plan on lunch together, and then we'll visit the Pirate Guru."

That was half an hour ago, he realized. Perfect. He moved to the head, washed his face, and pieced together a light breakfast. As he ate, his eyes swept the cabin, hands gathering stray clothes and tucking gear away with the practiced efficiency of someone long at home on the water.

He texted Faidh, *"Come by DM when you're done. I'll make us a lunch, and we can walk to see the Guru when we're ready."*

His pulse quickened when three dots flickered to life in the message window. He told himself she must have been waiting for his reply. Then the dots were replaced by "*kk.*" The uncertainty of her response unsettled him briefly, but

47

his mind clung to the memory of their goodbye hug the night before, still warm in his mind. In that hug was a glimpse of something deeper—a promise of connection or a fear of distance, he wasn't sure which. But whatever it was, it was enough to set his heart alight with hope and yearning.

It was shortly before noon when Junior heard a knock on the hull of Dream Maker.

"Request permission to come aboard, Captain?" came Faidh's giggling voice.

"Come on board, you silly girl. You're always welcome on Dream Maker." He heard Faidh's shoes thump as she kicked them off on the side deck, then sensed her energetic steps as she climbed into the cockpit.

"Where are you?" she called.

"Down in the galley, making lunch. Come on down!"

Dream Maker's salon exuded sturdy grace, where teak gleams under soft light. Leather seats squeak faintly, offering a warm embrace. The air carries a faint tang of salt, a constant reminder of the sea beyond. With the sun streaming through the windows, this is a place to face the horizon without pretense.

Its beauty, after all these years, took Faidh's breath away.

"I forgot how beautiful this boat is. It's like stepping into something out of a magazine—inviting you to sail around the world in her arms."

The steady clink of knives on the counter drew her attention. She turned to see Junior's hands at work, focused and sure, giving the greens a final, practiced toss in the bowl.

"I made us a chicken Caesar salad. I thought I remembered you loving salads."

"Sounds perfect." She stood there, just staring at Junior, beaming.

"We can sit here in the dining area, in the salon, or up in the outdoor dining area I had built since the last time you saw her."

"Let's sit up on the deck, in your new space. I can't wait to see it!"

Aft of the cockpit on Dream Maker lies a designer teak table, broad and true, folding down when the sea calls it to rest. It holds six comfortably, so with just the two of them present, it felt overkill. The benches are firm, but the cushions yield, molding to whoever finds them, as if carved for him alone.

"Wow, this is beautiful! Didn't this used to be a storage locker?"

"Yes, it was. The wood in it was rotted, so I took it down. Rather than rebuilding it as it was, I wanted to do something a little more fun."

"I'd say you definitely pulled that off. This is gorgeous."

They ate in easy rhythm, forks tapping quietly against their plates. Conversation drifted between them, unhurried and natural, as if carried on the tide. Junior found himself slipping into the tranquility of the moment, yet beneath the calm, he felt a flicker of worry about the future—what did this easy companionship with Faidh mean for them both? There was no need for pretense, no roles to fill—just themselves, honest and unguarded, with a cool breeze slipping beneath the soft cover stretched from the mizzen.

The ocean moved below, steady and silent, a presence felt more than heard, like a truth that needed no words.

Junior cleared the dishes with the same quiet efficiency he had brought to everything at sea, stacking plates and silverware, making space for Faidh to attend to her business on her phone. Faidh glanced at the screen, her stomach twisting as her mother's name flashed—another plea for help with her endless demands. Why now? Can't my family handle one crisis without involving me? She forced a smile, stepping away, her voice low and clipped as she murmured assurances into the phone. The adventure with Junior felt so close, yet this tether from home yanked her back, a quiet storm brewing inside her. While scrolling through messages, she recentered her focus as she returned two calls about the survey that had brought her here. Each answer was brief and certain, her eyes meeting Junior's now and then with a steady, reassuring nod before she ended each call.

Junior watched her return, brow furrowed. "Everything okay?"

Faidh waved it off, a bit too sharply. "Just some family stuff—nothing I can't ignore for now. And it looks like the buyers of the boat that brought me here are accepting it - so we are going to go to closing."

Junior nodded, "That's great news!", focusing on the business piece of her response, but his eyes lingered, sensing Faidh might be building a small personal wall between them. The moment passed, but a subtle tension hung in the air as they finished cleaning up after lunch.

They stepped off Dream Maker, boots thudding against the dock. Junior lifted a hand to shade his eyes, studying the sky where heavy storm clouds gathered over the mountains of Puerto Rico. He nodded toward the darkening

50

horizon as he spoke to Faidh, watching her out of the corner of his eye for her reaction.

She smiled, her words light but sharp. "That's fine. I'll take your shirt for an umbrella if I need it."

As they approached Restaurant Brisas del Mar, Junior and Faidh saw an old man sitting in a webbed yard chair, its nylon strands sagging under his slight weight, a chair that had held him through countless afternoons like this one, outside a steel building whose green paint had chipped away from years of salt air. His face was lined by sun and time, his eyes dark and steady. He wore a tilted straw hat and a guayabera shirt, yellowed but clean. His hands, gnarled as mangrove roots, rested on his knees. The air was thick with the scent of rain, and he sat still, watching boys kick a ball and women call to one another in Spanish. He did not speak, but in his stillness was the weight of years, of hurricanes endured, of fish hauled from the deep, of nights under distant stars. The building behind him groaned faintly in the breeze, and he nodded, as if they understood each other.

Junior spoke first, "Are you Domingo Montoya?"

"Si. Soy Dom."

"Hablas inglés, Dom?"

"Si...I mean, yes, pequeto." He said, holding his index finger and thumb close together.

Junior looked at Faidh and rolled his eyes slightly.

"Buen día, Dom, soy Junior y esta es Faidh." He pointed to Faidh, who was carrying a package. "Is it true that you are the local expert on Pirata Roberto Cofresí?"

"Si. No. I dunno. I know plenty 'bout him, mucho, and I like tellin' them pirate stories. But expert? Nah, I no call myself that."

"Can you tell me what you do know about him? I was told that you like Medalla. So I've brought you doce Medallas if you can help me with information about Pirata Cofresí."

"A'ight, I help you, eh, but no need for medalla, no. I love talkin' 'bout Pirata Cofresí, ese hombre." He sat there grinning a near-toothless grin, hesitating for effect. "But since you bring them cervezas for me, eh, I drink with you bof, happy, sí." And took the bag from Faidh's hands.

The old man opened the twelve-pack of cans, a master at breaking down the packaging, and took out three beers. He opened one for himself, took a big swig, and handed one to each Junior and Faidh.

Faidh just laughed, "I guess it's five o'clock somewhere."

Faidh and Junior each opened their beer and took a sip.

"I start wit the basics 'bout him, eh, then you ask questions if you want, 'cause I dunno why you wanna know 'bout Pirata Cofresí. ¿Bueno, sí?" Dom shared as he took another big drink from the can.

"I think so.", quizzically replied Junior. "Go slow, if you would, it's a little hard to understand you, k?"

"Ok. Pirata Cofresí, he born here in Cabo Rojo, raised here too. Since a little boy he love the sea, you know. Always happy listenin' to them sailors, their stories right here in town. He love fishin'. He learn how to make money carryin' fish, produce too, to other towns 'long the coast." Dom paused to swat at a persistent mosquito buzzing near his face. He chuckled softly, then tapped his can of beer, letting the hiss echo briefly in the air before continuing. "His parents, they no from Puerto Rico, but him, he soak up the island culture, eh. Stories say he wish he was Taíno, from the blood of Puerto Rico, but him not. His adventures when him young, explorin', that's how he know every port, every cove 'long the costa of Puerto Rico.

Roberto Cofresí, he start sailin' on El Scipión, eh, with him his cousin, who was the capitán." Dom gestured with his hand, mimicking the waves and the movement of ships at sea. "That cousin, he teach him how to, how you say, navigate dem seas...and how to lead men. Cofresí, he crew on El Scipión, two years maybe, before he say, 'I wanna be capitán him own ship.' He wanna use what he learn and go for his own treasures.

Pirata Cofresí, he no like them big ships, no, not like other piratas gettin' bigger ships when they can. He like small, fast ships, with small drafts. This let him sail more rápid than anyone chasin' him, usin' his knowing of the waters, of them shoals, them coves all 'long Puerto Rico costa and the islands 'round it. He was a master at escapin', even when them authorities think they got him trapped. Never doubt, if he needed to, he leave his ship, flee to land, and hide for as long as him need, no problem.

Cofresí, he rob ships under any flag, no matter, eh. Many times, he fly the Spanish to trick him target, then he attack. He stay much 'round the Mona Passage, but also go to East Coast of Puerto Rico if his contacts in the ports say, 'Ey, good treasures there.' He know him knowledge of the passage give him advantage over them big European ships passin' through, carryin' treasures and gold from South América, and even island to island."

Dom took a moment to let all of that soak in while he finished the first beer and took out a second beer.

Junior found himself not just seeking understanding, but an answer shadowed by urgency. The mystery of the stone tugged at him with a tension he couldn't quite place, like a storm on the verge of breaking - wondering if someone else, some treasure hunter, might be out there looking for the same artifacts. Junior dismissed them initially, but now felt a sliver of doubt behind each laugh.

"Wow, I think I got most of that," Junior said, his expression shifting to serious contemplation. Although Cofresí's history was easily accessible online, what he needed was more profound knowledge, folklore that could reveal the true meaning of the stone in his pocket. "Can you tell me anything about this?" Junior showed the stone to Dom.

"Wow! You find one dem amulet. That be amazing." Dom's eyes lit up seeing the amulet.

"I guess. What do you know about it?"

Dom continued, this time with energy and excitement in his voice - like he was a little boy, getting a bicycle on Christmas morning, almost finishing the second beer in a single gulp. "Like I say before, Cofresí, he a master of escapin', sí? And accordin' to legend, it say one time, Pirata Cofresí was bein' chased, almost trapped and caught. He make promise with Juracán, the Taíno God of Storms. You know him, Juracán?" He paused for a moment to let Faidh and Junior catch up.

Faidh and Junior looked at each other quizzically, both shaking their heads no. "We don't know who Juracán is."

"Juracán is God of Storms, spirit of biggen storms… You know Hurricanes, Maria, Fiona, you know? He is a Taíno spirit."

They both nodded, and the old man continued with his story. Dom put down his second empty beer and picked up another; apparently, he didn't want the beers to get warm.

"Cofresí, he beg Juracán, 'Make a big storm to scare them pursuers away.' He promise Juracán, 'If I escape, I leave all my treasure in a secret cave, and get bohitius, them taíno priests, to do ceremony to honor you, with four amulets, each with RC mark on the back.' Stories say that hurricane that ripped through south Puerto Rico and the Mona Passage, in September 1824, was really called by Cofresí. He escaped capture, but his ship, it get broke, he drifted to La Española, DR today, where they catch him and put him in prisión. But he escape. Him always escape. Then they catch him and prison again. Final, he escape one more time, they say with bribe to them guards, and he steal a new ship. He and his crew sail back to Isla de Mona.

Even though Cofresí swear to Juracán, with a promise to honor it, them amulets never make it to him secret cave where he keep him gold. No ceremony happened, nada. Soon the Americans catch Cofresí and he not escape, take him a San Juan, where they convict him and shot him. Bang, Bang". The old man pointed his index finger at Junior and Faidh, and shot them like with a gun.

Legend Cofresí no keep his promise, and that make Juracán angry, eh. That's why them Hurricanes they come through Caribbean every year in summer.

Stories say them amulets, they spread 'cross the Caribbean, each one on a different island, in one of Cofres'ís hideouts. Cofresí split 'em up, eh, so nobody find his treasure. And, people say, he left him daughter a letter telling her where the amulets are, but nobody believe she find them. I hear that if them amulets get back to the cave with his treasure, and a Taíno ceremony happens, like him promise to Juracán, he gonna be finally happy again and let go his grip on them annual storms and show where Pirata Cofres'ís Treasure been lost."

"No more hurricanes?" Faidh asked.

"Si. No tormentas."

"Do you know where we can find the rest of the stones?" asked Junior.

The old man started laughing. "Eh, if I knew, I go get them amulets myself, pa' mí."

"Right. Stupid question," Junior said.

"Legends say, when you find one amulet, you got every knowledge you need to find them all, even the cave where Cofresí hide him treasure."

"Unless this turtle is some clue, that doesn't help me at all. Cause the RC on the back doesn't help at all. Do you have any idea what the Turtle is supposed to mean?" Junior was a bit frustrated with what he was hearing.

"No, you know more than Dom, eh. I thought, maybe, the answer gonna be easy once you find one amulet." Dom laughed, finishing his third beer.

"Can you give us any insight where we might look for the other three Amulets?" asked Faidh, finding herself curiously engaged after hearing the old man's stories.

"Ha," chuckled the old man, "Where you find this amulet, maybe that give you help for the others, no?"

"Sure," replied Junior. "I found it on Mona Island."

"In a cave, you say?", surprised by the thought that the stone was from Mona Island.

"No, I was hiking and fell as I rolled my ankle on a rock. And when I looked down, I found it. "

"Out in the open, on trail? Very rare, eh. No story say them amulets just lyin' there on a trail. You find it like that, amigo?"

"No, I was off the main trail. I was walking from Cueva del Diamante to El Uvero."

"¡Caramba, eso es incredíble! Maybe, eh, the spirit de Cofresí send you to find that amulet. You think so, amigo?""

"I don't know about that. I didn't hear any voices telling me where to go. I was exploring the island and fell. I saw the stone and picked it up. Now, I'm just trying to understand exactly what it is that I found."

"I think that turtle, it's a Taíno zemi, sí? But that's all I can know, eh. You gotta talk with a bohitiu, a sacerdote Taíno. A Taíno priest. He gonna tell you what that turtle signifies, what it mean."

"Where do I find one of these Taíno Priests?"

"Jayuya, that's La Capital Indígena, full of Taíno espíritu. The Festival Nacional Indígena, it happen every noviembre, three days, celebratin' the Taíno cultura—music, danza, comida, artesanías, and them ceremonias. This weekend, it is. That's when they light the Fuego Taíno, make the pueblo come alive with yukayeque village and all. You should go, find a bohitiu there, a sacerdote Taíno, at the festival. They know the secrets of them zemi, like your turtle. Maybe they tell you what it mean, how it connect to Cofres'ís amulets. Nemesio R. Canales Plaza, that's where it's at. You go, ask, maybe you find the next clue for them other amulets."

57

"Fantastic. I'll figure out where that is and go there."

"Thank you so much for your time." Faidh demurely smiled her appreciation.

"Wait, before you go to Jayuya, you should see the cueva de Pirata Cofresí and his statue, eh. They not in Jayuya, they in Cabo Rojo, not too far, by the coast."

"He has a monument? And a cave?"

"Cofresí, he a héro local, eh. They say he like Robin Hood of pirates, stealin' from rich, helpin' the poor. Don't know if it's all true, but it's a great story, no? The cave, it's in the Refugio de Vida Silvestre de Cabo Rojo, near the Playa Buyé, north of Boquerón. Legend say Cofresí hide his treasure there, one time, with them stalactitas and stalagmitas, beautiful but mysterious. The statue, it's in Boqueron, part of Cabo Rojo too, but close, some say it's hard to find, in a park with a pond, not too much signs. You take PR-100 southwest from Plaza de Recreo José De Diego, then PR-102, 'bout 2.5 millas total, follow signs to the Refugio for the cueva. For the statue, ask locals, 'cause it's hidden. Worth it for the history, amigo. Sí, if you go to that cueva de Cofresí, take much water and a light, eh. That place, it's scary and wild, with many bats." Dom flaps his hands like a bat, "No wanna get lost or stuck out there."

"Do you think there is another stone there? Is it worth going to?"

"Eh, maybe you right, amigo. Lots de Puerto Rican kids been pokin' 'round that cueva de Cofresí, huntin' his treasure and they find nothin'. But maybe for you, Amigo. That first amulet, it show itself to you, no? Maybe the second gonna do the same, quién sabe. That Refugio de Vida Silvestre de Cabo Rojo, where the cave at, it's no all comercial like other caves. It's pure, natural, still got that mystery. You go, take that water and light, and keep your eyes open, eh."

"Gracias. We really appreciate your stories. It's fun to hear local folklore from the people closest to it."

"Oh, if you find the stones, eh, you gotta come back and tell me, amigo. Promise!"

"We promise."

Rain began to fall as they made their way back to Dream Maker, the first drops cool against their backs. With each step, the downpour gathered strength until they were running through puddles in the marina lot, the sky opening above them. Junior stopped, laughing, pulled off his shirt, and tossed it to Faidh, who caught it with a flourish. They jogged the last stretch together, breathless and soaked, water streaming down their faces, laughter echoing in the rain. As they stepped onboard, the familiar scent of wet teak mingled with the salty air, and above, the distant rumble of thunder reminded them of the journey that lay ahead. Dream Maker swayed gently, ready for the next adventure.

CHAPTER 6

THE STORM BREAKS

Junior and Faidh stood dripping wet in the cockpit, their clothes clinging to them like second skins, the acrid scent of brine mingling in the air. Above, the storm clouds churned violently, casting an eerie green hue over the water that mirrored the turbulence churning within them. Rain poured down all around them, hammering against the deck in a deafening rhythm that matched their racing hearts.

"I have dry clothes down below if you want to get dry."

"I'd like that, thanks. I feel like a drowned rat."

"The most beautiful drowned rat I've ever seen," he said under his breath, but Faidh heard him.

Junior bent to open the hatch, sliding back the companionway lid. As rainwater ran down his spine, doubt flickered briefly in his mind. Was he willing to risk the friendship that had been his constant anchor? But then Faidh's fingers traced his back, cold and electric, chasing away his hesitation. He straightened, turned to her, caught a handful of her hair, and drew her in until her chest pressed against his. He kissed her, the storm forgotten for a moment.

Rain hammered the deck. The boat rolled under their feet. Faidh's lips were warm on his cold skin. She pressed closer, gripping his shoulders. Her knuckles were tight. The world shrank to rain's sound, her heated breath, the salt's taste. He pulled back, searched her eyes, deep with fear and longing, words unspoken.

"You're shaking," she said, her voice low, almost lost in the storm. She was completely aware of what had just happened, not for a moment second-guessing it.

"So are you." He touched her cheek. Water streamed down his fingers, a shiver sparking between them. The boat groaned against a wave, and they stumbled, hands clutching. Her blouse clung to her, almost transparent now. He could see the beautiful curves of her body, each outline reminding him of the desire he'd harbored for so long. His chest ached with the realization—years of wanting her, nights spent longing for this moment pressing between them. As the boat steadied, Faidh felt a warmth blooming within her, a contrast to the chill outside. The scent of the sea and the sound of rain seemed distant, eclipsed by the quiet electricity between them.

They moved down the companionway, the air below chill but dry, with a soft smell of varnish and vanilla. He handed her a towel, then a dry shirt—his own, too big for her. She took it, her fingers brushing his, and he felt the jolt again, like lightning in his veins. She turned away to change, and he watched the curve of her back, the way her wet hair stuck to her neck. He wanted to touch her again, to pull her close and forget the storm outside.

"You've always been there," she said, not turning, her voice steady but soft. "All these years, and I never said it."

He stepped closer, not touching, just near enough to feel her warmth. "I didn't either. I should've."

She turned then, the shirt hanging loose, her eyes searching his. The boat swayed, and she fell against him, her hands on his chest. He held her there, his heart loud in his ears, louder than the rain. They didn't speak. They didn't need to. The years of waiting, the tension strung tight between them, snapped in that moment. He kissed her again, harder this time, and she answered with a hunger that matched his own.

The captain's cabin isn't big on Dream Maker, and the bunk is smaller than a queen, but it was enough. They moved together, clumsy at first, then, finding a grace unique to them, the storm outside faded to a dull roar. Her skin was chilled by the rain but warmed beneath his touch, radiating heat like the sun on a calm sea. They didn't speak of tomorrow, or what these moments meant, or the years they had spent wanting. The present consumed them, a fierce intimacy defined not by words, but by every heartbeat and breath they shared as the rain continued to fall.

Her heartbeat thudded against his chest, quick and strong, echoing the sea below. They paused, her breath uneven, her fingers pressed into his back. Light filtered through the portlights, shadows moving across her face, eyes half-closed, lips parted. She looked at him, silent, a calm that spoke more than words. He wanted to tell her how often he'd thought of her, how many times he'd stopped himself from reaching for her hand. The words stayed put, heavy as an anchor.

She leaned into him again. Her lips brushed his neck, soft and deliberate, and the world shrank to the feel of her. The salt on her skin, the creak of the boat. They moved to the bunk. The space was too small. Their knees bumped.

Their laughter was soft and fleeting. The storm was theirs now—not just the rain, but the years, the desires, the fear of what came next. Her hands found his face, pulling him closer. He felt the weight of her gaze, heavy with everything they'd never said. He kissed her throat, her collarbone— long and hard. The pulse there was quick under his lips. Her skin was sweet and salty all at once. She arched against him. Her breath caught. He held her tighter, as if he could keep her from slipping back into the friend she'd always been.

The boat rocked, and they moved with it, their bodies finding a rhythm older than the sea. Her fingers traced the lines of his back, slow and sure, and he felt the years peel away—the distance they'd kept, the walls they'd built. She whispered his name, just once, and it was enough to unravel him. He buried his face in her hair, breathing her in, the damp scent of her mingling with the rain. They were not gentle, but they were careful—each touch a question, each answer a promise neither could speak. Sunlight flickered in for a second, and the shadows in the cabin grew long, wrapping them in a world where only they existed.

They sank into the bunk. Their limbs knotted, the boat's sway a hush below. Her head pressed into his shoulder. Each warm, slow breath traced his skin. He pulled her in, arms holding tight, the weight of their past thick between them. Silence pressed in, providing a haven of relief and longing that had finally been released. Years of unspoken love flickered bare. Her fingers curled, seeking his heart's thump. He pressed his lips to her forehead, a vow sealed in warmth. Rain faded to a hush, and their breathing merged, steady as the tide. Just as sleep began to find them, a low groan from above reverberated through the cabin, a reminder of the storm-worn boat and the uncertainty of the journey ahead. The peace they tasted was new, yet the lurking worry about the noise hinted at the challenges that could test their newfound bond. The world was slipping away: only the close heat of their embrace and love rising, wordless and sure, between them.

In the dim light of the cabin, they lay together. The rain slowed, a soft patter now, and the boat rocked gently. When she woke again, she didn't know how long they had slept, but her head rested on his chest, her breath steady, her fingers tracing slow circles on his arm. He stared at the low ceiling, the wood grain blurred in the half-light, thinking of all the times they'd hung together, laughed together, even across the miles. He wondered why it had taken so long, why it had taken the rain.

"We can't go back." Her words were raw, carrying the weight of their meaning. She didn't lift her head, didn't look at him.

"No," he said. "We can't." The words sat heavy in his chest, marking both an end and a beginning. The friendship they'd shared was gone, replaced by something raw and uncertain, thrilling and a little frightening. He didn't know if it was better or worse, only that it was real, and it belonged to them.

She shifted, propping herself up to look at him. Her hair fell across her face, and he brushed it back, his fingers lingering. "I don't want to lose you," she said. Her eyes were steady, but there was fear in them, a shadow he hadn't seen before.

"You won't. I'm not going anywhere. I think I've always been right here," he said, the words heavy but straightforward. He pulled her close, and they lay together, the boat rolling gently with the leftover swell, rain tapping softly on the deck. The world outside could wait. For now, there was only this: her warmth against him, the hush after the storm.

She lifted her head and kissed him again, fiercer than before. It felt like a door opening, one they'd both wanted but never dared to cross. Her lips pressed hard to his, her hands pulling him close, as if she could hold him there forever. He answered, fingers tangled in her hair, holding on like she might slip away. The kiss was its own storm, fierce and deep, carrying all the years they'd kept silent. They broke apart, breathless, foreheads touching, eyes meeting in the dim light. No words, just the sound of their breathing filling the cabin.

She settled back against him, her body fitting into his like it had always belonged there. His hand rested on her hip, feeling the rise and fall of her breath, the warmth of her skin. The boat rocked gently, and the rain was now a distant murmur, a soft curtain around their world. He traced the line of her shoulder, moving slowly and deliberately, memorizing the feel of her. She sighed, a slight sound, and nestled closer, her leg draped over his, her fingers splayed across his chest. It was a quiet intimacy, a language of touch that spoke what their voices couldn't. The weight of what they'd done, what they'd become, settled over them like a blanket, warm and heavy.

He felt her relax. Her breathing slowed. Her body softened against his. His own eyes grew heavy. The rhythm of the boat lulled him. He thought of the years ahead, uncertain and uncharted. But for now, they were here. Together. The past and future held at bay. Her hand slipped down to rest over his heart. He covered it with his own, feeling the pulse beneath her skin, steady and sure. They lay like that, entwined. The cabin was a cocoon against the world. The portlights glowed dimly as dark clouds rolled in again. The shadows softened, wrapping them in a stillness that felt like love. Yet as the storm whispered above, a question lingered, unbidden. Could this fragile moment hold against the winds of the next tempest? Their bodies pressed close, holding fast to what they'd found in the rain, but the weight of the question tugged like an anchor, pulling at their newfound peace.

Faidh stirred slightly, her voice a soft murmur against his chest. "Didn't you say you have something dry for me to wear?"

He opened his eyes, the dim light catching the curve of her cheek. He smiled, a small thing, and reached for the shirt he'd given her earlier, still draped over the edge of the bunk. "I gave this to you before, but I rather like you out of my clothes more than in them," he said, his voice low and rough with sleep. He held it out, but his hand lingered on hers, not letting go.

She chuckled, the sound warm in the small space. "I forgot. I kinda like it too," she said, taking the shirt but not moving to put it on. Instead, she pressed closer, her skin warm against his, the dampness of their earlier clothes forgotten. "I don't need it right now." Her eyes met his, soft but certain, and he saw the truth in them, the same truth he felt in his bones.

He pulled her back into his arms, the shirt falling to the floor. The boat swayed, and the rain picked up again, tapping a beautiful rhythm on the deck. Her head found its place against his shoulder, and he felt her breath steady, her body relaxing fully into his. His fingers traced slow patterns

66

on her back, not urgent, just there, like the sea outside. She tilted her head, her lips brushing his jaw—not a kiss but something softer, something that carried all the years they'd known each other, all the moments they'd stopped short of this.

They didn't speak again. The silence was enough, heavy with the weight of what they'd crossed into. His hand settled on her waist, hers curled against his chest, and they fit together like pieces of a puzzle long scattered. The light was starting to fade as sunset drew near, casting a faint glow over their tangled limbs. The boat rocked them gently, and sleep came again, easier this time, pulling them under like a tide. They held each other, not tightly, but with a quiet certainty, as if they'd always been meant to end up here, in this moment, with the rain and the sea and the love they'd finally let in.

CHAPTER 7

DREAMS, STORMS, AND PACTS

The sea was black and heavy. Waves crashed over ten feet high, white foam spitting against Dream Maker's hull. I gripped the helm, knuckles pale, the wheel slick with spray. Water was coming over the gunwales and into the cockpit, pooling ominously around our feet, threatening to drown the electronics. Junior clung to the rail, his face taut, eyes scanning the darkness. I could see the fear in his eyes—fear of whoever was chasing us. The night was alive, wind howling through the rigging. Sails were taut and straining. We were running. Running hard, with the threat of sinking hanging over us like a specter. The motorboat's drone, a low growl, cut through the storm's roar. Its lights bobbed behind us, twin eyes in the murk, closing fast. Just a couple of hundred yards now.

The storm bore down on us, the air dense with salt and the kind of threat that settles in your bones. Rain lashed my face, each drop a needle, blurring my vision until Junior was little more than a shadow moving forward, forced to crawl out toward the bow. I hated that he had to go, but there was no choice. Dream Maker pitched and rolled beneath me, her timbers groaning as the sea's weight pressed in from all sides. My heart hammered a steady rhythm, loud in my ears, as I fought the wheel to keep her on course. Junior's voice was lost to the wind, his shout snatched away before I could make sense of it, but his arm pointed aft, urgent. The motorboat was still there, its hull knifing through the waves, relentless and closing.

Then he was there—Pirata Cofresí. Not a man, not flesh, but a shadow that shimmered. He stood on the deck where no man should stand. His eyes burned, dark and deep, like the sea itself. His coat was tattered, soaked, dripping with water that wasn't there. He spoke, his voice low. It cut through the wind like a blade. "Turn back, woman. The amulets are cursed. The treasure is death. You chase it, and the sea will claim you."

I stood rooted at the helm, hands locked on the wheel as Dream Maker lurched violently, a broadside wave slamming into us and sending water cascading across the deck. Junior's shout was lost in the chaos, but I couldn't tear my eyes from Cofresí. His face was carved with the years and the sea, every line a testament to storms weathered and battles fought—a pirate's face, unyielding. "You've seen the storm," he said. "This is nothing. Keep on, and worse comes. The sea don't forgive."

The motorboat's engine roared, its lights now glaring through the rain, blinding in the storm's gloom. I blinked, and Cofresí vanished, swallowed by the darkness as if he'd never been there. The helm felt impossibly heavy in my hands, Dream Maker resisting every correction, the storm pressing down with

69

renewed force. My breath came shallow, chest tight, and when I glanced at Junior—his face pale in the flickering light—I couldn't help but wonder if the pirate's warning was more than just a dream. The sea felt alive beneath us, vast and indifferent, and for a moment, I was certain it meant to take us.

Faidh woke gasping, chest tight, the sea's roar still echoing in her skull. The dark pressed in, and for a moment, she didn't know where she was—Dream Maker's helm or some other place, real or not. Her heart hammered, the pirate's warning sharp in her mind, his shadow-eyes burning. Then Faidh felt Junior's warmth, his skin against hers, steady and solid. Her breath slowed. The storm faded, the motorboat's growl gone. She was here, next to Junior, in his arms, not there. His arm shifted, heavy with sleep, and she anchored to it, the world settling back into place.

Junior stirred beside Faidh, his warmth pulling her further from the dream's grip. He propped himself up, his concern evident, eyes soft but sharp in the dim light of the dock peering in through the portlight, catching the tremble still running through her. "Are you okay?" he asked, voice low, steady, cutting through the last threads of the storm and Cofres'ís warning. She nodded, still shaken and seeking comfort, but not yet trusting words. Her hand found his, grounding her soul as the nightmare's waves receded.

Faidh's voice was soft, barely above a whisper, as she said, "Just a bad dream." Her hand stayed in Junior's, her trembling easing, but the weight of the sea's roar still faintly echoed in her chest.

70

Junior replied, steady, as he looked at Faidh, her hand still clasped in his. "Do you want to talk about it?" he asked, his eyes searching hers in the dim light, catching the flicker of unease that hadn't fully faded from her face. The tremble in her fingers had quieted, but the shadow of the dream hung heavy, unspoken, between them.

Faidh's voice softened even further, a faint smile breaking through the lingering shadow of the dream. "You'll laugh," she said, her hand still in Junior's, her soft breast warm against his chest.

Junior's voice was firm, quiet, his eyes steady on Faidh's. "No, I won't," he said. "I'll listen—truly listen and be a part of the dream with you." His hand tightened gently around hers. His other arm pulled her even closer, until their hearts began to beat together.

Faidh's voice was low, halting at first, as she began to unravel the dream for Junior. She described only the most intense moments—the black sea and the roaring storm that seemed to blur the line between reality and dream. She spoke of the relentless pursuit, how the motorboat's lights cut through the dark like predatory eyes, but most of all, the encounter with Pirata Cofresí haunted her. His ghostly warning about the cursed amulets and the deadly treasure felt as real as the salt on her skin. Faidh's words trembled slightly, the vividness still clinging to her, as though carrying the weight of the storm's phantom spray. Junior listened, his hand steady in hers, his eyes never leaving her face, sharing the weight of the dream that felt more like a vivid memory than mere fantasy.

Junior drew Faidh closer, his arms a steady anchor against the lingering chill of her dream. His voice, a soft whisper, was warm against her ear. "It was just a dream." Or

71

was it? The memory of his own dream the night before came rushing back into his mind. He wondered if he should share his memory, but chose against it, not wanting to scare Faidh. It was then that he could feel Faidh's body relax into his, letting herself begin to drift off once again, confirming his decision not to tell her.

The sun spilled through the cabin, warm and golden, bathing Faidh and Junior where they lay, still intertwined, their bodies pressed close as if letting go might unravel the moment. Neither moved, each fearing the other might vanish with the breaking of contact, the dream's shadow still lingering faintly.

"Morning," Faidh whispered, her lips brushing Junior's neck, soft and deliberate. "How'd you sleep?"

Junior's eyes met hers, sunlight warming his expression. "Amazing. Better than I have in a long time. I felt complete. How did you sleep?"

Faidh's gaze softened, though a flicker of unease passed through it. "Same, except for my dream last night. That was really scary." She paused, her fingers tracing his arm absently. "I think I might have had another dream about your pirate again just before waking up this morning, but it faded from my memory as quickly as my eyes opened. I tried to hold on to this one, unlike the last that I wish I could let go. This one didn't scare me as much as the first. I felt a comforting peace in this dream." The weight of Cofres'ís warning still lingered slightly, a ghost in the light, but Junior's steady presence held her fast, grounding her in the warmth of the new day. "Funny how dreams can be so vivid and feel so real, but in reality, they are literally figments of our imagination."

Junior leaned back, his arm still around Faidh, the morning sun casting lazy shadows across their tangled limbs. "What's on your agenda for today?" he asked, his voice light but curious.

Faidh tilted her head, a small smile breaking through the lingering haze of her dream. "Well, if you'll have me, I'd love to spend the day with you, especially if you are planning to explore and check out that cave that Dom told us about."

Junior's grin widened, his eyes catching the sunlight. "I was hoping you'd say that. We can have some breakfast, head over to the park where the Pirate Cave is, and see if we don't stumble on an amulet. I figure, since no one has found it in over 200 years, we're sure to find it in a single afternoon." Their laughter mingled, bright and easy, cutting through the last threads of the night's unease.

Faidh's expression softened, a flicker of hesitation crossing her face. "Can I ask you something?" she said.

Junior's gaze steadied on her. "You can ask me anything."

She took a breath, her fingers tracing the edge of his hand. "Do you believe in ghosts? I mean, I felt like there was something special about my dream. It felt like it was more than my subconscious doing whatever it does. It felt like I was there, at the helm, steering Dream Maker in a violent storm with a ghost standing in front of me."

Junior's brow furrowed slightly, thoughtful. "Honestly, I think it was exactly your subconscious. Not only was the old man's story on your mind when you fell asleep, but so was

73

a very real rainstorm, as well as you venturing into a potentially dangerous emotional situation with a very good friend you don't want to lose."

Faidh's eyes widened, a new perspective settling in. "Wow, I hadn't looked at it that way. I like your explanation way better than what's been running through my mind. But I gotta be honest, it seemed so real."

Junior squeezed her hand gently, his voice warm. "I'm sure it did. Dreams can be very powerful and feel very real, especially when you're on Dream Maker." The boat rocked faintly beneath them on cue, the sun climbing higher.

Outside, the marina roused itself by degrees, the sky shifting from gold to a clear, hard blue as the sun climbed above the horizon and spilled light across the glassy water. The boats nearby rocked gently, hulls creaking against the old docks, lines stretched tight and worn from years of salt and sun. Fishermen moved with the slow certainty of men who know the sea, boots thudding on the planks, nets slung over shoulders, faces weathered and set. Gulls circled overhead loudly, their cries blending into the atmosphere with an eerie familiarity. The smell of fish and diesel hung heavy, mingling with the briny tang of drying seaweed. A lone pelican stood sentinel on a piling, beak snapping shut as it watched the water for the flicker of baitfish. In the distance, the faint yet persistent call of a foghorn cut through the morning noises, a reminder of unseen obstacles and the hidden depths that lay ahead.

As they lay together in the warm comfort of Dream Maker's teak walls, engines coughed to life, low rumbles rolling across the water, stirring it to a faint chop. The clink of metal on masts rang out, crisp, as sails were checked and lines coiled. A woman's voice, hoarse, called out in Spanish, answered by a man's laugh, short and rough. The sea breathed steadily, waves lapping softly against the breakwater and the side of the boat, while the sun climbed higher, painting the boats' white hulls with fire. The marina pulsed, alive but unhurried, each sound and sight woven tight into the morning's quiet rhythm, as Faidh and Junior nestled quietly in each other's arms.

Faidh's eyes held a mix of curiosity and lingering dream-shadows as she looked at Junior, the morning sun warming their skin. "Do you think this amulet is going to lead to anything?" she asked, her voice soft but probing, tinged with cautious anticipation. "Two nights ago, I was making fun of you about it. Now, I feel like a little girl again—fantasizing about adventures and treasures. I suddenly can't help but feel excited to learn what is next, but also a little nervous."

Junior's grin was easy, his arm still draped around her. "It kinda already did, led to something that is. After last night, I kinda feel like I found my treasure." He chuckled, shaking his head. "And yes, I know I'm corny."

Faidh laughed, her fingers brushing his. "No, that's one of the things I like about you—you wear your emotions on your sleeve and you don't hold anything back."

"Thanks," Junior said, his voice earnest. "I don't want the people I care about in this world ever to wonder how I feel about them. Life's too short." His openness was unguarded, a quiet conviction in his words. "And to answer your original question... No, I think this amulet thing is just a myth, building legend around a local hero, even if he was a notorious pirate." He continued, "I think it'll be fun to find and explore the cave. But I don't expect to find anything.

Then I plan to find a way to get to Jayuya for the Indigenous Festival Dom mentioned. There, I'll donate the one amulet... or stone, that I found, and that will be that."

Faidh tilted her head, a spark of mischief in her eyes. "But what if we do find a second amulet?"

Junior's gaze locked with hers, steady and bold. "If we find a second amulet, then I want you to cancel your flight and join me and Dream Maker for what could be the craziest adventure either of us has ever been on."

"Deal!" Faidh said, her smile bright, sealing the pact as the sun climbed higher, casting light on the uncharted path ahead—cave, festival, and maybe something more.

CHAPTER 8

SECRETS IN STONE

The roads in Puerto Rico twist and climb, narrowing to a single car's width. Construction scars them, and off the main paths, dirt tracks rattle with craters deep enough to swallow small cars. Drivers on the island split two ways. Some crawl, courteous to a fault, halting mid-road to let others pass, regardless of lane or moment. Others, seemingly trained in the snarl of old New York cabs, weave and cut, pulling out sharply, forcing brakes to scream. Yet these opposites mesh in a strange dance along the island's battered veins.

The distance from Puerto Real to Reserva Natural Punta Guaniquilla is barely a mile. Still, by car, the drive stretches to fifteen minutes, winding around the harbor, climbing through hills, and skirting the crowded sprawl of Buyé Beach. When Faidh and Junior finally set out, the sun was already high, burning down with a heat that pressed against the glass.

The trail from Reserva Natural Punta Guaniquilla's entrance cuts through Cabo Rojo's wild heart. It starts easily, a dirt path under the sun, flanked by dry forest and scrub. They walk, their thoughts as vivid as the scenery. Junior thinks, I've never smelled salt this dry, a thought lingering like the aroma itself. Hiking shoes crunch underfoot. They pass mangrove edges where birds dart like thoughts. The air smells of the earth, carrying stories of the island's past. Every other step seems to alert a local: one of the many lizards and iguanas roaming the forest, their scampers hidden in dry leaves. Sometimes you see them. Most times not. Half a mile in, the path dips and limestone rocks rise, jagged as old bones. Ruins of Hacienda La Romana with weathered brick walls and crumbled stone dot a hill overlooking Laguna Guaniquilla in the foreground, its still water reflecting volcanic scars. Boqueron Bay lies beyond, filled with the crisscrossing white streaks of jet skis. The trail narrows, twists right, and climbs gently. Another mile, and the sea's breath grows quiet in the distance. The cave waits, a dark mouth in the rocks where Cofresí's ghost hides his secrets.

They stopped where the trail gave out, a limestone wall rising ahead, tangled in vines and scrub. Two entrances to Cueva del Pirata Cofresí waited. The first was a narrow hole, barely wide enough for a person, that dropped straight into darkness, breathing cool, damp air. Even Junior's flashlight could not cut through the black. Nearby, a larger opening gaped, its slope gentle, offering an easier way into the unknown. The sun pressed against their backs, but the cave promised relief. Junior's sandals stirred dust as he peered inside. He shrugged off his pack, heavy with water and gear, and set it in the shade, knowing the weight would slow him in tight spaces. Stories of Cofres'ís amulet, hidden deep and maybe cursed, had drawn them here. He turned to Faidh. "Wait here till I test the first steps. Can't see past ten feet down that hole."

Faidh nodded, her smile firm. "No bars on my phone," she said, waving it. "If you need me to help you, I'm on my own up here." Her tone was light, but her gaze held steady.

Junior entered the larger hole, the cave claiming him. Light vanished quickly. His flashlight pierced the darkness, catching stalactites that resembled jagged teeth and odd, round holes in the ceiling, smooth as if they had been carved by design. The floor dropped fast, opening into a broad chamber. He stood, letting his eyes adjust. Shapes emerged—rock walls, shadows in crevices. This was a junction, fed by both entrances above. He shouted, "Faidh, come down! The ceiling is low at first, but you'll soon stand upright. It's at least fifteen feet here."

Her form appeared, quick and sure, descending the larger entrance. "Hi, hi!" she called, her voice bright and her steps lively. Clearly, adventure ran in her blood.

"What's that sound?" she asked, cocking her head.

Bats, Junior said, his beam catching three shapes clinging to a hole in the ceiling, wings folded tight—the cave pulsed with their presence, a restless rustle, sharp as dry leaves. Air chilled. Light vanished. Wings beat in the dark, soft and frantic, a wild pulse echoing off stone. High, ceaseless squeaks cut the silence, a hum that made the rock itself seem to breathe. The sound pressed in, urgent, a warning to anyone who lingered too long in the cave's cold heart.

The air grew heavy, cool, and damp in their lungs, each breath edged with a quiet tension. They pressed deeper, hearts thudding, and entered a second chamber, the ceiling arching high above, vast as a cathedral. Faidh's light caught a glint—just quartz, not gold. She cursed under her breath, frustration tightening her words. Junior moved ahead,

79

silent and wary, the path sloping down, slick beneath his sandals. The sound of trees outside faded, leaving only their footsteps and the bats' restless chorus.

The main chamber opened wide, its walls ancient, gouged by time. Junior knelt, his light scouring the floor—dust, bat dung, nothing else. Faidh swept her beam over the walls, seeking a mark, a clue. Her light stopped on a crevice, narrow and deep, shadowed by a rock's overhang. She called Junior, her voice hushed, wary of the cave's ears. He reached in, his arm straining, his fingers grazing the stone. Empty. Their eyes locked, hope thinning but alive. They pressed on.

Junior raised his flashlight. Dozens of bats swirled above, their chaotic paths cutting the beam, shadows flitting like spirits. As their eyes adjusted, faint light trickled through holes in the roof, pale and ghostly, and below, a glow seeped around a boulder, hinting at another chamber and possibly a different entrance. The cave held more secrets, waiting to be discovered.

For over an hour, Junior and Faidh roamed the cave's depths—sometimes shoulder to shoulder, sometimes splitting to probe separate crevices, their flashlight beams occasionally crossing in the darkness. The main chamber's sandy floor was littered with loose rocks, but no amulet gleamed; no petroglyphs or ancient carvings marked the walls. They found six offshoots branching from the chamber, two leading to hidden exits—escape routes, perhaps, for a pirate cornered in his lair. They snapped dozens of photos with their phones, the flashes catching stalactites and shadows, and explored every nook of the vast underground maze. But no carved stones or clues to

Cofres'ís treasure revealed themselves. The bats' restless chatter followed them, a constant hum in the cold stone.

Junior paused, wiping sweat from his brow. "Let's head up," he said. "Take a break, drink some water. I've got nut bars if you're hungry."

"Sounds perfect," Faidh replied, her voice steady despite the hours of fruitless search.

They climbed out together, blinking in the sun's glare. A patch of shade near the cliff's edge offered relief, the ocean breeze cool on their skin. They sat, drinking water, nut bars breaking in their hands. The sea murmured far below, steady and indifferent.

Faidh stood, stretching, and quietly wandered down a worn path around a cluster of boulders, seeking privacy near one of the cave's other entrances. Minutes passed. Then her voice cut through the air: "Junior, come here!"

He bolted around the rocks, heart pounding, half-expecting to find her sprawled and bleeding. Instead, she sat casually on a rock's edge, smiling. "What's up?" he asked, catching his breath.

"I had a déjà vu," she said, her grin infectious. "Huge!"

Junior blinked, confused. "Okay…"

"Remember this morning," she said, "I told you about that dream I had just as I woke up—the one I couldn't recall, but felt. It's coming back now."

"Yeah, you said it felt comforting."

"Damn, you do listen." She laughed, then grew serious. "I was right here in the dream, sitting on this rock, exactly like this. Another woman with dark eyes was with me—a spirit, like Cofresí in my first dream. But she wasn't carrying a warning or trying to keep me from searching for the amulets and treasure. She was... kind and friendly."

Junior leaned closer. "You're remembering this now?"

"Yes, in this place. It just came rushing back. I can almost see her, standing there." Faidh's voice trembled between wonder and disbelief as she pointed to a spot where vines tangled with tree limbs. "She smiled and pointed at that small entrance." Her finger aimed at the narrow hole they'd seen earlier, barely big enough for a child. "I know it sounds crazy, but I can feel she wants me to find the amulet."

"We searched the cave," Junior said, frowning. "Nothing."

"We searched the cave, and you're right. Everyone who's been in the cave has searched for treasure. But we didn't search this entrance." Faidh insisted, her eyes bright with conviction.

He nodded slowly. "All right. Let's try."

The small entrance was a narrow gash in the rock, tangled with vines and branches. Neither could fit—Junior's shoulders too broad, Faidh too tall. Clearing the overgrowth took nearly an hour, Junior's knife sawing through stubborn vines, sweat stinging his eyes. At last, the hole lay open, a dark throat in the stone. Faidh dropped to her hands and knees, reaching in as far as she could. Her fingers brushed air, then stone, but found nothing. She sat back, breathing hard, her resolve unbroken.

Junior stood, brushing dirt from his hands. "Get up. Let me try," he insisted, nodding at the small entrance.

Faidh's eyes flashed with frustration, heat flaring in her cheeks. "Fine." She ignored his offered hand, grabbing a limestone rock to pull herself up. The stone shifted under her grip, and she stumbled, falling back to the ground with a sharp grunt. Her pride stung, she reached for Junior's hand this time, swallowing her irritation, and as she rose, her eyes caught something on the stone that fell—letters, RC, carved clear. She gasped, a mix of shock and hope flooding her, and flipped the rock over, expecting more. But the other side was smooth, polished by ancient water, no petroglyph in sight.

"What is it?" Junior asked, stepping closer.

"I thought it was the amulet," Faidh said, voice thick with disappointment. Her shoulders slumped. "But it's just Cofres'ís initials—RC—carved into the stone. It's not what we hoped to find."

"Really? Let me see."

She turned the stone in her hand, its warmth sinking into her palm, then passed it to Junior. He studied it, eyes narrowing. "Follow me," he said, sudden and sure.

He jogged back to their patch of shade, grabbing a water bottle from his pack. Faidh followed, drawn close. In the sunlight, he set the stone on the ground, smooth side up, and poured water over it. The liquid traced lines across the surface, and slowly, a petroglyph appeared—a tree, faint but unmistakable, its branches curling like a secret revealed. Junior grinned, knowing this was no ordinary stone. "It's called wet rock enhancement."

Faidh didn't wait. She grabbed Junior, spun him to face her, and kissed him hard, her lips fierce and lingering, her breath catching—relief and exhilaration colliding in that moment. When she pulled back, her eyes burned with new resolve. "I'm in," she said, two words, sharp and confident.

Junior blinked, caught off guard. "What? I mean, thank you, but what's 'I'm in' mean?"

"It means I'm in." Her voice was steady, alive. "I'm canceling my flight out of San Juan and returning my rental car. If you will have me, I'm with you until this adventure's done, whatever that looks like. I just have one request."

"What's that?"

"I want you to teach me how to sail. I've been on dozens of boats that I've sold, and I've helped captains when they need help, but I really don't know what I'm doing. I want to learn, and I want you, Junior, to be my teacher. I trust you."

He seized her, arms tight, lifting her as they spun. His lips found her neck, kissing hard, joy surging as the stone lay forgotten in the dirt. The sea roared below, and the cave watched, silent, its secrets spilling into the light. "I will teach you everything I know. But I have a feeling you know a lot more than you even realize."

"Like I said, I'm in!"

Junior and Faidh stuffed their gear into his backpack, the stone with its hidden petroglyph tucked safely inside. Excitement pulsed through them, a shared fire, but they chose the long trail back, winding through Reserva Natural Punta Guaniquilla. The path hugged Laguna Guaniquilla, its still waters reflecting volcanic rocks that jutted like old bones from the shore. They walked steadily, the sun high, their boots scuffing earth, eyes tracing the rugged beauty of the reserve.

By mid-afternoon, the breeze had died, leaving the air thick and heavy. The sun bore down, relentless, their skin slick with sweat. The trail veered close to open water, and a small beach appeared, its sand pale against the edge of the sea. They exchanged a glance, wordless, and dropped their pack. Stripping down to near naked, they plunged into the cool waves. The water washed away the heat, the dust, the cave's damp chill, leaving salt in its place. They swam, weightless, the sea cradling them, its rhythm slow and deep.

Junior slung the backpack over his shoulder, the petroglyph stone safe inside. "If it's okay with you, Faidh, I'd like to see that Cofresí monument Dom mentioned, then head back to the boat."

Faidh grinned, brushing sand from her hands. "If we find a place to eat on the way, I'll buy."

"Deal," Junior said. "I'm down."

They started walking again, the sun still fierce even for late in the afternoon. Junior glanced at her with a playful glint in his eyes. "Have you ever steered a boat by Orion's belt?" he teased, nudging her arm gently. "Tomorrow's Friday, and if we catch the morning tide, we could take our time, maybe reach Ponce by mid-morning Saturday. You know, so we're not rushing, and you could learn to sail Dream Maker, take the helm the whole way. What do you think? We could even anchor somewhere tomorrow night and see if we can spot some constellations, sleep on deck under the stars, just the two of us."

Faidh raised an eyebrow, her smile teasing. "Are you trying to seduce me, Mr. Wright?"

Junior's eyes held hers, unflinching. "No. I'm trying to help you fall in love with me."

She laughed, sharp and bright, the sound mixing with the sea's low roar. They walked on, the reserve's wild paths stretching before them, the promise of the monument and the open water pulling them forward.

Downtown Boquerón, in Cabo Rojo, is a small village carved into the coast, raw and unpolished. Once focused solely on fishing, now tourism is its lifeblood. Its heart, a single street, runs tight along the bay, lined with wooden shacks painted in fierce colors: red, blue, green, faded by salt and sun. Oyster stalls stand open, shells split on rough tables, the air thick with the scent of sea and lime—vendors with jewelry and souvenirs. Bars, small and loud, pour rum and beer, their jukeboxes spilling salsa into the dusk—flat voices of street karaoke echo on the south end of town. Everywhere you turn, the beat of native music surrounds you. There's a marina that houses many boats, small and weathered, rocking gently on the tide. In stark contrast, a weathered fisherman, his hands rough and practiced, mends his nets beside a sleek, glossy yacht docked nearby, its polished railings glinting in the sun. In the bay, a half-dozen cruising sailboats anchor, enjoying the protected waters, loud music, native food, and great nightlife.

Faidh eased the rental car into a spot at the north end of Boquerón, where the village's pulse beats strongest. They stepped out, choosing to walk—the main road choked with cars under the late afternoon sun. By night, this street would close, giving way to a flood of bodies—dancing, laughing, singing their Boricua pride. The beach ran close, its sand soft, the water clear and steady, lapping softly at the edge of the promenade. The air carried fish, sweat, and the promise of stars, raw and alive, tied deep to the island's roots. They agreed to eat later, after the monument, and set off.

To reach the monument's pond, they crossed a narrow canal, its waters feeding the other Boquerón marina. Along its banks, a sleek resort rose, flanked by million-dollar condos, each with a yacht moored in its backyard, gleaming like trophies. Junior and Faidh exchanged a glance, seeing two Boqueróns—one for the rich, one for the rest—the divide as clear as the canal's edge.

The Cofresí monument stood just west of the bay, a bronze pirate, fierce and unbowed, rising from a shallow pond. Bushes pressed close, veiling it like a secret kept. Standing tall and strong, sabre in hand, his gaze sliced the horizon, sharp as the seas he once ruled. No plaque told his story, only his name etched into the stone below, but the statue spoke—defiant, solitary, alive. Once he slipped through shoals and coves, a shadow to his foes. Now he stood in still water, hidden, but for all who searched for him.

The sun hung low, bleeding orange into the horizon as Junior and Faidh walked back to Boquerón's heart. They craved a restaurant with a bay view, a quiet spot to sit and breathe, but the village laughed at their hopes. The main street buzzed, cars and voices tangling, and no place offered the calm they sought. Even a clear view of the bay was scarce, hidden by shacks and crowds.

Faidh stopped, her eyes sharp. "Let's call an audible," she said. "Oysters and pinchos from one of those stands. Grab some mojitos, find a spot on the beach, and watch the sun go down."

Junior nodded, a grin breaking through. "Sounds perfect."

They wove through the promenade, stopping at a weathered kiosk. Oysters lie fresh. Pinchos sizzled, the air thick with the scent of smoke. Mojitos in hand, cold and sharp with mint, they found a stretch of sand. The bay stretched wide before them. The sun sank, painting the water a golden hue. They sat, silent, the village's pulse fading behind the sea's steady breath. They enjoyed the taste of Puerto Rico together.

Junior and Faidh returned to Puerto Real as darkness settled in, the air still and the docks quiet. They parted ways to handle final tasks before dawn's departure. Junior strode to the office, where the Dock Master lingered, his desk cluttered with charts and coffee mugs. "We're leaving at first light," Junior said, leaning on the counter. He explained that Faidh's rental car was due for pickup by the agency in the morning and asked for a place to leave the keys.

The Dock Master nodded, his weathered face creasing. "Standard service for cruisers passing through, just leave them on the desk," he said, waving off the request as routine. As Junior turned to leave, a sudden chill, accompanied by a faint scent of rain in the air, caught his attention —a sensory prelude breaking the humid calm. "Which way you headed?"

"East towards Ponce for now—maybe stop in Bahía de Guánica tomorrow evening. Why do you ask?" Junior replied.

The Dock Master had a mildly concerned look. "Have you seen any weather reports today? There's a late-season tropical low developing southeast of us. Currently, it's stationary and isn't expected to develop into anything. But I'd keep an eye on it, if I were you."

"Really? This late in November, huh? I appreciate the insight. I'll definitely keep an eye out. Buen día." Junior turned and headed down the docks back to Dream Maker. His mind spinning, he knew that November storms rarely grew serious, but there was no reason to take any risks. If the storm developed, he would take DM and Faidh to calmer waters until it passed. The amulets could wait.

Faidh, meanwhile, hurried to her Airbnb, a small spare room that was calm and quiet. She showered fast, the water washing away cave dust and sweat. Packing was quick—she traveled light, a habit honed flying back and forth to the tropics. Her bag zipped shut in minutes, and she checked out, leaving the key in the lockbox. Within an hour, she was back at the marina, her steps quick on the dock as Junior finished prepping Dream Maker. He tightened lines and checked gear, the boat swaying gently under his feet.

He took her bag, stowing it below deck, and helped her settle in. Exhausted, they collapsed together in the aft cabin, the day's weight—crawling through caves, chasing ghosts of amulets—pulling them under. Deep sleep took them in seconds, as the marina hushed around them—both happy to be in the arms of someone with whom they felt safe.

CHAPTER 9

FIRST LIGHT, NEW WATERS

In the morning, Faidh twisted in the sheets, the gentle sway of Dream Maker at the dock betrayed by the fury unfolding in her mind.

The sea churned like a living beast, waves towering fifteen feet or more, slamming into the hull with bone-jarring force that sent shards of foam exploding across the deck. She clutched the helm desperately, her arms aching from the wheel's violent jerks, water flooding the cockpit up to her knees, shorting out gauges in sparks of blue light. Junior shouted something lost to the gale as he clipped in and crawled forward, his body battered by the relentless spray, hands slipping on the slick foredeck. The pursuing motorboat's engines thundered closer, its hull slicing through the chaos like a predator, its lights piercing the night like accusatory beams. Then, in a horrifying instant, a rogue wave broadsided them—Dream Maker heeled sharply, the deck tilting at a deadly angle—and Junior's tether snapped with a sickening crack. He tumbled overboard, arms flailing, vanishing into the black abyss with a choked cry that pierced Faidh's soul, the sea swallowing him whole as she screamed his name into the void.

From the swirling mist rose Pirata Cofresí, his form more solid and menacing than before, standing defiant on the bucking bow where Junior had just fallen. His eyes glowed with unearthly fire, his tattered coat whipping like shredded sails, a cutlass gleaming in his grip as if ready to strike. "Foolish woman," he bellowed, his voice booming over the storm's rage, "the amulets demand blood! Continue this path, and the sea will claim him forever—your lover dashed on the rocks, his bones scattered to the depths." Faidh lunged at the wheel, trying to turn back, but the boat fought her, waves crashing down like hammers, Cofresí's laughter echoing as he dissolved into the spray, leaving only the image of Junior's empty harness dangling limp. The motorboat bore down, its bow aimed like a spear, and the cold water rose to pull her under, too.

Faidh bolted awake, gasping for air, her chest heaving as if she'd truly been drowning. The cabin was still, the night quiet save for the soft lap of water against the hull at Cabo Rojo. Junior slept soundly beside her, oblivious, his steady breathing a stark contrast to the horror still clawing at her mind. She pressed a hand to her mouth to stifle a sob, unwilling to wake him, the pirate's warning burning like salt in a wound. It was just a dream, she told herself, but the taste of seawater lingered on her lips, and the fear refused to fade. It took over an hour, most of the time spent staring at Junior to ensure he was safe, but eventually, sleep claimed Faidh once again. This time, it was a dreamless sleep.

Sunlight crept over the mountains as Junior and Faidh woke early, the air cool and clear. Junior thought he noticed a bird's sudden flight, disturbed from its perch for reasons unknown, but he dismissed it as morning rustle. Faidh brewed coffee below while Junior moved quietly on deck, checking lines and gear. She joined him in the cockpit, mug in hand, ready for the day's first briefing. The beauty of the morning was complete, yet he couldn't shake the impression of the bird startled into flight, a hint of unpredictability in the day to come.

"You're Captain. I'm the first mate. You take the helm. I'll cast off lines, push us free." The wind was still, the current weak—easy conditions for Faidh to gain confidence.

"Cast off, Matey!" Faidh called, beaming.

"Aye, aye, Captain." Junior jumped down to the dock, uncleated and tossed lines aboard, saving one. He looped it around a cleat, holding the boat. He climbed on, freed the line with a quick whip, and they drifted free.

Faidh took the wheel, eased the electric drive forward. Dream Maker slipped from the dock, silent and smooth. Junior stowed the bumpers, coiled the lines, and tucked them into the forward locker. The deck was clean, ready for open water.

It felt good for Junior to have someone to sail with. He loved the solitude of the sea—complete independence and the bright, clear air—but being on the water with someone he cared about as much as Faidh changed things. It brought a warmth and presence that felt like a gift. Trust ran both ways, and the shift from solitude to companionship left Junior feeling lighter, more content.

They left Puerto Real slowly, the scenery beginning to change as Faidh stood at the helm, hair streaming in the breeze while the boat cut through blue water. Her smile spoke clearly, setting the tone for the passage ahead.

Soon clear of land and well out into the Mona Passage, Junior recommended to the Captain that they turn into the wind—about a 130 heading—so they could set the sails.

Faidh spun the wheel hard to port. Dream Maker's bow met the wind. She shouted, "Prepare to raise the main!"

"Prepare to raise the main, aye, aye, Captain," Junior replied with a grin.

Rudder back to midships, the Captain gave her next order, "Raise the mainsail!"

Without hesitation, Junior stepped to the cabin's forward starboard deck, unlocked the main halyard, wrapped the line around the winch, and started cranking the main up. As he cranked, he could feel the taut rope vibrate under his palm, like a guitar string being plucked—a vivid reminder of the main halyard at work. "Raising the mainsail. Aye, aye, Captain." He was having fun, but also teaching Faidh the importance of communication, ensuring everyone is on the same page.

Mainsail up, halyard locked, line coiled and stowed. Faidh watched, learning to keep lines tidy, a habit Junior knew she'd embrace.

Faidh turned south, the mainsail filling as Junior trimmed for a port close reach. He'd save the finer points of sail trim for later. For now, he wanted her to watch the heading and read the water.

Just then, Faidh belted out her next order, "Set the Genoa!"

Junior just smiled—he'd always suspected she knew more than she let on. "Set the Genoa. Aye, aye, Captain."

He unlocked the Genoa furling line, loosened the port sheet, and cranked the starboard sheet on the winch. The Genoa flapped briefly, then filled. "Genoa set and trimmed for a port close reach, Captain."

Faidh beamed. "Thank you." A pause. "Can we turn the motor off?"

"What's your speed?"

"Six point two knots."

"Yes, ma'am. Throttle to neutral. Kill the motor."

The seas were calm, with light winds of five to eight knots. Without the engine, they held four point three knots —a good cruising speed since they were in no hurry.

Junior liked early starts—empty water, no ships in sight. He stood beside Faidh, flicked on the radar, and pointed out the land returns to port. One blip trailed behind: a motor yacht, another early riser.

They sailed down Puerto Rico's southwest coast, the land unfolding in quiet beauty. Green hills and low mountains pressed against dense forest. Beaches like Playa Sucia, Boquerón, and El Combate shone white against turquoise water. Rocky cliffs jutted out, sea-worn and sharp. Cabo Rojo's lighthouse stood stark above the cape. As they passed the rocks, Faidh took her first tack. She glanced at Junior, a fleeting worry crossing her mind. "What if the weather turns and we get caught out here?" she asked, the beauty of the cliffs still echoing in her thoughts. Junior smiled, his eyes reassuring under the brim of his hat. "We're prepared," he replied, his voice steady, guiding her back to the ease of the journey.

The water shifted from deep sapphire offshore to clear, vibrant green near the coast, revealing coral patches and darting fish. Mangroves clung to inlets. Small fishing boats dotted the horizon, pelicans diving for their catch.

In the distance, the town of La Parguera. Its stilted houses and docks stuck out from the lush green. Over the town, a blimp hung, white and long, tethered by a thin cable, its belly holding cold, silent radar. Against the wide blue, it was a pale dot above the hills and beaches. The wind moved, the waves rolled, but the blimp stayed fixed.

By early afternoon, they sailed into Guánica Bay. Junior dropped anchor in the west end, a quiet spot shielded from industry. Early arrivals meant picking a place where Dream Maker could swing free with the tides, clear of sandbars and other boats. Today, luck was good—no other vessels in sight.

Guánica Bay lay flat and wide, water smooth as a mirror under the brutal sun. Mangroves stood at the edges, their roots gripping the shallows. The hills rose sharply behind, guarding the harbor. No waves broke. The air was hot, heavy with salt and the faint rot of fish. The bay stretched silently, two miles of calm, holding the ghosts of old ships and men who came with guns. Quiet now, the town was small, the past carved deep into the shore.

Two decrepit smokestacks rose from the ruins of Guánica Centrale. Gaunt sentinels pierced the sky. Brick weathered, stained with age, crumbling at the edges. No smoke now. They stood hollow, holding the weight of a century— sugarcane's rise and fall, the sweat of enslaved men, the hum of machines long silent. The sun baked their surfaces.

95

Vines clawed up. Relics, stark against the fields, speaking of what was and would not be again.

Dinner was early—steaks and asparagus grilled on deck. After days of motion, they wanted quiet. They ate, opened a bottle of Malbec, and let the night settle in. No moon, just sharp stars overhead. Junior switched off the deck lights, leaving only the anchor light. They stretched out on bow cushions, a blanket over them, sea air cool and crisp, wine in hand.

Faidh rested her head on Junior's chest, easy and content. But something nagged at him. Junior wondered if his mind was playing tricks on him. Days of talk about treasure and adventure might have stirred him. He didn't think so. He was a man who prided himself on staying level, having been forged by Naval Aviation training to remain calm in the face of adversity. Yet beneath that quiet exterior, his pulse hammered despite the cool night air. But he trusted his gut, and it told him something was wrong. The bay had been empty at sunset. No boats creeping in under the dark. No anchor lights pierced the night. Yet voices—Spanish, low and urgent—carried across the water. They were close enough to feel real, maybe two hundred yards off. Sound traveled far over flat seas, especially under a star-filled sky. But this was no illusion.

Minutes later, engines rumbled to life, a low growl in the dark. A boat slipped away, its light a brief flicker on the water. As it departed, a faint scent of diesel lingered in the air, mingling with the salt and bringing a new edge to the night. The sound of the wake softly lapping against the hull added an eerie echo. Junior eased himself from Faidh's side and moved to the cockpit. He powered up the chartplotter, eyes scanning for an AIS signal to pin a name or type to the phantom vessel. The screen stayed blank—no trace of anything in the bay.

He didn't usually bother with the boat's alarms or cameras when he was aboard, awake to the world around him. But tonight felt different. The air held a weight, a whisper of something unseen. He armed the systems and let the cameras keep a watchful eye. Just to be sure.

Junior slid back under the blanket, Faidh's warmth pulling him close. She lifted the edge, her eyes soft in the starlight, and asked, "Is everything okay?"

"Right as rain," he said, voice steady. "Just checked the GPS tracker, made sure the anchor's holding." He kept his tone light, a shield against the unease coiling in his gut. No need for two sets of nerves tonight. He'd carry the worry for both, let her rest easy under the vast, quiet sky.

They slept under the stars on the deck of Dream Maker. The breeze was cool, and the waves rocked them to sleep, with nothing but the stars looking down on them.

Faidh lay peacefully under the blanket in Junior's strong arms, but sleep pulled her into chaos.

The calm was shattered by a howling gale that whipped the sea into a frenzy. Waves reared like beasts, twenty feet high, crashing over Dream Maker's deck in relentless fury, splintering wood and tearing at the rigging. The boat bucked wildly, her masts groaning under the strain, lightning cracking the sky like veins of fire. Junior fought his way forward, harness clipped, but the deck was a slick nightmare of foam and debris. A massive swell slammed broadside, heeling the vessel nearly on her beam ends, and Junior's feet slipped out from under him. His body smashed against the lifelines, the tether fraying with a sharp twang before snapping completely—he plummeted into the churning void, his scream swallowed by the roar as sharks circled below, drawn by the scent of blood in the water.

From the heart of the storm emerged Pirata Cofresí, his spectral form towering on the bow, cloak billowing like torn canvas, a rusted cutlass dripping seawater and gore. His eyes burned with malevolent glee, face scarred and twisted, teeth bared in a feral grin. "You dare defy the curse, woman?" he roared, his voice thundering over the wind, echoing like cannon fire. "The amulets are bound in blood—yours, his, all who touch them! Press on, and the sea will rip him apart, piece by piece, his flesh fed to the depths while you watch helplessly!" Faidh clawed at the wheel, trying to steer toward Junior's flailing form, but another wave hammered down, flooding the cockpit, instruments exploding in sparks. Cofresí lunged closer, his blade raised high, the motorboat from her previous nightmare now joined by a fleet of ghostly ships, their cannons blazing, splintering Dream Maker's hull as the boat began to disintegrate beneath her.

The vision intensified, Cofresí's laughter a cacophony blending with the storm's rage. Junior resurfaced briefly, gasping, only for a rogue wave to drag him under again, his eyes locking on hers in silent accusation. The pirate's form loomed over her now, cold breath on her neck: "Abandon the hunt, or his death seals your fate—eternal torment in the abyss!" The sea closed in, pulling Faidh down with icy

98

fingers, her lungs burning as darkness swallowed everything.

Faidh jolted awake with a sharp cry, bolting upright on the bow cushions, her heart hammering like a drum. The blanket tangled around her legs, and she gasped for air, the cool night breeze a stark contrast to the fury of the dream. Junior stirred beside her, his eyes snapping open, his hand instinctively reaching for her arm. "Faidh? What is it? You okay?" he asked, voice thick with sleep but laced with concern, sitting up quickly as he scanned the dark bay.

She pressed a hand to her chest, forcing a shaky laugh, willing her pulse to slow. "Yeah, yeah... just a bad nightmare. Nothing serious." Her voice trembled slightly, but she met his gaze steadily, the pirate's warnings echoing in her mind like a distant thunder.

Junior frowned, his thumb brushing her shoulder gently. "Sounded pretty intense. Want to talk about it? Was it the storm again, or... something with Cofresí?"

Faidh shook her head quickly, pulling the blanket up like a shield. "No, really—nothing like that. Just... rough seas, you know? The kind of dream you get after a long day on the water. Overboard stuff, but silly. Go back to sleep, Junior. I'm fine." She leaned in, pressing a quick kiss to his cheek, hoping her smile hid the lie, the taste of saltwater still phantom on her tongue.

The rest of the night stayed quiet, the bay's stillness unbroken. Junior figured his mind had run wild, conjured ghosts from treasure tales. They'd planned to sail at sunrise, but neither he nor Faidh felt like leaving the warmth of each other's touch. They lingered, tangled in blankets, for another hour, rising only when the mood struck.

Weighing anchor was simple, the routine familiar. Soon, Dream Maker glided out of Guánica Bay and into the Caribbean Sea, bound for Ponce. Junior kept watch, scanning the water. Only three boats dotted the inlet as they left—all apparently pulling out from Copa Marina, just east of the bay. Two were sport fishing rigs, low and sleek, built for speed. The third, a Sea Ray motor yacht, moved with lazy confidence. Each boat held its course, no sign of the shadow Junior had sensed. The sea sparkled under the morning sun, and the coast stretched out, green and calm, as they sailed on toward Ponce.

The sail to Ponce passed smoothly and steadily. Junior took the helm today, hands firm on the wheel. He wanted Faidh to feel the lines, to learn the pull and give of setting sails. She handled them well, her movements sure, a broad smile on her face. She loved it, every second. Faidh was at home on the sea, at least in the calm. Rougher days might test her later, but for now, she and Junior didn't know where they'd point the bow after Ponce. They hoped Jayuya, up in the island's rugged heart, would offer some clue, some spark to guide their next move. The coast slipped by, green and quiet, as Dream Maker cut through the blue.

An hour out from Ponce, Faidh's phone lit up with texts, a sudden storm of notifications. The texts buzzed in rapid fire—her mother's accusations flying about who should handle it. Not again. I'm finally free out here, living for once—why do they always pull me under? Guilt gnawed at her, mixing with resentment; the open sea called, but family chains felt unbreakable. Her face tightened, worry creasing her brow as she glanced at Junior. "You okay without me? Mind if I take a call?"

"Go ahead," he said, his voice tinged with concern. "Everything alright?"

Faidh's expression turned blank, her eyes going distant as the messages kept coming. She slipped below deck, pulling the companionway hatch shut with a soft thud. Junior watched, feeling the distance grow in seconds, worry stirring at the sudden change.

Faidh emerged, eyes distant, missing Junior's cue on the sails. "Sorry," she muttered, fumbling a line.

Junior paused, concern edging into some frustration. "You've been off since that call—what's going on? We're a team here."

She sighed, snapping back, "It's my family; they need me, okay? But I'm trying to be present." He softened, touching her arm. "I get it, but talk to me—don't shut me out." The exchange left a quiet strain, but they pressed on, the sails filling as awkwardly as the silence between them.

Junior let his words hang in the air, soft and open. "We're about half an hour from Ponce Yacht Club. I reserved a rental car with Enterprise. They'll meet us at the docks this afternoon to pick it up for the drive to Jayuya. You still good for the trip?"

Her eyes locked on his, steady and sure. "I wouldn't miss it for anything." She paused, her voice low and intense. "I want you to know, Junior, there's nowhere else I'd rather be than right here, right now."

"Same," he said, a smile breaking through, warm and genuine. "Sails are down, we're under power. I'll bring us into the dock. Mind being First Mate, handling the lines when we tie off?"

"Aye, aye, Captain!" she called, a flicker of her old spark returning. She moved to the deck, readying the fenders, her hands quick and sure despite the shadow lingering in her thoughts.

The sun burned high, a fierce white disc, as Junior steered Dream Maker into Ponce's harbor, bound for the Ponce Yacht and Fishing Club. The water shimmered, a sheet of molten glass flashing midday light. The city spread before them: pastel buildings faded but unyielding, gripping the shore like men braced against a storm. Catedral Nuestra Señora de Guadalupe stood firm, its twin towers carving the sky, a steady watcher over the din below. The air was thick with salt, diesel, and the faint, sweet bite of roasted coffee from the docks.

Junior's hands held the wheel, calm and sure, guiding Dream Maker through the harbor's pulse. To starboard, the yacht club's piers stretched out, crowded with sleek yachts and scarred fishing boats, nets slung like hammocks. The waterfront thrummed—vendors shouting, carts clattering, the sharp clink of bottles under the sun's glare. Sailors worked the dock, their movements slow but precise, as they coiled lines and prepared their boats for another adventure. Beyond, the hills rose green and heavy, folding into one another, unmoved by the clamor.

Dream Maker's bow cut true, her timbers creaking as Junior eased her toward the club's docks, where the next leg of their journey waited. Ponce stood raw, enduring, its heartbeat steady as the tide, alive with sweat and waiting.

As they approached, Junior felt the pulse of the port, signaling not just the end of a journey but the start of uncertainties yet to unfold. Whatever Faidh carried, she'd share when ready, but he knew that once they docked, everything could change. For now, the sea was calm, the sun high, and they sailed on together.

CHAPTER 10

THE MOUNTAINS, THE FESTIVAL, THE STONES

The approach to Ponce Yacht Club was smooth, and the dock lines were secured without a hitch. Junior guided Dream Maker in with a steady hand, while Faidh handled the lines as if she had been born to it. The boat settled against the dock, the harbor calm under the midday sun. Yet, just as Junior allowed himself to relax, he noticed an unusual ripple across the water, as though it were disturbed by something unseen beneath the surface. Stop it, Junior thought. You're chasing ghosts in your own mind.

A dockworker glanced over his shoulder, eyes narrowed, as if sensing something amiss. Junior shook off the feeling, letting the quiet thrill of the voyage fill him. Having Faidh aboard—her beauty, her quick smile, her charm that caught him off guard—made the boat feel more alive than it ever had. He glanced at her as she coiled a line, her hair catching the breeze, and thought to himself: Let this adventure stretch on forever. Give her every reason to keep sailing with him on Dream Maker. The idea settled deep, warm, and sure.

They climbed into the rental car, the sun pressing down on their shoulders, heat shimmering off the docks. The SUV waited, small but sturdy, keys left behind in the office—just right for the climb ahead. Junior eased onto the highway, steering north from Ponce, the road stretching toward Jayuya and the green spine of the Cordillera Central. The first miles rolled out smooth and wide, a modern highway built for speed, but the promise of mountains and wild country lay ahead, where the road would narrow and twist through rugged hills.

The drive would take an hour, maybe more if the mountains had their way. Out of Ponce, the road ran flat and easy, cutting through barrios—Sabanetas, Machuelo Abajo—where houses and corner stores pressed close to the pavement. Traffic thinned, the SUV humming steadily beneath Junior's hands. Faidh watched the world slip by, her shoulders loosening, the last of her tension fading with each mile. Fields rolled out, green and gold, then gave way to the first low hills, the Cordillera Central rising ahead, blue and distant.

Soon, the highway began its climb. The road twisted gently at first, then grew steeper, carving through the foothills. Curves tightened, and Junior downshifted, keeping the wheel steady as they navigated the sinuous path. The SUV handled the turns well, though some bends demanded focus—180-degree switchbacks that slowed their speed considerably. Faidh, unfazed by the winding road, kept her hands folded in her lap, occasionally pointing out a breathtaking view.

Off the main highway, the world tightened. The pavement held, but the road twisted hard, climbing steeper, sometimes narrowing to a single lane pressed between jungle and drop-off. They crossed the Río Grande de Arecibo, its headwaters flashing silver in the sun, and rolled over narrow bridges, each one a promise that the mountains would not be tamed easily.

The scenery shifted as they climbed. The hills grew greener, thicker with sierra palms, bamboo, and banana trees, their leaves catching the sunlight in flashes of emerald and gold. As they got further into the mountains, the air cooled, carrying the scent of earth and wet foliage. Faidh opened her window, letting the breeze ruffle her hair, a subtle gesture of release. Junior followed suit, feeling the cool air wash over him, unraveling the last threads of tension knotted in his chest. With each breath he took, filled with the freshness of the mountains, his senses seemed to sharpen, grounding him in the present. Yet, in the back of his mind, a sudden gust carried an undercurrent of doubt, teasing at the edges of his calm. He pushed it aside, focusing instead on the vibrancy of the journey and the road still unfolding ahead.

The mountains took command, peaks jagged and blue against the sky. Los Tres Picachos rose ahead, its three points cutting a sharp line above the trees. For a while, the Río Cerrillos kept them company, its water running clear and fast over the stones. Faidh spotted a waterfall tumbling down a cliff, its spray catching sunlight in a brief, bright arc. The forest pressed close, thick with impatiens blooming red and pink, their colors burning against the green.

With each turn they took, the scenery seemed to grow wilder. The road wound past barrio Guaraguao, where the land felt untouched, save for the occasional wooden house tucked into a clearing. The Río Grande de Arecibo sparkled below, its banks lined with smooth stones. On a clear day, Junior knew, you could see to the Caribbean coast from these heights, but today a few clouds softened the horizon.

The mountains seemed to breathe, their slopes draped in mist that clung to the valleys below.

Nearing Jayuya, the road passed signs for La Piedra Escrita, a boulder etched with Taíno petroglyphs, and the Museo del Cemí, its odd, triangular shape a nod to the island's indigenous past. Faidh's eyes lit up at the thought of exploring these, her earlier worries fading with the promise of discovery. The town itself appeared slowly, a cluster of buildings nestled among the peaks, surrounded by coffee fields and the shadow of Cerro de Punta, Puerto Rico's highest summit.

Junior let the SUV slow as the road leveled, Jayuya unfolding before them. The climb—uphill in more ways than one—had left its mark, the mountains offering a quiet reward after the uneasy night in Guánica Bay. Faidh leaned back, her smile easy now, ready for whatever waited in the heart of the hills.

The festival was on its second day. Junior and Faidh stepped from the car, the mountain air cool on their skin. Jayuya's streets were narrow, lined with low houses painted in bright colors. They walked toward the Nemesio R. Canales Recreation Plaza, drawn by a low hum of voices and the pulse of jíbaro music. The Festival Nacional Indígena was alive.

The plaza opened before them, a vast square ringed by booths. Smoke rose from grills, carrying the scent of roasted pork and mofongo. A fire burned at the center, lit in a Taíno ceremony, its glow sharp against the green hills beyond.

Drums beat, steady and deep, as bomba dancers swayed, their skirts flashing red. The crowd pressed close, locals and strangers shoulder to shoulder, laughing, eating cassava bread, sipping coffee grown in the slopes above.

Junior and Faidh wandered through the festival, their steps slow, eyes wide with the pulse of Jayuya's plaza. The air was thick with the scent of roasted pork and the sharp twang of coffee. They passed booths where artisans carved Taíno faces into wood, their tools scraping soft and steady. Women in vine-woven costumes moved with quiet pride, their shell necklaces clicking. The Yukayeque hut stood open, its thatch roof low, showing a glimpse of a world lost to time. Faidh lingered near a dancer, her skirt swirling to the beat of bomba drums, while Junior studied a petroglyph replica, its lines sharp under the sun. They took it all in, piecing together the Taíno's story, feeling the weight of the island's roots.

Junior's shoulders eased, the festival's rhythm settling him. He approached a booth where an older woman arranged clay cemís, her hands worn and sure. "Buen día, señora," he said warmly. "Soy Junior. Mucho gusto. ¿Habla inglés?"

She looked up, her eyes crinkling with a smile, and nodded. "Yes, I speak English," she said, her accent thick but clear. "Welcome to Jayuya."

"Can you tell me if there is a 'bohitiu' here that might speak English as well?" To ensure he said the word correctly, Junior had it spelled out on his phone and showed it to the woman.

She smiled. "Yes, my nephew, Guey, speaks English very well, and he is studying to be a 'bohitiu' with my brother, his father, as his teacher. He is walking around here somewhere. I can text him and have him come over if you would like."

"That would be great," Junior said, his voice steady, a spark of anticipation in his eyes. He and Faidh stood by the booth, the festival alive around them. Faidh shifted closer, her gaze drifting over the plaza's swirl of color and motion, while Junior kept one eye on the woman as she tapped out a text to her nephew.

Minutes passed, the crowd's laughter and music filling the wait. Then a young man approached, his steps quick, his face open. He spoke to the woman in rapid Spanish, their words a soft cadence. Turning to Junior and Faidh, he extended a hand. "Buen día, I'm Guey," he said, his English clear, tinged with the island's rhythm. "How can I help you?"

Guey stood before them, young and lean, his skin the color of the earth baked by Jayuya's sun. His eyes were dark, sharp like the petroglyphs carved into La Piedra Escrita, holding a quiet, knowing look. He wore Taíno garb —vines woven tight across his chest, shells and seeds strung low on his hips, clicking softly as he moved. His hair, black and straight, fell past his shoulders, tied back with a cord of braided palm. Bare feet gripped the plaza's stone, steady as the mountains around him. He spoke English clearly, but his voice carried the rhythm of the island, of drums and rivers. He was of Jayuya, born to its soil, raised in its stories, a bohitiu learning the old ways.

"Buen día, Guey," Junior said, his voice steady, hand outstretched. "I'm Junior, this is Faidh. We drove up from Ponce, hoping to find some answers. We have stones—amulets—with petroglyphs. We think they're Taíno. Can you help us understand them?"

Guey's dark eyes flicked to the backpack, then back to Junior. "I can try," he said. "If I can't, someone here will." The shells clicking at his hips shifted as he leaned forward.

"Perfect," Junior said, a spark of relief in his tone. He reached into his backpack, pulling out the stones, their surfaces worn but etched deep with symbols. He handed them to Guey, one by one.

Guey's hand trembled slightly as he took the first petroglyph, his eyes glazing over for a split second—as if seeing something beyond the stone. "This... it whispers of deep waters," he murmured, voice distant.

Junior exchanged a glance with Faidh, his instincts flaring: Who is this guy? Too young to know so much—could it be a con? But Guey's smile returned, warm yet enigmatic, pulling them in despite the unease.

"Where'd you find these?" Guey asked, turning a stone in his hand, the turtle petroglyph catching the light.

"It's a long story," Junior said. "Is there somewhere quiet, more private, we can talk? I'll tell you everything."

Guey glanced at his aunt, words in Spanish passing quickly and softly between them, a rhythm Junior and Faidh couldn't catch. He nodded, then led them through the festival's pulse—past the drums, the smoke of roasting pork, the swirl of dancers—to a large tent at the plaza's edge. It stood near the Río Grande de Arecibo, its waters murmuring past the museum grounds where the festival hummed. The tent was cool, shaded, the river's whisper a low counterpoint to the distant music.

They settled on woven mats, the air heavy with the scent of earth and water. Junior spoke, his voice low, steady. He told of finding the first amulet on Mona Island, its weight strange in his hand. He spoke of the old man, his tales of hidden caves and forgotten Taíno paths. He described the Pirate Cave, its damp walls, and secrets. As he named each stone, he passed it to Guey, who studied them, his fingers tracing the carved lines. Faidh added her piece, her voice hesitant but clear, sharing dreams that came unbidden—visions of storms and spirited figures. She wasn't sure they mattered, but Guey listened, his eyes sharp, curious, drinking in every word.

"I don't know much about Pirata Cofresí," Guey said, his voice thoughtful, "I have some cousins that live in Cabo Rojo who have told me some of his stories, though. But I've heard the legend of his four amulets. We thought it was just pirate talk, old stories spun for tourists." He held up the first stone, its turtle petroglyph bold under the tent's dim light. "Let's start with this one."

Guey held the stone with the turtle petroglyph, its lines worn but clear in the dim light of the tent. The amulet seemed to hum with its own weight, waiting for Guey's words. He turned it slowly. His voice came low, steady, carrying the weight of his father's teachings.

The turtle, he said, is sacred to the Taíno. It is Atabey's creature, the mother of creation, tied to the earth and sea. Its shell is a shield, a home it carries always, representing strength, protection, and endurance. To carve a turtle is to honor the journey, the slow, sure path through time. It speaks of survival, of carrying your roots wherever you go. The Taíno saw it as a guide, a sign to stay grounded, to trust the land and water to provide. Today, the spirit of the turtle persists as communities honor Atabey through ceremonies that pay homage to the earth and sea. They celebrate her through food harvest festivals and practice land stewardship to ensure the island remains bountiful for future generations.

He paused, his dark eyes meeting Junior's, then Faidh's. "This petroglyph, on an amulet, is no small thing. It could mark a place—a cave, a river—where the Taíno felt Atabey's presence. Or it could be a call to protect something, a secret kept safe, like the turtle's shell. Where you found this, on Mona Island... it makes me think it's tied to something older, something hidden."

Guey's fingers traced the turtle's outline, his voice steady as the mountains. "The turtle doesn't rush. It knows its way. Maybe it's telling you to keep going, to carry the weight of what you've found, and trust the path will show itself."

Faidh and Junior locked eyes, a silent pulse passing between them, the weight of Guey's words about the turtle still settling. The tent was cool, an easy breeze blowing quietly through. Guey held the second amulet, its surface rough under his fingers. "And now this one," he said, his voice calm, rooted like the mountains. "The one with the Tree petroglyph, you say."

He reached for a clay jug and poured water over the stone. The liquid caught the light, revealing the carved shape—a tree, its branches spread wide, roots deep, etched sharp and clear. Guey studied it, his eyes narrowing, tracing the lines with a steady hand. "The Cojobano Tree is life itself to the Taíno," he said. "It is Yocahu, the giver of cassava, the sustainer. Its roots bind the earth, its branches reach for the sky—connecting the underworld, the living, and the spirits. To carve it is to mark a place of power, a center where the world holds together."

He turned the amulet, water dripping to the woven mat below. "This symbol speaks of balance, of growth that endures. It could point to a sacred grove, a meeting place, or a site where the Taíno sought Yocahu's strength. This one found here on Boricua, in that cave, it might mean a hidden truth, something tied to the land's heart." His gaze lifted to Junior, then Faidh, steady and sure. "The Cojobano doesn't move. It stands firm. This amulet—it's asking you to seek the center, to find what holds the story together."

Guey continued turning the amulets in his hands, the turtle and Cojobano Tree petroglyphs sharp under the tent's dim light. "These Taíno petroglyphs carry deep meaning," he said, his face troubled, brow creased. "The turtle is protection, endurance. The Cojobano Tree is life, balance. But I can't see how the turtle would have led you to the second stone, or how the tree hinted at another on Mona Island. These stones haven't helped you in your search, but it could be that something spiritual has." As he said this, his eyes flickered with a brief shadow of doubt, his words hesitating as if caught on the edge of revelation. He shook his head, voice low. "I've asked my aunt to find my father. He's the eldest bohique in Jayuya. He knows the old Taíno teachings, things I haven't learned yet. He might see what I don't."

While they waited, Junior and Faidh pressed Guey with questions, hungry for the Taíno world—tales of Yocahu, the cem'ís power, the batey's sacred games. Guey answered, his words clear, rooted in the mountains, but the amulets stayed silent, their secrets locked tight. The tent held them close, the air thick with river damp and the weight of unanswered questions.

The tent flap parted, and Guey's father stepped in, a figure carved from the earth of Jayuya. Cacique Mabó, he was called, his presence heavy with years, his Taíno dress— vines tight across his chest, shells glinting at his waist— marking him as elder, bohitiu, keeper of old ways. His face was lined, his eyes deep like the rivers cutting through the mountains. Guey introduced him to Junior and Faidh, then spoke in Spanish, a rapid flow of words, catching his father up on the amulets, the turtle, the Cojobano Tree, and the talk of Pirata caves.

Cacique Mabó stood silent, a stone in each hand, eyes closed as if listening to the earth itself. The tent held its breath; suddenly, the drums were quiet, and the river's rolling splashes outside were the only sound. He spoke in Spanish, slow and deliberate. Guey translated, his voice steady, carrying the weight. "My father says these stones hold energy. Bad energy. They must be cleansed, but not here. No. All must be together, with Taíno ritual, in the place where the pirate treasure is—or was at one time. Only then will the evil lift."

Junior leaned forward, his voice low, urgent. "Does your father know where we might find the other two stones? Any clues in the Taíno symbols we're missing?"

Guey relayed the question. Cacique Mabó opened his eyes, dark and determined, and shook his head. Guey spoke for him. "He says the symbols—turtle, Cojobano Tree—have no clear tie to the places you found them. Cofresí picked them, but they seem random, no map in their lines."

Junior and Faidh nodded, their thanks quiet, heartfelt. They turned to leave, the festival's hum swelling as they neared the tent's edge. Guey's voice cut through, sharp, holding them. "Wait. Where will you go from here?"

Junior's face was heavy, eyes distant. "I'm not sure. We've got no more clues. We could dig into research, find another Cofresí expert, but right now, it's a dead end."

Guey's gaze held them, his dark eyes fierce, almost pleading. "Could I come with you? If you find more stones, I might be able to help decipher them. And my father and I agree—when all are found, you'll need a Taíno bohitiu to cleanse them. I could be that for you."

Faidh turned to Junior, a smile breaking through, light in her eyes. "Up for another crew member, Captain?"

Junior pulled Faidh aside in the tent's shadow, voice low. "He's sharp with the symbols, but a stranger on the boat? I'm not big on some stranger joining us—could be trouble, especially with that 'bohitiu' magic vibe."

Faidh bit her lip, glancing at Guey chatting with his father. "True, no matter what, a third on board complicates things. But he feels... destined. Let's see where this goes. But it's your call, and I trust your instincts."

They returned, Junior's questions probing: family, motives. Guey answered earnestly, but his eyes held a guarded depth, as if hiding personal stakes in the curse.

Finally, Junior agreed to the Taíno youth joining him. The three stood together, bound by adventure ahead and the promise of stones yet to be found.

Guey's face lit up, his joy sharp and unguarded, like a boy stepping beyond Jayuya's green hills for the first time. Born and raised in the mountain's heart, he'd only left a handful of times—trips to Ponce or San Juan for festivals or family matters. Now the sea and its secrets called, and he stood ready, his Taíno garb catching the tent's dim light.

"How soon can you be ready? And I ask this, not sure if you will need one, but do you have a Passport?" Junior asked, his voice steady, a captain sizing up his crew.

Guey glanced at his father, then back. "I need to settle a few things. I can join you in Ponce tomorrow morning, if that's okay. I'll find a ride and be there by mid-morning. As for the passport, I do have one, which seems crazy, but it's true. I was supposed to attend the Indigenous Peoples' Conference in Santo Domingo in the fall of 2020, but it was cancelled due to COVID. So I still don't have any stamps in it. Do you think I'll need it?"

"I don't know where we might end up—you might be the one who steers us to another country. Who knows?" Junior said, a faint smile breaking through. "And whenever you get to Ponce works. I wasn't planning to sail till we figured out a new destination, anyway."

Guey turned to his father, their Spanish quick and soft. Then Guey faced Junior again, his eyes earnest. "My father wants to study the stones more. Could you leave them with us? I'll bring them to Ponce tomorrow."

Junior paused, weighing the request. "Wow, that's a big ask. You know that, right? We have known each other for no more than a couple of hours, and you are asking me for what is possibly the map to a hidden pirate treasure."

"I'm sorry. I'm not presuming anything, Mr. Junior. My father and I were simply hoping to have more time with the stones before they were taken away."

He looked long and hard into Faidh's eyes. He wasn't looking for the answer there; he didn't want to be distracted in his thoughts by Guey's innocent smile. He reached into his pack, holding the turtle amulet in one hand, the Cojobano Tree in the other. "Here's a deal," he said, voice firm but warm. "In trust, I'll leave one with you, and you can take a picture of the other. That work?"

Guey relayed the offer in Spanish, his father's eyes narrowing, then nodding slowly. Cacique Mab'ós face stayed unreadable, but his hands closed gently around the turtle stone as Junior handed it over. Guey pulled out his phone, snapping a clear shot of the Cojobano Tree amulet before passing it back.

Junior met Cacique Mab'ós gaze. "Tell your father, when we find all the amulets and lift the curse, we'll donate them to the museum. Let them be seen by all. I'm not a collector. I'm just trying to do what's right."

Guey translated, and a smile broke across his face, bright as the festival outside. "That would be wonderful!" he said, his voice carrying the weight of Jayuya's pride. The three stood bound by a promise, the stones' secrets pulling them toward the sea.

Junior glanced at Faidh, his eyes catching the fading light of the tent. "Guess we should head back to Ponce before dark," he said, voice steady. "The mountain drive was fine in daylight, but I don't think it'd be as fun at night."

Faidh sighed, a smile breaking through. "I second that."

They both laughed, the sound soft, easing the weight of the amulets' mystery.

Guey leaned in, his Taíno garb rustling, his face bright with a boy's eagerness. "Would you like to see one of Puerto Rico's coolest sites on your way down?"

Faidh's eyes lit up before Junior could answer. "Hell, yes!" she called, her voice sharp with excitement.

Guey grinned, quick and real. "It's called Cañón Blanco, a white granite canyon carved by a small river—a hidden gem. If you get the chance, jump in and swim. The water's cool, refreshing. It washes your troubles clean."

"That sounds amazing!" Faidh said, her smile wide, her earlier worries gone.

"It's about thirty minutes down the road, on your way back to Highway 10," Guey added. "Your phone should guide you there."

Junior nodded, the idea settling like the promise of a clear sea. Cañón Blanco called—a place of white stone and cool water, waiting to be found.

Junior and Faidh left Jayuya, the sounds of the festival fading behind them. As they drove away, Junior muttered to Faidh, "Hope we're not going to regret this. Keep an eye on him."

She nodded in complete agreement.

The SUV wound through green hills, the air cool with the scent of earth and coffee. Their phones guided them to a turnoff near Utuado, where Cañón Blanco waited. They parked on a dirt pullout, the Río Grande de Arecibo glinting below, its waters carving a path through white granite. The canyon was close, hidden by a curtain of sierra palms and bamboo.

They stepped from the car, gravel crunching underfoot, and followed a narrow trail down. The path was steep, roots breaking the earth, the river's murmur growing louder. Faidh moved ahead, her steps quick, hair catching the late sun. The air turned damp, heavy with the smell of wet stone and moss.

The trail opened to Cañón Blanco. White granite walls rose sharply, smoothed by centuries of water, their surfaces pale as bone against the green forest. The river ran clear, cold, pooling in deep hollows between the rocks. Sunlight cut through the canopy, turning the water to glass. No petroglyphs marked the stones, not that they could see, but the place felt old, alive, like it held its own secrets - somehow magical.

Faidh kicked off her shoes, her laugh sharp and free. She stripped to her panties and bra and stepped to the edge of a pool, the water lapping at her toes. "It's perfect," she said, her voice bright. She ran in, clean and sure, breaking the surface with a splash that echoed off the canyon walls. The water closed over her, then parted as she rose, grinning, hair slick against her neck.

Junior watched, a smile tugging at his lips. He shed his shirt and shorts, the air cool on his nearly bare skin, and followed. The water was sharp, cold as Guey promised, biting his chest as he sank in. It woke him, washed the dust of the road and the puzzle of the amulets clean away. He swam to Faidh, her eyes catching his, bright as the river's shimmer. They floated, the current gentle, the granite walls standing guard.

The canyon was quiet but for the water's rush, the distant call of a coqui. No clues to the amulets surfaced, no carvings spoke. Yet the place held them, its cool embrace enough for now. They swam until the sun dipped low, then climbed out, water dripping from their skin, the stones warm under their feet. Cañón Blanco stayed behind them, silent, waiting, as they walked back to the car, the road to Ponce ahead.

Shortly after getting a good phone signal again while driving down the mountain, a notification sounded on Junior's phone. It was an alarm from Dream Maker. His heart skipped a beat, and his fingers tightened on the steering wheel. Someone unwelcome was on board, trying to get in. Junior's mouth went dry, a metallic taste filling his mouth as he opened his security app. The video recording of the incident flickered to life on the screen, delivering a cold jolt to his gut. Two men, strangers to him, were inside the cockpit of Dream Maker, trying to pick the lock on the companionway. The alarm clearly startled them, as they quickly chose to get off the boat.

"What the hell?" asked Faidh.

"Looks like someone tried to break into Dream Maker." For the first time, Junior said the words out loud that had been scratching at his mind for more than a day now: "I think someone knows that we have the Amulets, and I think they're following us."

His words settled between them, heavy as an anchor. The drive back to Ponce passed in low voices and long silences, both of them turning over what to do next, the road winding on beneath a sky that seemed to hold its breath.

By the time they arrived back at Dream Maker, it was nearly 11:00 pm, but Faidh was in no mood to sleep. She hadn't said anything about it all day to Junior, but Faidh was, in fact, afraid to close her eyes or to let her mind dream - knowing that dreams likely meant seeing Cofresí again.

That left Faidh restless in the bunk, the hum of Dream Maker's stillness in the Ponce waters, a fragile comfort after the long drive back from Jayuya. The amulets, one left

120

behind with Guey and one left sitting in Junior's backpack in the salon, seemed to pulse with a quiet menace, their weight pressing on her chest as she stared at the ceiling, dread coiling tight. Sleep loomed like a trap, the memory of Cofres'ís threats from her last dream clawing at her resolve.

Junior sat up beside her and took her hand, "What's wrong? I can see that something is bothering you. Is it the alarm from earlier? I'm gonna inspect the boat in the morning when we have good light, but I don't think anyone got inside Dream Maker today. Or is it the phone call you received earlier that is bothering you? Do you want to talk about it?" Junior realized he was asking too much and not letting her talk, so he decided just to shut up and let Faidh find her voice, if and when she was ready.

Faidh hesitated, the weight of her mother's urgent voicemails pressing down—another family fight over her brother and his mental health issues, pulling her from this dreamlike escape. If I tell him, will he think I'm not committed? But keeping it in is eating me alive. She shook her head, forcing a smile. "It's nothing big—just family drama. Let's focus on the adventure. We'll get there. Right now, I want to stay focused on what's ahead of us here." Inside, the distraction festered, her mind split between the sea and home.

Junior pressed gently, "It doesn't seem like nothing—you've been quiet all day." Faidh's temper flared briefly. "I said it's fine! I don't need to dump my mess on you." He backed off, hurt flickering in his eyes, but nodded. "Alright, when you're ready." The moment created a subtle distance, amplifying her internal guilt as they continued into the night.

Five minutes of silence passed, and it felt like an eternity.

Then Faidh turned to Junior and said softly, "But there is more than just my family issues that are keeping me awake. I keep having dreams every night—storms, you falling overboard, and that pirate yelling at me to stop chasing the amulets. I'm scared to close my eyes."

Junior's eyes opened wide, soft but alert, and he nodded. "I'm so sorry. I know it's easy to say, 'it's just a dream,' but I do understand dreams can get inside your psyche and affect you to your core. Why haven't you told me?   Do you feel like this is too much?

Quickly and maybe louder than she meant, Faidh blurted out, "No! After everything we learned today, I think this is bigger than us. I believe this is something we must do. I'm just scared. It'll pass."

"Ok, but please stop keeping these dreams to yourself. I want to hear about them." Junior hesitated for a long pause before continuing, "I probably should have told you the first night you shared yours with me."

"Told me what?" Faidh interjected.

"That I have had two nightmares myself, before you came aboard." Junior shared. "But I thought they were just my subconscious dealing with the amulet that I had found and everything I had learned through research on the subject."

"Yeah, you probably should have told me that first night." Faidh scolded him.

"I didn't think they were related. The subconscious is pretty powerful, and I thought maybe you were just coping with our first time being together. But now that you say you've had one every night since, I think there is some weird going on."

Faidh looked into Junior's eyes. "And they have become more graphic with each night. At the beginning, it was just threats, but each night now, I'm actually losing you overboard, in a massive storm, with a motorboat right on top of us." She hesitated to regain her composure. "And Cofresí is getting bigger and bigger each night; not only is his size growing, but so is his anger. I'm not a believer in the supernatural, but I'm starting to wonder if his threats are real. If maybe the curse is actually something we need to be afraid of."

Junior leaned over Faidh, put his arms around her, and held her tight, whispering in Faidh's ear, "Remember, they are just dreams; they can scare the hell out of you, but they can't hurt you."

"I know." She said softly, letting herself relax in his arms.

It was nearly 1 am by the time Faidh finally fell asleep. Junior stayed awake, holding and comforting her until he was certain she had fallen asleep. And once he was sure, sleep overcame him as well.

The sea raged, a black maw of waves towering thirty feet, crashing over Dream Maker with a roar that shook her bones. Lightning split the sky, illuminating Junior as he fought forward, harness taut, only for a monstrous swell to hurl him overboard. His body slammed against the hull, blood streaking the water, and sharks circled with frenzied jaws snapping. Faidh screamed, lunging for him, but the deck buckled, sending her sprawling as the boat began to break apart. Cofresí materialized, his figure towering and skeletal, cutlass raised, eyes glowing red. "The amulet's curse hungers!" he bellowed, slashing the air, the blade grazing Junior's flailing form as he sank. "His death is your price—stop, or watch him bleed out!" The sea surged, dragging Faidh under, her lungs filling with icy water as Cofres'ís laughter drowned her cries.

She jolted awake with a choked gasp, thrashing against the blanket, her elbow jabbing Junior in the ribs. He grunted, bolting upright, his hand gripping her arm. "Faidh! What the hell—was it him again?" His voice was rough with sleep and concern, the dim cabin light catching the worry in his eyes as he steadied her. He caught a glimpse of the time; it was nearly 7:00 am.

Faidh nodded, pulling the blanket tight around her shoulders, her breath ragged. "This time, you went overboard to the sharks, and Dream Maker was disintegrating under my feet. And Cofresí is not only growing, but he looks more like death each time I see him. There was something different this time. I felt a desperation in his voice this time he appeared. It was like he was as scared as I was." Her voice cracked. "I'm not sure I can handle another night of this."

Junior held her tight, feeling her body tremble against his. It was clear to him that, even though she had gotten some sleep the night before, nearly six hours, it would be even harder for her to fall asleep later that evening. That was something they would deal with when the time came. For now, he held her tight, and before long, they both nodded off for what seemed an eternity and woke up fresh, ready for another day of this evolving adventure.

CHAPTER 11

THE MAP REVEALED

Guey sat alone in his Jayuya home, the night deep and quiet, the mountain air still. A restless energy hummed in the room, centered around the turtle amulet, which lay heavy on the table. Rumors whispered that it held the power to unlock secrets of the past, a guide to hidden treasures. The festival's echo was gone, the stars sharp through the window. The petroglyph on the amulet caught the lamplight, its carved initials 'RC' almost daring him to uncover its truth. Beside it, a photo of the Cojobano Tree amulet glowed on his phone. He stared at them, eyes tracing the lines, searching for what he missed, what they all missed. Junior's story rang in his mind: one amulet leads to the rest. How?

Petroglyph on one side. RC on the other. He turned the turtle stone in his hand, its surface cool and stubborn. He poured water over it, slowly and carefully, watching for shapes to emerge, for a clue lost to the years. Nothing. The lines held their silence.

Could it be the bad energy his father spoke of? Guey's thoughts returned to the words of his father, weaving a thread through the years. His father had always warned about the risk of losing touch with their heritage, a fear that sometimes crept up on him like a shadow. Guey wondered if the stones held some magnetic pull, like the lodestones the ancients used, tied to wood, floating in water, that pointed north and south. But even if this turtle were magnetic, it couldn't point to another stone, far off on another island. It simply wouldn't work that way. Yet, the thought snagged at him, the possibility of failing to uncover the truth his ancestors left hungry in his mind. Another island. He couldn't shake the feeling that he needed to succeed, not just for himself, but to honor the legacy he carried on his shoulders.

Cofresí knew islands. Mona, where Junior found the first amulet, was the pirate's base, a jagged outpost for raids. The second stone came from Puerto Rico's hills, Cofres'ís boyhood home, its paths etched in his bones. Where else did he go? What islands held his shadow?

Guey set the amulet down, its weight final, and opened his laptop. The screen's glow lit his face, his Taíno garb folded nearby. For three hours, he scoured the internet, chasing Cofres'ís ghost. He read about the pirate's raids on Spanish gold ships and his escapes from American and British fleets. He found tales of Vieques and Culebra, lawless isles where crabs scuttled and timber grew thick, perfect for a pirate's resupply. He learned of Tortuga, a pirate haven off the coast of Haiti, its waters hiding shipwrecks, its beaches once alive with buccaneers. Nassau, in the Bahamas, also emerged as a stronghold for men like Blackbeard, whose swift ships were well-suited to its shallow waters. Cofres'ís name is tied to Puerto Rico's coast —Rincón, Boquerón, Cabo Rojo—but also to whispers of caves on Vieques' Monte Pirata, where he might've stashed loot.

No clear map emerged, nor was a list of companions named. The pirate left little trace, his crew's names lost to time or legend. But the islands—Mona, Puerto Rico, Vieques, Culebra, maybe Tortuga—felt like a thread. Guey leaned back, the turtle amulet glinting. The stones were tied to Cofres'ís world, his routes, his hiding places, but they seemed to evade Guey.

Finally, exhausted, Guey lay down and fell asleep almost immediately, the mountain air cool. His bed was simple; the night was black, and the stars were sharp through the open window. In his dream, shapes danced.

A turtle appeared first, carved in a triangular stone, its lines deep, worn by time. It moved slowly through a sea of shadow, its shell a shield, heavy with the earth's weight. Its eyes, like polished obsidian, held his, then faded. A Cojobano Tree rose on a circular background. Yocahu's tree, giver of cassava, glowed green, then blurred into mist.

Other shapes drifted in, unanchored. A jagged spiral spun, sharp as a blade. A broken circle pulsed, steady as a heart. A triangle, its tip burning, floated and fell. They crossed the turtle's path, tangled in the tree's roots, moving without pattern or meaning. The shapes pulled him, a tide of light and shadow, toward a cave where water dripped, cold and slow. The turtle crawled over the stone. The tree's branches brushed the cave roof. Spiral, circle, triangle circled them, whispering, drawing him toward what waited in the dark.

He woke, Jayuya silent, the room still. The shapes lingered, sharp in his mind, the turtle and tree interlaced with the chaos of spirals, triangles, and circles.

The haze of his dream cleared, and Guey sat up with a bolt. "Shapes!" he yelled.

Guey grabbed the Turtle Amulet, sitting on the desk. Its edges were worn, and he raised it to the lamplight. The stone was shaped like Puerto Rico itself, its outline clear—long and narrow, with curving edges. The hole where a cord once hung pierced the southwest corner, right where Cueva del Pirata Cofresí lay near Boqueron. His breath caught, sharp and quick. "That's it," he said, voice low, to the empty room. The amulet's shape wasn't random—it marked the place where the next stone was found.

Guey now sat, the turtle amulet heavy in his hand. He grabbed his phone, pulling up the photo of the second amulet, the Cojobano Tree. Its shape stirred something, a memory tugging hard. He opened Google Maps, fingers quick, and zoomed to the islands east of Puerto Rico. There —Vieques, Isla Nena, its outline nearly a twin to the stone. The hole for the cord pierced the south-central coast, the Vieques Bioluminescent Bay glowing nearby.

His pulse quickened. He searched for an hour, the phone's glow sharp on his face. Ensenada del Pirata—Pirate's Cove—sat right where the hole marked the stone. Once a Navy ordnance range, now part of the Vieques National Wildlife Refuge, it was the kind of place a stone could hide for centuries. A crumbling lighthouse, now just rocks, stood nearby. Land was hard to reach, but trails fanned out from the cove, leading to hidden bays. No Taíno legend named the spot, but its name—Pirate's Cove— echoed Cofresí, the shadow behind the amulets. The turtle had pointed to his cave; the Cojobano Tree pointed to Vieques, to this cove.

The stones were a map, carved by a pirate or maybe by hands older still. Tomorrow, he would meet Junior and Faidh in Ponce and show them what he'd found. Junior would want a destination: Vieques, where the cove waited, silent and certain. But where in the cove? That was the question.

Guey leaned back, the turtle amulet warm in his hand. He set his phone down, heart pounding with the pull of new shores, the promise of a boat, Vieques and its secrets, the amulets' truth coming clear. In a day, Jayuya's quiet had turned to a call for adventure. He climbed into bed, the night cool, stars sharp, sleep coming fast, the shapes of islands and stones alive in the dark.

Guey stepped onto the dock at Ponce Yacht Club just before noon, the sun high, the harbor calm. He'd texted Junior earlier, giving his ETA, and his ride down the mountain from Jayuya was smooth. He carried a small duffel bag slung over one shoulder, a backpack on the other —light, ready for the sea. His Taíno garb was gone, traded for a simple shirt and shorts, but his eyes still held the spark of the festival, of the amulets' pull.

His father, Cacique Mabó, stood by the car, his face lined and quiet. Guey wrapped him in a tight hug, words soft in Spanish, a goodbye heavy with pride. Junior approached, offering a tour of Dream Maker, the boat gleaming white against the dock. Mabó shook his head, his gaze already turning back to the mountains, to Jayuya and the festival's final hours. He climbed into the car, the engine humming, and was gone, the road swallowing him up.

Guey turned to Junior and Faidh, the turtle amulet safe in his pack, its shape—Puerto Rico itself—still sharp in his mind. The Cojobano Tree amulet, with its Vieques outline, waited too, a map to the southern central part of the island. The sea stretched beyond, bright and wide, promising answers.

Guey stood on the dock at Ponce Yacht Club, the noon sun glinting off Dream Maker's hull. His duffel and backpack rested at his feet, the turtle amulet safe inside. He looked at Junior and Faidh, his eyes bright, voice sharp with discovery. "I know where to go next."

"Where?" Faidh asked, her voice alive with excitement, leaning forward.

"Vieques. Ensenada del Pirata," Guey said, the words quick, sure.

Junior raised an eyebrow, his hand steady on the dock line. "Is that a guess, or did you figure something out?"

Guey grinned, pulling the turtle amulet from his pack. He held it up, the stone catching the light, its edges tracing a familiar shape. "The stones are the clue to the next. This one," he turned it for them to see, "it's Puerto Rico. The hole sits right where Cueva del Pirata Cofresí is, in the southwest, where you found the second stone." His smile faltered slightly, his eyes flickering with a moment of doubt. "Just a hunch," he added with a nervous laugh, "but I think it's got to mean something."

Junior reached into his pocket, pulling out the Cojobano Tree amulet, and handed it to Guey. The harbor was quiet, the sea flat, waiting. Guey took the stone, his fingers tracing its outline. "See this? It's Vieques, almost exact. And the hole—" he pointed to the small puncture in the stone's south-central area, "—that's where a cove known as Ensenada del Pirata sits."

Guey's certainty unnerved Junior—How did he figure that overnight? Feels like more than guesswork. "Impressive," Junior said, probing, "Any... visions from your training?"

Guey hesitated, a shadow crossing his face. "Sometimes the ancestors speak in dreams. But it's not always clear."

Faidh shot Junior a look. This whole thing was unnerving and too easy. It was like Guey knew more than he was sharing.

Junior nodded slowly, accepting the input from Guey with some hesitation. The pieces are falling into place almost too easily.

"Well then, I think we should get underway. We have a long trip ahead of us."

Faidh took Guey below decks and showed him where his quarters would be, and gave him a quick tour of Dream Maker, while Junior started preparing for their departure. She shared how excited she and Junior were to have him come along.

Guey just beamed. "Thank you. I'm very excited and to be quite honest, a little nervous."

"Don't worry, you're in great hands. Junior is a great captain, and Dream Maker is ready for anything."

Guey managed a smile, uncertain but real.

Guey climbed topside, his face pale, eyes bright with the thrill of the journey despite the mountain air still clinging to him. Junior fixed him with a steady look, the Ponce Yacht Club Office quiet behind them. "If you're joining this adventure, you're not just coming along for the ride," Junior said, voice firm but warm. "Everyone on a sailboat is crew. So, my new friend, you're going to learn to be a sailor. There might be a few moments of regret—probably today— but you'll end up loving the sea."

Guey grinned, his excitement raw, untested. He was green, greener than the Jayuya hills he'd rarely left. Boating was a mystery, the sea even more so. Junior knew he couldn't lean on him for maritime work yet, and that was fine. Guey's value lay beyond the ropes and sails—in the amulets, the Taíno whispers he carried.

Junior turned to Faidh, her hands already on the helm. "Take us out. I'll show Guey how to untie the lines and stow them with the fenders in the forward locker."

The departure was smooth, Faidh's skill at the helm sure as Dream Maker slipped from Ponce's harbor. Guey fumbled at first but learned fast, coiling ropes under Junior's steady eye, stowing gear neatly and tightly. As they moved into open waters, Junior called to Faidh, "Turn into the wind. Let's set sail." The winds were light, the seas calm at one to three feet, rolling slowly every twelve seconds. Junior aimed for Palmas del Mar by nightfall, pushing for full sail with the main, mizzen, Genoa, and cutter. As the canvas caught every breath of wind, Guey felt a thrill pulse through him, mingling apprehension with exhilaration. The Caribbean stretched infinitely bright and wide before them, a vast mystery he was only beginning to understand. Before he could blink, they were under sail, cutting east at eight knots, and he was part of an adventure he only dreamed of.

The gentle swell was too much for Guey, his face paling further, yawns betraying the first tug of seasickness. Junior saw it, his voice calm. "Keep your eyes on the horizon, Guey. Don't watch the boat's roll." He offered the helm, a distraction, but Guey shook his head, unsteady.

Faidh, her eyes soft with pity, spoke up. "Want some crackers?"

Guey waved her off, his voice weak. "No, thanks. Dad got me lunch on the way down. Pinchos—chicken, and a fried pork empanada. Bad choice for the sea, I'm thinking."

Faidh giggled, unable to help it, her laugh light in the salt air. "Not the best for your first sail. Here—" she handed him a cold bottle of water, "—hydrate. It always helps."

Junior kept watch as the boat steered steadily at eight knots, with Palmas del Mar five to six hours off. The coast buzzed with Sunday life—jetskis darting like flies, center console fishing boats trolling for marlin. But one boat caught his eye, a Sea Ray, maybe the same one from Guánica Bay. It wasn't following, not exactly, but it zipped past Dream Maker three times, playing some game of tag, taking turns as "it." Junior's jaw tightened. He grabbed his binoculars, sighting the name and home port: El Tiburón, Puerto Real—no AIS signal, despite its size. The hairs on his neck stood up.

He turned to Faidh, voice low. "Can you find a boat's owner with just the name and home port?"

Faidh tilted her head, curious. "It'd narrow it down, but if you've got make and model, I could likely get the owner's name. Why?"

Junior pointed at the Sea Ray, now a speck ahead. "That boat. Gives me a bad feeling. I want to know more, put my mind at ease."

"Sure," Faidh said, already moving. "Let me grab my laptop. Can you take the helm?"

Junior looked at Guey, pale but standing. "You up for the helm? It helps when you're feeling under the weather. Forces you to watch the horizon, not the boat's bob in the water."

"Sure," Guey said, reluctant, stepping to the wheel, hands unsteady.

Junior sat beside him, voice calm. "Hold the heading, zero nine three, best you can." He pointed to the display. "She'll slide a couple of degrees with the waves. Don't chase it—let her find her way back. Small wheel movements if she doesn't."

"Aye, aye, Captain," Guey said, forcing a smile through the queasiness.

"We'll make a sailor of you yet," Junior said, clapping his shoulder, the sea stretching east, El Tiburón a shadow in his thoughts.

Junior guided Dream Maker into Palmas del Mar as the sun sank, the sky bruised purple over the Caribbean. The harbor was vast, calm, its waters glass-smooth, reflecting the lights of yachts and the low hum of wealth. Beyond the docks, the resort sprawled—villas of white stucco, red-tiled roofs, nestled among palms that swayed softly in the evening breeze. Golf courses stretched green, their fairways cut sharp, rolling toward hills dusted with guava and mango trees. The beach curved long and pale, waves lapping gently, leaving foam like lace on the sand.

Condos loomed at the edge, their windows catching the last light, staring out to the sea. Restaurants lined the marina, their tables spilling over with laughter, the clink of glasses, and the scent of grilled fish and rum. A few locals fished off the pier, their lines taut, patient. The air was warm, heavy with salt and jasmine, the night alive but quiet, holding its breath.

Faidh stood on Dream Maker's deck, the Palmas del Mar harbor quiet under the bruised evening sky. She pointed to the far end of a dock, where El Tiburón sat, its sleek hull glinting like a blade. "I've got info on our not-so-friendly follower," she said, voice low, sharp with discovery.

Junior turned, eyes narrowing. "What'd you find?"

"It was stolen yesterday," Faidh said. "Owned by a Puerto Rican couple from San Juan, but it's registered down in Cabo Rojo. They keep it on a mooring ball in the bay. They don't know when it was taken—hadn't checked on it for a couple of days. They're weekend cruisers, and when they went to dinghy out yesterday morning, they found the ball empty. They've been trying to track it ever since. No luck."

Junior's jaw tightened. "Seriously? Where'd you dig that up? I didn't think your sales systems were that good."

Faidh grinned, quick and sly. "Facebook. Friends of Puerto Real Group, Puerto Rican Cruisers Group. Took some translating, but I pieced it together."

Junior nodded, his face set. "I'm going to the Dock Master."

Faidh's eyes flicked to El Tiburón, worry creasing her brow. "Be careful. They got here before us. You don't know who's local, who's from that boat."

"I will," Junior said, pausing. "Stay here, both of you. Don't let anyone aboard."

Faidh tilted her head, half-smiling. "How're we supposed to stop them?"

"Scream. Sound the foghorn. That'll scare off the foggy characters." His grin was brief, but his eyes stayed sharp.

Junior strode to the marina office, the night air thick with the scent of salt and jasmine. Faidh watched from the deck, Guey beside her, his face still pale from the sea. Junior spoke to the Dock Master, a short man with a clipboard, gesturing toward El Tiburón. The Dock Master pointed at the boat, but Junior knocked his arm down, quickly, keeping their suspicion hidden. The man pulled out his phone and dialed the police.

Too late. El Tiburón stirred, lines flung aboard, engines roaring. It pulled away fast, reckless, nearly clipping a motor cat docked in front. The harbor's calm broke, ripples spreading. Before the police could arrive, the Sea Ray was gone, no lights, steaming south, a shadow swallowed by the dark sea.

Guey stood on Dream Maker's deck, the harbor lights of Palmas del Mar flickering across the water. His face was still pale, the sea's sway lingering in his gut. He looked at Faidh, his voice soft but steady. "The danger's gone, for now. If it's okay, I'm going for a walk. Solid ground might settle my stomach."

Faidh nodded, her smile warm, understanding. "Absolutely. I'll tell Junior where you went when he's back. We're eating here tonight. We'll wait for you."

As Guey stepped onto the dock, the rhythm of his steps became a steadying force. With each footfall on solid ground, the uncertainty that had gripped him since setting sail began to ebb away. His thoughts drifted to the amulets and the adventure ahead. A resolve began to form within him, a whisper of determination to see this journey through, not only for the treasure it might uncover but for the story he would write in his own heart. He felt a quiet shift, a readiness for tomorrow's challenges blooming with each breath of the salt-laden breeze.

"Thanks," Guey said, a faint laugh breaking through. "I'll try to lose the green on my face."

Faidh leaned against the rail of Dream Maker, the harbor's lights soft on the water, the night warm with an easy breeze. "I promise, tomorrow will be easier for you," she said, her voice gentle, steady, carrying the hope of a friend. And she thought to herself, I'm hoping my night will somehow be easier than the past couple of nights.

Guey managed a weak smile, his eyes grateful but tired. "Hope so," he said, stepping onto the dock, his legs finding the earth's stillness. He walked off, the marina's hum fading behind him, chasing solid ground to quiet his stomach. Faidh watched him go, the promise of Vieques and its secrets waiting in the dark.

After dinner, Guey settled into the forward berth, the gentle rock of Dream Maker tied to the dock at Palmas del Mar lulling him despite the unease churning in his gut from the day's events. The harbor lights danced faintly through the porthole, but sleep claimed him swiftly.

Suddenly, Guey found himself pulled into a dim, echoing chamber he didn't recognize—walls of jagged rock slick with moisture, the air thick with the scent of earth and salt, torches flickering in unseen drafts. He stood at the center, the four amulets arranged in a circle on a rough stone altar, his hands trembling as he chanted words that felt ancient and unfamiliar, drawn from some deep well of heritage. Junior and Faidh flanked him, their faces solemn in the wavering light, the cave's shadows twisting like living things as the ceremony built toward release—the curse lifting, the treasure's location shimmering into view like a mirage.

From the darkness beyond the altar emerged Pirata Cofresí, his form materializing like smoke coalescing into flesh, tricorn hat casting a long shadow over his scarred face, eyes gleaming with spectral fire. He stepped forward, cutlass at his side dripping with phantom seawater, his voice a gravelly rumble that echoed off the rocks. "Foolish guardian of old blood," Cofresí snarled, pointing a gnarled finger at Guey, "the amulets demand a toll! Cease this ritual, abandon the hunt, or the curse will claim a life—yours or those you drag into the abyss!" Guey froze, the chant dying on his lips, but the energy in the cave surged, the air crackling with unseen power as if the stones themselves rejected the pirate's warning.

Then, without prelude, a bolt of lightning erupted from the cave wall, arcing like a serpent's strike straight toward Faidh. It slammed into her chest with a deafening crack, her body igniting in a blaze of unnatural blue flame, screams tearing from her throat as she writhed, flesh charring and crumbling *to ash before Guey's horrified eyes. The fire spread hungrily, consuming her in seconds, the acrid stench of burning filling the chamber as Cofresí's laughter boomed, the treasure's glow fading into darkness. Junior reached for her, but it was too late—the cave collapsed inward, rocks tumbling like judgments.*

Guey bolted awake, drenched in sweat, his heart thundering against his ribs as he gasped in the quiet berth. The harbor's calm lapped against the hull, a mocking serenity, but the dream's horror clung to him like smoke, the image of Faidh's fiery death searing his mind. He sat up, hands shaking, unwilling to voice the terror aloud just yet, the amulets' curse feeling all too real in the still night.

CHAPTER 12

SHADOWS AND PURSUIT

Four Days Earlier

Dega Reyes awoke with a violent jolt, the piercing light of the Puerto Real morning slicing through his throbbing skull. The remnants of last night's rum clung to his tongue, a bitter reminder. Anger surged through him, more potent than the hangover. It filled the void that had become his life —no job, no future, nothing but the empty promise of another drink with the Santiago-Rivera brothers, Bruno and Tomas. Maria lay beside him, serene in sleep, unaware of the darkness festering within him. Once, not long ago, he'd had steady work at Propper International and a future with Maria in his sights. Now, his hands, once soft and gentle, were a stark reminder of the rage that had taken root within him.

She looked at him, hopeful, her voice light. "I heard a really cool story last night. Might cheer you up." She told of a sailor and his girlfriend at the restaurant, a stone he'd found, marked with Pirata Cofres'ís signs, maybe a clue to his lost treasure. "Isn't that cool?" she said, eyes bright. "After all this time, someone might find Cofres'ís treasure. It could be worth hundreds of thousands, maybe millions."

Dega sat up, sharp, like a blade drawn. "Who's this sailor?"

"Docked last night at the marina. A sailboat, I think."

"His name, woman?"

"Junior, I think. His girlfriend called him that."

"The boat's name?"

"Don't know." Maria's voice stayed soft, eager to please. She hoped that good news might help restore what she and Dega once shared—a connection now frayed. "Alejandro, the Dock Master, would have it. Want me to ask?"

"No. I'll handle it." His words were clipped, eyes narrowing. "What else about him? He leaving today?"

"I don't think so. I told him to find Dom, the old man in the chair at the end of the street who talks Cofresí nonstop. I said Dom could tell him everything he needed to know about the Pirate."

Dega nodded, his mind turning, hard and fast. "Make breakfast," he said, voice flat, already elsewhere. Maria rose, her steps quiet, while Dega sat, the weight of the story —treasure, a sailor, a stone—burning through the haze of his anger.

Dega pushed away his plate. The eggs and coffee were barely touched, the morning's haze thick in his head. No shower. No shave. He didn't care. He felt trapped by his reliance on Maria, who worked two jobs to keep them afloat and to keep him content, or at least to try to do so. The sun cut through Maria's blinds, sharp and hot in Puerto Real. He grabbed his phone, dialing Tomas and Bruno, his 'partners in crime.' The term came from their high school days. The three stole a car for a joyride, a lark that landed them in juvie for a month. It was the police chief's car. A dumb move, but they were sixteen. Their records were wiped clean at eighteen. The real weight on Dega's mind, though, was the gnawing belief that he was destined for failure, that his life would always come back to the same dead ends. Maria's story of the sailor, Junior, and the stone tied to Cofresí's treasure offered him a flicker of hope, a chance to disprove that misbelief and change his life. This was his way to escape the shadow of dependency on Maria. He saw a way out, gold, not anger. He wanted the brothers in. He didn't want to split the bounty, but he also knew he couldn't do it alone.

They met at Maria's apartment that afternoon, the air heavy with coming rain. Dega hadn't told them why, keeping the plan close to avoid their reckless streak. Tomas sprawled on the couch, and Bruno leaned against the wall, both waiting. Dega's eyes were hard, his voice low. "You still got access to your uncle's center console?"

Tomas shook his head. "Nah. He got pissed. We kept running it dry, not refueling."

"Useless," Dega snapped, fist clenched.

"What's up?" asked Bruno.

Dega shared the whole story with the brothers— everything Maria had shared with him earlier. "I think we're gonna need a boat. Something to follow this guy, see where he's headed, figure if his stone's worth anything before we waste time trying to chase a 200-year-old treasure that no one else has ever found." He paused, feeling the weight of his decision, his mind churning. This was more than a grab for gold; it was his chance to reclaim control, a lifeline to pull him from the abyss he felt swallowing him. The brothers, however, saw only glinting coins, their motivations straightforward. Dega fixed them with a stare, understanding that any misstep could turn allies into adversaries, and violence might plunge him further into the darkness he feared. "I'll find us a boat. You two go talk to Dom, the drunk old man who rambles about Cofresí. You know the one I'm talking about. Find out what the sailor said, what Dom told him."

Thunder cracked outside, sudden and sharp. Rain poured, heavy, drowning Puerto Real in sheets that lasted into the evening. The brothers nodded, undeterred by the storm, eager for a shot at the treasure themselves. Years of hustling and getting by had worn them down, and the idea of real money, a final score, was enough to push them forward. They stepped out, while Dega sat, his anger smoldering, the treasure a flicker of light in the shadows that darkened the apartment.

Later in the evening, the air finally settled in Puerto Real, now with a fresh, post-storm smell. Dega Reyes sat in a dim bar, the kind where the stools creaked and the bottles were dusty. His eyes were sharp, like a shark's, cutting through the haze of cigarette smoke. Tomas and Bruno leaned in, their voices low, faces rough with stubble and greed.

"What'd you two learn from Dom?" Dega asked, his words clipped, a man who didn't waste breath.

Tomas spoke, his voice gravelly, eager. "The old man spilled it all. Says the stone's real. Talked like the treasure's just waiting to be found. Needs four stones, though, to get it. Nobody knows where the other three are, but he said one's enough to find the rest. Thinks the sailor's onto something—called him chosen by Cofres'ís spirit to find it. The old man was half-drunk, but he believed every word. Says the treasure might actually be found."

Bruno snorted, leaning back, his bulk filling the chair. "I don't buy spirits or ghosts, but it's damn strange a gringo found that stone."

Dega's eyes narrowed. "Did Dom say where they're headed next?"

Tomas nodded. "Told 'em to check Cofres'ís cave and his statue. Then sent 'em to Jayuya for the Indigenous Festival this weekend. Thought the Taíno folk there might know something about the carving on the stone."

Dega's jaw tightened, his fingers tapping the table. "The cave's a dead end. We've combed it dozens of times. And so has every kid within 50 miles of here. Nothing but bats and their shit. No treasure there." He paused, his mind turning. The hope of treasure fueled him—he needed to believe this story meant more than the empty dead ends of his past. "I might have a line on a boat, though. I'll know more tomorrow. Talked to Alejandro at the marina. Says the sailor's name is James Wright, goes by Junior. His boat's an old sailboat, Dream Maker."

Tomas grinned, teeth yellow in the dim light. "No matter the boat you find, we'll outrun a sailboat. And it's three of us to one of him. Well, one and a half, with his girlfriend along."

Bruno laughed, a low rumble. "We can take that boat whenever we want. I say we let the gringo do all the hard work, then take the treasure when he finds it. I ain't any good at solving problems, and," looking around the bar, "from the likes of our present circumstances, neither are you two."

The three men laughed, loud and sharp, the sound cutting through the bar's haze. The night outside was still, but Dega's eyes glinted, fixed on the hunt, on Junior and his stone, the treasure just beyond reach.

The next day, Dega sat in a shadowed corner of a Boquerón bar. The air was thick with the damp scent of the sea and the pungent aroma of cheap rum. His friend, a marine electrician's apprentice, leaned in, voice low. "The boat's a Sea Ray Sundancer 380 on a mooring ball in Puerto Real. Badass. I worked on it a couple of weeks back, installing LEDs. Owners keep a spare cabin key under the port bench seat in the bridge for workers like us. Inside, the ignition keys hang on a rack, plain as day. Get to the boat and it's yours." He paused, sipping his beer. "Owners live in San Juan, come down some weekends to party. If you wait till Saturday, it might be gone."

Dega nodded thanks, eyes sharp, mind turning. He didn't want to dally around, so he picked up the tab for the beers and headed out. That evening, his phone buzzed. Alejandro, his marina contact, spoke fast. "Dega, it's Alejandro. You asked about Dream Maker. Owner says they're leaving at first light tomorrow."

"Where to?" Dega asked, voice flat.

"East, toward Ponce," Alejandro said.

Dega grunted thanks and hung up, his fingers already dialing the Santiago-Rivera brothers. "Meet me at Boquerón

Marina, noon tomorrow. Bring beer, food, and clothes for a couple of days. And any guns you got." He hoped the guns would stay cold, just a threat to keep the sailor in line when they took the stones—or the treasure.

That night, Dega slipped into the harbor, swimming out to El Tiburón with his belongings sealed tight in a bag at his waist. The water was black, cool against his skin, the world hushed and sleeping. He climbed aboard, silent as a shadow, and found the key tucked under the port bench where it waited. Inside, the cabin gleamed—polished wood, chrome shining in the dim light. He ran his hands over the controls, unfamiliar but promising. He was used to center consoles, not yachts, but a boat was a boat. The tanks were full. It would serve.

He set his alarm on his phone for 4 a.m. He wanted to slip out before the world woke. He'd drift outside the inlet and wait for Dream Maker to show in the morning. Then, he would tail her to Boquerón. There, he'd grab Tomas and Bruno, stock up, and chase the sailboat down again. He laughed to himself, low and sharp. The thought was clear: pirating was easy when your boat roared and the others crawled under sail. The night was still. The Sea Ray waited, its shadow from the moon long across the still water.

The next day broke clear, the sun a sharp blade over Puerto Real. Dega fired up El Tiburón at 4 a.m., the engines growling low, the harbor still asleep. He eased her out past the inlet, drifting in the dark, waiting for Dream Maker. He didn't have to wait long. Just after sunrise, the sailboat puttered out, slow and steady, her sails rising as she turned southwest, then tacking back south. Dega watched, a grin curling his lips. "I could swim faster than that thing," he muttered to himself. "Like taking candy from a baby."

He hung out for a bit, biding his time, scanning the horizon for signs they weren't being followed. Then he steered El Tiburón to Boquerón by noon, intent on getting Tomas and Bruno as quietly as possible. The brothers climbed aboard. Their arms were heavy with beer, food, and duffels stuffed with clothes, preparations for a trip they all knew would last longer than a day. Guns were tucked out of sight—they planned to stay out of trouble if they could, but weren't taking chances. Dega didn't want trouble, but he'd be ready. To keep off the grid, he grabbed a pair of wire cutters and snipped the AIS system's power lines. No circuit breaker for him, just like during those reckless teenage years when he and the brothers knew every back alley and shortcut, making sure they were ghosts to anyone who tried to track them. El Tiburón was a ghost now. Untraceable.

The Sea Ray roared around Cabo Rojo, the Caribbean flashing blue under the hull as they searched for Dream Maker's trail. No sails in sight. The brothers grew restless, thinking it was a wild goose chase. How could he lose such a slow boat so quickly?

By the time El Tiburón turned east, Dream Maker had already reached Guánica Bay. Junior, wanting to take it easy on their first day at sea, had turned into the bay and dropped anchor, settling for the night in the bay's west end. Focusing only on what was ahead, Dega overshot the Guánica Inlet at first, looking desperately for sails on the horizon. Then he took a second to think, cursing under his breath before finally checking the chartplotter. Dream

Maker's AIS signal blinked—a lone dot in the bay, behind him. He'd found her.

He eased El Tiburón back, hanging off the coast as the sun sank, painting the water gold and purple. Under the cover of darkness, he slipped into the bay, anchoring far enough away to stay unseen and unheard. He thought he was hidden. The night was quiet, the stars sharp, Guánica's hills a black shadow against the sky. Dega forgot that sound traveled easily across still water, like Guánica Bay, especially when surrounded by hills that acted like a grand hall, every little peep billowing to the audience in the back seats. The acoustics here, eerie and deceptive, whispered doom lurking in the shadows, hinting at unseen ears tuned to their plans, setting an ominous stage for a confrontation yet to come.

Dega, Tomas, and Bruno sprawled on El Tiburón's deck, the night black around them, Guánica Bay still as glass. They drank cold beers, bottles sweating in the warm air, chatting up what each would do with the treasure, their laughter low, certain no one knew they were there. Dream Maker's anchor light glowed faintly across the water, a quiet target. The stars burned sharp, the hills a dark wall against the sky.

Suddenly, blue police lights flashed on shore, cutting the dark. The three froze. Dega cursed, finished his beer. Tomas and Bruno tossed empties overboard, bottles splashing softly. They scrambled, pulling on the anchor, the chain rattling. Dega gunned the engines in the darkness, no lights. The yacht slipped out of the bay, unseen by police or Junior. The Caribbean opened, swallowing their wake as they sped south, night hiding their escape.

They waited another hour before heading back into the cover of land. Dega slid El Tiburón into a small cove just east of Guánica Bay's inlet, the water dark and still, the shore a shadow of mangroves and low hills. The yacht rocked gently, hidden from the bay's open eyes. Dega stood on the deck, the night thick with salt and quiet, his face hard under the starlight. He turned to Tomas and Bruno, their figures dim against the rail. "We're on watch tonight," he said, voice low, sharp. "Bruno, you take first. Tomas, you're next. I'll take last."

He knew the final watch was his—best to sleep deep, be sharp when Dream Maker's sails rose at first light. Bruno nodded, settling by the helm, eyes scanning the dark. Dega and Tomas went below; the cabin was cool, with the hum of the sea outside. The cove held them close, its silence a shield, the hunt for a treasure waiting like a tide ready to turn.

The sun broke over the horizon, painting the sea gold as El Tiburón bobbed in the quiet waters outside Guánica. Dream Maker sailed past an hour after sunrise, her sails taut, cutting east. Dega Reyes stood at the helm, his eyes sharp, tracking the boat's path. He'd anticipated their move, known their course. Below, the brothers, Bruno and Tomas, slept hard, their snores echoing throughout the boat. Dega let them rest. No need to rush. He knew where Junior was headed—Ponce.

An hour later, the brothers stirred, their faces heavy with sleep but ready. Dega fired up El Tiburón, the Sea Ray's engines growling to life. They didn't trail Dream Maker, didn't linger in her wake. Dega pushed the throttle, and the boat surged east, slicing through the calm Caribbean waters at speed. They reached Ponce two hours before the sailboat, still a slight haze over the bay from an overnight fog. Dega chose a small bay right at the marina, dropping anchor where the water was deep and quiet, not so close as to grab attention, but near enough to watch. The stolen boat sat low, unnoticed, its lack of AIS a shield against prying eyes.

Dream Maker arrived just after noon, tying off at the T of a dock, her crew quick and sure. Dega leaned against the rail, binoculars steady, the brothers at his side. Junior and his girlfriend stepped off, met by a waiting car. The SUV pulled away, dust trailing up the road toward Jayuya.

Dega's lips pressed thin. He knew the mountain town, its festival, its whispers of Taíno secrets. The amulet was likely with them, but the boat called.

"They're gone for hours," Dega growled, voice rough as gravel. "Jayuya's a haul. Three, four hours, easy."

Bruno, thickset and steady, scratched his jaw. "Stone's with them, sure. But the boat? Might hold something."

Tomas, eyes sharp as a hawk, nodded. "Papers, notes, crumbs, they forgot. Any money you can find. Worth a peek."

Dega's gaze stayed on the dock. Dream Maker was alone now, bobbing gently. "We search it. Quick, quiet. No trace. But let's wait a couple of hours to make sure they didn't just go to a nearby store. I'll drop you two off on the dock where the sailboat is. Then I'll pull away, minimizing our exposure and attracting as little attention as possible."

150

The three waited, El Tiburón anchored in the quiet bay off Ponce Yacht Club, the sun sinking low. Dega's eyes stayed on Dream Maker, tied to the dock, her hull still in the evening light. They'd decided to move near sunset, when the marina staff would be distracted—shift changes, hunger pulling their focus—a chance to slip aboard unnoticed, silent as shadows.

As the light began fading, Bruno raised the anchor, the chain clinking softly. Dega eased El Tiburón forward, guiding the Sea Ray to an open slip on Dream Maker's dock. The boat settled, engines cut, the harbor's hum covering their steps. Bruno and Tomas leapt off, their boots light on the wood, moving quickly toward the sailboat. They knocked, a casual rap, like friends dropping by. No answer came. The boat was empty, as expected.

They climbed aboard, taking care with their steps, heading for the cockpit. The hatch was locked, a bolt barring the way. Tomas knelt, pulling a small pick from his pocket, his fingers working the lock's pins. Seconds passed, the metal clicking softly. Bruno hesitated, a heartbeat of doubt crossing his mind, the weight of the moment deepening the risk. His hand shot out, stopping Tomas in his tracks. His eyes flicked up—a security camera, its red light blinking, staring straight at them. The brothers froze, their breath held, the marina's quiet pressing in.

"No alarms," Bruno whispered, voice low, rough. "We go."

Tomas nodded, pocketing the pick. They slipped off Dream Maker, moving fast but smooth, back to the dock's edge. As he stepped off the boat, Bruno decided to leave something behind—a warning. He reached up with a knife and cut the starboard Genoa sheet nearly clean through.

That'll make things a little trickier—failing at the worst opportune time, he thought.

Dega was there waiting for them, El Tiburón idling, a shadow in the dusk. They climbed aboard, the boat rocking gently under their weight.

Back at the anchor spot, the brothers told Dega what happened, their voices tight. "Camera," Bruno said. "Red light. Right on us."

Dega's jaw clenched, his eyes hard, but he nodded. "You did right. One alarm, and we're done."

They settled El Tiburón in the bay, the anchor dropping with a soft splash. The harbor lights flickered in the warm night. Junior and Faidh would return soon, likely with the amulet in their hands. Dega and the brothers waited, eyes on the dock, the sea quiet, the game not yet over.

Dega stood on the deck, the night air thick and quiet. Dream Maker sat tied to the dock, clearly in his view, a silent shadow under the stars—the glow of the dock lights warm around her hull. He turned to Bruno and Tomas, his voice low and rough, like coral. "We keep watches again. We've stayed on them this far; no losing them now. Don't know which way they'll sail come morning, if they leave at all."

Bruno nodded, leaning against the rail, eyes scanning the dock. Tomas checked his watch, ready to take the first shift. They'd held Junior's trail through Guánica all the way to Ponce, the amulet's pull never out of reach. The night was still, but Dega's gaze stayed hard, fixed on his target, the game alive in the dark.

The sun rose over the southern coast of the island, the harbor still, Dream Maker quiet at the dock. No movement stirred her decks, no sign of life. Dega watched from the fly bridge of the Sea Ray, anchored in the bay, his eyes sharp, single-minded. Junior and Faidh had returned late last night, their figures dim in the marina's glow, slipping below deck to sleep. Dega, Bruno, and Tomas kept their watches, wondering if Jayuya had given the couple answers or sent them back empty. The amulet's shadow hung heavy, unanswered.

By ten, the dock remained silent. Then Junior and Faidh appeared, stepping out from below decks, onto the dock, then climbing into their SUV, and driving out of the marina. Dega's jaw tightened. A quick errand or a day's absence? He couldn't tell. He checked their stores—food and beer holding steady, enough for now. If they needed more, a small village, east or west, would do. No marinas, just quiet shores where a stolen boat like this one could slip in and out, unnoticed.

An hour later, the SUV returned. Junior and Faidh carried grocery bags, provisions stacked high—preparing to sail, maybe soon. Dega's pulse quickened. Then a third figure appeared—a young man, native to the area, with sharp features, likely of Taíno descent. He boarded Dream Maker, his step uncertain, carrying a duffel. Dega's eyes narrowed. They'd found something in Jayuya, a guide, a key to the next stone.

He ducked below deck, the air cool, the brothers lounging and staring at their phones. "They're back," Dega said, voice low, rough. "Brought a new one, Taíno, looks like. They have a plan, possibly leaving soon. Be ready to move."

Bruno grunted, checking his knife. Tomas stood, eyes like a hawk, peering through the porthole. El Tiburón swayed gently in the bay, the sea calm, but the chase was alive. They were ready and anxious.

Dega stood on El Tiburón's bridge, the stolen Sea Ray idling, the midday sun beating down. His eyes followed Dream Maker as it slipped its lines, the sailboat cutting clean through the water. "Interesting," he muttered to himself, his voice low, rough like the gravel of his youth in Puerto Real. "The woman was at the helm, steady, her hair catching the breeze. Junior and the new kid—some mountain boy, green as palm fronds—stowed lines, cleared the deck, their movements quick but untested."

Out of the harbor, Dream Maker turned east. Dega nodded to himself. East made sense, with sixty nautical miles of reef-strewn coast leading to potential stops in small villages like Santa Isabel or Salinas, which were suitable for resupply. He gunned El Tiburón's engines, passing the sailboat, aiming for a quiet dock. Santa Isabel was a bust. Every slip was full. The marina was crowded. Dream Maker moved faster than he'd figured, sails full, catching up before he could blink. He cursed under his breath, pushed the throttle, and raced ahead to Salinas Marina. Too much activity there, eyes everywhere, and El Tiburón's stolen shadow loomed large. He couldn't risk being spotted.

Dream Maker caught up again, relentless. The day was souring, not bending to Dega's plan. "Unless Junior's an idiot," he thought, "he'll notice a boat that keeps leapfrogging him, then waiting." He swung El Tiburón close to shore, hugging the coast, hoping the sailboat's crew watched the open sea, not the shallows. No stops today— fuel was half-full, food and drinks holding, but Bruno and

Tomas were restless, their voices low, grumbling about giving up. Dega's jaw tightened. He needed something to keep them sharp, or he'd lose them.

Dream Maker's AIS track blinked on his chartplotter, veering into Palmas del Mar. Dega turned El Tiburón, risking the marina. The charts showed slips far from the office—perfect to hide from Junior's eyes. He'd use an alias name, unsure if the owners had reported the theft. The brothers, Bruno and Tomas, manned the rails, leaping to the dock, tying off clean as the Sea Ray slid into a far slip. Nightfall would cover them, allowing them to restock and refuel at dawn.

Then he saw Junior step from the marina office, the Dock Master at his side, pointing straight at El Tiburón. Dega's gut clenched, a surge of panic hitting him like a wave. For a split second, the reckless kid who'd spent a stint in juvie screamed in his mind, the same one who thought he could outrun any trouble but ended up caught. 'Grab the lines!' he barked to Bruno and Tomas. 'Get back on—now. They're onto us.' The brothers scrambled, lines flying aboard. Dega gunned the engines, pushing away the flash of insecurity, ignoring the 'No Wake' signs, the boat roaring around the last dock, lights off, plunging into the inlet's dark. The night swallowed them, the sea their only shield.

CHAPTER 13

VIEQUES AND THE PIRATE'S SECRET

Junior and Faidh rose early after each having enjoyed a deep, dreamless sleep. Over Palmas del Mar, the sky stretched pink and gold, the Caribbean Sea flat and gleaming. Yet, an unfamiliar tension hung in the air, a feeling more unsettling than the morning breeze. On Dream Maker's deck, Faidh cupped coffee in her hands, the warmth spreading through her. Junior gripped an ice-cold glass of Diet Coke, beads of condensation slicking his fingers. A whisper of wind carried a distant, crackling radio signal, a brief warning lost in the hum of waking life. Morning dew softened the air. Below, Guey slept, worn out from his first day at sea; his green face pressed into the pillow, he welcomed the quiet. Junior glanced at his phone, the screen's glow bright in his palm as he checked the Caribbean weather, his brow furrowing slightly.

A low-pressure system, 300 miles southeast of their position, just west of Saint Lucia, crept along—barely moving. It had dumped heavy rain but only intensified into a depression last night. NOAA now gives it a 20 percent chance of becoming a storm within two days and 50 percent in seven days. Not likely, but not nothing.

Junior turned to Faidh, his voice low, steady. "It's late in the season. Odds are that this storm will stay a depression, possibly fizzling out. It's relatively close, but it's not moving much. Just giving you a heads up, could mean trouble if it spins up."

Faidh sipped her coffee, eyes on the horizon. "We've got options—Vieques, Culebra, even back to Ponce or San Juan, if it turns ugly, right? Think it's worth the risk?"

Junior nodded slowly. "Yep, I think we keep going. Vieques isn't far. If it shifts, we duck into a safe harbor. This late, it'll likely just be rain and wind anyway."

She met his gaze, her smile faint but sure. "Then we sail. Ensenada del Pirata's waiting."

The sea stretched east, calm for now, Cofres'ís Treasure's pull more substantial than the storm's shadow. They let Guey sleep for now.

Junior moved across Dream Maker's deck, the harbor still and bright. He fired up the generator, the hum steady in the morning air, and switched the boat from shore power to ship's systems. Disconnecting the water line, unplugging the power cord, he stowed each with practiced hands. Dock lines coiled tight, tucked away. At the helm, Faidh gripped the wheel, eyes fixed on the horizon. Junior looked up. "You ready?"

"You betcha. Cast off," she said, a quick smirk and a giggle.

"Aye, aye, Captain," Junior said, grinning. He slipped the lines free. Faidh eased Dream Maker out, tapping the jet blasters—quick bursts to clear the docks and buoys.

She glanced at Junior, her eyes bright. "I love these jet blasters. Tight turns and tough slips—they make it easy, even for me."

The boat's motion stirred Guey below. He stumbled up the companionway, hair mussed, face less green than yesterday. "Good morning," he said, voice rough.

"Good morning, Sunshine!" Faidh called, her smile wide, warm as the sun.

"You guys have coffee?" Guey asked, rubbing his eyes.

Faidh laughed, the sound light on the breeze. "Yeah, but you have to make it yourself. Keurig's in the galley, on the counter. Cups are in the cabinet on the aft wall. Water tank is full, pop in a K-cup and hit start."

"Got it," Guey said, turning. "Anyone want anything while I'm down there?"

"No, thanks," Junior and Faidh said in unison, Junior stepping into the cockpit, lines stowed, hands free.

He looked at Faidh, the sea flat, the sky clear. "Despite the weather southeast, it looks like a beautiful day ahead."

"No doubt," Faidh said, her eyes scanning the water. "Wonder if we'll see El Tiburón today, or if last night scared them off."

Junior chuckled, the word sharp on his tongue. "Pirates, arghh. I don't think we've seen the last of them." But beneath his laughter, a flicker of unease crept in, memories of past encounters with real danger surfacing, only half-acknowledged. Could they really trust the relative calmness of their current adventure? His voice steadied, back on task. "Winds are east today, trade winds mixing with the storm's counterclockwise pull. We'll tack across to Vieques, hold close to the wind. Good practice for you and Guey."

"Sounds like fun." Faidh was just thrilled to be at sea again.

Guey came up to the cockpit, coffee in one hand, a slice of bread in the other. Junior glanced over. "I can make you breakfast, something more than bread."

"Nah," Guey said, managing a smile. "Bread's good for my stomach."

They laughed, the sound drifting over the water. Ahead, Vieques waited, its pirate cove hidden in the east.

Faidh felt relaxed at the helm now. She looked at Guey, "Tell me about the Taíno," she said, her voice soft but hungry. "Who were they, really?"

Guey sat thinking for a moment. He was going to share his dream from the night before, but it soon slipped his mind as he reached into his pocket and felt the turtle amulet. Junior had let him keep it with him, its weight grounding him. "The Taíno were the first here," he said, voice low, steady like the mountains. "They came from the Orinoco, paddling dugouts across the sea, centuries before Columbus. They settled Borikén—Puerto Rico—and the islands around, living by the rivers, the forests, the fish. They cultivated cassava, constructed villages, and carved petroglyphs on stones similar to the ones we hold. Their gods, Yocahu and Atabey, lived in the crops, the rain, the caves. They played batey, a ball game, sacred, fierce. Their world was alive, tied to the earth."

He paused, the sea quiet, the harbor's hum distant. "Then the Spanish came, in 1493. They brought swords, disease, hunger, and slavery. The Taíno fought—Chief Agüeybaná, others—but their numbers fell, fast and brutal. By the 1500s, most had disappeared, either mixed into the island's bloodline or lost to history. But their words—

hamaca, barbacoa—remained. Their DNA runs in us, sixty percent of Borikén's people. The amulets and petroglyphs are what's left, whispering who they were." His eyes met Faidh's, sharp, carrying Jayuya's weight, the Taíno still alive in him. "I think this adventure could bring new energy to the Taíno people. If you let me, I would like to share the story when we return—maybe even with the media."

Junior fixed Guey with a solemn look, "This is your story, Guey," he said, voice low, steady. "I think I speak for Faidh when I say we're happy you let us join this adventure."

Guey's eyes softened, "Thank you, sir," he said, his voice clear, "If mi padre were here, he'd thank you too. You're too kind."

Junior clapped his shoulder, a grin breaking through. "Guey, what do you say we set sail?"

"Love to," Guey said, his face bright, eager. "Can you show me? I want to learn it all."

"Show you?" Junior laughed, sharp and warm. "You're doing it. I'll coach you through."

"Okay," Guey said, his voice steady despite the sea's newness.

Faidh turned the helm, nosing Dream Maker into the wind, her eyes flicking to Junior. "Prepare to set the Main and Genoa," she called, a sheepish glance checking her words.

Junior nodded, his smile quick, sure.

"Preparing the main and genoa, aye, aye, Captain," Guey echoed, his hands already moving to the lines, Junior's voice guiding him.

The sails rose smoothly, the canvas catching the east wind, and Dream Maker came alive. The boat leaned into the sea, tacking east toward Vieques.

Just north of Palmas del Mar, hidden in Bahia Lima, Dega drank coffee at the helm of El Tiburón as Dream Maker pulled out of the marina. The brothers slept below, recovering from overnight watches. Dega felt no rush. He was perfectly hidden until he learned where Junior's crew was headed.

His patience paid off. Watching the track on his chartplotter, it was obvious that Dream Maker was heading to Vieques. That's perfect, he thought. He can call his cousin in Santa Maria and restock/refuel the boat there. The best part is that the island is small enough that he'll still be able to keep track of Dream Maker, wherever she goes.

When Bruno and Tomas woke, Dega filled them in on what he'd learned and what the plan was. Surprisingly, the two brothers were excited, not only about restocking food and beer supplies, but also about possibly taking a walk around Vieques. Neither of them had ever been there.

Dream Maker sliced through calm Caribbean water, Vieques' mountains rising on the horizon. Faidh held the helm, tacking to port, sails tight. A sharp pop split the air. The genoa snapped loose, flapping wildly in the wind. Instinct took over; her mind raced through the sailor's checklist: ease the mainsheet to reduce pressure, maintain the heading to steady the boat, and secure the flogging sail to prevent damage. Junior moved swiftly beside her, their training and experience colliding with a sense of urgency.

"Holy crap!" Faidh yelled, her hands tight on the wheel. "What did I do?"

Junior laughed, his voice steady, cutting through the chaos. "You didn't do anything. Starboard genoa sheet snapped. Odd though, I replaced all the rigging six months ago. Should've lasted years." He stepped forward, eyes scanning the deck. "Hold this heading. I'll furl the genoa to stop the whipping, then tie a new sheet into place. We got a spare below."

He showed Guey the furling line, his hands quick, guiding. "Stop when the clew—corner of the sail—nears the furler," he said, pointing. Guey nodded, green but focused. Junior ducked below, grabbing a spare line from the forward locker, the boat rocking gently beneath him.

Ten minutes later, the new sheet was tied and rigged back to the cockpit. Junior glanced at Faidh, a grin tugging at his mouth. "Ready to reset the genoa, Captain?"

She laughed, hearty, barely getting the words out. "Reset the genoa."

"Resetting the genoa, aye, aye, Captain," Junior called, unfurling the sail. The canvas caught the wind, balancing Dream Maker again, main and genoa full, slicing east at eight knots.

Earlier that morning, as part of his routine, Junior had thoroughly checked Dream Maker's rigging, walking the deck to inspect all lines and sheets. The habit was ingrained from years at sea, each inspection a promise of safety.

Junior coiled the broken sheet, hands steady. He'd send it to the manufacturer, see if they could explain the failure.

At the end, he paused. The line wasn't just broken. It was sliced clean, three-quarters through, the rest frayed. He thought that he would have seen it earlier in his inspection, but the slice was so clean that it clearly didn't stand out as an obvious, impending threat. "That's strange," he muttered.

"What's weird?" Faidh asked, glancing over, her eyes sharp.

"This sheet didn't just break, it was cut," Junior said, holding up the end.

Faidh frowned. "Could it have caught on something? Maybe nicked something when we were tacking?"

"Nothing on the deck would have cut it this clean," Junior said, passing her the line. The cut was surgical, the fray a result of the break.

Her face tightened. "You think our 'pirates' did this? From El Tiburón? When they snuck on the boat in Ponce?"

"Could be," Junior said, his jaw set. "Probably thought it'd slow us more. They don't know how resilient Dream Maker is. I'll check the lines I can reach now and then inspect the rest when we anchor at Ensenada del Pirata."

"Be careful," Faidh said, worry creasing her brow, her voice soft but firm.

"I always am," Junior said, his eyes on the sea. The wind held steady, Vieques growing larger, the cove's secrets waiting.

As Monte Pirata passed off their port beam, Junior had Faidh turn on the electric motor and put Dream Maker back under power. Then he had her turn fully into the wind so he and Guey could lower the sails. Once complete, he came back to the cockpit and politely asked to take the helm. "I want to take her into Puerto Ferro, and it's a narrow inlet, so if you don't mind…"

Faidh happily turned over the helm. "Our current heading is zero-niner-six. Our speed is 4.2 knots under power. The helm is yours, sir."

"Thank you, Faidh, I've got the helm."

Dream Maker slipped past Mosquito Bay, its waters black on the port side, the famous bioluminescence lost in daylight. Junior eased the throttle, slowing to just over two knots. He pointed out Ensenada del Pirata and the ruined lighthouse, now only rubble. He steered into Puerto Ferro's bay. The water was glass, still as breath. Mangroves crowded the edges, roots clawing the shallows. The beach was narrow, sand and pebbles mixed, driftwood scattered like bones. Low hills rose behind, scrub and cactus baking in the sun. The sea shifted from turquoise to deep blue, calm and waiting.

Junior dropped anchor, Dream Maker settling off the shore, steady. Faidh and Guey stood quietly, Ensenada del Pirata's secrets close, calling through the silence. "I'll lower the dinghy," Junior said, his voice low and sure. "We'll head to the cove in a bit, but I think we should eat lunch first and pack lots of water. No telling what we'll find or how long we'll be."

"I can cook bacon and we can have BLTs," Faidh offered, her smile quick, breaking the stillness.

"I'm in," Junior said, nodding.

"Me too," Guey added, his face less green, eager. "Anything I can do?"

"Yeah," Faidh said. "I'll fill water bottles. You load them into the dinghy and grab anything else you want to take."

They ate on deck, BLTs sharp with peppered bacon, sun warm, bay quiet. Junior chewed slowly, eyes fixed on the shore. "There's a trail south that ends at the water. We'll dinghy over, start searching. Ensenada del Pirata is about a mile hike. No idea what we're looking for, so we stick together. If there's a cave or crevice, anything that needs a closer look, no one goes alone."

Both Faidh and Guey agreed.

Lunch finished, they climbed into the dinghy, the motor's hum low as Junior steered for the trail's end. He tied off to a gnarled root, rope taut, and they stepped ashore, sand crunching underfoot. The path to Ensenada del Pirata wound ahead, narrow through scrub and stone, secrets waiting in the heat. Junior paused, boots firm on the shore, sun hot on his neck. He looked at Faidh and Guey. "If I were a pirate in the early 1800s, like Cofresí, I'd anchor here. A small, fast boat could vanish in Puerto Ferro's shallows. I'd post a lookout where the lighthouse stood, someone I trusted, eyes sharp for trouble. And I'd find a quiet place—a cave or hollow—where my crew and I could lie low until the hunters passed. Let's hope this cove has such a place."

Faidh nodded, her eyes scanning the path, eager. Guey clutched his pack, his face set with purpose. The trail beckoned, the cove's secrets buried in its sand and stone, waiting under the Vieques sun.

The trail wound through low hills, soil dry and cracked, dusted with cacti and thorny acacia. Sierra palms leaned overhead while their fronds rustled in the light breeze, casting jagged shadows. Forced single file by the narrow path, Junior led, Faidh followed, and Guey brought up the rear. Quick as thought, lizards skittered across rocks. Coquis chirped; their calls cut sharply in the heat. The climb was gentle but steady, the ground tripped with roots and loose stones. Sweat beaded on their necks as the sun beat down, but a hint of sea breeze brought relief. Through the brush, old Navy bunkers—rusted and crumbling—peeked out, reminders of Vieques' past as a target range. The trail curved, dipping into a shallow gully, then climbing again.

After a mile, the path opened, the scrub parting to reveal Ensenada del Pirata below. The hike took thirty minutes, their steps slowed by the heat and the need to watch the ground. They paused at the crest, the cove spread out like a secret kept by the island.

The cove was small, a crescent carved into Vieques' southern shore, its waters clear and inviting, lapping softly against a thin strip of sand. Mangroves crowded the edges, their roots twisting into the shallows like veins in the earth. Low cliffs, rocky and worn, flanked the bay, their faces pocked by wind and salt.

Junior, Faidh, and Guey stood at the cove's edge, the sand warm underfoot, the third amulet somewhere in the stone and shadow. The sea whispered, the cliffs stood silent, and the ruins above waited, all heavy with what they had kept hidden for centuries.

They walked in and around the cove, searching for something that could be hidden anywhere. They swam in the refreshing waters, hoping they might find a hidden alcove or crevice in rocks that would reveal a clue—a petroglyph or initials. They needed some sign from Cofresí.

Unfortunately, the day's search in Ensenada del Pirata turned up nothing—no caves, no carvings, no third amulet. The sun was setting, its light glowing softly orange near the horizon. All three walked back to the dinghy together. Junior and Faidh, worn out, were ready to return to Dream

Maker in Puerto Ferro, set to search again at dawn. Guey decided to stay, a sharp pull in his chest. "I'll check the lighthouse ruins and sleep up there," he said, his voice steady. "I'm used to sleeping outside under the stars. I do it all the time in the mountains around Jayuya. It'll give me time to listen to my ancestors."

Junior paused as Guey spoke, considering his words for a moment. Then he nodded and handed over a flashlight and a radio, making sure Guey had both before turning back toward the dinghy.

"Be careful," Faidh said, her worry soft as she watched Guey prepare to stay. The dinghy's hum faded across the bay as she and Junior made their way back to Dream Maker. During the silent ride, their shared looks conveyed more than any words that passed between them.

Dega leaned against the rail of El Tiburón, the Sea Ray tied off at a weathered dock in Santa Maria, a quiet street stretching toward his cousin's house. The sun was still high overhead, hot and unrelenting. He'd sent Bruno and Tomas to scrounge groceries, their steps fading into the town's glow. He stayed behind, unwilling to leave the stolen boat alone. If someone asked questions, he'd spin a story—better than letting them weave their own. His cousin had promised when they chatted earlier to bring a razor blade to scrape El Tiburón's name from the stern, a task Dega would handle later under the cover of darkness.

His cousin arrived, blade in hand, and they talked low, the dock creaking beneath them. Dega's eyes flicked to his phone, the AIS tracking Dream Maker. She'd stopped, anchored in Puerto Ferro, her signal steady. He grinned, sharp and quick. Good news—as long as Junior's boat stayed put, he, Bruno, and Tomas could hole up in Santa Isabel, safe in the shadows, waiting for their next move.

The sun was gone, hidden behind Mount Pirata, leaving Puerto Ferro's bay dark, the Vieques mountain a jagged shadow against the starlit sky. Dream Maker rocked gently, anchored close to shore, the day's heat lingering in the air. Junior and Faidh returned from Ensenada del Pirata, sweat-soaked, the search for the third amulet fruitless. Guey stayed behind, his Taíno pull keeping him at the lighthouse ruins. They stepped aboard, the deck cool under their feet, the sea quiet.

They showered, the water cold, washing away salt and dust. Faidh's hair hung wet, clinging to her soft shoulders, her skin glowing in the cabin's dim light. Junior watched her, his eyes steady, a smile tugging his lips. They climbed into the narrow berth, the boat's sway soft, the mountains looming through the porthole. Her fingers found his, warm, sure, pulling him close. Their lips met, hungry, the day's weight falling away. They moved together, passionate, fierce, the shadows of Vieques holding them, the sea's rhythm matching their own. The night was still, but their love was loud, alive, a fire burning in the dark. Their passion is truly two halves, coming together to make each of them whole.

Faidh drifted into sleep, her body heavy and warm against Junior's, the gentle lap of Puerto Ferro's bay fading into a distant roar. But the calm was shattered in an instant.

The sea erupted into a monstrous tempest, waves forty feet high slamming Dream Maker like hammers from the deep, splintering her hull with cracks that echoed like thunder. The ketch bucked wildly, rigging snapping like brittle bones, sails tearing to shreds in the gale. Junior fought forward on the deck, his harness straining, but a colossal swell broadsided them, heeling the boat until her masts kissed the foam. His tether ripped free with a whip-crack, and he hurtled overboard, body twisting in the air before vanishing into the churning black, blood blooming in the water as sharks tore into him, his screams swallowed by the storm's fury. Faidh clung to the helm, her cries lost, the boat disintegrating beneath her, planks floating away like driftwood from a grave.

From the heart of the chaos towered Pirata Cofresí, his form colossal now, a skeletal giant rising from the waves, twice the height of the masts, his flesh rotting and peeling like ancient parchment, eyes hollow sockets glowing with desperate, infernal fire. His tricorn hat hung in tatters, his coat a shroud of seaweed and barnacles whipping like serpents, a rusted cutlass the size of an anchor gripped in bony claws. He loomed over Faidh, his voice a deafening wail that shook the sea, frantic and unhinged: "Foolish wretch! The amulets are sealed in blood— mine, eternal! Cease this madness, or the curse

169

devours all! Your lover shredded in the depths, your vessel a splintered corpse on the rocks!" His massive hand swept down, nearly crushing the cockpit, his decaying face twisting in rage as the storm intensified, lightning cracking like whips across his form.

Cofresí's desperation peaked, his colossal frame leaning closer, breath a foul gale of salt and decay. "The curse reaches far—beyond these cursed isles! Your daughters, safe in their distant beds, will feel its grip: shadows in their dreams turning to knives, accidents claiming them piece by piece, the sea's hunger pulling them under no matter the shore!" Faidh screamed, trying to steer away, but another wave hammered down, flooding everything, Cofresí's skeletal laughter booming as he dissolved into the vortex, the sea closing over her, cold and absolute, her daughters' distant cries echoing in the abyss.

Faidh jolted awake, a strangled gasp escaping her lips, her heart thundering like the storm in her mind. Sweat slicked her skin despite the cool bay air filtering through the hatch, and she clutched at Junior beside her, his steady breathing a lifeline. The pirate's final threat lingered, sharp as a blade—his curse reaching her daughters, far beyond the Caribbean's grasp. She pressed closer to Junior, unwilling to wake him, but the fear coiled tight, the quiet bay mocking the terror that refused to fade.

She lay awake for what felt like hours, unable to let herself sleep. But her will was overcome by exhaustion, and Faidh fell into a dreamless sleep - again, a sleep that lasted all the way until morning light.

CHAPTER 14

THE THIRD AMULET

Guey climbed the headland, the night warm, stars sharp over Vieques. The lighthouse ruins lay broken, stones like scattered teeth above the waves crashing against the southern shore. Mosquito Bay glowed faintly, a spirit's breath to his northwest. He sat under the stars on the rocks just outside the ruins. From his pack, he took a pouch—a Y-shaped tube and cohoba, Taíno sacred powder, ground from cojóbana seeds, his father's gift for seeing beyond. He held the tube, carved from bone, smooth from the years of hands that had handled it. He put the cohoba powder in a small wooden bowl; its scent was sharp, like crushed leaves and earth after a rain. He then carefully scooped it and poured it into the tube's hollow ends.

He pressed the tube to his nostrils and inhaled hard. The powder hit fast, a burn that climbed into his skull, sharp and clean. His breath caught, then slowed, each inhale and exhale anchoring him. The world shifted. Colors bled into the dark; reds, golds, streaks of light that weren't there. His heartbeat drummed steadily in his ears, a tether to reality as the spirits came then, not loud but steady, like waves on the shore. They spoke in shapes, in flashes of the hunt, the sea, the ancestors' faces. He saw the future in fragments, clear as a stream, then gone. He lay back, just absorbed the energy that surrounded him, grounded by the rhythmic beating of his heart.

He could feel Taíno energy all around him. This spot wasn't random. He felt the same energy he did when he and his father would go up to Cerro de Punta, the highest peak on the island of Puerto Rico. Cerro de Punta was an ancient Taíno ceremonial site, where they could be closest to Atabey, open to her energy. He thought this rocky point facing south must have been a Taíno ritual site, long before it was a lighthouse. He could hear the spray of the water— distant but clear.

Suddenly, a chill came, no wind to stir it. She stood there —a young woman, a shadow with obsidian eyes, her form flickering like the bay's glow. Silent, she pointed to the Spitting Cave, a jagged crevice beside the ruins, where waves hissed and sprayed and the Caribbean Sea pounded the island. Guey followed, the cohoba sharpening his steps, his flashlight beam dancing on wet rock. At the top of the cliff, overlooking the cave, her hand, pale as mist, touched a narrow split deep in the stone. She vanished, the night still.

Guey knelt, heart loud, the sea's pulse in his ears. He reached into the crevice, arm deep. Nothing. He then lay down on his belly, feeling the heartbeat of the island against his, to see if he could reach further. His fingers grazed damp stone until they found something—oilcloth, rotted, brittle, heavy with time. He pulled slowly; it broke free. When he got it out, he laid it on the ground—a stone came free, noticeably smaller than the first two amulets, its shape very simple. There was a petroglyph—eternal lovers, two figures entwined, carved sharply. And a hole piercing the stone at one end. And he flipped it over. On the back, "RC." He found the third amulet. All at once, the world was quiet, stars bright, the stone alive in his hand, whispering of love and secrets yet to find.

Guey lay on a blanket among the lighthouse ruins, the Spitting Cave below hissing with each wave, its spray cool in the Vieques night. The sound was steady, a lullaby woven from sea and stone, pulling him under. Sleep came softly— he welcomed it. His body was heavy from the day's search, the cohoba's faint hum still in his veins—slowly beginning to fade. Both amulets rested in his pack. He felt the rocks' energy, as his father had said, pulsing. Not evil, though— no, something else, something alive. The stones, now so close, seemed to align, their power shifting and turning toward light. The stars burned sharp above, the waves sang, and Guey slept, the island's heart beating with his own.

Junior stepped onto Dream Maker's deck, the morning air heavy, the Puerto Ferro bay still. The sky was red, a fierce glow where the rising sun struck high cirrus clouds, thin and streaked, spilling from the south. The Caribbean lay flat, but the air felt wrong—thick, charged, like a held breath. The hair on his neck stood up, sharp, instinctive. He didn't need the weather app to know that the tropical depression, 300 miles southeast, had crept closer overnight, its shadow reaching for Vieques. The mountains loomed dark, and the sky warned of trouble coming soon.

Faidh climbed topside, the red sky over Puerto Ferro casting a glow on Dream Maker's deck. Junior stood at the rail, his face tight, worry sharp in his eyes. "What's up?" she asked, voice light but searching.

173

He tried to mask it, his smile thin. "Haven't checked the weather app, but I feel it. The storm's moving, likely toward us. We need to leave today, one way or another, or risk being caught here. Hopefully, we'll have better luck finding the third amulet before we go."

Faidh hesitated, thinking for a second that she would share the night prior's dream. Then she decided against it, feeling that it wouldn't help anyone to share it. That's when she turned on her beautiful 'Faidh' charm, like she was turning on a switch. Her eyes sparked, and her confidence was a flame. "Junior, today's going to be amazing," she said, her voice sure, cutting through the heavy air. "A red sky won't dim my fire."

He laughed, the sound warm, real. "Damn, I love your energy. The way you grab life."

She stepped closer, her smile coy. "You bring out my best, Junior. I completely trust you."

He stood taller, chest full. "Let's find Guey and that amulet."

"As I've said in the past, Mister. I'm in," she said, her look playful, certain.

They packed Junior's bag—water bottles, the Cojobano Tree amulet, and a flashlight. The dinghy hummed, carrying them two hundred yards to the trailhead, the sand and pebbles crunching as they stepped ashore. The path to the lighthouse ruins stretched ahead, Vieques' hills a little darker, as the clouds now shielded the sun.

When they arrived at the lighthouse, they could see Guey sitting out on a point of rocks, staring at the sea. He was clearly meditating or praying, likely hoping to connect spiritually as part of his search for the amulet. They didn't want to disturb him. So they walked around, checking out the ruins and the Spitting Cave while waiting for him to finish.

Then, suddenly, as if he knew they were there, Guey stood up and turned around—an enormous smile on his face.

"Did you have a good night?" Faidh asked.

"It was an amazing night. I found this." He reached into his pocket and pulled out the third amulet.

"Holy shit! You found it! Where? How?" screamed Faidh as she ran to him to give him a huge hug, eager to understand how he succeeded where they'd been struggling.

Junior walked to Guey as well, nodding and smiling with his eyes as he mouthed, "Well done," without actually saying a word.

Faidh grabbed the amulet. "Let me see it."

Guey happily handed over the stone, content to let his friends marvel at the discovery, waiting for the excitement to settle before sharing the story of the night before.

"What is this petroglyph?" asked Faidh, pointing at the symbol etched into the stone.

"Eternal Lovers—it's two figures entwined, their lines simple but alive." He traced the carving, his voice low, steady, holding the weight of the Taíno people in every word. "The eternal lovers, in Taíno tradition, are the bond of life. They are man and woman, sun and moon, earth and sea, joined forever. Not just love, but balance—two halves making one whole, holding the world together. The Taíno saw them in the stars, in the way rivers meet the ocean. They carved this on stones and on cave walls to honor what endures, what creates life. My father told me the lovers are a zemi, a spirit power. They guide families and villages, maintaining harmony when the world is shaken. This petroglyph, on an amulet, means something sacred—a vow, a union, maybe a secret kept between two. It's no accident Cofresí chose it. He hid it where the Spitting Cave sings, where the sea and stone meet, like the lovers themselves. The hole, here—" he pointed to the edge of the stone, "—it's pointing us somewhere, maybe another cove, where the bond holds strong." His eyes met Faidh's, then Junior's, the island's pulse in his words. "But I'm not sure what island the shape of this one represents."

Guey handed Junior the third amulet, its weight much lighter than the other two, the eternal lovers carved deep—two figures entwined, their lines alive. He turned it over, exposing the RC initials and highlighting the stone's shape, clear in the light. "This doesn't look like any islands I recognize," he said, voice low, steady. "To me, it looks like a long, skinny kidney bean. I'm not familiar with any islands that match that description. We'll need to dig, figure out where it points next."

"How'd you find it?" Junior asked, his gaze sharp, the stone still in his hand.

Guey's eyes softened, the lighthouse ruins behind him, the Spitting Cave's hiss continuing in almost a rhythmic way. "At the lighthouse, I felt it—energy, like my father said. Perhaps a Taíno ritual site, long ago, and sacred. I used cohoba, the powder I brought, because I believed it would help me see what was hidden. It opened things up, making the world hum. Then she came—a young woman, a spirit, eyes dark like obsidian. She led me to a crevice by the Spitting Cave, right over there," he pointed. "I reached in,

found the stone, wrapped in oilcloth, rotted but holding."
He passed the brittle cloth to them, its edges crumbling. "I
think I was meant for this, meant to find it. It came easily
once I stopped searching and began listening to the spirits,
the earth, and even listening to my own voice."

Faidh laughed, her voice light, cutting the weight.
"That's a metaphor for life if I ever heard one. Didn't expect
life lessons on a hunt for 200-year-old pirate treasure." Her
humor sparked, lifting them.

Junior interrupted the conversation. "I think we should
head back," he said, voice firm, eyes on the horizon,
motivated by the need to keep everyone safe. "It appears
that the tropical depression is moving toward us. North or
west are our safest choices."

Guey nodded, his pack slung over one shoulder, the third
amulet safe inside. "I'm packed. Ready when you are," he
said, a bounce in his step, the stones' energy aligning,
lifting them all.

They walked the trail back to the dinghy, the air thick
with promise. The distance passed quickly, their steps light.
At the shore, they loaded the dinghy, the motor humming as
they crossed the bay to Dream Maker, anchored steadily in
the calm.

Guey ducked below to stow his gear, while Faidh and
Junior prepped the boat. Junior lifted the dinghy, securing
it, then freed the anchor, its chain rattling as it rose from
Puerto Ferro's sandy bottom. He looked at Faidh. "Take the
helm. Get us out of the cove. I'll set the storm sail on the
cutter stay—just in case we need it later." The storm
loomed—Junior liked to be ready.

Faidh steered Dream Maker from the bay, her hands
sure, turning west at Junior's call, the sea flat but heavy

with warning. Junior went below, started the generator, and its hum was steady. He'd run the electric motor. Just easier on the short trip he was expecting. He knew he could maintain a speed of five to six knots for days without draining the batteries in this setup.

When Junior climbed back into the cockpit, Guey was already there, staring at the screen of his iPad. He handed Faidh her laptop and opened his own. "Let's find a kidney-shaped island—Dream Maker needs a new destination," he said. In the meantime, he set a course for the Safe Harbor Marina in Fajardo—probably one of the best choices for holding out if the storm continued to develop. He handed control to the autopilot. And just like flying, he didn't blindly trust the autopilot. He monitored the ship's track, but it also gave him time to peck away at his own computer.

The cockpit was quiet, only wind whistling through the rigging and fingers tapping keys breaking the silence.

Faidh, looking to talk through the problem, her eyes bright and curious, said, "I hate to be master of the obvious." Laughing at herself, she continued, "We have stones with three different petroglyphs so far—a turtle, a Cojobano Tree, and eternal lovers. Right?"

Guey looked up, his voice calm, steady. "Yes. And before you ask, I don't know if they mean anything together, or with a fourth. I'm still working on it."

Faidh grinned, undeterred. "Wasn't going to ask, but good to know." She continued, "And each stone's from a different island—Mona, Puerto Rico, Vieques. Right?"

"That's right," Junior said, his eyes on his own screen.

Faidh hesitated, thinking. "Correct me if I'm wrong, but the only other major island tied to Puerto Rico is Culebra, right?"

Neither Junior nor Guey replied.

She continued, "But Culebra's shape doesn't match the stone. Is there a part of Culebra that Cofresí was known to frequent?"

Junior's face lit, a spark catching. "That's it, Faidh! You're a genius!" His voice was loud, ecstatic. "It's not Culebra. The stone's the shape of Cayo Pirata—a small islet in Ensenada Honda, Culebra's big harbor. The small island is actually named for Cofresí. And many years ago, they even found some of his treasure there—gold coins."

Faidh and Guey pulled up their screens, their fingers flying as they read quickly. Cayo Pirata's shape—long, skinny, kidney-like—matched the amulet, its eastern hole pointing to a new secret. They nodded, agreement sharp between them. "Cayo Pirata's next," Faidh said.

Guey, "I think that's it!"

"Ok, I'm setting the course," Junior said, hands on the nav, the autopilot humming as Dream Maker turned north, the sea open, Culebra's promise calling.

Bruno and Tomas sprawled on El Tiburón's aft deck, the Santa Maria dock creaking under the morning sun, plates of cold rice and fish half-eaten. Vieques is quiet again after the morning ferry brought the first load of tourists for the day. Dega had gone to stretch his legs and visit his cousin's family, leaving the brothers to watch the stolen Sea Ray.

He'd stayed close to the boat since Cabo Rojo, wary of eyes, letting Bruno and Tomas wander alone. They didn't get to see much of Vieques—only what was within walking distance yesterday. However, they did find a couple of chinchorros, small roadside bars, where they learned about life on Isla Nena—the local name for Vieques. It was over a drink that the brothers learned of a late tropical depression —organizing, growing—just southeast of them. Fishermen by trade, they knew little of boats, but hurricanes they knew: Fiona, Maria, storms that tore their lives apart. A small boat was no place to face one.

They'd watched ferries churn between Vieques and the big island, their hum steady, tempting. If Dega didn't move soon, they'd jump ship, ride the ferry back, and leave him to his chase. This hunt for Junior's stones was turning into an obsession, and they knew obsessed men made bad calls —dangerous calls. Just then, Bruno looked up, saw Dega striding down the dock, his grin sharp, like a cat with a kill. "You're back quick," Bruno said, squinting.

"They're moving," Dega said, voice low, sure. "Dream Maker's AIS shows them leaving Puerto Ferro. I think they found another stone. No need to rush, but we should follow, see if they head to the big island or another."

Tomas leaned forward, his plate forgotten. "You checked the weather, Dega?"

"Yep," Dega said, quick, confident. "Storm's southeast, couple of days out at least. Might not even develop."

Bruno's eyes narrowed, his voice hard. "We don't want to be caught at sea if it comes."

Dega shot back, "Neither do I," but his voice wavered slightly, betraying a sliver of uncertainty beneath his bravado. For a brief moment, memories of past storms

180

flashed in his mind — moments of chaos at sea, the relentless wind and rain, and the fear he had to suppress to keep going. He shook them off, finding strength in the goal that pushed him forward. "Nor Junior, I bet. Here's the deal: as long as they sail away from the storm, and they will, we follow, since our goal is to recover the stones without undue risk. If it turns toward us, or they head into it, we quit. Find shelter. Pick up their trail after the storm passes. Junior's left his AIS on this whole time. No reason he'd stop now." Dega's laugh, though meant to sound diabolical, carried a hint of something more profound, a fragility masked by his exterior confidence.

The brothers nodded, slowly, their eyes on the sea, the deal settling like the weight of the coming storm.

CHAPTER 15

HARBOR OF SHADOWS

Dream Maker slipped into Ensenada Honda by early afternoon, the sun blazing, heat pressing down on Culebra's rocky spine. The sea shifted from turquoise to deep sapphire, thick with salt and the scent of seagrass. Sailing around Vieques had stretched the day, but the beauty here made the miles fall away. Water mirrored their purpose, the harbor biting into the island's side. Junior stood at the helm, eyes sharp, watching mangroves curl into the shallows and cacti bristle on the hills, old Navy bunkers rusting in their shadows. The wind held steady from the east at eight knots, seas gentle at two feet. Dream Maker cut through under power, smooth as a blade.

The harbor buzzed with life: center consoles roaring past, jetskis darting, fishermen hauling lines, tourists chasing the sun. Yachts rocked at anchor, hulls bright, scattered like stars across the blue. Small sailboats clung to the mangroves, ferries churned by, their wakes rippling out. Culebra's pastel roofs peeked through the palms. At the bay's north, Cayo Pirata crouched low and rocky, fringed with seagrass and dark mangroves, reefs lurking just beneath. The place was vibrant and loud, but heavy with watching eyes—too many boats, too many shadows for El Tiburón to slip behind.

Junior eased the throttle to three knots, carefully guiding Dream Maker through the harbor's mouth. He kept his voice low and spoke without looking away from the water. "Busy today," he said, glancing at a catamaran gliding past while its crew waved. "Faidh, keep a lookout up front for hazards—coral, buoys, and other boats. Don't want to clip anyone."

"Got it," Faidh replied, her voice bright and steady as she leaned over the rail to get a good view ahead. She waved back at the catamaran, then focused on the water. "Traffic's wild—like a regatta and fishing tournament rolled into one. There's room on Cayo Pirata's west side, though. It's shallow, but we can fit." She looked over her shoulder at Junior, her smile coy. "You sure you can thread this needle, Captain?"

Junior grinned, sharp and sure. "Watch me." He steered past anchored yachts, their lines pulled tight. Coral heads flashed below in the clear water. The harbor smelled of diesel and salt, the air thick with engine hums and the faint thump of music drifting from shore.

Guey gripped the starboard rail, his seasickness gone, the sea's sway now a friend. "This place feels alive," he said, voice soft, a smile in his voice. "Definitely louder than the Vieques' cove." His chuckle delayed his question, "Cofresí hid here, didn't he? It is said that Cofresí once outsmarted the Spanish fleet by vanishing into these very waters. He was said to have a secret route, known only to the Taíno, that allowed him to disappear like a phantom."

"No doubt," Junior said, eyes on the depth sounder. "Cayo Pirata was named for him. Small, hidden—ideal for a pirate. I'd like to vanish like he did—unseen by every boat in this harbor. But Dream Maker's a ketch. She stands out wherever she goes."

Faidh nodded, her face tight. "I feel like we're being watched. I liked it better in Puerto Ferro, Vieques. It felt safer being alone in the cove. We don't know—any of these boats could be the pirates that were following us on El Tiburón. Or there could be different ones who've been told about our adventure." The sliced Genoa sheet lingered in her voice, an edge of caution.

Junior swung Dream Maker wide toward Cayo Pirata's west side, turning the bow into the wind for a controlled approach. He checked the islet's dark mangroves and noted the reefs stretching out a hundred feet. The charts showed twelve feet of water at 250 feet off, which was enough for Dream Maker's swing. He spotted a single boat anchored to the south, leaving the north clear. The west side was most sheltered, away from the worst of the harbor's churn and the trade winds' push. "Guey, get the anchor ready," Junior called, watching the depth. "We'll drop it just off the islet, bow into the wind."

"Aye, aye," Guey said, moving to the bow, hands quick on the chain, his grin wide. "Sailoring's growing on me, huh."

Faidh laughed, warm, light. "Told you, Sunshine. Just don't trip over the chain."

Junior eased Dream Maker down to two knots, the engine nearly silent as they drifted into place. Eyes on the depth sounder, he called, "Drop it now, Guey. Let out a hundred feet of rode — six-to-one scope with our freeboard." The anchor rattled down, chain hissing as it bit into the sand. Junior reversed the motor, feeling for the set, and watched as the boat held steady among the crowd. With so many hulls close, there was no room for error.

Faidh leaned back, eyes on Cayo Pirata, its low shape sharp against the water. "We're close, I can feel it," she said, her voice soft, sure.

Junior looked at Faidh, a sly smile shadowing his face. "Oh, so now you sense the stones' energy too?" He coiled a line, jaw set, the storm's shadow in his mind. "If you two are up for it, I'll dinghy you to the island. Scout the land. I'll check the southeastern edge by water, get another angle," he said, pausing for effect. "But stay together and on alert. I'm with Faidh—I doubt we've seen the last of El Tiburón or her crew." His gaze swept the harbor, the hair on his neck prickling.

Guey held the third amulet for the other two to see it, eternal lovers carved deep, its kidney shape a map. "The Taíno hid in plain sight," he said, voice low. "Cofresí learned that. Whatever's here, it's waiting for us to hear it."

Faidh and Junior just nodded in agreement.

Dega trailed Dream Maker from Vieques to Culebra, keeping El Tiburón's stolen hull at a distance, a shadow on the horizon. The Caribbean stretched wide, the sun high, its light sharp on the water. He'd watched Junior's ketch slip into Ensenada Honda, and he knew better than to follow too close. No one had bothered them in Vieques—the authorities weren't hunting, not yet. Junior and his crew were the real threat; their eyes sharp for the Sea Ray's shape, even with its name scraped off, they would likely notice it. Distance was safety, and Dega meant to keep it that way.

He steered El Tiburón into Ensenada Fulladosa, a small cove west of Ensenada Honda's mouth, Culebra's hills low and green around it. The water was calm, shallow, and fringed by mangroves; the air was thick with salt and the hum of coquis. He dropped anchor in six feet, the chain rattling, the boat settling quietly. The fuel tanks were nearly full, and there was enough food and beer for three, maybe four days—no need to draw eyes by docking in the busy harbor. The cove hid them, its seclusion a pirate's trick, like Cofresí himself.

Dega knew Junior's crew had found at least one more stone—maybe two—since Cabo Rojo. The AIS track showed Dream Maker anchored off Cayo Pirata, a kidney-shaped islet in the big harbor. To stay close without being seen, Dega set a new plan. No watch on El Tiburón—the boat was safe here. Instead, the brothers would watch Dream Maker. Bruno and Tomas would take turns, six-hour shifts, on shore. Dega would ferry them on El Tiburón to a public access point on Ensenada Fulladosa's western edge, a short walk to a rise overlooking Ensenada Honda. From there, they'd see Dream Maker, track any move—dinghy trips, searches, anything tied to the amulets. At night, they'd stand down, the dark too thick to spot details, Dega always staying aboard, his eyes on the radio, the AIS, the sea.

Bruno leaned on the rail, his face set, chewing a crust of bread. "This better pay off, Dega," he said, voice low.

"It will," Dega said, sharp, sure. "They're close to something. We stay patient, stay hidden. Junior's AIS is still on. He doesn't know we're here." The cove was still, the hills silent.

The dinghy bumped Cayo Pirata's small dock, a weathered platform nestled on the islet's west shore. Junior tied off; Faidh and Guey stepped onto the planks, the sun high. The islet was low, fringed with seagrass and tangled roots. The southwestern point, where the amulet's hole was hinted at, lay about 300 feet away, along a jagged path. They shouldered packs—water, flashlights, amulet pocketed—ready for whatever secrets the place held.

The trail began at the dock's end, a narrow cut through coarse sand and low bushes. Cacti spiked the edges. Guey led, his boots crunching, eyes scanning for loose rocks or hidden roots. Faidh followed, her steps light, her gaze flicking to the harbor—boats humming in the distance. The islet was quieter than Ensenada Honda's bustle. The path twisted south, climbing gently. The ground was dry, cracked, and scattered with pebbles and dried palm fronds. Seabirds called, sharp and fleeting. Lizards darted across the trail, quick as thought. The air grew warmer, the sun unrelenting, but a breeze off the water carried relief, faint and cool.

The trail dipped into a shallow gully as mangroves closed in. The path narrowed, branches brushing arms. A half-buried Navy marker jutted from the scrub—a relic of Culebra's past. They climbed a low rise. The southwestern point came into view—rocky outcrop over the sea, waves lapping, a lone twisted tree. The harbor sparkled, but here the islet held its breath, secrets close.

Guey paused, wiping sweat from his brow, the view sharp—turquoise water, green hills, the town's pastel glow faint in the distance. "This is it," he said, voice low, steady. "The hole points here, southwest. Look for anything—carvings, crevices, something Cofres'íd hide behind."

They spread out; the southeastern point was small but heavy with possibility, the hum of the sea urging them on. Junior came into view 100 feet away in the dinghy.

Junior shoved off from Cayo Pirata's dock, the dinghy's engine humming in the thick heat. Sun hammered down, water clear as glass, coral flashing beneath. He steered for the southeastern shore, where the islet's edge turned jagged and the mangroves pressed close, roots tangled in the shallows. The harbor's noise faded behind him, replaced by a hush heavy with secrets. He cut the motor, letting the dinghy drift, eyes searching the rocks for a pirate's hiding place.

Junior leaned forward as the dinghy bobbed gently, steadying himself with one hand on the tiller. Scanning the coastline, he spotted a narrow split in the shore's rock face just above the waterline, barely wide enough for a hand. It was low and hidden — the kind of place a pirate might trust for a secret. With the boat drifting, Junior decided to radio Faidh and Guey to check out the crevice together.

The afternoon waned, the sun low over Cayo Pirata. Junior, Faidh, and Guey scoured the southwestern point for the fourth amulet — nothing turned up. Heat pressed, harbor hummed, dusk crept close. Junior called Faidh and Guey on the radio: "Head back to the dock. I'll meet you there."

The three reunited at the battered dock, its weathered planks warm underfoot, the islet's mangroves looming against the dusk. Junior's dinghy bobbed silently, motor idle. He looked at Faidh and Guey, their faces tired but content from a long search, and grinned, easy but weary. "Let's call it a night. After days at sea — or at a lighthouse," he said, nodding to Guey, his smile gentle, "how about we head into town, grab some food and maybe a drink or two? Let's start at dawn. Maybe we rotate roles — someone else takes the dinghy tomorrow."

Faidh's eyes lit, her laugh quick. "I call dibs on the dinghy. Fewer bugs out there, I'm thinkin'."

They laughed, the sound light, cutting the day's weight. Junior steered for town, harbor alive with yachts and ferries, wakes rocking the small boat. At a public dock, he tied off and locked the dinghy. Packs grabbed, amulets safe, they stepped ashore into dusk.

Junior turned to Guey, his voice warm. "You've never been here, but you know the language, the culture. You pick the restaurant. I'm buying."

Guey grinned, pointing across the street to Zaco's Tacos, its sign bright on Calle Pedro Marquez. Faidh and Junior burst out laughing. "Seriously?" Faidh asked, raising her brow.

"I'm Taíno," Guey said, his smile wide. "It's always traditional meals or Puerto Rican food. I'd kill for tacos if you don't mind."

"Fine by me," Junior chuckled.

"Works for me," Faidh added, her voice bright.

Zaco's Tacos pulsed with life, a small spot at the heart of Culebra. The patio sprawled under a patchwork roof, trees throwing shade over tables, lanterns flickering as night crept in. Local art adorned the walls, the floor worn down by the sandy boots of visitors. Tacos arrived hot, wrapped in corn tortillas, salsas bright with tomatillo and habanero. Chickens strutted through, pecking at crumbs, matching the island's rhythm with their steps. The crowd was loud, locals and travelers laughing, voices sharp against the hum of boats in Ensenada Honda. The food was honest, Caribbean, and Mexican flavors mingling beautifully.

"I swear, if those chickens start a conga line, I'm joining," Guey joked, nudging Faidh.

She chuckled, "As long as you save me a taco before you start a new career as a dancing farmer."

Junior ordered a pitcher of margaritas and raised his glass. "To the three stones we've got," he said, voice warm, not dwelling on the one still missing. Chips and salsa disappeared fast, plates stacked with leftovers, stomachs full before they knew it. Three pitchers in, Junior—usually quiet, reserved—was loose, face flushed, stories tumbling out. He talked of flying, Navy days, open skies, and tight missions, each word drawing Faidh and Guey in, their eyes wide, caught up in the telling.

❖

When the crew of Dream Maker headed to town in the dinghy, Tomas called Dega and told him what was going on. Dega, getting impatient and growing weary of Bruno questioning his every move, told Tomas to go to town and follow the crew. Find out where they are going and if they go to a restaurant, to get a table next to them.

Tomas, surprised by the change of plans, asked, "Should I try to talk to them and learn what I can?"

"Absolutely not. Just get a table for three. Listen to everything you can from their table and wait for me and Bruno to get there. It's gonna take us about 45 minutes to get there, so ask the waitress to give them slow service if you can. I think it's time that I had a face-to-face with our dear Captain Junior."

What Junior didn't notice was the three sailors at the table sitting and drinking, listening to every word he said. And when Junior got up to use the restroom, one of the sailors followed him.

Junior stepped into the shadowed bathroom of the seaside restaurant, the murmur of the dining room fading as he rinsed his hands. The door swung open with a creak, and Dega slipped inside, his bulk filling the space, a smirk curling his lips as his eyes locked onto Junior. "Captain Junior," Dega drawled, pulling a gleaming knife from his belt, its edge catching the fluorescent light as he advanced. "I know that face—seen it on your fancy boat. That treasure you're sniffing out? It's mine when you find it. I'm just givin' you fair warning. You will hand it over, or this blade carves a message into you and your pretty missy out there."

Junior's pulse quickened, his instincts urging caution as he edged back, hands raised slightly. "I don't know who you are, but you're making a mistake. Back off."

Dega chuckled darkly, pressing closer, the knife tip grazing Junior's shirt, his voice low and threatening. "Oh, I know you, aviator. And I know you have three of the four stones. Plan to hand over the treasure when you find it, or none of you survive, and Dream Maker's next — sunk with you on it."

The tension snapped tight, Junior calculating his next move, when the door burst open. Two drunk sailors staggered in, their slurred laughter shattering the moment, one bumping into Dega. The pirate's knife vanished as he stepped back with a snarl, and Junior seized the chance, brushing past the sailors and exiting into the humid night, his mind racing with the encounter's weight.

The last words that Junior heard as he slid out of the bathroom were Dega's voice, "We will be right behind you. Don't think you can outrun us."

When Junior stumbled to the restroom, Faidh leaned toward Guey, her voice low, a smile playing. "I've known him for years, seen him handle anything. Always in control, never indulging like this. This is new."

Guey smirked, his eyes warm. "It's awesome. Feels like an honor, him trusting me this much."

Faidh's smile grew, soft, real. "He trusts you completely. So do I."

Guey grinned, humbled, then hesitated. "Can I ask how long you two have been together?"

Faidh laughed, light and easy. "Less than a week." She paused, her voice softening, as her eyes slid away thoughtfully. "But we've been friends for five years. Different paths, till now." The words hung briefly, a trace of unspoken question weaving through the air, as if acknowledging the unpredictable dance of friendship and romance.

Guey nodded, his voice quiet. "That's amazing, you two feel completely natural, like you've always been together, always will."

Faidh blushed, her eyes bright. "Thanks. It's the most natural I've ever felt. We accept each other for who we are. Not something easy to find."

Junior popped back, swaying slightly, a blank, almost fearful look on his face. Sternly, he asked, not really caring about the answer, "Are you two ready to head back to Dream Maker?"

"Are you ok? You look like you just saw a ghost?" Faidh asked with a concerned look.

Looking around the restaurant for Dega, "Yeah, I'm fine. I think we've all had enough, and tomorrow is gonna be another big day for us." Junior struggled with not sharing what had just happened in the bathroom, but he didn't want to cause any more fear in either of his crew members. This was his burden for now.

Faidh said, standing, her arm around him, a big kiss on his cheek. "Ok, let's go, but I'm driving the dinghy, though."

"Works for me," Junior said, his head on a swivel, a smile returning slightly.

They walked back to the dinghy peacefully, the night warm. They pulled away from the dock, Faidh at the helm, Guey sitting next to her, and Junior on the bow, looking aft. As Culebra's rhythm carried them back to the sea, Junior could see the man he encountered in the bathroom, standing side-by-side with two other sailors. And it flashed across Junior's mind that the three were sitting right behind him the whole time they ate dinner.

CHAPTER 16

THE LAST AMULET

Junior bolted upright in the berth, the dim glow of Ensenada Honda's lights seeping through Dream Maker's aft portlights. Faidh startled, her eyes wide in the dark. "You okay?" she asked, voice soft, urgent.

He chuckled, reaching for the water glass by the bed. "I'm great. I need water, but I'm fine. Oh yeah, and I had a dream. I might know where the last stone is."

Faidh sat up, her hair spilling over her shoulders. "Wait— how? Was it her again, the woman with the dark eyes?"

"Yes," Junior said, his grin sharp. "To both."

"Did she show you where to look?"

"Yep. Kinda."

"Stop it," Faidh said, crossing her arms, a playful huff in her voice. "Stop dragging this out. This isn't fair. I get the nightmares, and you get a dream that shows you where the next amulet is hidden. Tell me what you know, Mister."

Junior laughed, settling back, the water glass cool against his palm. "At first, everything was dark—blurry, like looking through fogged glass. I couldn't place myself. Then it became clear: I was underwater, diving off what felt like the southeast tip of Cayo Pirata. I can't swear to it, since the dream began and ended beneath the surface, but you and Guey both dreamed near

193

stones. I'd wager this is the same." The excitement in his chest was sharp, the dream's location suddenly vital to their search.

"What'd you see?" Faidh's voice was eager, leaning closer.

"I was swimming alone, along a reef. A shadow appeared, like the sun ducking behind a cloud or a boat passing over. Then it took shape—a young woman, waving me to follow, like a siren. Weird thing was, I could see her, but through her at the same time." He took a long gulp of water, the memory sharp. "I followed her. I don't know for how long. Then she stopped, pointed to a hole in the rocks—a small cave."

"Would you recognize it?" Faidh asked, eyes bright.

"Maybe," Junior said, his brow furrowing. "Not sure."

"Think," she urged. "Anything stand out around it? Something you'd recognize?"

He shook his head, slowly. "Don't know."

"How big was the cave?"

"Three, maybe four feet wide. About the same height. I think I actually swam past it—I didn't see it until she pointed. Then I woke up."

Faidh's mind raced. "Do you have dive gear on board?"

"Yeah," Junior said, nodding. "I have a portable tankless system, battery-powered. I use it to clean the hull."

"Perfect," she said, her smile quick, certain.

Junior looked at her, the porthole light catching her face, her eyes alive, her beauty sharp in the dark. He thought about how much lighter the journey—and his burden—felt with her support. How did I get so lucky, he thought, to have her here, on this chase with me? His heart felt full, the weight of the journey and of life lighter with her near.

"You okay?" Faidh asked, tilting her head, her voice soft. "You look like you're deep in thought."

"Things couldn't be better," he said, his voice warm. Then he lay back, pulling her close, his arms wrapping tight, her body warm against his. "I'm so damn happy you're here, Faidh. Right now, life's perfect."

"Me too," she whispered, curling into him, feeling his strength, his warmth. Their bodies fit, hearts beating as one, Junior's breath soft on her neck. Sleep came fast to both Faidh and Junior, the sea rocking Dream Maker, Cayo Pirata's secrets waiting in the dark.

Unfortunately, in the forward berth, Guey was experiencing a very restless sleep; the gentle sway of Dream Maker at anchor off Cayo Pirata was a fragile shield to the nightmare that came.

Suddenly, the mist dissipated, and he found himself in a cavernous cave, the walls glistening with damp rock, the air heavy with the tang of salt and decay; torches cast eerie shadows that danced like specters. He stood at a stone altar, the four amulets glowing faintly as he chanted, hands trembling with the weight of the ritual, the curse's energy pulsing beneath his feet. Junior waded into the cave's shallow pool, water lapping at his waist, assisting with the ceremony, but a sudden roar filled the chamber as a massive wave surged from the darkness, flooding the space with icy force. The current swept Junior away, his body tumbling helplessly, head striking a rock with a sickening thud before he vanished into the churning depths, his muffled cry echoing off the walls.

From the shadows loomed Pirata Cofresí, now a towering figure twice the cave's height, his form a grotesque caricature of death—skin sagging and blackened like charred flesh, eyes hollow pits of glowing embers, his tricorn hat a crumbling ruin atop a skull-like head. His anger radiated in waves, his rusted cutlass trembling in his skeletal grip as he advanced, voice a thunderous snarl that shook the cave: "You dare defy the curse's will, Taíno fool? The treasure is mine, sealed in blood! Stop this blasphemy, or the sea will claim your friend, his bones crushed and lost forever!" Guey stumbled back, the chant faltering, but the pirate's rage grew, his form swelling further, tendrils of seaweed and rot dripping from his frame as he raised the blade high, desperation etching deeper lines into his decaying face.

The cave trembled, and a jagged bolt of lightning erupted from the rock ceiling, illuminating Cofres'ís monstrous silhouette as it struck the water where Junior had fallen, sending steam hissing into the air. Guey fell to his knees, the amulets' glow dimming, the ritual unraveling as Cofres'ís laughter boomed, a sound of fractured madness. "The price is life—yours or his!" the pirate roared, his voice cracking with frantic urgency, before his form dissolved into the mist, leaving Guey gasping in the flooded cave, the weight of the dream's terror pressing down like the sea itself.

Guey jolted awake, his breath ragged, the berth's confines a stark contrast to the cave's chaos. Sweat drenched his shirt, and he clutched the edge of the bunk, the image of Junior's disappearance searing his mind. The quiet of the night outside offered no solace; his heart was pounding with dread of what the next dream might bring. He did all that he could to stave off further sleep, but exhaustion overcame him. Guey tossed and turned the rest of the evening, but no other nightmares appeared in his sleep.

The morning broke gray over the bay, the sky heavy with clouds, the wind sharp, stirring up chop in the harbor. Junior and Faidh woke with a spark, like kids on Christmas morning, eager for the fourth amulet, its promise close after Junior's dream. Faidh bolted to the galley, her hands quick on the Keurig, coffee brewing, its scent sharp in the cabin. Junior moved forward, ducking into the bow's storage to pull out his tankless dive system. He checked the charge—full and ready—but knew a recharge would take three hours if the first dive were to fail. He opened the hatch in the forward space and lifted the equipment onto the deck above.

Junior went aft to the Captain's Quarters for his phone. The weather app's warning glared: Tropical Depression now Tropical Storm Wendy, two hundred miles southeast, tracking west-southwest at fifteen knots—stronger and faster than the models had called. St. Croix and Vieques were under warnings; Culebra had a small craft advisory. The wind's bite and the harbor's restless chop confirmed it—Wendy was on the move. As he grabbed a Diet Coke, a granola bar, and an orange from the counter, a knot of worry tightened in his stomach, mirroring the storm outside. The cautionary breezes whispered doubts in his mind, questioning the path ahead. The harbor was quieter than usual, most boats staying put, but the dinghy ride would be rough, waves slapping hard against the hull, reflecting the turbulence inside his own thoughts.

He loaded the dive gear—wetsuit, fins, mask, flashlight, knife, breathing device—and a small anchor into the dinghy, then ducked below to find Faidh and Guey. Guey was up, coffee in hand, eyes bright. Faidh had already shared the dream, her words tumbling out with excitement. Junior broke in, "Our tropical depression has a name now—Wendy. She's a storm, moving fast, but not straight for us. Still, with the way the forecasts have been,

I wouldn't bet on them knowing her next move. I want to get a dive in this morning, the southeast tip of Cayo Pirata, just like the dream pointed out. If I don't find the stone, we'll recharge and try again around noon, weather permitting." The need to beat the storm pressed at him. He turned to Faidh. "Will you take me out in the dinghy and wait?"

She nodded, her coffee steaming in a to-go mug. "Let's do it."

He turned to Guey. "You're welcome to come, but I'd rather you hold down Dream Maker. Keep her and the three amulets we have safe."

Guey grinned, calm. "I'll stay. I'll call my dad, see if he's found any link between the petroglyphs—turtle, Cojobano Tree, eternal lovers." Keeping Dream Maker safe was a priority, but Guey was also determined to help unravel the mystery from afar.

"Perfect," Junior said, chuckling. "Just don't sail off without us."

"Not going anywhere," Guey shot back, his smile wide.

Junior glanced at Faidh. "Gear's loaded. Whenever you're ready."

"I'm set," she said, grabbing a hat. "Coffee's in the mug. Let's go."

They climbed aft, the dinghy rocking in the chop. Faidh took the captain's seat, her hands sure on the wheel. Junior smiled, warm, steady. "She's yours, Captain. Let's find that stone."

The ride was quick, a few minutes across the harbor's restless water, Cayo Pirata's southeast tip looming, its rocks dark against the grey sky. Junior slipped into the wetsuit, fins, mask, and the breathing device, with the light on his chest. He checked the battery one last time, then slid into the sea, the water cool, the reef below alive, waiting for the cave his dream promised.

The reef below was a patchwork of coral and shadow, the sea alive under Ensenada Honda's grey sky. His mask was tight, the tankless dive system humming softly on the surface, its battery strong as he kicked down, fins steady, following the dream's pull. He turned on the GoPro he had mounted on his head. He thought it might be good to review the recording when he got back to the boat - maybe the camera would catch something his eyes missed in real time. The eastern reef stretched jagged, its edges sharp with brain coral and sea fans swaying in the current. He swam slowly, eyes scanning for the cave—just a bit bigger than a trashcan lid, he thought to himself, the woman's shadow pointing in his mind. Rocks piled against the islet's base, their faces pocked, crevices dark but too shallow, too narrow for a pirate's secret. The water was clear, fish darting like sparks, but no cave, no carving, no sign of the fourth amulet.

He circled wider, the current tugging at him, his breath steady through the regulator. The eastern shore was rough, coral giving way to smooth stone, then sand, but nothing matched the dream's shape. A shadow passed overhead—a boat, not a spirit—and Junior's heart jumped, the harbor's bustle close. He checked the battery gauge—still good, but time was short, the storm's chop above making the dive harder. He probed a final crevice, his fingers brushing against mossy rock, which was empty. The reef held no answers, only silence. He surfaced, the dinghy's hull bobbing nearby, Faidh's face sharp with hope. Nothing, he thought, the dream's cave still hidden, Cayo Pirata keeping its secret tight.

At sunrise, Dega eased El Tiburón from its anchorage in Ensenada Fulladosa's quiet cove, the Sea Ray's engine a low growl, cutting through Culebra's grey morning chop. The sky was heavy, clouds thick, the wind sharp with Tropical Storm Wendy's distant threat. Bruno stood on the bow, his eyes on the public dock at the bay's western edge, where Dega aimed to drop him. It was his turn to watch Dream Maker, anchored off Cayo Pirata, to track Junior's crew and their hunt for the stones. The harbor was waking, ferries humming, but the chop kept smaller boats scarce. Dega tied off at the dock, the wood slick with dawn's dew, and Bruno stepped ashore, his pack light, a radio clipped to his belt. "Six hours," Dega said, voice low. "Radio if they move." Bruno nodded, his boots heavy on the planks, and headed for the rise overlooking the harbor.

From the hill, Cayo Pirata was a low shadow in Ensenada Honda, Dream Maker's ketch rig clear against the water, her hull steady at anchor. Bruno crouched in the scrub, his eyes fixed on the boat: the wind bit, the harbor restless, waves slapping the islet's reefs. An hour after dawn, he saw the dinghy pull away, the woman at the wheel, Junior in dive gear, heading for Cayo Pirata's southeast tip. Bruno's pulse quickened—they were hunting, sure as Cofresí. He watched Junior slip into the water, a splash, then nothing, the dinghy bobbing as Faidh waited. For an hour, Junior dove, his head breaking the surface now and then, searching the reef. Bruno squinted, the distance blurring details, but no stone came up, no signal of a find, no celebration. The radio stayed silent in his hand, the harbor's hum and the storm's weight pressing close, Dream Maker's secrets still out of reach.

The dinghy rocked back through the chop, the sky feeling heavier now, amplified by their morning failure. Faidh took them back to Dream Maker, staying silent beside Junior, their hopes for the fourth amulet sunk in the morning's dive. Cayo Pirata faded behind, its reefs hiding the cave from his dream. As they tied up to Dream Maker's stern, a sudden ripple beneath the water caught Junior's eye, a shadow moving swiftly, darting away with a flash of silver. He hesitated, pulse quickening for a beat—was it just the play of light or something more sinister lurking below? The question ate at him as he climbed up on deck, dive system battery in hand, yet he said nothing to Faidh, the burden of the unknown fanning a quiet urgency inside him. Guey met them, his eyes reading their defeat in an instant.

"No luck, huh?" he asked, voice soft, as Faidh climbed back aboard.

"Nothing," Faidh said, her hat pulled low. She felt his disappointment and chose not to push him, deciding that encouragement, not pressure, was what Junior needed now. "I didn't push him. His face said he didn't want to talk about failure."

Junior hauled the dive system's battery forward, hooking it to the charger, its hum low in the forward space. He took a quick shower to clean up, salt and sand clinging to his skin. In the salon, Faidh and Guey sat, the air warm, the boat's sway gentle. Junior returned, his GoPro in hand, and plugged it into the TV. "I recorded everything in front of me," he said, voice steady but edged. Junior was determined not to let frustration blind him; if he missed something, he wanted the others' help to spot it. "But it doesn't mean I saw it all. Let's review it, if you don't mind, see if I missed something."

The screen flickered, showing the reef's jagged sprawl—coral, sea fans, fish darting—but no cave or significant holes in the rocks or reefs. The tape ended, the salon quiet. Junior looked at them, his eyes tired but sharp. "I searched the eastern side of the southeast tip this morning. I plan to go back and do the same thing to the western half this afternoon. Thoughts?"

Guey shook his head, calm. "Nothing you haven't already thought of, Junior."

Faidh met his gaze, her heart heavy at his anguish. "I've got nothing," she said, voice soft.

The battery took four and a half hours to recharge—longer than Junior hoped. The afternoon sun broke through the thinning gray clouds, Wendy still tracking west, now only 160 miles out, her rain bands starting to brush north of Vieques. The harbor's chop lingered, wind steady at twelve, gusting fifteen—rough, but manageable. Junior and Faidh loaded the dinghy, stowed the gear and anchor, and set out again for Cayo Pirata's southeast tip. The water slapped the hull, the islet's rocks looming dark ahead, the cave from his dream still waiting, hidden.

Junior slid into the water for a second dive. A small break in the clouds allowed sunlight to penetrate; the sea was cool and restless. His fins kicked steadily to where he started in the morning and then off to the western half of the reef - coral jutted like broken teeth, and rocks piled dark against the islet's base. His dream's shadow guided him, the woman's dark eyes pointing to a cave. He wished she were down here to guide him.

Just then, as he thought of her, ten feet down, he found it—a hole, just wider than his shoulders, and not much taller, carved into the rock face by hundreds of years of wave action, half-hidden by swaying sea fans and seaweed hanging down. He swam in, the passage tight, water murky, his breath slow through the regulator. Ten feet in, the cave widened just a bit, and there it was: an old chest, no bigger than a shoebox, crusted with barnacles, wedged in a rocky shelf.

He worked fast, fingers digging at the chest, rough wood scraping his knuckles. He drew his knife, wedged it under the lid, and pried. Minutes dragged by, his breathing slow, the cave tight against his back. The chest loosened. With a final wrench, it popped free, heavy in his hands. Junior kicked backward, shoulders scraping the stone, the cave's mouth a dim sliver ahead. He surfaced, chest gripped tight, the dinghy rocking close, Faidh's eyes bright with hope. He heaved the chest aboard with a thud, voice breaking out: "Look what I found!" Sea spray hit his face, the weight of the chest promising the amulet inside.

The sun was nearly directly over Culebra, the grey clouds seeming to thin a little. The wind steady now, maybe picking up, stirring whitecaps across the harbor. Dega motored El Tiburón back to Culebra's public dock again. It was early afternoon, time to swap Bruno for Tomas, keeping their watch on Dream Maker sharp. Tomas stepped off the boat while Bruno climbed aboard, his face weathered, eyes squinting against the glare. As they pushed off, the boat bouncing through the chop, Bruno leaned close, his voice low over the motor's hum. "Junior dove this morning, southeast tip of Cayo Pirata. He was down for an hour, but seemed to come up empty. The girl waited in the dinghy. They're hunting hard, but no stone yet." Dega nodded, his jaw tight, afraid their chance was slipping away, being so close, but possibly being lost with the approaching storm.

Tomas, meanwhile, trudged from the dock to the rise overlooking the harbor, his boots heavy on the sandy path, scrub and cacti lining the way. Tomas settled in the brush, his radio clipped, eyes fixed on the distant dinghy. He hadn't seen Junior go down for the second dive; it must have happened while he was hiking up, but as he watched, Junior broke the surface, his mask glinting, something small—a box, maybe—tossed into the dinghy, followed quickly by Junior. The girl gunned the motor, the dinghy racing back to Dream Maker, spray flying in its wake. Tomas's pulse quickened; they'd found something. He grabbed the radio, his voice urgent. "Dega, they're back. Junior pulled something up and threw it in the dinghy. They're heading to the boat fast."

Unfortunately, Dega never heard his transmission - he had unintentionally turned off his radio.

The dinghy raced home. Thirty minutes after leaving, they were back, closing in on Dream Maker. Junior gripped the barnacle-crusted chest in his right hand, no bigger than a shoebox, its weight heavy with promise. Faidh's grin flashed, her eyes alive, the morning's failure forgotten. Guey stood at the stern, his gaze catching their faces—good news, even as the clouds started blocking out the sun's rays again. Junior tied the dinghy, the rope taut, and they climbed aboard, the chest dangling, its rusted edges glinting in the sunlight.

Junior set the chest on the deck; the wood was dark and swollen, the lock and hinges eaten by rust. The three crouched close, the harbor's hum distant, the chest old, heavy with time. It wouldn't budge; the lock fused, hinges brittle. Junior ducked below, returning with an angle grinder. "Turn around and cover your ears," he said, voice steady, sure. Faidh and Guey turned, hands to their heads, as the grinder whined, sparks flying, metal screaming. The lock fell away, and the hinges crumbled. "Alright, turn back around," Junior called. He lifted the lid, the wood creaking, revealing an oilcloth inside, rotted but whole, just like the one wrapping the third stone. He reached in, fingers careful, and unwrapped it. A stone emerged, its petroglyph clear—a semicircle with jagged edges, containing a spiral in the center and below that, two crossed lines. He turned it over, the letters "RC" etched roughly on the back, Cofres'ís mark. The air stilled, the amulet's truth burning in their hands.

Junior handed the stone to Guey. "Do you recognize the symbol?"

Guey handled the stone, his touch reverent, as he felt a profound connection to his ancestors. "Yes, but it's more than one symbol. The spiral symbolizes water or energy. That is a standard Taíno symbol. The semicircle above the spiral usually represents a cave. The Taíno people believe the cave is the foundation of life, from which we were all born," he explained, his voice carrying the weight of past generations. His grandmother had often told him tales of Taíno warriors and their sacred caves, where spirits whispered the island's secrets. "But I'm not familiar with the two crossed lines underneath at all." He turned the stone over in his hands, the two crossed lines looking more like the RC than they do the other symbols. Guey then took a picture of the stone and sent it to his father.

Junior added, "And the shape looks like Mona Island. What a brilliant method of hiding the stones. The legend the old man spoke of was right: if you have one, you can find the rest."

Junior looked at Faidh and Guey. "What do you say we grab some lunch? I'm suddenly famished. Then let's try to decipher the four stones. What do they mean? Where are they telling us to go next? We need a new destination. It's time to find Cofres'ís hidden treasure."

CHAPTER 17

PIRATES!

The four amulets rested on Dream Maker's salon table, their petroglyphs—turtle, Cojobana Tree, eternal lovers, cave over water—carved deep, each line holding the weight of Cofres'ís secrets. Afternoon sunlight slanted through the portholes, painting the table in gold, while Ensenada Honda's chop slapped the hull and the wind rattled the rigging; Tropical Storm Wendy pressed closer with every gust. Junior absently tapped his finger against the table, the gentle rhythm a counterpoint to the hull's persistent thud below. He leaned back, steady-eyed, watching Faidh and Guey. "We've got all four stones. Legend says they're the map. Let's each dig into where they point, pick a spot, and defend it. If we agree, that's where we go." They nodded, screens glowing in the dim cabin, the only sounds the generator's low hum and the slow, restless creak of the boat.

By three o'clock, Guey broke the silence, his voice calm, carrying the weight of the Taíno culture in it. "My dad and I think it's Norman Island, BVI."

"Ok, tell us why?" Junior asked.

Guey spread the stones across the table, his fingers tracing each one as he spoke. 'The turtle fits Norman's waters—turtles crowd the reefs and dive sites, The Indians, Brown Pants, The Caves, even Angelfish Reef. The Taíno saw turtles as the start of

206

life itself, tied to Deminan Caracaracol, one of their heroes.' He paused, a memory flickering in his eyes, revealing its emotional depth. 'I remember once, when I was a kid, snorkeling with my dad on the southwest part of the island. We saw this great turtle glide effortlessly beneath us. Dad said it carried the spirit of the ocean. I felt...connected, like that turtle was guiding us just like now.' Guey focused back on the table. 'The Cojobana Tree matches the island's green hills, sacred for its power, a bridge between nature and spirit. The eternal lovers zemi calls to Norman's hidden coves, the way the island draws in adventurers and lovers, the balance the tribe sought.' He paused, weighing the stones. 'With just these three, it could be any number of islands in the Caribbean. But the fourth cave over water, crossed lines beneath—it's Norman's caves. They're famous, tied to pirates, the Nuestra Señora de Guadalupe in 1750, perhaps even the spark that inspired Treasure Island. Those caves are the island's heart. And the crossed lines, they aren't Taíno. My dad and I searched —there's no petroglyph like them anywhere. We think Cofresí carved them himself, his 'X' to mark the spot. It's Norman Island.'

Junior grinned, leaning forward. "Holy crap, Guey. I was guessing Turtle Cove, St. John, USVI, but it was a shot in the dark. Your logic's tight, way more than anything I could defend."

Faidh nodded, her eyes bright. "Amazing work, Guey. I checked Cofres'ís haunts, found Norman mentioned a couple of times, but I was stuck on the USVI, closer to Puerto Rico. I think you've got it."

"Alright then," Junior said, standing, his voice firm. "We set a course for Norman Island, BVI, after clearing customs at Tortola's West End. Everyone got their passports?"

Guey patted his pack, smiling. "Right here."

Faidh just smiled. "Of course! I'm always ready for an adventure!"

❖

Junior checked the weather app, his face grim. Wendy had strengthened, turning north in the last hours, now 150 miles south-southeast of Culebra, moving at fifteen knots. Her winds roared at 60 knots, gusts to 75. Culebra now faced a Tropical Storm Warning, the harbor restless under grey skies. He called Faidh and Guey to the salon, his voice steady, and described the change in weather. "We can stay anchored, ride out the rough weather here, or sail east toward Norman Island, outrun the storm. Staying risks loose boats breaking free, smashing into us. Sailing means a long night, 10-12 foot seas most likely until we get some protection north of the USVI. Probably some scary moments. But Dream Maker's built for it—full keel, heavy ballast. We'll rig the storm sail, double-reef the mizzen, and keep bare steerage. What do you two think?"

Faidh glanced at Guey, then met Junior's eyes, her trust clear. "It's your call, Captain. We trust you!"

"If it were just me, I'd leave now," Junior said. "Better to face the back of the storm at sea than risk its eye in a crowded harbor. It'll be scary—big waves, spray everywhere. But the boat's solid, and we've got the electric motor if we need it. You two ready?"

Faidh nodded, hesitant but game. "This'll be a story for the ages."

Guey's eyes burned. "Juricán won't stop us this close to breaking the curse."

Junior gave orders, 'Secure everything—gear, dishes, amulets. Grab dry clothes and towels, keep them handy. Foul-weather gear's in the aft locker—pick what fits.' He climbed topside, the wind gusting to twenty knots, light rain stinging, Wendy's breath close. The ketch rocked in Ensenada Honda's chop, Culebra's boats swaying uneasily. Junior moved fast, his boots gripping the wet deck, readying Dream Maker for the gale-force winds they were likely to face. The Genoa was furled tightly to minimize wind resistance. The sheets were coiled and lashed to stanchions with double sail ties to prevent movement; extra wraps bound it to the forestay to ensure it stayed secure. The main sail was flaked neat in its jack stack and zipped shut, with additional ties cinched to hold it down during the storm. Halyards were cleated, taut, and chafe-free, critical to avoiding damage during high winds. The storm sail, with hanks clipped to the inner forestay, lay ready to hoist for better control in heavy winds. The mizzen was stowed for the moment, planned for double-reefing later to help balance and distribute the center of effort in rough seas. Jacklines ran bow to stern, clips firm for harnesses, setting a safe path for movement on deck. The dinghy was hauled up and lashed tight to the stern, reducing the risk of it being torn away by waves. Loose gear, like fenders and buckets, was stowed below, and hatches were dogged shut, preventing water intrusion. Dream Maker stood lean, taut, and ready for the battle with the sea.

Faidh and Guey emerged, geared up in yellow foul-weather bibs, as they threw their jackets onto the side deck next to the companionway, life jackets with harnesses clipped, ready for jacklines in case they needed to leave the closed cockpit. Faidh's gloves were grippy, her boots steady on the deck, and she hadn't tightened her harness yet. Guey, less sure, wore the same, his harness very tight. The gear was heavy and warm, but it kept them dry and safe. "Faidh, take the helm," Junior said, his trust in her absolute. "Guey, you and I'll handle the rest. We'll set the storm sail and mizzen once clear of the harbor, before the winds climb."

Faidh settled at the helm, turning the key to the electric motor, its hum low. "Ready when you are."

"I'll take her till the anchor's up," Junior said, pulling his remote control. "Stay here." He stepped onto the port deck, his foul-weather jacket red, lightweight, hood cinched against the rain. Grey bib overalls, waterproof, moved with him, his life jacket auto-inflating, tethered to the jackline. Non-slip boots bit the wet deck, a knife and whistle clipped to his belt. He eased Dream Maker forward, slackening the anchor chain, raising it slowly as the wind fought against him. Four times, he created slack, the chain rattling, until the anchor broke free and slid into its roller. He locked the windlass, securing the chain to prevent a slip in the rough seas ahead. He signaled Faidh, her nod sharp, and she steered clear of Cayo Pirata, threading through the harbor's anchored boats. Junior returned to the cockpit, peeling off his jacket, life jacket back on, the sea's challenge waiting.

Dream Maker cleared Ensenada Honda's mouth, Junior's head on a swivel, looking for El Tiburón. The sky was now very dark and low, with steady rain, as Culebra's hills faded astern while Faidh steered east toward the Virgin Islands. The wind howled from the southeast, steady at twenty knots, gusting to thirty, the seas rising, six to seven feet, their crests curling white. Junior and Guey moved fast on the wet deck, their foul-weather gear—Junior's red jacket, Guey's yellow—slick with spray, harnesses clipped to jacklines. Junior hoisted the storm sail, its hanks snapping onto the inner forestay, the small triangle taut and steady. Guey raised the mizzen, double-reefed as planned, its reduced canvas balancing the ketch, the sheets tightened hard— Junior checking his work.

In the cockpit, Faidh held the helm, the electric motor quietly pushing the boat forward, almost six knots. Junior kept the motor on, its power letting them point higher into the wind, meeting the waves bow-on to cut their roll. The sea hissed, spray stinging the dodger's windows. Junior scanned the horizon, the storm's edge close, his eyes sharp for squalls. "Hold her steady," he told Faidh, voice calm, trust absolute. Guey stood by, ready for any call, the ketch carving through the swelling seas.

Tomas crouched on the rise overlooking Ensenada Honda, the wind gusting, rain stinging his face. Dream Maker's ketch rig pulled away from Cayo Pirata, steamed south out of the harbor, and as he saw her turn east, he could see her storm sail and mizzen rising as she cleared the inlet. Tomas grabbed his radio, calling Dega, but static filled the air—nothing. It was 4:30 p.m., his shift not done till 6:00, but the empty harbor mocked him. No point watching a ghost. He slung his pack, boots crunching down the sandy path to the public dock, hoping to spot El Tiburón or signal Bruno. He was dripping wet and frustrated. The sea churned, Culebra's hills dark, Wendy's breath close.

At 5:30, Dega cursed in El Tiburón's cockpit, anchored in Ensenada Fulladosa's cove, noticing his radio was off. "Damn," he muttered, flipping it on, static crackling. "Tomas, you there?" Tomas's voice broke through, urgent, soaked from the rain. "Dream Maker's moving, headed east. Tried you all day— nothing." Dega dropped the mike and yelled to Bruno, "Get the anchor, now! Junior's on the move." They motored to the dock, picking up Tomas by 6:00, his clothes dripping wet, his face grim. "Radio was dead," Tomas said. "Tried my phone, no signal. What happened?" Dega shrugged, "Turned it off by mistake. No bars here either." Bruno glanced at the darkening sea, Wendy's warning heavy. "Locals say it's a Tropical Storm Warning, maybe a hurricane by tonight. You sure about this, Dega?" Dega's eyes were sharp, AIS glowing on the screen. "They've got a 12-mile lead. We're faster—we can catch them in an hour. They're running behind the storm, not waiting here. Let's do the same. Better than sitting, hoping no other boats smash us." Tomas hesitated, then nodded, Bruno following. El Tiburón roared to life, chasing Dream Maker's signal into the swelling seas.

Faidh felt Dream Maker rise and fall as the seas began to swell, now at least seven to eight feet, the hull tracking steadily despite the eight-second swells rolling beneath her. The storm sail thrummed in the wind, driving the boat at 7.5 knots with the electric motor humming quietly at relatively low power. Every couple of minutes, a rogue wave crashed over the bow, sending cold spray sweeping across the deck. The boat felt stable, her deep keel biting into the water, reassuringly safe despite the relentless pitching.

Junior stood braced in the cockpit, his glance bouncing between the seas aft of the boat and the ship's instruments. The wind was pegged at a steady thirty knots, gusts shrieking through the rigging. At her current speed, Dream Maker was making solid headway, the storm sail's pull complemented by the motor's silent torque. He considered easing the throttle to conserve battery, but the boat's high angle into the wind kept her bow slicing through the swells without excessive pounding. He decided to hold course and speed for now.

Darkness pressed in swiftly after sunset, thick clouds suffocating the last glow of daylight. The cockpit's dim blue lighting cast shadows on Faidh's tense face, anxiety ready to tip overboard. Junior kept his voice steady, assigning tasks to channel their focus. "Faidh, keep her steady... hold this course," he said. "Guey, scan the horizon for lights — any ships not showing on radar or AIS. Focus your attention aft." The lookout task in this murk felt almost futile, yet it kept Guey at ease. Junior's mind lingered on El Tiburón, a threat he knew must be weaving through the darkness. He glanced at the radar screen, heart thumping with each sweep. There, he saw a single blip. Eight miles astern. "Faidh," Junior's voice cut through, sharper now. "We need eyes on... anything moving." The radar blip taunted him; his thoughts began to fragment, mirroring the quickening pulse in his veins.

Fifteen minutes later, the target closed to six miles, gaining fast. Junior's jaw tightened. "Might be El Tiburón," he said, reluctant, his eyes meeting Faidh's. "Push the throttle to eight knots. Tell me the RPM when it's stable." Faidh nodded, her hands firm on the helm, easing the electric motor up. The ketch surged, cutting the waves sharper, spray rattling the dodger.

"Eight knots, 1400 RPM," she called after two minutes. "Why do you think it is El Tiburón? We haven't seen them since we left Palmas del Mar."

Junior nodded, calculating—two, maybe three hours of battery at that pace before the generator kicked in. He'd avoid it if he could—preferring not to run the generator in rough seas. He looked solemnly at Faidh, "Because I know they are following us. I know they want the treasure."

Guey stepped in, "How could you know that?"

Junior hesitated, then blurted out, "Because her Captain pulled a knife on me in the bathroom at the restaurant last night. He told me they were going to take the treasure once we found it."

Faidh screamed, "WHAT?!"

Junior looked directly at Faidh, "I'm sorry, I didn't want to scare you."

Guey spoke up now, "What else are you holding back from us? You told us that leaving Culebra was the right decision due to Tropical Storm, but you didn't provide us with all the information you had. You didn't tell us that the pirates were right on top of us."

"Would it have changed your answer?" quipped Junior, now looking at Guey.

"We'll never know, because you didn't give us a chance." Guey's response was quick and to the point."

"Ok, I screwed up." Junior didn't hesitate to fess up. He knew getting belligerent or stronghanded at this moment would only further erode their trust in him, "I didn't share with you everything I knew because I felt it was my burden to shoulder as a Captain. Sometimes I forget that I'm no longer in the military. I'm guessing we are all hiding something to protect each other. All I know is that I think the crew of El Tiburón is growing increasingly impatient. If they are truly following us, I think they mean us all harm. I believe they will try to board us and take Dream Maker. If it's not them, then I humbly ask for your forgiveness. We'll turn around and return to Culebra. Either way, I need to know if you trust me enough to captain us going forward."

The cockpit was silent as the waves crashed over the bow of Dream Maker, and she rolled slowly, riding the growing swells.

Finally, in a soft but firm voice, Faidh looked deep into Junior's eyes and said, "I told you, I'm in. I trust you, Junior. But if there is anything else you are hiding, please tell us now."

"I've told you everything. I know this is scary, but I think I have a plan to get us through this, without them boarding us, or even bothering us anymore." Junior stood tall as he spoke.

"Junior, I'm scared as hell. I'm not a fighter. I'm studying to be a bohitiu. I'm counting on you to keep us all safe."

Junior looked directly at Guey, "I promise you, I will do everything in my power to protect you."

Guey dropped his head and replied, "Ok, I'm with you - whatever it takes. Just know that at this point, I'd happily give up the amulets and whatever treasure may be out there, if that meant getting myself safely back to Jayuya."

Junior touched the young man's face, lifting his chin until they were eye-to-eye, and said, "I promise to get you home safely."

With that, Junior's posture changed. He took on a commanding presence that Faidh had never seen before. "Guey,

Faidh," he said, his voice calm, sharp. "We are gonna go dark and turn off the AIS. Then we'll come about to a southerly heading, and see if they're dumb enough to follow."

Faidh glanced at him, her eyes bright under her cap. "Think we'll lose them?" Junior's grin was thin, sure. "They're leaning on our AIS, I'm guessing. I want to make it even harder for them — create a problem to solve while we drag them into heavier seas."

Guey leaned forward in Dream Maker's cockpit, "Turning south puts us closer to Wendy, doesn't it?" he asked, his voice sharp.

Junior nodded, his face calm, sure. "Yep. And it'll help us, believe it or not."

Faidh's head snapped up, her gloves tight on the helm. "Wait, what?"

Junior's grin was thin, steady. "Dream Maker's got a displacement hull, built for heavy seas. El Tiburón's a planing hull, made for speed, not storms. Bigger waves—ten to twelve feet, four to five second intervals—shift the edge to us. We'll outrun him." As Junior spoke, the bow edged south, steadying against the rising waves. The thundering spray lessened, and the ketch found her groove, the sea's fury hinting at the advantage of their tactic. The radar glowed, the target six miles astern, closing.

Faidh's eyes narrowed. "Into a tropical storm?"

"Hopefully not," Junior said. "I'm betting he turns back first. If he doesn't, he's no match in those seas." He flipped off the AIS, then the nav lights, deck lights, every glow but two dim cockpit bulbs, making Dream Maker a ghost in Wendy's churn. Stepping to port, he grabbed the storm sail sheet, his boots firm on the wet cockpit deck. "Faidh, come about—heading 180, due south." The ketch hesitated, her bow heavy, then a wave slammed port, shoving her right. The storm sail fluttered; Junior released the port sheet, leapt across the cockpit, and hauled the starboard sheet tight, setting the sail for a port close haul. The double-reefed mizzen snapped taut, the ketch slicing south, the sea hissing, El Tiburón's light shifting from astern to their starboard beam. He looked at Faidh and told her to turn port until she saw the storm sail flutter just a bit, and then back off a couple of degrees.

She did exactly as she was told. And they all stared at the radar to see what the track following them would do.

On board El Tiburón, Dega gripped the helm. His clothes were slick with spray. The wind howled at 30 knots now, Wendy's outer bands pushing from the southeast. At twelve knots, the boat climbed each wave—her bow rising sharply, then slamming down. The impact was jarring. Water crashed over the windshield; wipers thrashed. The engines roared, steady but strained. The hull shuddered as it planed, skimming the troughs, only to meet the next swell's wall. Bruno and Tomas braced in the cockpit, their clothes soaked. Life jackets were tight, hands clutching rails as the deck pitched. The horizon tilted. Dream Maker's lights were gone. The AIS return was aging, but no one noticed. All they saw was that they were gaining faster than before. The sea's hiss and the storm's growl were loud in their ears.

Each wave lifted El Tiburón. The props bit hard to keep the speed up. The seas' interval gave just enough rhythm to settle into, but the height kept Dega tense. His eyes scanned constantly for rogue waves. Spray stung his face through the open helm window. He needed the fresh air outside to stay calm. Bruno cursed low, knuckles white. Tomas checked the chartplotter—its screen dim, Dream Maker's five miles off our bow now. The boat was fast but fragile in this churn, built for speed—not endurance—unlike the ketch they chased.

At twelve knots, Dega and crew caught up to the aging last reported position of Dream Maker in just about 20 minutes. They slowed down when they were within a mile of the position. But they saw nothing. Dream Maker was truly a ghost.

"Damnit!" yelled Dega. "They've turned off their AIS. We're looking at a signal on the plotter that's twenty-five minutes old. Bring up the radar on the screen!"

They looked, and there was a single blip, about 4 miles due south of them.

"There they are. They can't get away that easily," Dega said, turning the boat south and pushing the throttle up until he saw 12 knots on the gauge again.

Bruno spoke up, worry clear in his voice. "Dega, we're really pushing the boat too hard in these seas. We need to slow down before something goes wrong."

"We're fine."

But the seas were clearly getting rougher—El Tiburón was taking a beating that wasn't sustainable.

Dream Maker continued south through the Caribbean's seething waters, the seas climbing to nine feet, their crests sharp in the limited light. Winds screamed at thirty-five knots, now gusting to forty, rattling the rigging, Tropical Storm Wendy's outer bands clawing from the southeast, her center getting closer with each minute. Junior hunched in the closed cockpit, rain hammering the dodger—the noise very loud in the cockpit. He tried the Starlink, calling the U.S. Coast Guard in San Juan, but the signal flickered, drowned by the storm's heavy rain. He cursed low, knowing even a connection might bring no help in time. The radar glowed, El Tiburón's blip four miles astern, matching their southerly turn after twenty minutes of chasing a ghost.

Faidh gripped the helm, her yellow bibs slick, eyes sharp under her cap. "They're back on us," she said, voice tight. "The AIS trick only worked for a bit."

Junior nodded, calm, his gaze steady. "Didn't expect them to quit. Just wanted them to sweat. The most important thing now is that they are likely frustrated and not thinking clearly, following us straight into Wendy." He glanced at the gauges, the speed bouncing at 7.8 knots. He would like to turn off the motor, but not yet. "Winds are thirty-five now, gusting forty. Seas are rougher, aren't they?"

Faidh agreed, her hands firm.

"Yeah, and we're slowing." Junior's voice stayed even. "El Tiburón won't be able to keep their speed in this. They're definitely taking a beating. We're built for it." He paused, then added, "Faidh, if you need a break, I'll take the helm."

She shook her head, grinning faintly. "I like it here. Keeps my mind off the storm—focused on Dream Maker and keeping her tracking properly. And in case you're wondering, so far, tonight feels nothing like my dream. I completely trust you."

Junior's eyes held hers, silent, warm, saying what words didn't. Then Junior said, "I need a Diet Coke. Does anyone else want anything from below deck?"

Guey spoke up, nervous but quick. "I'll go get it, Junior. I feel safer with you up here."

Junior chuckled, the sound thin, tense. "Was gonna show you that things are fine, even without me for a second, but if you prefer—"

"I prefer," Guey cut in, bolting for the companionway. Their laughter broke—nervous, sharp—the sea hissing.

Guey climbed back into Dream Maker's cockpit, the companionway hatch slamming shut behind him, rain drumming the dodger. He handed Junior the Diet Coke, the can cold, beaded with condensation. Junior popped it open, took a sip, and set it in the cup holder, the ketch pitching as Faidh held the helm steady. Junior grinned, his phone glowing in his hand. "Know what we need?" he asked, thumb tapping the screen. AC/DC's "Thunderstruck" loudly crackled through the cockpit speakers, guitars sharp over the storm's hiss.

Junior's eyes lit, his grin wide. "Music!"

He cranked the volume, the beat cutting through Wendy's roar all around them. Faidh laughed, her shoulders easing. Guey's laugh joined hers, nervous tension breaking like a wave, their faces bright in the dim cockpit glow. The radar blip was getting closer—just over three and a half miles astern, El Tiburón fighting the seas—but for a moment, the music drowned the chase, Dream Maker charging south, alive.

Faidh's mind flashed to the image of dozens of helicopters attacking a beach in Vietnam with The Ride of the Valkyries blasting over loudspeakers in the movie, Apocalypse Now.

Unseen by both crews, Wendy roared into a Category 1 hurricane by 8:00 p.m., her 75-knot core just 90 miles south, fueling chaos. El Tiburón pressed after Dream Maker, but her speed bled to ten knots. The ride turned brutal, twice as violent since their southerly turn, winds tearing at forty knots. Bruno and Tomas clung to the cockpit, soaked, pleading with Dega to abandon the chase.

"It's not worth dying for," Tomas urged, his voice thin against the gale.

Dega's eyes stayed locked on the radar, three miles from Dream Maker, his obsession burning. "We're closing."

Tomas snapped, "Then what? Board them?"

Dega replied, his voice hard. "Yes, we board them and take what they've got. No more waiting—we're going on the offensive."

Bruno's frustration broke, his shout fierce. "That's what I needed to hear! If we're just trailing them, I'm done. But if we are taking what they have, I'm all in!"

Dega nodded. "Bruno, get the guns below. Load them and be ready."

"Damn straight," Bruno said, ducking below, the boat lurching, the hunt now deadly.

Guey squinted at the radar in Dream Maker's cockpit, the glow sharp against the dark, rain lashing the dodger. "Two miles separation, Junior," he said, voice tight.

Junior nodded, eyes calm, calculating. "They're closing at under two knots now." He turned to Faidh, her hands steady on the helm. "You holding up?"

Faidh met his gaze. "I'd rather be snuggled in bed with you, but if we get that later, I can survive anything right now."

Junior grinned. "Deal." He checked the wind gauge—thirty-eight knots, gusts to fifty—speed bouncing around seven point five knots. "Seas are pushing twelve to fifteen feet. El Tiburón's ride must be hell."

Guey, gripping the rail, voice uneasy, said, "This isn't exactly smooth here, Junior."

Junior chuckled, low. "We're better off than they are, trust me." He looked at Faidh, his smile sharp. "Prepare to come about. We'll turn left, through the wind, back to an easterly heading. We're close enough to the eye—time to lose them."

"Ready to come about, aye, aye, Captain," Faidh called, her voice bright over the storm's roar.

Junior's tone softened, firm. "Come about, Faidh. Bring her port to zero-nine-zero."

"Zero niner zero, aye," she shouted, spinning the wheel left. Dream Maker swung, the bow cutting through a wave, Junior working the sheets, the storm sail, and the mizzen snapping taut.

"This'll pull El Tiburón closer," Junior said, eyes on Faidh. "They'll angle to cut us off. When they're within a couple of hundred yards, I'll take the helm, if that's okay." Faidh nodded, brow furrowed, unsure. He continued, "Then we'll ease northeast, about 60 degrees off the wind—a close reach, not a close haul. It'll get rough—really rough — for a couple of minutes. Waves will come over the starboard bow pretty aggressively. We'll list hard port, maybe 20-30 degrees of heel. You both sit starboard, more for comfort than ballast. The good thing is that our keel's long, heavy—built for this. El Tiburón won't stay upright if she tries to stay with us. We'll push them past their safe limit, maybe before they even realize it."

By 9:00 p.m., the Caribbean was churning violently under Hurricane Wendy's wrath. El Tiburón closed to about 300 yards on Dream Maker, the Sea Ray's lights sharp at Junior's stern through sheets of rain. Salt spray veiled Dream Maker, her form barely visible to Dega's crew, as the 15-foot seas crashed and the winds howled. Junior met Faidh's eyes in the cockpit, the dodger rattling. "It's time. I'll take the wheel."

Faidh nodded, "She's yours, Junior. What's my job now?"

"Grab the starboard storm sheet," he said, voice steady. "Ease it out slowly to keep the sail trimmed. I'll give you the signal." He turned to Guey. "Same for you with the mizzen traveler sheet." Guey, his face taut, nodded concurrence.

Junior eased the helm to the left, turning so slowly that it was almost unrecognizable. Dream Maker's bow shifted northeast to 60 degrees off the wind, a heading about zero seven five. "Ease the sheets, slow," he called to Faidh and Guey. The ketch surged, speed climbing from 7.5 to 8 knots, then 8.6 as Junior nudged the throttle to 2000 RPM. Waves broke over the starboard bow, the boat rolling to 25 degrees, then settling to a 15-degree heel, her long keel biting deep, steady. The ride jarred, but held.

Sharp pops cracked through the storm—Junior's jaw tightened. Either they were firing at us or they were starting to come apart. He thought it would be foolish to fire at Dream Maker, but Dega likely meant to scare them, to force a slowdown for boarding. Not a chance, Junior thought. He flicked on every light—nav, deck, spreaders—Dream Maker blazing like a beacon.

Just then, the winds gusted over 100 knots, a 40+ knot gust, and Dream Maker started to roll left with wave after wave coming over the starboard side of the ship. And that quickly, Dream Maker was knocked down on her port side. Junior first looked at Guey and Faidh to make sure they were safe. He yelled, "Hold on, she will right herself in a second."

Then he looked aft, knowing the knockdown was going to give El Tiburón a chance to get even closer.

The 'second' as Junior described it, felt like hours to Guey and Faidh, who were holding onto the railing in the cockpit with dear life. But he was correct, Dream Maker did right herself, but she did so without a functioning storm sail. The sail was still in place and looked functional, but the port sheet was torn, leaving the sail flapping in the wind violently and the loose line banging hard against the port side of the boat.

The boat was now upright, and Junior could immediately feel the change in balance as she steered; she was pulling hard to starboard, trying to turn back up into the wind, even as the waves crashed against her starboard side, trying to push her back port.

Faidh screamed, "What can we do?"

Junior looked aft and couldn't believe his eyes. El Tiburón was bouncing violently, but still closing. They clearly weren't quitting. So close that he could see the man who drew the knife on him, standing on the lit bridge.

He looked at Faidh. "I'm gonna need you to take the helm. I need to go forward and attach a new sheet to the storm sail or cut her loose so we can deploy a minimally furled cutter. Can you take the helm?"

"No!" Cried Faidh, the nightmares of losing Junior as he steps forward, filling her mind. "What about my nightmares?"

Junior pointed towards El Tiburón, screaming over the howling winds, "We need to do this, or they are going to catch us, and it could be even worse than your nightmare."

Faidh nodded, a complete look of terror in her eyes as she could see the lights of the motorboat chasing them. It was everything she had seen in her nightmares, and now Junior was going forward. All she could think was that Cofresí was going to appear and take Junior from her. And Guey and she would be lost without him.

She then took a deep breath and slid behind the helm, the water running down her face was more than just seawater, "Ok, what do I need to do?"

Junior put his two wet hands on either side of Faidh's face, trying to relay comfort and to make sure she understood what he needed. "Hold this heading. The gust that knocked us down was rogue, not something I expect to see again. Right now, we are stable with 15 degrees of heel. The boat is bouncing around a lot, and occasional waves are coming over the starboard gunwale, but things are relatively stable. She's gonna pull to the right on you - just do your best. I trust you with my life."

223

Faidh pulled him close and kissed him. "Please be careful." Tears running down her face. She took the helm, and Junior grabbed an extra line to use as a replacement sheet, tying off a carabiner on one end. Then, he tested his lifeline, ensured his harness was secure, and moved outside up the port side of the boat, water rushing over the port gunwale, making it difficult to step forward. He looked over his left shoulder and saw that El Tiburón was bouncing violently in the waves, and he couldn't figure out why they hadn't backed off.

Then Junior looked at Guey, "We got this, but I need you to stay here and help Faidh. She might need help keeping her steady in these winds."

Guey was clearly filled with terror and could hardly think. He sheepishly replied, "Aye, aye, Captain."

Slowly, Junior made it up to the loose sail, as it violently slashed in the wind. Methodically, he reached out with one hand for the loose sheet, the other firmly holding the railing on top of Dream Maker's cabin. "Got it!" He yelled to no one. Then he pulled out his knife when a big wave crashed over the starboard bow and knocked Junior to the deck. He could faintly hear a scream from the cockpit.

He slowly stood back up, giving a wave to let Faidh know he was ok, and cut the old sheet clear. As quickly as he could, he slapped the carabiner with the new sheet attached to the flopping sail and started working his way back to the cockpit slowly, threading the new sheet through the appropriate blocks back to the cockpit. He was working as quickly as he could, knowing that time was of the essence with El Tiburón still bearing down on them.

As he finally got back to the entrance of the cockpit, Junior looked aft and saw El Tiburón; the boat was within about 50' now, but it looked like she was losing control. The boat was bouncing on the waves, and her bow was moving back and forth nearly 45 degrees with each bounce. The captain clearly lost control and was trying to keep her steady, overcorrecting each swing of the bow.

As Junior climbed back into the cockpit, he heard a loud pop. When he looked up, a flash of lightning revealed the bridge's top ripping off its foundation and blowing away, exposing the Captain at the helm, looking angry, but completely defeated.

He turned to Faidh and smiled, "I'm back!" Then he turned around and set the sheet on the storm sail to help bring balance back to the rigging of Dream Maker. The sail snapped full of air, and the boat immediately heeled to almost 25 degrees. He turned and yelled out, "Faidh, ease her starboard to 090. I'll bring in the sheet. And that will smooth out our ride a bit.

The last thing Junior did before sitting down in the cockpit was pull out his phone. He tapped his phone, Metallica's "Enter Sandman" thundering from the speakers, a defiant roar over the waves, as El Tiburón slowly drifted away. The ketch powered on, her lights and music a taunt, pulling away as the pirates' boat faltered in the breaking seas.

Dega was feeling like they had finally caught Junior. From what he could tell, they were still gaining, and they could see them now, probably about 300 yards off the bow. Junior's little trick of turning to the east only made it easier for El Tiburón to close the distance between them.

He needed to act quickly, though. He wasn't sure how much more the Sea Ray could take, nor how much he and his crew could handle. El Tiburón battered through the Caribbean's fury. Waves broke white; each crest slammed the Sea Ray like a fist. Winds screamed at 40-50 knots. The wipers could barely clear. The boat climbed steep swells, bow pitching high, then plunged into troughs. The hull shuddered. The engines roared, now barely holding eight knots. Their whine was strained as the props bit air

225

between waves. The short interval gave no respite. The seas were too tight for the powerboat's design. Her speed faltered, every impact rattled fittings, threatening to crack the fiberglass.

Tomas had all but given up on the chase. He clung to the cockpit rails, begging Dega to turn around. Even Bruno was struggling, despite his recent refocusing, as they thought they were going to board Dream Maker.

Dega didn't notice the turn that Dream Maker was making. He called for Bruno to fire some warning shots. But before he knew it, the boat stopped pitching as much as it had previously. The waves started rolling El Tiburón fiercely. Suddenly, a rogue wave reared—eighteen feet, breaking white. El Tiburón climbed its face, bow high, rolling hard to port, nearly forty degrees. Then she plunged, snapping back to starboard. The crash was jarring. A deck fitting snapped loose, pinging across the cockpit. The radar flickered.

Bruno shouted, his voice raw, "Dega, she's breaking! Slow down!" Tomas clung beside him, life jacket tight, eyes wide as water surged on the deck of the bridge, the hull shuddering, a low crack echoing from the starboard chine. Dega's jaw clenched, eyes locked on Dream Maker, who he could see was now knocked down. "We got them! Look!" He yelled, pointing at the large sailboat on their side. They were suddenly gaining faster. But the Sea Ray was faltering as well; speed dropped to six knots, the engines choking on the strain, with the port engine starting to overheat. Another wave hit, spray blinding, the windshield frame rattling. The boat wasn't built for this—not like Dream Maker. Then, suddenly, Dream Maker was back upright. It was becoming increasingly challenging to keep El Tiburón steady. She was bouncing from wave to wave, mainly tracking straight, but it was more luck than anything he was doing.

Smoke was billowing from below, the port motor completely overheating now, he pulled the left throttle to idle. The boat veered sharply to the left due to the loss of power. Dega countered the movement with the wheel, but given the circumstances, he overcorrected. Suddenly, Dega found himself in an oscillatory struggle - the boat swinging wildly left to right and back again. He knew the only solution was going to be to throttle back the right motor, but that would mean giving up the chase, and that wasn't going to happen.

That's when another random gust came from the south, at the same time he was correcting the boat's bow starboard. A loud pop, and the top of the bridge broke clear from its stanchions and flew off into the sea, exposing the entire bridge and its captain to the elements.

Tomas yelled in a fearful voice, "Please, Dega, break it off before you get us killed."

Dega didn't want to yield, but he could see Dream Maker pulling away from him, the gap opening. He lost her. He was furious, but he knew there was nothing else he could do. And now, Dega realized that if he didn't shift his focus back to safety, he might not live through the night. The waves continued to pound his starboard side, rolling the boat further and further with each wave.

Bruno yelled out, "We're taking on water. I don't know what happened, but we need to stop rolling, one or two more waves, and we are going to roll over."

That's when Dega finally realized what had happened: Junior had been lured into an easy turn until they were nearly abeam to the rolling seas. He quickly turned back southeast, into the wind and waves. The waves didn't relent, but at least they stopped rolling. Next, Dega throttled back, slowing down to three or four knots—just enough to maintain control. His pursuit of Dream Maker was over. His hope of any treasure, gone.

The last thing he could hear was the faint pulse of Sandman, coming from the direction of Dream Maker, and he knew he was defeated.

CHAPTER 18

WENDY

Salt-spray stung Junior's eyes as the pirate bow lights vanished into the murk. For hours, the threat behind them had eclipsed even the storm, but now, with danger fading astern, his thoughts returned to Dream Maker and the work ahead, guiding their home safely through Wendy's unsettled seas.

With the distance growing between them and the other boat, Junior brought Dream Maker back on an easterly course. He asked Faidh and Guey to trim the sails for a starboard close haul, and the change was immediate—the boat steadied, the wild rolling giving way to a more predictable pitch. This heading would widen the gap from El Tiburón and carry them out of Wendy's worst. Junior's aim was clear: put at least twenty miles between themselves and the pirates, enough to disappear for good. He suspected the pursuers had run into trouble—maybe engine trouble, maybe just burned too much fuel in the chase—but he couldn't know for sure. Either way, it seemed unlikely they'd be coming back.

For the next three hours, Dream Maker steamed east, the seas beginning to settle slightly with each passing minute. Junior asked Faidh and Guey to take the watch, and he went below to rest. It was still going to be a long night, and even two to three hours of rest would do him good. He went down to the salon, resting on the couch—one of the best places to lie in heavy seas because it is almost directly over the center of gravity. While he could feel the roll and pitch of the boat, he was on the fulcrum of the seesaw, not the end. As he lay there, a flicker of unease stirred in his mind. Memories of the storm during his North Atlantic crossing at twenty-one surfaced, the gale etched in his nerves as indelibly as salt into wood. Those dreams had been haunting his nights ever since.

At Midnight, as requested, Guey came down to the salon and woke Junior up. After years in the Navy, standing watches and sitting alerts in planes on the carrier deck, Junior was accustomed to waking up cold and being ready to go.

"Thanks for waking me up," Junior alertly continued. "You look exhausted, Guey. If I were you, I'd try to get some sleep. Dream Maker and I will keep you safe." Then he grabbed a drink and went up to the cockpit to see how things were going.

Faidh immediately welcomed him, "Hi Sleepyhead, how was your nap?"

"It was short, but refreshing. What's going on up here?"

Faidh, excited to report, "We are still heading east - a starboard close haul, with the storm sail set and mizzen reefed twice. The winds are down to 35 knots, and the seas have subsided considerably."

"That sounds like walking in the park", Junior laughed. "I would like you to hang out for a little bit. I'm going to Heave-To Dream Maker and I want you to see how it is done."

"Very cool. I always love learning - especially from you," Faidh said with a loving look that filled her whole face.

"It can be a tough maneuver in many sailboats, but it's very easy in Dream Maker - the full keel helps her hold heading very well through the process", Junior said, taking the helm from Faidh. "I just want to check the radar real quick - make sure El Tiburon is no longer in range." Taking a quick look at the chartplotter, he could see the screen was clear, adding, "All clear."

Faidh added, "Their blip disappeared from the screen about 30 minutes ago."

Junior eased the helm to starboard, bringing Dream Maker's bow through the wind. The storm sail fluttered briefly before he backwinded it, hauling the port sheet tight to hold it against the starboard side. "You see, all we are doing is coming about, without releasing the storm sail's port sheet, so that it backwinds." He said to Faidh, "Go ahead and ease the mizzen sheet, let her balance." She grabbed the traveler sheet and followed Junior's instructions exactly. The mizzen slackened as the ketch settled, her bow 45 degrees off the wind, drifting slowly at 1-2 knots. The long keel bit deep, steadying the boat as the waves slid beneath. The heel softened to about 8 degrees. Junior locked the helm, the rudder hard over, and the ketch found her rhythm, bobbing gently. Her balance muted the gale's roar. Junior checked the jacklines and hatches to ensure everything was secure, then nodded to Faidh. "She'll hold. Dream Maker is now basically sailing herself. We will wait out Wendy here, keeping all of us rested and the gear spared from unnecessary strain." The cockpit's shelter kept them dry. Their quest paused but unbroken as Dream Maker danced with the storm, unshaken.

Faidh and Junior spent the night in the cockpit. Junior kept watch, the wind humming in the rigging, while Faidh slept, her head resting in his lap.

The sun broke through a dawn overcast, casting a faint glow over Dream Maker's deck. Junior and Faidh stood in the cockpit, their faces warmed by the light. The night's survival was a quiet triumph. Hurricane Wendy's wrath had eased. Her core was now distant, leaving only 20-knot winds and 3-6 foot seas. It was a gentle roll compared to the gale's fury. The radar screen sat blank. El Tiburón was gone, swallowed by the storm or turned back—nobody really caring which. Junior glanced at Faidh, still in her yellow foul-weather bibs, eyes bright. "Guey's probably out for a while," he said, voice steady. "Let's head north. We can make it to the BVI Customs office before it closes. If you take the helm, I'll derig the storm sail, strike the mizzen, and hoist the genoa and main. With these winds, we'll make good time—a bit rolly to start, but it'll settle down as we get closer to the islands."

Faidh nodded, her hand firm on the wheel. "I'd love to. Anything else I can do?"

Junior grinned, his cap shading his eyes. "Nope, this is perfect. She's rigged for one if needed, but I'm not gonna lie, I'm getting used to my First Mate—especially one who snuggles all night."

Faidh's smile widened, soft but fierce. "This is the time of my life. I don't want it to end."

"You know, it doesn't have to," Junior said, his voice low, warm. "Once we're rigged, how about I whip up some breakfast burritos below?"

"As long as I get to drink coffee with mine. None of that Diet Coke crap, for me."

They both laughed, and Junior got to work rigging Dream Maker for the day ahead. And about 45 minutes later, Dream Maker was on a starboard close reach tracking zero four zero, straight for the Pillsbury Sound, between St. Thomas and St. John islands.

Taking their time, Junior and the crew reached Pillsbury Sound around noon, the day unfolding into one of those rare, perfect sails. By then, everyone was up—Guey emerged from his cabin after ten, looking rested. After breakfast, Junior handed him the helm, and for the next few hours, Guey sat beaming, steering Dream Maker through the Caribbean.

Junior joined Guey in the cockpit. "How are we doing?"

"Just coming up on Pillsbury Sound, like you said. Winds are still out of the East, and we're tracking zero four two degrees at seven knots.

Junior looked at him. "Thanks, do you mind if I take her through the Sound?"

"She's all yours, Captain. I'm gonna grab my iPad and do some more research on Norman Island - see if anything, besides the obvious 'The Caves', jumps out as a starting place for us when we get there."

"Sounds Great," Junior said as he sat at the helm, opened his phone, and started playing a Jimmy Buffett playlist - thinking, 'everyone loves a little fun island music.'

Dream Maker glided through Pillsbury Sound. The sun was high, its light splintering across the turquoise water, flecked with whitecaps. Winds now showed fifteen knots from the southeast. The ketch's genoa and main swelled, her hull slicing clean, a steady eight knots toward Tortola's West End. St. John's green hills loomed to starboard. Their slopes were dense with tamarind and frangipani, while St. Thomas sat to port, a low shadow of cruise ships and rooftops. The sound's current tugged gently. One to three foot swells rolled easily, their rhythm soft—what a difference a day makes. Junior stood at the helm, cap low, his hands light on the wheel, feeling the boat's pulse, alive with the wind. After a short nap and a long shower, Faidh came up to sit with him. She sat in the stadium-style seating, her hair loose, eyes tracing the coral shallows and their colors flashing below the surface.

The air was warm, salt-sharp, carrying the scent of seaweed and distant rain. Dream Maker heeled slightly to port, her deck warm underfoot, the rigging humming low as the sails caught each gust. The sound was alive—gulls wheeled overhead, a pelican skimmed the waves, and a schooner's silhouette ghosted far off, bound for Jost Van Dyke. The swells rocked the ketch, a cradle's sway, but Junior held her true, the rudder answering crisp. Faidh smiled, her voice soft over the wind's murmur, "This is why we sail, huh?" Junior nodded, silent, the boat's motion and the sound's beauty enough.

Faidh's phone rang. She looked at the number and mumbled, letting it go to voicemail. The caller ID screamed urgency—her mom again, probably escalating the issue. They don't get it; I'm out here chasing something real, but the guilt... it never stops. She silenced it, but the vibration echoed in her chest, a reminder that home's chaos waited, threatening to drown her joy in the waves.

"Family again?" Junior asked, his tone laced with worry.

Faidh nodded tightly. "Yeah, and it's getting worse. But I don't want it ruining this."

He sighed, frustration creeping in. "You're carrying it alone— let me help."

She pulled away slightly. "It's my burden, Junior. Just... give me space." The exchange hung between them like a squall, but the wind's call pulled them forward.

"Not trying to push, but you know I'm here if you need someone to talk to, or just bounce ideas off of," Junior offered, loving eyes staring straight at her.

"I know", she hesitated, then went on. "There is so much going on right now, we are starting a new stage of our relationship, and we are on this big adventure. We don't need the added pressure that family always brings to the table. I tend to be pretty internalized and protective of my family. When the time is right, after this adventure, I will share everything with you. I'm not trying to be secretive, just not ready to share."

"Ok, just know that I am always here."

Sitting in the cockpit together, alone, Faidh grabs Junior's arm, firmly, but lovingly, "Junior, I know you are. That's why I'm here." Again, she paused and then softly added. "That's why I don't want to leave."

His eyes, soft and warm, stared at her as he put his other hand on the one holding his arm, "And you don't have to, ever."

Dream Maker glided through the northern neck of Pillsbury Sound. The water began to change from soft turquoise to a deeper sapphire as it deepened. Congo Cay and Lovango Cay rose to port. Their green slopes and rocky edges sat low against the horizon. The channel was wide but busy. The air carried a faint scent of cedar. Junior held the helm steady, eyes sharp. Faidh perched by the rail, scanning ahead. Guey was below decks. Just then, a 35-foot Hatteras fishing boat charged from Congo Cay's lee, southbound. Its engines roared, and the wake curled white. The boat cut across Dream Maker's bow at 25 knots, rods flashing, crew shouting, a hundred yards off and closing. Constant bearing, decreasing range— all that ran through his mind was a flashback to early flight training in the Navy.

Junior yanked the wheel to starboard, the ketch heeling hard, sails flapping briefly as a swell rocked her. "Brace!" he shouted. Faidh clutched the coaming, her hair whipping, while Guey stumbled topside, grabbing the sides of the companionway. The Hatteras thundered past, no more than 30 yards to port - less than a couple of boat lengths. Its captain tossing a careless wave, unaware of the near hit. Dream Maker settled, her keel steady, sails catching the wind again as Junior returned to course, his face calm but pulse quick. Faidh let out a sharp breath, "Idiots."

Then Guey muttered, "What the hell was that?" The sound widened, the lingering swells subsiding.

Junior, anger brewing inside, did his best to laugh it off, "Guess you've got to be on your toes around here. Not everyone is paying attention, kinda like driving on the islands, huh?" Junior quipped, glancing at Guey.

"You got that right!" replied Guey.

The rest of the trip into Soper's Hole was uneventful. As they left US territory and entered BVI, Junior struck the genoa and main, the ketch gliding under motor, and hoisted the yellow quarantine flag—Q flag—high on the starboard spreader, signaling their arrival and intent to clear customs. The flag fluttered, a bright marker of their un-cleared status, the boat's papers and passports stowed below, ready for inspection.

Dream Maker eased into Soper's Hole, Tortola's West End, the water relatively calm under an early afternoon sun. The BVI's hills rose green and quiet, their slopes flecked with white villas. Junior stood at the helm, Faidh by his side, Guey readying lines below. The customs dock loomed, a low pier with flags snapping, the marina alive with yachts and chatter.

Junior nosed Dream Maker to the customs dock, Faidh tossing fenders over the side, Guey securing lines to cleats, their movements sure despite the morning's near miss off Congo Cay. The customs office, a squat building with open windows, hummed with officials in crisp uniforms. Junior stepped ashore, ship's registration, crew passports, and clearance from Culebra in hand, his cap low, voice steady as he declared their arrival: no goods, no weapons, just three souls bound for Norman Island. The officer, eyes sharp, checked documents, asked about their voyage—Wendy's gale, the route through Pillsbury Sound—then stamped their papers, granting entry. The Q flag came down, replaced by the BVI courtesy flag, its colors catching the breeze.

Back aboard, Junior fired the motor, Faidh and Guey casting off, Dream Maker free to sail on.

Since the day was getting late and Junior didn't want to try to fight for an anchorage over at Norman Island, they decided to anchor in Sopers Hole and enjoy the evening at Tortola. A short dinghy ride and they could walk the streets, enjoy a great meal, and of course, hit Pusser's Landing for a "Painkiller".

At dinner, they sat next to several crew members from a local charter catamaran. Faidh overheard them talking about 'The Indians' and 'The Caves,' so she went over, introduced herself, and started a conversation. After everyone at both tables gave quick introductions, Junior bought a round of drinks for everyone and invited the newcomers to join their table. They readily agreed, sliding their chairs over to combine the tables and create space for all seven—no self-respecting sailor refuses free drinks or a chance to swap stories.

"Where are you all from?" Junior asked before the drinks arrived.

Harry, as he said his name was, "Ey, Mate, I'm from Down Under." He pointed to the gentleman sitting next to him, "This here is Willem, my South Africa mate." Then to the young woman across from him, "And here's Aisling, our lone lassy from Dublin, a proper legend." "And finally to the tallest of us—notice I didn't say oldest, even though he is, I say with a cheeky grin to the bloke loomin' over Aisling like a palm tree in a squall. Peter's our only locally born and bred right here in the BVI, and he's chock-full of tales, ain't ya, mate?

Peter just smiled, calmly waiting for his drink, "Maybe after I wet my lips a might."

Then Harry continued, "And before you ask, we are the crew on the Lagoon Seventy7, SOBAD. How 'bout you?"

Faidh piped up, "I'm from the Northeast part of the States, mostly up in Massachusetts. Junior here", putting her hand on his arm, very intimately, "is from," she hesitated.

"I'm from Pennsylvania. But that was a long time ago. Lived all over since." Junior jumped in, saving her from embarrassment.

"And this young man is from Puerto Rico. This is his first adventure off the island," finished Faidh.

"How long have you all been sailing in and around Norman Island?" Junior asked, the waitress delivering the round of Painkillers, all level 2.

The three foreigners each answered only a couple of years, but Peter responded after taking a big drink of his painkiller, "Oi, mate, you wanna know how long I've been divin' and pokin' around Norman Island's waters? Most of my life, that's the short of it, but lemme spin you the full tale! I was barely taller than a conch shell when I first started splashin' about these reefs, prob'ly sneakin' out on my uncle's skiff before I could even spell "scuba." Born and bred in the BVI, so these islands—Norman especially—have been my backyard forever. I was maybe 10 when I first dove The Caves, chasin' after parrotfish and gettin' my mask all fogged up from excitement. By the time I was a teenager, I was hookin' up with the local dive crews, learnin' every nook, cranny, and coral head from The Bight to Soldier Bay.

Been at it nigh on 30 years now, mate—explorin' every inch of those underwater canyons, dodgin' currents, and spottin' eagle rays when the seas are kind. Norman's like an old mate; she's got her secrets, but she'll show 'em to you if you treat her right. From the wild days divin' off rickety boats with nothin' but a tank and

238

a prayer, to now, guidin' folks through spots like Brown Pants or those quiet little overhangs nobody's named yet—it's been a proper adventure. Ain't nothin' like droppin' into that clear blue, feelin' the island's pulse under the waves. Stick around, and I'll show ya a corner of Norman that'll make your jaw drop, guaranteed!"

"Ok, Peter, you are the man I was hoping to find, but didn't expect to be sitting at my table," Junior stroked Peter's ego a bit. "Do you know of any water caves, other than The Caves, on the island? Ones that may not be as glamorous or even as big as The Caves, but filled with adventure?"

"Ahhh, you're askin' about water caves on Norman Island, eh? Not the big, flashy ones like The Caves up on the northwest side —those are proper famous, with all the snorkelers and day-trippers swarmin' like bees to honey. You want the quieter ones, the little hideaways that don't get all the fuss but still have that magic. Fair enough, I know a few spots that us locals keep close to the chest, tucked away from the charter boat crowds. These ain't as grand as The Caves, mind you, but they've got their own charm, like secret nooks carved out by the sea herself. Let me spin you a yarn about a couple of lesser-known spots that'll get you grinning underwater.

First off, there's a little gem we call Mermaid's Hollow, just a stone's throw south of The Bight, near where the cliffs start to crumble into the sea. It's not much to look at from the surface— just a narrow slit in the rock, barely wide enough for a dinghy to notice. But slip beneath the waves, and it opens up into a cozy cave, maybe 10 feet deep and 15 feet across. The entrance is shallow, sittin' at about 8 feet, so even snorkelers can poke their heads in on a calm day. Inside, it's like a wee underwater cathedral, with sunlight streamin' through the opening, dancin' on the walls covered in soft corals and tiny sea fans. You'll spot little critters like juvenile parrotfish and sergeant majors dartin' about, and if you're lucky, a spiny lobster might be hidin' in the shadows. The current's usually gentle here, but watch your fins — kick too hard, and you'll stir up the silt and ruin the view. It's not glamorous, but it's peaceful, like the sea's whisperin' just for you.

Then there's Crab Grotto, a bit further east along the coast, closer to Soldier Bay. This one's a proper sneaky spot — most folks sail right past it without a clue. It's a low, wide cave, more like a deep overhang, sittin' at about 20 feet down. You'll need to dive to get the full effect, but it's worth it. The entrance is fringed with gorgonians and sponges, and the back wall's got these funky little ledges where crabs — hence the name — love to scuttle about. You might even spot a moray eel or two, peekin' out with that grumpy look they've got. The water's clear as gin most days, and the cave's just big enough to swim through without feelin' cramped. It's not some massive cavern like The Caves, but it's got a rugged, untouched vibe that makes you feel like you've stumbled on buried treasure.

Another one worth a mention is Starfish Nook, tucked around the southeast side of the island, near where the rocks get all jagged and the swells pick up. This one's a bit trickier to find — ask your boat captain to hug the shoreline and keep an eye out for a cluster of boulders that look like they're tumblin' into the sea. The cave itself is small, maybe 6 feet high and 12 feet deep, with a sandy bottom at about 15 feet. What makes it special is the starfish — dozens of 'em, all colors, clingin' to the walls like little jewels. You'll also see anemones and the odd octopus if you're patient. It's a dead simple spot, nothin' fancy, but it's like the ocean's own little hideout. Just mind the surge if the wind's up — Starfish Nook can get a bit lively when the seas are rough.

These spots don't get the love The Caves do, and that's just fine by us locals. They're not on every dive shop's itinerary, so you'll likely have 'em to yourself, 'specially if you go early before the charter boats start buzzin'. You don't need a big dive boat to get there—a small skiff or even a kayak'll do, as long as you know where to look. Just respect the reef, keep your hands to yourself, and don't go pokin' at the critters. Oh, and if you're divin' with one of the local crews like Blue Water Divers or Sail Caribbean, drop a hint you're after somethin' off the beaten path —they'll know exactly where to take you. These little caves are like Norman Island's best-kept secrets, and once you've slipped inside one, you'll get why we don't shout about 'em too loud."

Harry, Willem, and Aisling all sat back and let Peter go. He was unstoppable once he got going.

"Are you serious? Are those for real?" asked Faidh.

Laughing out loud now, "You're askin' if Mermaid's Hollow, Crab Grotto, and Starfish Nook are the real deal, eh? Are those for real? Haha, I'll level with ya—those spots are straight outta my head, cooked up to sound like the kinda secret hideaways we'd whisper about over a cold one at the Willy T. Norman Island's got plenty o' little nooks and crannies under the waves, mind you, with corals and critters just like I described, but those names? Pure local-style storytelling, my friend. I leaned hard into the BVI vibe—turtles glidin' by, eels givin' you the stink-eye—to make 'em feel proper authentic. No chart's got 'em marked, but if you're divin' round the island and stumble into a cave that fits, you go ahead and slap one o' those names on it. Tell the dive crew you heard it from a salty local, and I'll buy ya a rum next time you're in The Bight!

Everyone at the table started to laugh.

And Peter continued, "Oi, wait. You all are lookin' for treasure, huh? And you want to know where you could look that others might not be aware of. Is that right? Haha, I see that glint in your eye — chasin' after some pirate gold, are ya? Well, you've come to the right salty dog. This island's got more secrets than a rum-soaked pirate's diary."

"Not really," Junior jumped in, absolutely enthralled with listening to Peter. "We had a friend tell us about a cave, deep in one of the wave-cut ravines on the west side of Sabu Mathila Bay. Have you ever heard anything like that? We just wanted to do something a little different. You never know what you'll find in sights that are off the beaten path."

"So your friend's been spinnin' tales about a cave tucked deep in a cut ravine on the west side of Sabu Mathila Bay, eh? I'm picturin' one of them narrow gashes in the rock where the waves have chewed away at the island, maybe hidin' a small cave or overhang that don't get much chatter. There's plenty of little crevices out there, not as famous as The Caves, mind you, but just as likely to spark a bit of adventure. Could be your friend stumbled on one of them unnamed spots — divers and fishermen round here sometimes keep quiet about their favorite hideaways, 'specially if they're off the beaten path like you're after.

Lemme paint you a picture of what might fit the bill. This one is real. Over by the west end, near where the cliffs drop sharply into the sea, you've got some shallow cuts and overhangs, some no deeper than 20–30 feet. These ain't proper caves like the big ones at Treasure Point, but they're tight, shadowy spots where the rock's been hollowed out just enough to swim into. You'll see sponges and soft corals clingin' to the walls, maybe a nurse shark nappin' in the back or a spiny lobster givin' you the eye. The ravines out there can feel like secret passages, with the current pushin' you through and the light dancin' off the water. If your friend's cave is real, it might be one of these—tucked in a gully where the reef meets the cliff, easy to miss unless you know where to look.

Now, since you're lookin' for somethin' different, I'd say check the stretch between Treasure Point and Soldier Bay. It's quieter than the main snorkel spots, and the coastline's got a few nooks that don't make it into the guidebooks. One place I've heard whispers about—mind you, it ain't got a name—is a narrow cut just south of The Caves, where the rock splits and forms a kinda half-cave at about 25 feet down. It's not deep or glamorous, but it's got that wild, untouched feel, with schools of glassfish swarmin' inside and the odd barracuda patrollin' nearby. You'd need a calm day and a good boat captain to moor up safe, 'cause the swells can get feisty. Bring a torch to light up the corners, and who knows? Maybe you'll spot somethin' shiny your mate was hintin' at."

Everyone around the table just stared at Peter as he was completely dominating the conversation.

"You mentioned Brown Pants earlier. What can you tell us about the cave at that site?" Guey jumped in and asked.

"Brown Pants, eh? I knows it. It's exposed to the open Atlantic, so the seas can get a bit choppy, and mooring up can be tricky if the swells are up. The National Parks Trust has set some mooring balls out there to make life easier, but you'll still want a calm day to really enjoy it.

When you drop in, the water's usually crystal clear, giving you cracking visibility—10 to 30 meters, no bother. You'll start at a shallow 10 feet or so, maxing out around 40 feet, so it's perfect for open-water divers, even if you're starting out. The site's all about these rugged underwater cliffs and canyons, like something carved by the sea gods themselves. You've got ridges and grottos galore, with one proper standout: a big open cave in one of the canyons. Bring a dive torch, and you'll see sponges in every color of the rainbow glowing in the shadows—bright reds, oranges, and yellows that'll make your eyes pop.

As you drift down, keep an eye out in the blue for turtles and eagle rays cruising by—real beauties, those. Closer to the cliffs, you'll spot small gangs of barracuda giving you the side-eye, plus schools of palmetto, queen angelfish, and whitespotted filefish darting about. There's a fair few lobsters and eels tucked into the nooks and crannies too, so take your time poking around. The whole place feels alive, with soft corals and sponges clinging to every surface, making it a proper underwater playground.

Locals love Brown Pants for its raw, untouched vibe—none of that yacht-crowded nonsense you get on the north side of Norman. It's just you, da sea, and a cracking good dive. Just watch the currents, as they can sneak up on you, and make sure your boat captain knows the lay of the land. If you're diving with a crew like Sail Caribbean Divers, they'll have you sorted with the best routes through those canyons. Go early before the other boats roll in, and you'll have this slice of underwater magic all to yourself."

Junior bought a second round of drinks. Peter and his crew then took turns sharing more stories. However, the crew of Dream Maker, still tired from their fight with pirates and their night with Wendy, said goodnight to their new friends and began to leave. As they headed out, Faidh looked over her shoulder and asked, "I've been meaning to ask, does SOBAD stand for anything?"

The four at the table all laughed. "Figure it out," said Aisling, "Here's a hint. It's what we do when we don't have any customers on board."

"If you see any of us again, and guess right, we'll fill you up with rum," said Peter, bowing in thanks for the drinks.

Walking out the door, Faidh yelled back, "Slippery Oysters Bouncing Across Deck."

Aisling laughed out loud, "Good try, but not even close!"

The evening was just what everyone needed: good drinks, great food, and fantastic company. And of course, they all bought something to take home from Pussers' store. Junior got an eclectic island shirt, akin to a shirt most people would recognize as something Cosmo Kramer would burst into Jerry's apartment wearing, and, of course, a bottle of Pusser's Gun Powder Proof Dark Rum.

Faidh bought herself a Pusser's ball cap, as she said, "To keep the sun off my light skin and my hair out of my eyes." Junior just thought to himself how sexy she looked when she tried it on, pulling her hair into a ponytail.

Last but not least, Guey bought small souvenirs for his immediate family: his mom, dad, and younger sister. After everyone spent some time enjoying steady legs ashore, they all returned to Dream Maker and settled in for a good night's sleep, ready for a big day tomorrow.

While Guey headed below to unwind, Faidh and Junior lingered in the cockpit, the harbor lights twinkling across the water. They climbed up to the bow and lay on the cushions under the stars - both a little tipsy from the earlier painkillers.

The stars wheeled overhead as Dream Maker rocked gently at anchor in Soper's Hole. Faidh sat beside Junior, the earlier tension from her ignored call still simmering. "It's my family," she finally admitted, voice breaking. "My brother has mental issues and is an addict. He has been clean and sober for a couple of years, but my mom thinks he fell off the wagon again. My mom and I fight over how best to care for him—sometimes the texts and calls are nonstop, guilting me for being 'away adventuring.' It distracts me, makes me question if I deserve this freedom."

Junior pulled her close, his frustration melting. "You do deserve it. And you don't have to face it alone—tell me next time. We're in this together." She leaned into him, relief washing over her. "I was scared it'd pull me away from you."

He kissed her forehead. "It won't. Let's call them together tomorrow—share the load." The confession lifted her, the internal storm easing as the sea whispered on.

"No, we don't need to do that. However, once this is over, I need to fly back to Boston for a couple of weeks to assist. I just needed to let you in, and trust you." She kissed his stubbly cheek. "You've been so understanding. I can't tell you how much that means to me. I'm not used to men standing by me when things get tough, and you have never shown me anything but support." Tears are running down Faidh's face now. "Thank you, Junior."

CHAPTER 19

JOURNEY TO NORMAN ISLAND

Guey hovered on the edge of wakefulness, the faint light of dawn seeping through Dream Maker's porthole at Soper's Hole, but sleep's grip yanked him back into the abyss.

The cave materialized around him, vast and oppressive, its walls pulsing like a living heart, slick with brine and echoing with distant thunder. He knelt at the enlarged stone altar, the four amulets throbbing with malevolent light as he intoned the ritual, his voice cracking under the strain. Junior and Faidh stood nearby, their faces etched with determination, but the cave's waters rose suddenly, a tidal surge roaring in like a beast unleashed, flooding the chamber to chest height in seconds. Junior was caught first, the wave slamming him against jagged rocks, his skull cracking audibly as blood swirled in the foam; he gasped once before the current dragged him under, his body vanishing into a whirlpool that gurgled like laughter from the deep.

Then, towering from the flooded shadows, erupted Pirata Cofresí, his form now a colossal monstrosity filling the cave's expanse, three times the height of a man. His skeletal frame was exposed through rotting flesh that sloughed off in chunks, bones gleaming yellowed and cracked like ancient relics. His eyes were

*bottomless voids spewing crimson sparks; his tricorn
was a tattered crown of thorns, and his cutlass was a
massive, serrated scythe dripping with gore and algae.
Fury contorted his deathly visage, veins bulging like
rivers of tar as he bellowed with unhinged rage, his
voice shattering stalactites from the ceiling: "Insolent
cur of forgotten blood! The curse devours all who
meddle—halt this sacrilege, or watch your companions
ripped asunder, their souls chained to the abyss
forever!" Guey recoiled, water surging to his neck. Still,
Cofresí's anger exploded, his massive fist smashing the
altar, scattering the amulets as lightning forked from his
claws, striking Faidh in a blaze that vaporized her in an
instant—her scream cut short as her form dissolved into
ash and steam, the stench of charred flesh choking the
air.*

*The pirate's desperation twisted into madness, his
enormous body convulsing as he leaned in close, his
breath a hurricane of decay blasting Guey's face. "The
price is absolute—a life for the treasure! Yours now, to
spare the rest, or the curse claims everything, your world
crumbling like this cave!" The walls buckled, rocks
tumbling in a cascade that buried the ritual site, the
flood rising to swallow Guey whole, his lungs burning as
Cofresí's skeletal grin filled his vision, laughter a
deafening cacophony of doom.*

Guey surged awake with a guttural gasp, bolting upright in
the berth as morning light flooded the cabin, his sheets soaked in
sweat and his chest heaving like he'd truly drowned. The quiet
lap of water against the hull at Soper's Hole grounded him, but
the dream's horrors clung like barnacles—the deaths of Junior
and Faidh, Cofresí's escalating fury, the demand for his own
sacrifice. He rubbed his eyes, heart still racing, knowing he

couldn't keep this buried any longer; he'd have to tell them soon, before the curse made the visions real.

Morning crept over Soper's Hole, slow and quiet. Faidh and Junior were still weighed down by the sleepless night after Wendy's gale. Sunlight flashed sharply, the marina's water flat and blue as glass. Junior was up first, stepping onto the deck, the air already thick and warm. Faidh followed, coffee in hand, hair tousled, pajamas loose. They sat together at the cockpit table, the mizzen boom's shadow casting a patch of coolness over them. Beyond the dock, Tortola's green hills waited, silent.

"Do you think we will really find something at Norman Island?" Faidh asked, her voice soft, a child clinging to a half-lost dream.

Junior leaned back, eyes glancing at the horizon. "Hard to say what's true anymore," he murmured, a faint smile playing on his lips. He adjusted the sails quietly, letting the wind guide the moment. "This trip's shown me stranger things than I ever expected." Junior paused, one hand lightly touching the helm, sensing the sea beneath them. "But right now, sailing and living at sea—that's what matters. It's always the journey." He let the wind ruffle his hair, the sea's salt lingering in the air. "Navigating by wind, like sailors did centuries ago, is a gift. The sea puts you in the middle of nature's raw edge." He tapped the table, the wood solid under his hand. "Sure, it feels good to reach a destination, but the real heart of it is out here." Junior's voice softened, eyes reflecting the ocean's endless expanse.

"Dream Maker's simple, gadgets or not. People laughed when I swapped her diesel for electric. 'Diesels are reliable,' they'd say. I just grinned. She's a sailboat, moved by wind," he said, glancing toward the horizon again, "same as Columbus crossing these waters. What was his backup? Men with oars." He paused, a chuckle escaping. "Me, docking under sail? I could do it if I had to. That's how sailors learn. That's how I learned, forty years back." He gazed beyond the stern, the laugh still echoing softly. "But honestly, I'd probably just call a tow boat."

"Look at me," he said, waiting as she set her mug down. "When this is over, stay aboard. Sail with me. I know you sell boats—do it from here, on Dream Maker, exploring the world together. Think of the cruisers, the boats needing buyers. You're magic with people. With me. These last two weeks—they've been the best, not because of what I was doing, but because of who I was sharing it with." He hesitated, letting the weight of his words settle, then added, "No pressure now, just something to think about."

Faidh's eyes glistened as she responded, tears catching the light. "I've thought about it, more than I'll admit." She dabbed at her eyes with a napkin. "I'd love to. Every minute since you docked in Puerto Real has felt alive. But there's a catch—not stopping me, just a delay. Personal matters need settling, or those calls and texts I get will keep coming, maybe even get worse."

Junior nodded, his voice soft and sincere. "No rush. I just wanted to let you know how I feel. We've been friends so long, becoming more feels so right."

Faidh smiled softly, her voice certain. "It's funny, I thought it was gonna complicate things. But it didn't. It made them clear, like this was meant."

"I know, right?" Junior said with a wide grin. "I didn't hear you wake up last night. Are the dreams gone? I know you haven't had one in a while, but I'm not sure if you are just hiding them from me."

Faidh grinned at him, "You already know me too well, Mr. Wright. I did have another nightmare when we were in Viegues, which I didn't share with you. But I haven't had one since. In fact, my sleep has been completely dreamless, as far as I can remember."

Junior gave her a big hug and stood up. "That's good to hear. I was worried they were a sign about us and our newfound relationship. But enough mushy stuff, we have work to do. What do you say we find Cofresí's treasure and end Juracán's curse?"

"I'm in," Faidh answered firmly, eyes bright.

Dream Maker slipped free of her mooring in Soper's Hole, morning sun bright, water flat and blue. Faidh took the helm, hands steady, guiding the ketch under motor through the marina's bustle—yachts drifting, a catamaran docking, a dinghy buzzing past with a fisherman's wave. Junior, first mate now, worked the lines, cap pulled low, coiling the mooring line as Tortola's green hills rose to the north, white villas scattered on the slopes. St. John's peaks stood to the south, thick with tamarind, the Sir Francis Drake Channel shining beyond, gulls crying overhead. Faidh eased the throttle, Dream Maker clearing the harbor, her hull cutting clean, the BVI's beauty all around.

Guey came up as the bay opened wide, sails rising under Junior's quick hands, catching wind at seven knots. He sat beside Faidh, eyes on the harbor falling away, masts swaying like reeds, a schooner slipping out to starboard. Tortola's cliffs faded in the haze, St. John's shores wild and green, colors bright against the sea's shine. The channel widened, traffic thinning, Dream Maker sailing free, deck warm, wind humming steady, the islands' quiet majesty close around them. He said, out of the blue, "I have something I have to share with you both."

"Fire away!" said Junior.

"Ok, this is kind of weird." Guey hesitated while looking down at his feet. Then he looked straight at Junior, opening up. "At first, I thought it was just nightmares caused by the seasickness. However, I haven't been sick for days, and the dreams continue to happen. Once every night."

"Are they of Cofresí?" Faidh interrupted him with a startled look on her face.

"Yes. And let me tell you. He is a terrifying dude." Guey continued.

Junior chimed in this time. "We know, and we've both seen him."

"What? Are you kidding? You've seen him in the cave?" Exclaimed Guey.

"No." Interjected Faidh. "We saw him here on Dream Maker, in the storm. You saw him in a cave?"

"Well, I don't know for sure that it was a cave, but it felt like one." Guey shared his dreams and how they have been escalating in fierceness with each night. And he shared his fears of losing either Faidh or Junior during the ceremony as tears welled up in his eyes. "I'm sorry I hid these dreams from you, but I didn't know how to share them.

Junior looked firmly at him. "Guey, are you shooting straight with Faidh and me? Telling us everything you know?"

Guey stammered, "I, I, I think so."

"What does that mean?" Junior poked further.

"I mean," Guey choked back more tears. "I don't think I know anything more that I should be telling you."

"It's just curious how easy you have made the search for the stones since you joined us. I mean, seriously, I literally stumbled on the first stone. Faidh and I didn't even know what we were doing when we found the second stone. But you have given us not only the map to the stones, but have told us exactly where the treasure seems to be. It feels like you know more than you are sharing and that you are just sharing what you need to share to keep stringing us along."

Guey sat up straight, wiped the tears from his eyes, and spoke directly to Junior. "Junior, I didn't seek you out; you found me. I think you and Faidh are feeling the same way; this has been a journey that has been more than just finding a treasure. I feel like I've grown in so many ways. I wish I could explain exactly how I figured out that the shapes of the stones were actually pointing to different islands. And I wish I could help you better understand how my ancestors speak to me. I don't know. It just happens. The dreams I just shared with you are not from my ancestors. They have been scaring the crap out of me because I feel like I'm going to be asked to sacrifice either you or Faidh when we find the cave with the treasure. I want them to stop, because honestly, I'm afraid to close my eyes anymore. My ancestors don't talk to me through night dreams; they do so through the cohoba pipe. These dreams are coming from the stones. And believe it or not, I think they are tied somehow to this boat. There is some magic in Dream Maker that we are eventually going to have to discuss."

Junior stood up and looked around at the open sea surrounding Dream Maker. "I'm sorry to doubt you, Guey. Thank you for that. Listen, I would love to say that nothing is going to happen and that it's just a dream. Unfortunately, this trip has been marred by unusual events. However, the fact is that there is no guarantee of anything. There are no promises of good weather to a sailor, and there were never any promises that we are actually going to find any treasure on this adventure. I do know for sure that I'm not backing down, especially to a Pirate who has been dead for nearly 200 years. I say we go for it, and we do whatever it takes to find this treasure.

Faidh looked up at him, "Not to sound like a broken record, but I'm in. I have been since the moment we found the second amulet."

Guey looked at Junior with the same eyes that a five-year-old boy looks at his father, "Junior, I know trust isn't something simply given, but earned. In so many ways on this journey, you have earned my trust. I'm with you, Junior, to the ends of the earth. I just had to share what I've been feeling. And I hope that I can earn your trust."

They all stared at each other in silence, what felt like an eternity, until Junior broke the silence. "Ok, that settles it. We do this. We find the secret cave. Guey performs the ceremony, and come what may, we find the treasure."

An hour out of Soper's Hole, the Indians punched up from the sea, a ragged fist of rock off Norman Island's north side, black spines slashing the morning sky. Dream Maker headed southeast, sails tight, cutting through swells that nudged her hull. The rocks loomed a mile ahead, their faces raw and scoured, with guano-white patches bright against the basalt, scrub gripping the cracks. Beneath the surface, the current twisted unpredictably, a hazard waiting to catch the unsuspecting. Waves churned white at their base, the reef's teeth hidden, spitting foam—dangerously shallow shoals lay here, some charted at just eight feet, threatening the unsuspecting hull. Gulls wheeled overhead, their cries lost in the wind, an iguana sunning itself on a hot ledge.

The plan was to stop at the Indians and see if there was anything worth pursuing, so Faidh engaged the motor again and turned Dream Maker into the wind. On cue, Guey furled the Genoa and Junior lowered the main—like a well-oiled machine.

The rocks stood low, no taller than a ship's mast, but fierce, refusing the sea's slow grind. Coral flashed red and gold below, fish darting through shadows. The Indians marked the way, as old as the pirates who once slipped past their reefs, sloops dodging cannon shot. The air hung thick with salt, the rocks' silence heavy, a gate to secrets. Junior dropped anchor just north of the Indians, close enough for easy reach to both the rocks and Pelican Island.

Junior, Faidh, and Guey slipped over the side, masks tight, fins kicking, snorkels hissing. Guey's gear didn't fit, Faidh's was a little off, but it worked well enough. Small swells pushed them toward the Indians' black spines, Norman's cliffs a shadow past

Pelican, the sea's pulse slow and easy. They swam on, strokes cutting the chop, reef colors—coral red, gold flashes—blooming below as they neared the rocks, the cave's mouth dark and low in the stone.

The Indians' reef pulsed with life, parrotfish weaving through brain coral, a barracuda's silver flash hanging close. The cave loomed, half underwater, walls slick with green algae, shadows thick inside. Junior led, kicks smooth, Faidh and Guey close behind, breaths sharp through their snorkels. Inside, the cave narrowed, light splintering through the entrance, barnacles crusting the rock, sea fans waving in the surge. A school of grunts darted past, yellow stripes catching the dim light. The water pressed them against the walls, gentle but firm, the cave's belly tight, secrets lost in the murk. They lingered, eyes searching the dark, then kicked back to the reef's bright sprawl, the Indians' edges raw, the sea's beauty pulling them out. Junior took out his snorkel and said, "No sign of treasure or Taíno here. I know we're eager to find it, but what do you say we enjoy the swim, see what the Indians have to offer? We're here, and it'd be a shame to miss such a beautiful spot."

Both Faidh and Guey nodded in agreement.

Junior advised, "I recommend we stay close together, but if you feel like you want to head back, just let the others know, okay?"

More nods. Junior could see the smile in both their eyes.

Before heading back, Junior led the others over to Pelican Island, just in case they missed a hiding spot. Pelican Island crouched low in the channel, a speck of rock west of the Indians, its shape blunt against the noon sun. Little more than a reef-fringed mound, its surface was streaked with guano and salt-bleached stone; scrub was thin, and waves lapped softly at the edges. Gulls and pelicans circled above, shadows flicking over the shallows, a lone crab scuttling on the rocks. No crevices, no caves.

By the time they got back to Dream Maker, everyone was famished. Junior grilled up some chicken at the stern BBQ while Faidh prepared a salad below deck, chopping vegetables at the galley counter. Guey rinsed off their snorkel gear with freshwater at the stern, carefully stowing it up in the bow locker. When their tasks were done, all three gathered at the aft table, hungry and ready for a good meal.

Dream Maker crept east from her anchorage north of the Indians, motor humming low, sails furled, holding two knots in the small swells. The Indians' rocks faded behind, Pelican Island a low hump to starboard, water sparkling in the trade wind. Cumulus clouds puffed white, scattered across the sky, edges soft against St. John's distant green hills. Norman Island loomed to the south, cliffs dark, fringed with sea grape and cactus, Money Bay's cove a tight crescent of sand. Faidh steered, Junior scanned the horizon, and Guey stood on the bow with binoculars, searching the shoreline for any sign of an overhang or cave.

Dream Maker curved south, then west, Norman's spine rising —Benures Bay's shallow arc, Soldier Bay's rocky edge, caves gaping black in the cliffs. Cumulus clouds towered over the island, gray and heavy, swallowing the sun. Junior pointed out the empty Brown Pants mooring balls as they passed the southern side. The ketch turned north along the west shore. Privateer Bay's narrow inlet slid by, waters deep and shadowed by tamarind. Suddenly, a downburst roared in, wind spiking to 48 knots, rain lashing the deck, washing salt spray from Dream Maker, forcing Guey to dash for the cockpit. For a while, the sea churned, swells sharpened, and visibility dropped to a gray blur. At the helm, Faidh glanced at Junior beside her. He nodded, urging her to hold steady and motor on into The Bight's wide arms. The rain eased, clouds parted, the cove's sand beach glittered in the sun, and yachts bobbed at moorings. Norman's hills fell quiet, the caves' mouths locking away secrets. The trip around the island took a couple of hours, time well spent, as it gave them a lay of the land.

By mid-afternoon, they moored in The Bight, Dream Maker's hull still in the calm bay. Norman Island lay low in the blue, crystal water all around, hills dark and tangled, a jagged silhouette in the sun. Water lapped emerald at the shore, caves yawning black in the cliffs, mouths carved by the tides.

The island whispered of pirates, its history sharp as a cutlass. Named for a corsair, Norman was a haunt for men like Blackbeard and Cofresí, their sails ghosting these waters centuries past. The caves, deep and narrow, hid treasure—chests of Spanish doubloons, jewels stolen from galleons, buried in sand or sunk in pools. Locals spoke of Roberto Cofresí, the Puerto Rican rogue, stashing his loot here in the 1820s, his ship dodging British frigates, his curse tied to Juracán's wrath. Wreckage of old sloops littered the reefs, their timbers gnawed by time, stories of ambushes and betrayals clinging to the rocks. Junior felt the weight, the amulets' hum, the island's secrets waiting, its past alive in the wind's low moan.

Once the boat was settled and secured, Junior turned to Faidh and Guey. "What do ya'll think about taking the dinghy in and going for a short hike to the southeastern part of the island? I noticed a trail that starts behind Willy T's and crosses the island. We should be able to tie up right at the trailhead. After the hike, we can grab a bite to eat at Pirate's Bight before coming back for the night. Maybe we'll catch another story or two from some of the locals."

"Sounds like a plan. But I wouldn't put much faith in anything anyone around here says. They all seem to like to sew a good yarn, as they like to say." Faidh gave her two cents, then added a third, "And tonight, dinner is on me."

Everyone got their hiking attire together: Faidh pulled on her hat and boots, Guey checked the laces on his shoes, and Junior found his pack. Junior lowered the dinghy into the water and started the motor. Then, he packed two bottles of water into his backpack and tossed it up by the bow as he secured the backpack. Faidh and Guey returned, ready to go ashore.

The dinghy ride was quick and easy. Junior beached the boat and then tied it off to one of the trees lining the beach. The three were off on another adventure, this one over land.

Junior, Faidh, and Guey stepped ashore from the dinghy. The beach south of Willy T's was firm underfoot, the late afternoon sun low, the sky spotted with clouds, but there were no signs of any impending storms. Norman Island's hills rose sharply, tangled with sea grape and acacia. They climbed the path from The Bight, stones crunching, sweat beading, the trail snaking up to a ridge. At the fork, they turned right, heading east toward Privateer Bay, the ground rough and roots twisting underfoot. The eastern path traced the hill's spine, the rocky cliffs of Sabu Mathila Bay's curve glinting below, dropping steep to turquoise water. Four crevices caught their eyes—deep gashes in the rock, eroded dark, hinting at caves, their mouths too far downslope to reach. Two were on the west side of the bay, two on the east side. The two on the east side notches are easier to see with the setting sun shining directly on them. Junior paused, his cap shading his gaze, Faidh sketching the spots in her mind, Guey squinting at the shadows, all three silent, the island's secrets close but locked.

Then they backtracked, taking the western path, the trail dipping through scrub, Privateer Bay's narrow inlet now behind, Soldier Bay's far off to the north, but it was Bluff Bay just below them to the south that caught their attention. Two more crevices hidden in long shadows of the western shore, edges worn, black slits too steep to probe from above, the sea's crashing waves rising from below. The island's spine hid more, its folds tight, caves possible but unseen. After an hour, legs heavy, they descended to The Bight, the path easing, Pirates Bight's lights glowing warm, the bar's hum drifting over the beach. Tables sat scattered, fish grilling, rum sharp in the air. They took an outside table, on the beach, the day's hike etched in their bones, the crevices' dark promise waiting for tomorrow's dinghy run to the south side.

Unlike the night before in Soper's Hole, the crowd here was mostly tourists—they didn't see any locals offering up exciting tales of their adventures in and around Norman Island. The view, the atmosphere, and the dinner itself, though, were all magnificent, and the company of each other, as it turned out, was enough for tonight. Each had but one thing on their mind—the treasure of Pirate Cofresí.

Maybe it was the couple of mojitos that he had at dinner, but when they returned to Dream Maker, Junior decided to take action. He felt that somehow, the negative energy of the amulets was causing the dreams. He didn't know how or why, but he thought, if he got them off the boat, maybe all of his crew could get a good night's sleep. So he grabbed all four amulets, put them in his backpack, and left the bag on the dinghy, which he then set adrift, tethered to Dream Maker.

He looked at Guey and Faidh smilingly, "There, the stones are off the boat. Maybe we can all get a good night's sleep tonight."

Faidh and Guey each smiled as they looked at each other and then at Junior, then sighed in unison, "Thank you."

CHAPTER 20

A STORM OVER PRIVATEER BAY

The crew of Dream Maker all woke from deep, dreamless sleep to a morning thick with something unspoken, a sense that the day would not be ordinary. No one said a word about it, but the feeling ran deep, a silent current between them. The air pressed close, heavy and damp, already 85 degrees before breakfast, the kind of heat that clings to skin and slows every movement. Norman Island's hills stood dark and watchful, cumulus clouds building over the cliffs, their edges smudged and gray, hinting at rain. The sky's warning was quiet for now, but it was there, growing stronger by the minute.

If the weather stayed calm, the plan was simple: move Dream Maker to Privateer Bay, close to The Caves, anchor where they could swim ashore without needing the dinghy after their run along the south side. Junior left the dinghy trailing behind, its line pulled tight in the still water, easier than hauling it up for such a short trip. Guey worked the bow, freeing the mooring, while Junior guided Dream Maker clear of the crowded moorings in The Bight, rounding the rocky shoulder of Treasure Point and slipping into the quiet arms of Privateer Bay. By eight, the anchor was down, the ketch holding steady. Two charter boats had beaten them there, their crews already in the water, fins flashing as they disappeared into the caves' shadows, chasing secrets the island kept close.

The crew piled into Dream Maker's dinghy, rocking in Privateer Bay's light swells. A cooler of water and snacks sat heavy, snorkel gear stacked beside it, Junior's backpack with the amulets at the bow. Clouds loomed dark and swollen with rain, while the sky to the south, toward Sabu Mathila and Bluff Bays, was lighter, urging them on. Crews on the nearby charter boats hustled, snorkelers retreating quickly, spooked by the weather shift. Junior sat at the helm, the outboard snarling, steering south around Caravel Rock's edges. Faidh watched the cliffs; Guey gripped the gunwale, their eyes tracing yesterday's routes, the island's secrets sharp in the wind.

The first stop was on the far side of Bluff Bay, the large peninsula that sat between it and South Bay beyond. Guey had noticed this spot when they sailed by it yesterday morning. It was a deep V cut into the cliff, about fifty feet deep. When they had passed the day before, it seemed to hide a possible overhang, but as they approached, the rocks proved very sharp, the waves crashing. It was clearly not somewhere a pirate would risk approaching—too dangerous and too difficult to access or escape from easily. Guey reminded the others, "Remember, the Taíno believed in hiding in plain sight—Cofresí would have done the same. This place is too remote and inaccessible."

The dinghy nosed toward Bluff Bay, a peninsula jutting between it and South Bay. Guey had spotted a deep V in the cliff yesterday—its shadows hinting at an overhang. As Junior slowed the dinghy, waves crashed on jagged rocks. However, it was clearly too treacherous for a pirate's hide.

They pushed west along the coast, the dinghy slapping hard against the chop, every notch and crevice in the cliffs echoing what they'd seen on yesterday's hike. The eastern peninsula of Bluff Bay was all jagged rock, reefs lurking just beneath the surface, ready to rip open a hull. Waves hammered the cliffs, spray stinging their faces, the sky pressing down with heavy, dark clouds. Junior kept the dinghy close to shore, Faidh and Guey scanning every break in the stone, every shadow, searching for a sign. But nothing opened, no cave revealed itself, no secret called them in. The promise of the south side faded, hope thinning to a whisper in the wind. They turned back, the outboard's steady growl the only sound, Dream Maker waiting in Privateer Bay, the plan unraveling, the island's silence unbroken.

After their search along the cliffs, the dinghy rounded Caravel Rock, returning to find Dream Maker alone at anchor in Privateer Bay—the charter boats now scattered by the morning's squall. Clouds billowed black, swelling fiercely in every direction, darker than before, the air thick with the threat of rain.

Faidh's eyes met Junior's. Faidh glanced at the sky. "Should we move her before the storm hits hard? Her mast's the tallest metal in the bay—lightning's a risk."

Junior nodded, voice low. "I think that's a prudent call."

Guey cut in, sharp. "I think we should stay."

Faidh turned. "Why?"

Guey's gaze held steady. "The storm's not a threat to Dream Maker. It's Juracán, marking the treasure." Junior's jaw tightened.

Junior interjected, "One bolt of lightning could gut the ship, every wire fried in a flash."

Guey stood calmly. "You asked me to trust you when you sailed us into a tropical storm. Trust me now."

Junior's eyes narrowed. "I trusted my ship, five years rebuilding and living on her - knowing her limits. You're asking for faith in a 200-year-old curse?"

Guey's voice softened. "No, trust me—my people. You brought me because I can sense more than what's seen. That's why we're here."

Rain fell lightly, then harder, the ketch closer now. Junior grunted. "Let's board, haul the dinghy. We'll talk about it on board."

They climbed aboard, Guey stacking the dripping snorkel gear and wet backpack aft, Faidh hauling the cooler below. Junior hoisted the dinghy, opened the drain, and let rainwater and sea spray pour out, the storm's hum growing louder all around them.

The three sat in Dream Maker's cockpit, silent at first, the storm hammering Norman Island, rain drumming moderately on the ketch's deck. Ripples danced across Privateer Bay, swells small, 2-3 feet, belying the black clouds' menace overhead.

Guey broke the quiet. "Yesterday, if you remember, the storm didn't start coming down until we turned north around Caravel Rock into Privateer Bay. And it stopped once we cleared Treasure Point and entered The Bight. Then, today, it started again when we arrived at the anchorage, and then stopped when we headed south on the dinghy. It only started back up when we came around Caravel Rock again, and the stones were back in Privateer Bay."

Faidh nodded. "Yeah, that is what happened."

Guey's eyes sharpened. "It's not us. It's the stones."

Junior leaned forward. "So, Guey, what is our next step then?"

Guey's voice held steady. "I think that we should snorkel over to The Caves. Then I will conduct the ceremony that my dad taught me before I left Jayuya. That should break the curse, and if there is a treasure, expose it to be found."

Faidh's brow lifted. "You think it's that easy?"

Guey nodded. "I do. I think that Cofresí didn't hide the treasure—I suspect it was left in relatively plain sight. And when he failed to deliver the stones, as promised in his prayers, a storm, also known as the spirit of Juracán, effectively hid the treasure until they were returned. And now the storm is here, waiting for us to return the stones."

Outside, the storm hung still, rain pounding the island, lightning arcing cloud to cloud, no bolts striking earth. Junior's jaw tightened, torn, prudence urged him to sail Dream Maker clear, test Guey's claim from a safe distance, return by dinghy if true. But life's mark lay in bold moves, not cautious steps, the kind others shunned.

He met Guey's gaze. "Ok, Guey, you have my trust. Let's do it!"

Guey's face lit. "Thank you, Junior. You have no idea what that means to me."

Faidh's smile signaled her nod.

Junior's voice quickened. "Well, I don't think we should tempt fate longer than we have to. Let's gear up and swim to The Caves."

They stepped into the rain, shedding the cockpit's shelter, and donned snorkel gear. Junior slung his backpack, heavier than he had anticipated. He looked at Guey, "What's in this backpack? It weighs a ton."

Guey smiled, "I can carry if I need to. It has the amulets, as well as a few items that I need to do the ceremony to break the curse."

"No, I got it. The weight took me aback. I thought it was just the amulets."

They plunged into Privateer Bay's churn, the seas tossing them just a bit, winds pushing them out to sea. The swim to The Caves was tough, with the winds and seas challenging their commitment. They floated momentarily, lungs burning, storm roaring overhead, a beat of silence stretching around them. Their strokes fierce, they reached the northern cave's dark mouth, its shadows deep and dark.

The water was clear, blue, and alive, pounding on the rocks more than usual with the storm directly overhead. They swam toward the dark opening in the cliff, slow and steady. The Northernmost cave actually had two entrances, one on the sand and one from the sea. Three snorkelers entered the latter - the entrance was wide at the mouth, and the sea pulled slightly inward, as if something waited in the dark. The coral clung to the walls in soft colors—purples and oranges and reds—like forgotten flags from old ships. Fish moved quickly and brightly beneath them. Parrotfish. A grouper watching from a shadow.

Inside, it cooled and darkened - with faint rumblings of thunder from outside. Their arms moved without sound, and the only noises were splashes of water inside the cave. Junior climbed out of the water onto a sandy shelf, pulling off his backpack. The other two followed. Guey opened the backpack, first taking out the amulets and laying them out in a diamond. Then he pulled out and placed three small, statue-like figures carefully in the middle of the stones.

"This is probably what weighed the most," He said, pointing at the statues. "They are zemi idols of Guabancex, Atabey, and Yúcahu." The cave's half-dimmed light highlights the carved faces of the figures.

Faidh looked at Guey, "Does this cave feel familiar, like your dreams?"

Guey replied, "No, but the caves were just background to the nightmare, I can't be sure." Then he pulled out what appeared to be four quart-sized ziplock bags. The first was filled with feathers. The second contained what seemed to be a piece of flatbread. The third was a Y-shaped tube and a small packet of white powder. And the fourth held what looked to Junior like the dried tobacco and a lighter. Finally, Guey pulled out two shell necklaces and a single small shell with a hole in it. But to both Faidh and Junior's surprise, Guey didn't put the necklaces around his neck; instead, he slid them up his leg to his knees.

Faidh exclaimed, "Ok, this is getting weird."

Junior burst out laughing. "So, let me get this straight: two weeks ago, I tripped over a stone on an uninhabited Caribbean island that led me to three stones, requiring a girl in three different dreams to tell us exactly where they were. We had modern-day pirates chasing us while sailing through a tropical storm, so we could sail to another uninhabited Caribbean island in search of lost, cursed pirate treasure." He was laughing so hard he could hardly continue. "And now, you think leg shells, bread, a little white powder, feathers, and some leaves are weird?"

Faidh nodded, "Mm-hmm!"

By this point, they were all laughing uncontrollably. It was a combination of what would usually be considered a crazy situation, as well as an absolute release of penned-up emotions from the past week.

"Ok, now that we have gotten all that out of our systems, I'm gonna need your help with some things." He handed a piece of the cassava bread to Junior. "When I tell you, I need you to throw that in the water."

"Ok."

Then he rolled up one of the dried leaves and handed it, along with the lighter, to Faidh. He said to her, "When I look at you, I need you to light the tobacco leaves and swirl the smoke around the three of us, like this"—swinging his arm in a circle over their heads.

Then he closed his eyes and said, "Let's do this!", taking out the feathers and putting the headdress on his head.

Guey blew into the holed conch shell, a fotuto, its sharp cry bouncing off coral. Then he chanted low, feet shuffling in a small areíto dance, his voice calling to the storm goddess: "Guabancex, still your winds." The sea lapped at the entrance, cool and steady.

Guey then took the cohoba pipe, inhaled a small amount of the white powder, hesitated, then passed it to Junior and Faidh. They shook their heads, so he set it down.

It didn't take long for the cohoba to hit Guey. Almost immediately, he felt the rush of spirits through his body and an attachment to the earth, as if his legs extended to the center of the earth. He reached out and softly touched each amulet surrounding the zemis, saying something in either

Spanish or Arawak, the language of the Taíno; Junior wasn't sure which it was. Guey could feel the power of each stone with his touch - running through his body.

He then nodded at Faidh. She quickly lit the tobacco, smoke curling all around the cave. After a couple of seconds, he took the burning tobacco leaves from her hands and put them between the zemis.

He then looked at Junior, this time nodding his way. Junior, without hesitation, tossed the cassava into the water - the splash drawing a feeding frenzy from fish just below the surface.

Then Guey reached down, filled his hands with seawater, and sprayed it into the air, invoking Atabey's calm. And that's when he started dancing, as if he were playing an instrument with the shells around his knees and chanting, "Cacique of the Wind, spare our shores."

But nothing happened.

A silence stretched, not just around them but within. The failure sent a shiver of fear through Guey, the kind of fear that questions everything—his faith in his heritage, the stories he believed, and the very purpose of their journey. For Faidh, there was a sudden overwhelming doubt, a gnawing question of whether the chase for legends had eclipsed reality. Junior, normally unshaken, felt a flicker of awe at the immense power that seemed just out of reach, like the storm itself: potent, untamed, and indifferent to their plans. These ripples of emotion caught them off guard, as if the island itself was holding its breath, waiting.

"Seriously?" Faidh's voice filled with frustration. "That quick."

"I simply don't feel it." Guey continued. "If it were here, I would feel the energy. I can feel the energy of the stones and the zemis. Heck, I think if the treasure were in fact here, based on the power of the stones and these zemis, you both would feel the energy. But there is nothing here. Nothing for the Taíno energy to release."

"Well, what do you want to do next?" asked Junior.

"I want to try the other caves," he hesitated before continuing. "Let's try the southernmost one first. I think that's the biggest, and I think it's where Henry Creque found a bunch of doubloons in the late 1800s."

"We're following your lead," Junior stated, trying to assure Guey of his confidence in what they were doing.

The three packed everything back up in the backpack, ensuring that everything would be ready for the next ceremony, if needed.

Junior looked at Guey, "You know, I have dry sack bags back on Dream Maker. We could have packed everything in one of them and made sure nothing got wet, without a bunch of ziplocks."

"Sorry," replied Guey, "I never heard of such a thing."

Junior just laughed. "Next time, we'll use a dry sack." He then donned the backpack again, and each put on their snorkel gear, and they headed back out into the storm.

As they left the cave, it was clear the storm had gotten worse since they went into the cave. The seas were up to 3 feet or more, and the rain was coming down in sheets now. Junior just thought to himself, 'This better work, or we are gonna have to leave real soon. Or even worse, we won't be able to swim back.'

CHAPTER 21

THE CEREMONY

The southernmost cave yawned deep. Its mouth, a shadowed maw that swallowed light, presented a lonely dark that seemed to trap time itself. Outside, the sea raged, gray and violent under storm-heavy skies. Waves hammered the jagged rocks with a roar that carried ancient secrets. Rain hammered down in relentless sheets, obscuring the entrance. Guey, Junior, and Faidh floated at the threshold, their bodies rising and falling with the swell of the water. The lingering presence of a barracuda, sleek and sharp, watched them with cold, unfeeling eyes. It drifted aside, a silent guardian that pledged neither allegiance nor opposition.

They swam in slowly and deliberately. The water cooled their skin as the overcast hue faded behind them. The cave's walls, slick with algae, closed in tightly. Junior's fingers grazed the rough stone, stirring tiny bubbles that caught the faint glow. Parrotfish flashed below—streaks of green and gold. A grouper lurked in shadow, its bulk a quiet warning. The ceiling curved low, trapping air that carried their breath back in hollow echoes. Each exhale was a whisper of something lost, something buried. The cave felt alive, heavy with memory, as if it knew what they sought and guarded it still.

They moved deeper, darkness closing in until only the splash of their kicks remained. As they swam further, a knot of anxiety tightened in Junior's chest. He couldn't shake the thought of being trapped, unable to find his way back if the sea's mood shifted. Junior's flashlight swept ahead, catching a narrow ledge, barely wider than his shoulders, jutting from the wall—no sandy shelf here, just cold, wet stone, too tight for any dance.

They treaded water, lifted their goggles, and spat out their mouthpieces. Junior's eyes met Guey's. "What now?" he asked, his voice low, almost drowned by the sea's pulse.

Guey's face was calm, but his eyes burned. "This cave feels different, almost familiar. It has a heavy feel, like there is a huge burden in these walls. I say that I do the ritual again, the best I can." He hesitated a moment, then continued, "I think this is the one."

Junior nodded, glancing at Faidh. "You two climb up. Faidh, help him any way you can. I'll stay in the water. Please don't leave me here for too long. I prune easily."

Guey and Faidh hauled themselves onto the ledge. Water streamed from their bodies, pooling on the stone. Junior looked around the cave, sweeping the flashlight. The cavern stretched back eighty, maybe a hundred feet from the entrance. Nothing but walls carved by the sea, he thought. The blackness drank the light.

Guey opened the backpack and laid out the sacred tools. He held two shell bands—conchs and cowries strung tight, clinking like sea pebbles—and shook them in his hands. There was no room to tie them to his knees. His headdress gripped his brow, its twelve parrot feathers—green, red, blue—rising a foot high. They trembled in the damp air. Their colors caught the flashlight's glow, flashing like the eyes of zemi. He placed the three zemi idols—Guabancex, Atabey, Yúcahu—in a tight triangle on the ledge. Their carved faces were stern in the half-dark. The four amulets—a turtle, a tree, eternal lovers, and a pirate's cave—waited in the backpack. Their time had not yet come.

"Alright, here we go," he said.

Guey blew the fotuto. Its wail pierced the cave, echoing long and deep, a cry that seemed to wake the stone itself. The sound lingered, vibrating in their chests. He felt it—something stirred here, different, alive. He chanted, soft as a breath, "Guabancex, still your winds." The cave answered with a low hum and a rhythmic pulse as winds swirled, defiant, tugging at his headdress. The feathers on his head quivered like leaves before a storm. Guey pressed the band tighter, securing it against the swirling draft. He nodded to Faidh. She struck flint, sparking life into tobacco leaves. Their smoke curled thick and gray, swirling over their heads like a zemi's breath. Guey tossed cassava bread into the water, its splash a small offering to the sea. He then took the burning tobacco from Faidh and set it in the middle of the zemis. The swirling winds carried the smoke throughout the cave.

He lifted the Y-shaped cohoba pipe and inhaled deeply this time. The white powder burned his nose, pulling him into a deep vision. He offered it to Faidh; she inhaled the powder. Her eyes widened as the cave's energy surged. Not a dream, but a vision, with orange light bright as a sunset streaming from the zemis, filling the space with warmth. The cassava in the water bubbled, alive, sparking the sea with tiny bursts. Guey placed the amulets around the zemis, one by one: A Turtle, a Cojobano Tree, Eternal Lovers, and a Water Cave with a Treasure. Each added a new hue to the glow: green, red, gold, blue. As they watched the spectacle, Guey sensed a shift—a boundary that could not be crossed without consequence lingered in the air. Whatever the zemis offered, their power was finite, bound by rules unknown. Choosing to invoke this energy was not without risk, perhaps invoking a price that would reveal itself in time—the cave pulsed with color, a living tapestry. Then a flash of lightning from outside flooded the space, revealing petroglyphs—hundreds of spirals, faces, waves—etched on the walls, ancient and watching.

An enormous wave roared in, lifting the water at least three feet, lapping at the ledge. Guey scooped seawater, sprayed it high, shaking the shell bands, their clink sharp against his chant: "Cacique of the Wind, spare our shores." The feathers swayed, their colors a beacon in the chaos.

Then silence. The wind died. The tobacco's glow snuffed out. The cave's light vanished, dark as before.

Guey reached for Faidh's hand. "You there?" he whispered.

"Yeah," she said. "Junior?"

Nothing.

"Junior!" Faidh yelling.

Silence.

She dove into the pool of water.

"Wait, Faidh. Let me get some light in here." Guey yelled, trying to stop Faidh, but it was too late. She was gone as well.

Just then, sunlight started to shine through the entrance, filling the cave with a soft glow.

Meanwhile, Faidh was under the water in the pool, looking around, trying to see if she could see Junior. She lost track of time, but her lungs reminded her with a growing burn that she would soon need fresh air again. He was nowhere in sight. However, a soft glow of light emanated from deep within the cave. She swam towards the glow - the burn of her lungs growing stronger with each stroke.

As she reached the glowing hole, her chest felt like it was going to explode from holding her breath too long. She knew she was at a decision point. Turn back to the surface or she was going to drown, right here, right now.

Just then, a hand grabbed her arm and pulled her through the glowing hole and into fresh air.

Faidh reached the surface of the water and gasped for air. She had used every ounce of oxygen in her lungs, and the pain was nearly intolerable. It took a moment for her eyes to adjust to the dim glow, but when they did, she saw Junior staring down at her, smiling.

Faidh coughed, "Where are we?"

"You tell me, you are the one who swam here. I only ended up here because of the wave swallowing me up and pushing me through that hole that I pulled you through." He replied.

"This must be a cavern hidden deep within the cave." She looked up to a tiny hole in the top of the cave, "And the sun is shining precisely through the hole."

"Yeah, I'm guessing this cave is only filled with light for a couple of minutes a day, when the sun is shining."

"Had the storm not blocked out most of the light in the main cave, and the sunlight shining precisely as it did, I wouldn't have seen the glow and not found you."

"I would have swam out. I just needed to figure out how to do so with this." Junior showed Faidh the treasure chest that he found in the new cavern.

Faidh's voice cracked with excitement, echoing off the damp walls of the southernmost cave. "Holy crap, you found it! We found it!" She gave Junior a huge hug.

Already, the light in the small cavern was starting to dim as the sun's direct light was beginning to shift.

Faidh stared at the chest's weathered wood, its grain dark and swollen with age. Iron bands were rusted but firm. The cave's air was heavy and cool, smelling of salt and stone, as if it held the chest's secret close.

"Can we drag it back to Dream Maker?" Faidh asked, her voice trembling with hope, her hands gripping the ledge.

Junior grinned, his teeth flashing in the dim. "If Cofresí hauled it in, we can haul it out. But first, let's drag it back to the main part of the cave. Guey is probably freaking out by this point."

"Right, right. I'll go first. But Junior, you'd better be right behind me." Faidh looked deep into his eyes.

"Don't worry, I want out of here as bad as you do." Junior smiled.

The two swam back through the small hole and into the main cavern. She thought to herself, it was actually a leisurely swim, knowing where you are going.

When both surfaced, Guey was elated to see that they were both alive. "Where have you two been?"

Faidh climbed up on the ledge with Guey. "There is a small cavern through a hole just on the other side of that rock", she pointed to the back wall of the cave.

As Junior got to the small ledge, now holding both Faidh and Guey, he swung the chest up between the two of them. "Look what we found."

"Is it...the treasure?" Guey asked, gasping as he spoke.

"I think so." Junior smiled. "We'll drag it back to Dream Maker and open it to see. What do you say we get out of here? I'm ready to get out of the water and dry off. Are you ready to go, or do you need time picking up all the stones?"

Guey shook his head, still wearing his headdress. "All packed, whoops, except this," he said. He took off the headdress and put it into the backpack. "Zemis, amulets, shells, tobacco—safe. And as far as I'm concerned, we're not gonna need any of it anymore today." His laugh was low and warm. The thought of wet sacred tools was absurd in light of what had just happened.

Faidh nodded, playful. "I can tell you that I'm done after that one, no matter what."

Junior chuckled, his voice bouncing off the coral-crusted walls. "Same." Junior reached up to help the two down from the ledge, "Here," he called from the water. "That was a hell of a light show, Guey, even from down here."

Guey nodded, unsure. "I think so. Did you see all of that? Junior?"

"Colors everywhere, then lightning outside, and everything going black? Yep, saw it all. Right before the wave swept me away. Wasn't I supposed to?" He mumbled the last part, then added, "Sorry I doubted you, Guey."

"To be honest, I had no idea any of that would happen," Guey said as he started to laugh.

As they turned to swim out, sunlight pierced the cave's mouth, flooding the water with gold. The sea glowed, alive, dancing with light that painted the coral—purples, oranges, reds —in colors so vivid they burned the eyes. Parrotfish darted, their scales flashing like emeralds. A barracuda glided past, silver and sleek, no longer guarding, just watching.

Faidh gasped, her breath catching. "The colors... the fish... It's breathtaking. I missed it coming in; it was too dark, and I was too focused. But now..." Her voice trailed off, stunned, as the cave transformed into a cathedral of light and life.

Guey paused, mouthpiece dangling, his headdress feathers quivering in the faint breeze. He scanned the walls, his face shadowed but sharp. "Those petroglyphs covering the walls—did you guys see them when the lightning flashed? Or was it the cohoba?" His voice carried the weight of centuries, of a Taíno world nearly lost to time.

Faidh's eyes met his, steady. "I saw them. Spirals, faces, waves - everywhere!"

Junior nodded, treading water, the chest bobbing beside him. "Me too. But they're gone now. What's it mean?"

Guey's gaze lingered on the walls, now blank in the sunlight, their secrets hidden again. "More energy here than we know," he said, his feathers swaying, their colors a quiet prayer. "The zemis spoke. Maybe the treasure's theirs. I don't know." His voice carried a hint of an old chant from his heritage, "What was given by the earth returns to the earth, and what the sea claims, it keeps," adding a layer of ancient wisdom to his words.

❖

The sea cradled them as they swam from the cave. The chest trailed behind Junior, its weight tugging at his arms. He broke the surface. Water streamed from his face. He blinked against the western sun. The storm had fled. Its roar was silenced. Clouds tore apart, revealing a sky of deep blue. The sun's rays were warm and sharp, glinting off the ripples that lapped softly against the rocks. The Trade Winds barely stirred, hushed by Norman Island's green hills—steep and still. Junior's breath caught. The world felt new. Washed clean. He thought, If I weren't here, seeing this with my own eyes, I wouldn't believe a word of it. The cave's darkness lingered in his mind. Its petroglyphs and zemi glow: a memory too vivid to doubt.

Guey led the way, the backpack bobbing with each stroke. Faidh followed, her strokes steady, eyes bright with the thrill of what they carried. Dream Maker loomed ahead, its hull white and sleek, rocking gently in Privateer Bay's calm embrace. The sea smelled of seaweed, the air cool, tasting of freedom after the cave's heavy stone.

They reached the yacht's stern, waves slapping softly against its fiberglass. Guey climbed first, water cascading from his skin. The backpack was heavy. He tossed it onto the deck, its thud muffled by the canvas cover. Faidh scrambled up next, her hands sure on the ladder, hair plastered dark and wet. She darted forward, bare feet slapping the deck, and seized the spinnaker halyard. Its line was coiled tight and clean. The rope moaned as she lowered it. The pulley sang a high, thin note. Junior treaded water below, the chest bobbing beside him. Its wood was dark, and the iron bands were pitted with rust. He looped the halyard around the chest's splintered handle, knotting it fast. His fingers were raw from the sea's bite. "Ready," he called, voice sharp, eyes squinting against the sun.

Faidh pulled hand over hand. The halyard was taut, the chest rising slowly. Water streamed from its seams like tears. It cleared the rail, swinging heavily, and landed on the deck with a hollow thump. Wood scraped fiberglass. Junior hauled himself aboard, fins dangling from one hand, his chest heaving. The three stood over the chest. Its surface was scarred and silent, holding secrets older than their dreams. The sun warmed their skin, drying the salt to a faint crust. Dream Maker rocked, steady, as if it knew what they'd done.

CHAPTER 22

THE TREASURE OF NORMAN ISLAND

When Junior finally climbed out of the sea and onto the boat, he yelled to Guey and Faidh, "Bring the chest into the cockpit!" He ran below to grab a crowbar and his angle grinder to cut open the chest.

The three arrived in the cockpit nearly simultaneously. Huddled together in Dream Maker's cockpit, they placed the chest —a rectangular box of splintered mahogany with rust-flaked iron bands —on the bench seat. The cracked wood was slick with rain as Junior turned on the grinder, sending sparks as he cut the lock off. Guey pried the lid open, which groaned with age, revealing the contents: a stack of twenty-two gold doubloons and eighteen silver pieces of eight; two smooth, palm-sized Taíno-inspired stones, one carved with spirals and another with zigzags; a heavy silver crucifix on a tarnished chain; and a curled logbook fragment in a water-stained, waxed pouch. As they stared, their breaths caught; the cockpit felt thick with history, the dark cliffs and Juracán's shadow pressing in.

The coins—forty in all—gleamed faintly: twenty-two thick, weighty gold doubloons and eighteen large, rounded silver pieces of eight, stacked loosely and each marked by rough, scarred faces. Eighteen doubloons, dated 1710–1725, were oval and bore crude crosses and faded Spanish crests, while four were newer, stamped with Ferdinand VII's distinctive signature, along with the pieces of eight, all minted 1805–1815. Their rims were uneven, edges chipped as if handled by pirates; one silver coin was cracked nearly in half, another deeply scratched with an angular anchor, hinting at Cofres'ís raids. Each coin was the size of a thumb, heavy and dull, cold with the weight of the sea and time as Faidh traced their intricate, weathered curves.

Two Taíno-inspired amulets lay side by side, each palm-sized and carved from smooth basalt that felt warm despite the damp. The first was gray-green, etched with tight spirals around a central, jagged oval with radiating lines, resembling the Guabancex storm symbol. Its edges were chipped and scratched, dirt filling the grooves. The second was darker, heavy in the hand, its surface carved with sharp zigzags and concentric arcs like those at Cañón Blanco. Across one side stretched a faint crescent scratched into the stone, as if pointing into Jayuya's heart. Their surfaces were timeworn, the carvings shallow and deep in turn, humming between Guey's fingers as he studied them.

The crucifix was crafted from heavy silver, now blackened and rough with tarnish, suspended from a thick, knotted chain whose links showed pits of green and gray corrosion. Four inches long, with blunt arms and a smooth back, it bore a single, scratched "S" near its base, standing out in raw metal against the aging patina—evidence of a past owner. The chain's clasp was fused shut by rust. As Junior held it tightly, the simple cross's heft and battered surface stood in stark relief under the cockpit's light.

The logbook fragment consisted of brittle, curled pages wrapped in a cracked, translucent waxed pouch. Its cover was stiff and mottled, while the edges of the pages were frayed, the black ink now gray and blurred by years of salt. Spanish script in faded lines stood out on one exposed page—a captain's careful hand, possibly Cofres'ís—recording a bearing: "NNW of the cave's shadow, Norman's mark." The word "oro" was repeated several times, "escondido" underlined, next to a diagram showing a cliff's curve, the ink mostly faded but still legible enough to recognize the cave's outline. Guey carefully unfolded the page along its weakened crease, the paper quivering in the wind but still strong enough to hold its secrets. More pages, similarly aged and stained, rested in the pouch, but the exposed fragment—the only one marked with a sketch—held their focus.

Faidh looked at Guey. "Do you have any idea what either of those stones is trying to say?"

"No. They are very complex petroglyphs. It'll take time to decipher them. But I will love devoting my life to answering that question."

"Junior, what are you thinking right now?" Faidh asked Junior as he was clearly deep in thought.

Honestly, I'm torn. I look at those stones and that diary, and all I see are questions more than I see value. They hold secrets, mysteries that whisper of the past, their importance deeper than anything I could measure in dollars. But the coins and this cross," he said, lifting the crucifix and chain, "I'm guessing combined are worth in excess of $100,000. It's like holding someone else's fortunes in my hands, stolen moments from history now weighing on me. While I hoped we would find the lost Cofresí treasure, I had no idea we would actually end up with anything of real value. Now, my mind is filled with ideas on how to move forward. Do I keep it, report it, or find some compromise? I want to make the right choice here, not just for us, but for the story this treasure tells. It's like standing at a crossroads, knowing each path alters the course not just for me, but for the echoes of those who came before."

Faidh quipped, "Well, we found it. It's ours—just like in the movies."

Junior chuckled, "We could argue that. But I doubt the BVI's or even our own Customs authorities would agree with us.

Norman is a privately owned island. We found the chest buried on the island, not floating in the water. Some would argue that if we don't report the treasure, it makes us thieves."

"Of course not. Any more than the US settlers were thieves when they came to America for the first time. Right?" Faidh then stopped herself and laughed. "Ok, not a good example, but you know what I mean."

"Faidh, I don't know. This is a very tough one. Before we even start debating, we must consider the legal ramifications—salvage laws in the Virgin Islands are strict, and cultural property statutes may require us to declare these finds immediately to local authorities. To me, it's clear that Guey needs to take all the stones, both from the treasure and from the other islands, back to the Jayuya museum as mementos of great historical value to all Taíno descendants. It feels like the right thing for their legacy. But the coins and the cross, I think, are different. They are something that needs to be turned over to the authorities and donated to a museum where the artifacts can be displayed for everyone to see. I want to respect history and the law, even if that means letting go of something we found."

"Wait, what?!?"Faidh jumped up and nearly hit her head on the cockpit's ceiling.

"I just don't think we have any other options."

Guey finally jumped into the fray. "I tend to agree with Faidh. These items have been lost for over 200 years. No one even knows they exist. If you were to pick up a beautiful shell or a stone off the beach in The Bight, you wouldn't report it to the authorities, would you?" Rhetorically, he answered his own question, "Of course, you wouldn't. So what if you took that stone home, cleaned it up, and found out it was a diamond? Would you return it to whoever owned that beach?"

Junior looked at Guey, "I've got no argument for that or Faidh's comments, except that it doesn't feel right." Junior continued. "This struggle over whether to keep a clear artifact that I found didn't start an hour ago when this chest presented itself to us. It started two weeks ago for me, when I tripped and found the first stone on Mona Island. The questions of whether to keep it, put it back where I found it, or take it to an authority or museum have challenged my moral compass since the day I started this adventure. Part of me wants to honor the past by returning these items, but part of me feels a personal connection to the discovery. That conflict is what's making it so hard to decide."

Guey and Faidh both listened intently, and Junior shared his moral struggles.

Was it just luck that I found the stone in the first place? Was it the stone that brought me to you, Faidh? And to you, Guey? Or was something bigger than all of us? Karmic? My intention at each stage of this adventure has been morally grounded, never just trying to enrich myself with wealth. Instead, as I shared with Faidh just yesterday morning, as a sailor, I love the journey, living each moment as it comes, embracing the sea for what it is: freedom, adventure, and self-reliance, not as a means to get somewhere. The destination is merely the final stop on a journey. I didn't set off on this journey to find a treasure to get rich. And I didn't think you two did either. Before embarking, I knew Guey was drawn to the sea because it always reminded him of his ancestors, who once roamed these islands. His respect for his heritage and desire to uncover its truths have always resonated deeply with me. Faidh, your love for stories and history has often guided our conversations and decisions, which is why I value your perspectives so much. This adventure has been about exploration and finding the truth behind a legend that has existed for centuries. And as I've walked that path, each of you has joined my side, consciously or not. I don't think the adventure is over. I believe there are more truths to explore for the Taíno, for Cofresí, for Guey, for Faidh and me, and honestly, for Dream

283

Maker. We need to keep our compass pointed North as best we can and continue to search for truths. Ultimately, I want our actions to honor more than just ourselves.

"Damn you and your moral compass, James Wright." Faidh stared into Junior's eyes, expressing both admiration and love.

"So what do we do now? Who do we share our discovery with?" asked Guey.

"I actually looked it up the other day. We need to call the BVI Department of Culture or the BVI National Parks Trust. They will come and collect the treasure. We were supposed to leave it where we found it, but to me, that seems ridiculous, because someone else could've come along and taken it before the authorities even showed up. And that's what I plan to tell them if they ask."

Guey looked at Junior and asked, "What should we do with the stones?"

Junior sneered, "I say we take the advice of your ancestors and hide them in plain sight. Take all six and line them up on the shelf in the Salon. Nobody would even remotely suspect they were associated with a pirate treasure." He giggled, then added, "Hell, I know they are integral to the treasure, and I wouldn't suspect them. As Faidh said, when she saw the first one, it looked like something a young child would make in art class. But maybe these simple carvings unlock something far greater than we realize. It's not just clever—it's a way to protect their meaning until the right time and preserve their connection to your heritage, Guey. Who knows what secrets they might hold?"

"Hey!" interjected Faidh, then looked at Guey, "I meant no disrespect to your ancestors. I was just teasing Junior."

They all laughed together.

Junior then looked at Faidh and asked her to take the Logbook down to his quarters and put it on the shelf with the charts and sailing books next to their bed.

She smiled, "Right, in plain sight, next to our bed."

It's a strange twist that grips government men when you offer them treasure to haul away. The clerks who would usually turn you back, closing in an hour and telling you to come back tomorrow if you need a permit or a nod, drop their timetables like dead weight when gold enters the conversation. The anticipation was palpable as Junior's call still hung in the air, the silence on the deck filled suddenly by the distant rumble of engines drawing nearer. Three RIBs cut into Privateer Bay, their gray hulls swaying a stone's throw from Dream Maker, engines pulsing with the recent run, the whole crew assembled in less than two hours. The flash of uniforms caught in the waning sunlight, striking a note of both dread and excitement as they approached.

They came aboard Dream Maker with force, ten agents climbing the ladder, boots thudding hard on the deck, sea spray streaking their jackets. Junior stood at the rail, welcoming each with a steady nod, his smile holding a trace of caution. The leader stepped up, Senior Investigator Hodge, his voice slicing through the wind as he introduced himself. He pulled Junior aside, voice low and direct. "I'd like to make this quick. Can my agents search the boat?"

Junior's grin spread, easy and open. "Search away."

Investigator Hodge directed six of the agents to search the boat, telling them to do so politely. Meanwhile, two other minions were directed to take the chest and its contents onto one of the RIBs. Finally, Hodge and some sort of secretary, taking notes, sat down in the cockpit with Dream Maker's crew and asked them about the treasure, where, when, and how they found it.

Junior spoke for the three, keeping the story simple, avoiding any mention of Taíno stones. He spoke of the storm, the lightning, and the earth shaking from what he could only assume was a lightning strike on the surface. And he finished explaining how the wave came crashing into the cave and how he was washed into the small cavern with the force of the water. Faidh and Guey sat stoically, listening intently so they understood the storyline, should they be separated and questioned.

That's when the Hodge yelled out to one of the RIBs, apparently telling a bunch of divers where to look.

He then looked at Faidh and asked, "Why did you guys open the chest instead of leaving it for us to open it?

"Are you kidding me? We were curious. We had no idea what we found, but when we opened it and saw the doubloons and the crucifix, we all agreed that this was pirate treasure from centuries past, and we absolutely needed to get you involved, right away!"

Hodge then looked at Guey and asked, "Was there any other treasure in the chest? Anything other than what was there when we arrived?"

"Nope," He stated firmly. "Like Faidh said, as soon as we saw the contents, we realized we were in way over our heads. And didn't want to make things worse by taking anything."

It wasn't long after the swimmers arrived at the cave that the radio on the Hodge's side started buzzing with chatter. He pulled it from its carry case on his belt and joined in the conversation. Evidently, the divers had found no signs of the small cavern and needed further instructions on how to find it. Hodge handed the microphone to Junior, and he gave them the instructions they would need to find the hidden hole and cavern, recommending that they have a light, as the hole wouldn't be glowing too well now that it was getting dark. With that, Junior handed the mike back to Hodges, who waited to hear when they found the cavern.

It took about ten minutes until the divers radioed back that they had found the cavern. It was a tedious ten minutes as everyone in the cockpit just sat and waited, staring at each other.

Hodge then asked two questions of the divers. The first question was whether there were any signs of additional treasure. The second was whether any chisel marks or scrapes around the edges appeared to be man-made. The answer to both questions was a clear "No". And then the diver on the other end added, "Also, Chief, I'd be surprised if anyone would have found this cave intentionally. With no light coming from the other side of the hole, just poking around, it would be nearly impossible to find the cave, especially since most snorkelers wouldn't be able to hold their breath long enough to see it and feel safe enough, actually, to explore it.

Hodge then looked back at Junior and asked, "Ok, Mr. Wright, what are your plans from here?"

Junior smiled, "Well, once you and your staff clear us, we were planning to sail back to San Juan, Puerto Rico. My Godson here, he pointed to Guey, was only able to get a week off from work, so I need to get him home so he doesn't get in any trouble."

"Sounds nice. I hate to do this to you, but I'm gonna need you to sail up to Sopers Hole tonight. We are going to quarantine this entire area and try to piece together what happened here. We appreciate you calling us immediately - most people would try to sneak away with the treasure, not reporting it. We have your contact information and will follow up with you regarding any possible reward or finder's fee, but it will likely be months before any decision along that line is made."

Then he looked slowly at all three. "The final request I have for you all is that you not discuss anything about this find with anyone until you see a press release from our staff. The last thing we need is a rush of treasure hunters overwhelming our quarantine, before we are ready."

287

They all nodded enthusiastically, and Junior added, "No problem. We never expected any of this. We were just here wanting to enjoy some great snorkeling."

Senior Investigator Hodge stood up and yelled down to the salon. All six men came up the ladder, one by one, and immediately stepped out on the port deck. He queried each of them if they had found any treasure below. All shaking their heads, he released them back to the RIB they came on.

Hodge then looked intently at Junior. "Mr. Wright, I've notified the Sopers Hole Customs Office. They will be closed when you arrive tonight, but they are expecting you to check in first thing in the morning. Please don't miss your appointment with them. That would not go over well." He paused and then continued cordially, "I want to thank you for your patience and cooperation. As I said, our Front Office will follow up with you in the coming months regarding a reward. We are disembarking your vessel, and as I mentioned, we kindly request that you leave immediately. Do you have any questions for me or my staff?"

In unison, they all said, "No, sir."

As soon as the BVI Government Agents were gone, Junior looked at Faidh, "You've got the helm."

She dutifully stepped to the helm and turned on the key to the motor. "Aye, aye, Captain."

"I'm gonna take control of the motor from the remote, haul up the anchor, and then hand everything to you. When I give you the signal, I want you to back us away from these Government boats, and once we are clear, take us north." Then Junior looked at Guey, "Guey, please go below and check the stones and the general condition of the spaces. There is nothing we can do if they took something, but I'd like to know before we leave."

288

"Aye, aye." Nodded Guey.

In no time, Dream Maker was clear of the Government RIBs and heading north, on her way to Sopers Hole, to make sure they made their appointment with the BVI Customs Office, first thing in the morning.

The night swallowed Dream Maker as she cut north through the dark swell, her engine quiet, pushing through the night seas. Junior chose to run on the motor to simplify the night journey and keep them moving to their next destination. The sky was speckled with bright stars, with Norman Island's cliffs fading into shadow behind. Faidh held the helm steady, her eyes on the compass glow, feeling a mixture of relief and hope guiding her steady hand. When they arrived back at Sopers Hole, a glow from all the lights on the shore, a feeling of calm washed over them. Junior pointed Faidh to an open mooring ball, which they claimed as their home for the night, feeling a sense of satisfaction tinged with the anticipation of what lay ahead. Guey leaned against the rail, his silence marking the contemplation of their incredible day. Staring at the quiet streets just a hundred yards south, he felt a deep connection to the history they uncovered, yet slight anxiety lingered in his mind about the days ahead. The bay was quiet, broken only by the splash of fish around the bay. The ketch rocked gently, moored near the lights of Tortola. The government's Privateer Bay quarantine was now a distant memory, but Customs' presence lingered in the damp air, leaving them with a sense of unresolved tension amidst their achievements.

CHAPTER 23

RUMORS, RELEASES, AND REVELRY

Sunrise cracked over Sopers Hole, painting the bay in soft gold. Junior stirred first; the breeze felt cool against his skin. A single thought nagged at him, the question looping with the dawn —would customs come aboard and find the stones? The air held that perfect November morning crispness, only 75 degrees. A breeze rustled the palms along the shore, and humidity stayed light for the season. Below deck, Faidh and Guey slept, but the bay buzzed: dinghies darted between moored boats while vendors called from the docks. Customs launches idled near the pier as their crews eyed Dream Maker. Junior stretched. The sea was calm, the storm's memory washed clean. Yet the day felt charged, as if the island's secrets still whispered through the clear sky.

The sun climbed higher above Sopers Hole, its light dancing on the ripples, when two customs launches sliced through the bay toward Dream Maker. Six crew members were aboard, uniforms crisp, the November breeze carrying a hint of salt. The launches pulled alongside, engines dropping to a low hum. The lead officer, a broad man with a weathered face, called up, "BVI Customs. We're boarding." Junior, already on deck, nodded. The first aboard introduced himself as Agent Maduro, clearly the lead —tall and intimidating, his uniform pressed and badge glinting. He stated they had orders from above for Dream Maker's crew to remain on board to prevent leaks about the previous day's events. He looked directly at Junior. "It's a request that I'm told is more of a statement. There will be a press release later today, but they need a little more time before anything gets out."

The rest of the team climbed aboard, boots soft on the deck. Maduro handed Junior a clipboard. "Paperwork, please. Registration, passports, and arrival clearance." Junior fetched the documents from below. The crew's eyes were sharp as they scanned the horizon, alert. Faidh and Guey stirred, footsteps padding up from the salon and rubbing sleep from their faces—the sudden arrival yanked them into the day. The officer reviewed the papers with a nod, while three others moved below deck. Their steps echoed as they checked compartments with quick, practiced hands.

Faidh, ever the host, stepped forward, her voice bright and cheery. "Coffee? Tea? I can whip up some breakfast—eggs, maybe?" Maduro raised a hand, a faint smile breaking his stern look. "Coffee's fine, thank you, ma'am." The others declined, focused, their silence heavy with yesterday's shadow. Faidh brewed a pot, pouring a steaming cup for the officer, who sipped as he watched the inspection. The team returned topside, one muttering, "All clear," with no trace of the chest or its secrets lingering. The lead nodded to Junior. "You're in order. I have to take your documents to the office. I'll get your release so that you can be on your way—please, don't try to leave." He then looked at Faidh, handing her back the half-empty cup. "Thank you for the coffee."

The launches pulled away, leaving Dream Maker rocking gently, the bay's bustle resuming under the perfect Caribbean sky.

Late afternoon settled heavily over Sopers Hole, the sun dipping low and casting long shadows across the water. The air carried the faint scent of salt and diesel from the idling launches, a sensory thread connecting the morning's tension to the current moment. And still no signs of any customs agents returning to Dream Maker.

Finally, Junion and Faidh watched as a lone launch left the customs dock, a single man on board. Upon arriving, the man tied his boat to the hip of Dream Maker. His attitude was completely different than that of the previous agents who visited, as he didn't bark his intent to board; instead, he asked permission with a nod, respectful in the fading light. Junior stood at the rail, welcoming him with open arms. The ladder creaked as the agent climbed aboard, boots steady on the deck.

"Good Afternoon, Mr. Wright. My name is Agent Lettsome. My apologies for the delay in processing your release. We were waiting for permission from the Premier. Your discovery has garnered a lot of attention throughout our Government, and after the press release that was just released, there is buzz all over social media."

"Well, we certainly didn't want to cause any raucous. We were just trying to enjoy everything your lovely country has to offer," replied Junior.

"Anyway, I have your release paperwork, your registration, and your passports," he said, handing all of the paperwork back to Junior. "Please accept our apologies for any inconvenience this might have caused."

"No worries," Junior said, smiling.

"Can we offer you a cold drink?" asked Faidh.

"No, thank you, Ma'am. I have to get back to the office - you'd be surprised by all the paperwork associated with finding a treasure." He chuckled as he stepped off the boat.

Junior asked before the boat pulled away, "Can we go into town and have dinner tonight?"

"You are free to do what you want. Your paperwork shows you will be out of the BVIs by tomorrow at midnight, so feel free to come into town and enjoy a Painkiller at Pusser's," he said, looking up and grinning.

The launch's engine coughed to life, water churning behind it, the agent's figure fading into the dusk as Dream Maker rocked gently in the swell, the crew watching from the deck, papers rustling in Junior's hands.

Junior turned to Guey and Faidh, the dusk settling over Sopers Hole, the harbor lights flickering on the water. "What ya say we go in and celebrate?"

Guey sprang up, voice bright, "My treat, as long as we go back to Pussers. That place was awesome! I might even try a level 3 tonight."

Junior laughed, deep and easy, "Deal! And don't worry, if you have a little too much, I owe you one."

They lowered the dinghy into the water, its hull slapping the swell, and then motored over to Pussers. The dock bustled with evening activity. They found a table, the wood worn smooth, and squeezed in together. Faidh leaned forward and whispered into Junior's ear, "I feel like everyone is staring at us." Before they could call for a waiter, a man approached, three Painkillers balanced on his tray, and smiled widely. "These are on the house," he said, setting the drinks before them.

The three looked up, faces blank, and Faidh spoke, "Thanks. What's the occasion?"

"The manager wants to thank you for finding the treasure on Norman Island. He said business is going to explode when word gets out."

The three exchanged glances, Junior muttering under his breath to Faidh and Guey, "Just roll with it." Then he looked up at the waiter, brow raised, "Where did you hear that we found a treasure?"

The waiter laughed easily, "Sir, this is a tiny set of islands. News travels fast. But big news, like a treasure, travels faster than lightning. We have seen Dream Maker in the harbor since this morning. We were hoping you would come in again after you didn't leave all day. You are famous." As the crew processed the waiter's words, a low buzz of excitement spread through the bar. Patrons turned in their seats, curious eyes focused on the newcomers, their murmurs rising like a tide. The atmosphere was lively, the room filled with the colorful clatter of island life— laughter, glasses clinking, and the steady strum of a local guitarist adding rhythm to the scene. Locals whispered amongst themselves, clearly intrigued by the sudden notoriety of Junior and his crew.

After ordering dinner, the clink of plates filling the air, Faidh's eyes caught Peter and Harry, from SOBAD, perched at the bar. They leaned forward, shirts bright, clearly fishing for an invite, their glances sharp. She turned to Junior, "Are you ok if I invite Peter and Harry to join us?"

"Absolutely," he said, finishing his Painkiller, the glass sweating in his hand.

She waved them over, and quick as a tide, they dragged two chairs to the table, three extra drinks in tow, settling in like old mates. Faidh yelled at the top of her lungs, "Sailors Of Bold And Daring!"

"G'day Mate, thanks for waving us over," Harry said, his Australian accent rolling smoothly. "Nice try, Faidh, but no cigar. We weren't gonna intrude, but we were hoping to get a minute to talk to you."

The table buzzed now, voices blending with the harbor's night sounds, the Painkillers glowing amber under the lights, the crew's fame a weight they hadn't expected.

Peter leaned back at the table, the lantern light flickering over his lean Tortola face, a grin cutting through the hum of Pusser's. "You knew all along there was treasure on Norman Island, didn't you, mon?"

Junior sipped his Painkiller, the glass cool in his hand, and chuckled. "Yeah, we had a pretty good idea, just weren't sure exactly where."

Peter's eyes narrowed, playful but sharp. "Do you mind telling me how you knew?"

Junior paused, the night air thick with salt and rum, and glanced at Guey and Faidh. "What do you know about the legend of Pirata Cofresí and the four Taíno amulets?"

Harry, his Australian drawl easy, broke in with a laugh. "I only know a little of Pirata Cofresí. I know nothing of any, how you say, Taa-ee-noo Amulets?"

The table quieted, the clink of glasses fading, as the crew's secret hung heavy, the harbor's dark water lapping beyond the windows. Junior felt a coil of tension wind around his chest, his heart pounding against the silence like a drum. What once felt like shared camaraderie suddenly teetered on the edge of exposure. Faidh's hands fidgeted with a napkin, her smile a brittle mask covering a wave of apprehension. The thrill of the adventure left traces of anxiety, as if they were on the brink of crossing a line. Guey's gaze darted, caught between the urge to remain stoic and the flutter of adrenaline threatening to spill over. This wasn't just a secret—it was a weight of responsibility that could change everything.

Junior looked calmly at Faidh and Guey, smiled and whispered, "In Plain Sight, right?" Then he looked at Peter and Harry.

"It all kicked off a couple of weeks ago when I tripped over a root on a remote island, landing hard on a stone etched with a symbol and the letters "RC"—Roberto Cofresí's mark, bold as you please. That fall set us on a path we couldn't ignore. Faidh and I dug into the stone and discovered the lore of the notorious 19th-century pirate, Roberto Cofresí, whose exploits were legendary in the Caribbean. Legends spoke of a curse tied to his treasure, one that would only be lifted by discovering four Taíno amulets, each imbued with the spirit and story of the islanders. Ancient tales whispered that these amulets held the key to Cofresí's hidden wealth. Along came Guey, joining the hunt, and together we tracked down those other stones, each one humming with a story of its own. Once we had all four and chased off the pirates pursuing us, the stones pointed toward Norman Island, though the exact spot remained a mystery. We chatted with y'all right here a couple of days back, fishing for hints, but came up empty-handed. So, we hit The Caves, figuring it was the best place to start, and—boom—the treasure revealed itself, like it had been waiting all along. Quite a journey to get here, wouldn't you say?"

Peter set his drink down hard, the glass thudding on the table, and fixed Junior with a steady gaze, his eyes sharp. "That's a horrible tale, Mate. Com'on, you've got to come up with a better one than that."

Junior, Faidh, and Guey all started laughing out loud.

Just then, the waiter slid the adventurers' meals onto the table. Plates steamed with spiced fish and rice. The aroma didn't slow Peter and Harry. They leaned in, eyes glinting, eager for juicy sea stories and the trio's treasure hunt. Lantern light danced across the worn wood as the harbor's murmur blended with their prodding. Forks clinked, drinks sloshed, and the mood built.

The rest of the evening swelled with tales from both sides, a mix of truth and decades-old yarns. Neither side spoke fully honestly nor entirely spun from air. Guey, after one Level 3 Painkiller, slumped with a grin, his head heavy, ready to be hauled back to Dream Maker. It wasn't just limited to the five around the table. With each tale, the crowd at the table grew. The story of the treasure had gotten out. More importantly, the rumor of the heroes sitting in Pussers was all it took to gather crews from all over Tortola's West End.

All in all, the night was a roaring success. Junior, Faidh, and Guey let off steam that had built up over their two-week odyssey. Laughter cut through the salt air. When they woke aboard Dream Maker the next morning, sunlight crept through the portholes. They realized none had spent a dime—all drinks and meals gifted, a strange bounty from their fame. The adventure had not just been about treasure; it had transformed them. Junior, resting his hands behind his head, reflected on how their shared trials had deepened their bonds. He felt an unspoken understanding with Faidh and Guey, a camaraderie forged in the crucible of high seas and hidden secrets. They had navigated not only the waters but also their fears and uncertainties, emerging stronger. Junior leaned back, his mind drifting to old Navy port calls— Hong Kong, Thailand, Singapore, Australia. Nights of revelry in exotic harbors stacked up in his memory. He reckoned last night stood tall among them—a good night ashore, etched in memory.

CHAPTER 24

SAYING GOOD-BYE

The Jayuya festival grounds were alive with the hum of hundreds gathered under a vast, starlit sky, their faces turned toward him with reverence. Dressed in a full Taíno ritual gown—vibrant feathers and woven fibers cascading over his shoulders, a ceremonial headdress crowning his head—he stood as a bohitiu, his voice steady and resonant as he led the ceremony. The four amulets lay before him on a woven mat, their glow soft and harmonious, surrounded by offerings of fruit and tobacco, the air thick with the sacred scent of cohoba smoke rising from a clay burner. The crowd chanted in unison, their voices weaving a tapestry of hope and heritage, as he raised his hands, calling upon the zemis to bless the ritual and guide the revelation of the treasure.

This was a celebration of life, rather than a commemoration of death. He moved with grace, tracing patterns in the earth with a carved staff, the amulets pulsing in rhythm with his chants, their curse unraveling into a blessing. The crowd swelled, their faces alight with awe as the ground beneath trembled gently, not with destruction but with the promise of renewal—a vision of the treasure chest emerging, not from violence but from the earth's willing embrace, its

298

lid opening to reveal gold and history for all to share. Pirata Cofresí was absent, replaced by a quiet presence of ancestral spirits, their approval a warm breeze that lifted his gown, filling him with a sense of purpose and pride as the dream bathed him in a golden dawn.

Guey awoke slowly, moonlight filtering through the porthole casting a soft glow on his face, a faint smile lingering as the dream's peace settled into his bones. The weight of his nightmares had lifted, replaced by a clarity that felt like a gift from his ancestors, a vision of his role not as a victim of the curse but as its healer. He sat up, the memory of the festival crowd's trust lingering, knowing this dream marked a turning point in his life—in his path. Guey quickly dozed back off to sleep.

Junior didn't wait for Faidh and Guey to wake. He rose quietly, went topside, and prepared Dream Maker for a quick departure. He wanted to leave the BVI before the authorities could reconsider letting them go. The morning sun brightened Soper's Hole as Dream Maker bobbed gently. Junior stretched, inhaling the salty air, and readied the boat. He checked the rigging, tightened the mooring, and listened to the harbor's early bustle. His heart raced with anticipation. With the mainsail ready, Junior felt the weight of leaving the BVI fade as colorful buildings slipped into the haze.

Junior moved to the bow, untied the mooring, and Dream Maker slipped into motion. He quickly hoisted the mainsail, planning to keep things simple, and aimed southwest toward Cruz Bay. Tortola's hills rolled by to starboard, the smaller cays glinting to port. The sound of waves and a brief visit from dolphins kept him focused as he crossed from the British to the U.S. Virgin Islands.

Approaching Cruz Bay, the water deepened to sapphire and the hills of St. John rose steeply. The harbor buzzed with arriving boats and faint music. Junior furled the sails and motored to anchor just outside the mooring field, feeling relieved. Spotting the U.S. flag, he gathered his paperwork before heading ashore to clear customs; the transition between isles was marked more by the shared wind and sun than formalities.

It must have been the sound of the anchor dropping; Faidh and Guey both woke up from their evening slumbers. Junior handed each of them a morning coffee and told them he'd be back in 30-60 minutes, if things went smoothly; longer if not. He was going to dinghy in to clear customs.

At the Cruz Bay customs dock, Junior tied up the dinghy, the wooden boards creaking underfoot as he stepped ashore. The CBP office was a small, air-conditioned haven, where he presented his documents and answered routine questions about his journey. The officer's stamp on his paperwork marked his official return to the U.S., a moment that felt oddly ceremonial for such a short sail. Stepping back outside, Junior soaked in the sights of Cruz Bay—colorful shops, the chatter of tourists, and the scent of jerk chicken grilling nearby. Dream Maker sat proudly at anchor, her hull gleaming under the midday sun, a testament to his growing confidence as a sailor. The brief passage had been more than a physical journey; it was a bridge between the laid-back BVI and the familiar pulse of the USVI, all under the endless Caribbean sky.

As Dream Maker slipped out of Cruz Bay's bustling harbor, Junior handed the helm to Guey. The boat's bow cut through the sapphire waters of the U.S. Virgin Islands under a morning sky streaked with wispy clouds. The anchorage's reggae rhythms and ferry wakes faded, replaced by the gentle slap of waves and the hum of the trade winds, a steady 15 knots from the east-northeast. Once clear of the harbor, Junior, with Faidh's help, hoisted the mainsail and mizzen. The crisp white canvas snapped into place as Dream Maker heeled gently, eager to run. With the wind on a broad reach for the 70-nautical-mile passage to Fajardo, Puerto Rico, Junior unfurled the spinnaker. The vibrant, billowing sail bloomed against the turquoise horizon, and the boat surged forward, propelled by the raw power of the wind. The sensation was electric, a rush of freedom. Dream Maker danced across the open sea, untethered from engines or schedules, guided only by the elements and Guey's steady hand.

Sailing under the spinnaker was like harnessing a living force, the sail's colors glowing under the Caribbean sun, pulling Dream Maker with a quiet intensity that felt both wild and serene. The boat glided at nearly 8 knots, the hull slicing through gentle swells, each crest sparkling like diamonds in the midday light. Junior stood on the foredeck, the warm breeze tugging at his hair, feeling the pulse of the ocean beneath his feet and the vastness of the sea stretching to the horizon. To port, St. John's emerald hills receded, while ahead, the faint outline of Puerto Rico's coastline shimmered like a promise of adventure. The spinnaker's gentle hum, the creak of the rigging, and the occasional splash of a flying fish skimming the surface wove a symphony of freedom. For Junior, Faidh, and Guey, this was the essence of sailing—a fleeting escape from the world's constraints, where time slowed, and the wind's embrace felt like flying.

With the isinglass windows rolled up, the cockpit of Dream Maker was open to the warm Caribbean breeze. The winds carried the scent of freedom. Junior, Faidh, and Guey sailed in near silence, the boat gliding on a broad reach toward Fajardo. Guey stood steady at the helm, his hands light on the wheel, while Junior sat beside him, Faidh nestled close, her head resting on his lap, her fingers gently tracing the contours of his strong arms wrapped around her. The rhythmic song of the rigging and the soft rush of waves against the hull filled the air, blending with

301

the distant cry of a gull. Each of them absorbed the beauty around them, St. John's emerald hills fading astern, the endless horizon shimmering ahead. Junior reflected on how he'd grown more confident as a leader, steering them through storms, both literal and metaphorical. Guey found himself pondering the skills he had learned and how the sea felt like home, a place of new beginnings. Faidh thought about the courage she'd discovered within herself, facing dangers she never imagined and finding a more profound sense of purpose. The open sea, under the power of the wind, felt like a sanctuary, a place where time stretched and the world's weight lifted, leaving only the dance of Dream Maker and the elements.

Guey broke the silence, his brow furrowed as he glanced at Junior. "Junior, I have to ask you. Why did you choose to turn into a tropical storm when we were leaving Culebra? We didn't know the boat behind us was El Tiburón; it was just a blip on the radar. And it hadn't really taken any aggressive action toward us yet."

Junior's eyes flicked to the horizon, then back to Guey, a faint smile tugging at his lips. Inside, however, a mix of emotions churned. The thought of potential danger surged like a storm within him, balancing on a fine line between fear and determination. He felt a deep-seated pride in his crew and their journey so far, but an even stronger need to protect them from harm. "Call it instinct. Call it training. And, if I'm candid, it was greater fear of the known versus the unknown," he began, his voice steady despite the turmoil within. "When we started that afternoon, I knew we were taking a chance. Most sailors would rather tackle a storm in a safe harbor than risk potential gale-force winds and severe seas. The Captain's threat with the knife was real in my mind. I knew we had to get away from them, or we would have to stop the pursuit of the treasure. Then, when I noticed it was steaming quite fast, given the conditions, with no AIS broadcast, I was pretty confident it was El Tiburón. And after they followed us south, toward the storm, I was certain they not only intended to catch us but meant to board us. There was no other reason for them to follow—they could easily track us on both radar and their AIS."

"But that doesn't completely answer my question—why into the storm and not away?" Guey pressed, his curiosity unshaken.

Junior leaned back, his arm tightening around Faidh. "It was like a dogfight, but on the ocean. One that the captain of El Tiburón didn't even know he'd gotten into. I needed to play to our strengths while highlighting his weaknesses. As a sailboat, Dream Maker is slow and less maneuverable than a motorboat. She's big, with a mast height of nearly 75 feet—we couldn't just turn and hide; he'd always see us first, even on radar. But she's strong. And steady," Junior said, pounding the cockpit bench for emphasis. "One-inch-plus-thick fiberglass hull, carrying nearly 18,000 pounds of ballast in her full keel. I knew she could handle anything Tropical Storm Wendy threw at her as long as we were setting the terms. El Tiburón, on the other hand, was under 40 feet, and her captain wasn't familiar with her—he'd just stolen her. The likelihood of him knowing how to handle her in rough seas, let alone seas well outside his boat's safe limits, was slim."

Faidh looked up, her eyes bright. "Junior didn't pick the fight, but when it was inevitable, he knew how to make sure the other guy didn't land any punches. And then he walked away."

Guey nodded, a grin spreading. "So you guessed and got lucky?"

Junior chuckled. "No, I knew the limits of both vessels. I sailed Dream Maker to her edge, knowing he couldn't follow. Where I got lucky, maybe, was his ego—he wasn't going to let a 'slower' boat, a sailboat, get away."

The conversation settled, and silence returned, but Junior, restless with the quiet, pulled out his phone and opened his Spotify app, selecting his Sailing Collection. The first notes of

"Cool Change" by Little River Band drifted through the cockpit, its lyrics of freedom and the sea resonating with the wind-filled spinnaker and the open water ahead. The song wove into the moment, amplifying the sense of release as Dream Maker surged toward Fajardo's distant shore, the palm-fringed coastline slowly emerging under the golden evening light. The anchorage near Puerto del Rey Marina awaited, a haven after their journey. Still, for now, the trio basked in the wind's embrace, the spinnaker pulling them forward, each note and gust a reminder of the boundless freedom found only on the open sea.

Junior went below deck and brought up a small plastic bag wrapped tightly. His voice wavered, heavy with emotion. "I have something for each of you," he said, unrolling the plastic bag with a trembling hand. "I know your Dad is going to meet us when we get to Fajardo, Guey." He stopped, met Faidh's eyes, and his own threatened tears. "And you, we will have tonight together, but you are flying back to the mainland tomorrow, with no return flight scheduled. So I thought before the journey ended, I would give you these." He unrolled the plastic bag, revealing three gold doubloons, and handed one to each of them, holding the third tightly in his hand. The doubloons were more than just tokens; they symbolized their shared journey and the unspoken promises made along the way. For Guey, the doubloon was a connection to his heritage, a piece of the past that would guide him as he embraced his Taíno legacy. For Faidh, it embodied hope and a bond that would transcend the miles soon to separate them, a promise of return. For Junior, the gifted doubloon was a closure to this chapter and the start of many more adventures yet to come. His words faltered; the gift was meant to capture the meaning of their bond. "We each take one with us as a memory of this amazing adventure."

Tears rushing down Faidh's face, she kissed him deeply, hugging him hard and long. Her embrace was fierce, her gratitude and longing clear. "First, and foremost, I'm coming back to you and Dream Maker for as long as you'll have me. I told you, I just need to take care of some things back home. And second, I thought you were struggling with the moral dilemma of keeping the treasure. What happened to the lecture you gave Guey and me about doing what's right?"

"I told you I struggled with the moral dilemma - I didn't say I was perfect," he laughed, then continued. "Besides, I know there won't be any finder's fee for our discovery, and we deserve to take away something in exchange for our hard work."

Guey just looked at Junior, "Thank you," a long pause, "for everything!"

"Thank you, Guey, we couldn't have done any of it without you and the Taíno traditions."

As they neared Fajardo, the sea grew calmer, and the lush, palm-fringed coast of Puerto Rico came into view, with the distant lights of Puerto del Rey Marina glinting in the evening haze. The spinnaker, still taut, carried them effortlessly, its colors mirrored in the water's glassy surface. Guey, grinning at the helm, adjusted the course slightly, the boat responding with a graceful turn toward Fajardo's harbor. Junior and Faidh worked together to douse the spinnaker, folding its fabric as the mainsail and mizzen took over for the final approach. Pulling into the sheltered waters near Puerto del Rey, the trio felt a shared exhilaration, their day's journey a testament to the wind's power and the sea's allure. Junior took the helm and guided Dream Maker to a T-slip on the end of one of the docks. Guey and Faidh, seasoned sailors at this point, tied her off neatly, securing Dream Maker against the backdrop of Puerto Rico's vibrant shore, where the hum of evening life mingled with the lapping waves. The freedom of the open sea lingered in their bones, the spinnaker's dance a vivid memory of a day unbound, carried by the wind to a place where the world felt infinite.

Cacique Mabó, the Taíno bohitiu and Guey's Dad, stood waiting, his weathered face etched with pride and anticipation. Like Faidh two weeks earlier, he had been in the marina office when Junior's voice crackled over the radio, announcing their arrival. A local concierge rep had escorted him to the dock, allowing him to witness his son, Guey, now a seasoned sailor, return from distant seas. The sight of Dream Maker gliding in under the fading light, her hull steady in the calm waters, filled Mab'ós heart with a quiet joy he had never known. His son had ventured into the unknown and returned stronger, a man forged by the wind and waves.

Junior stepped off the boat, his feet steady on the dock as Guey disappeared below deck to gather his bags. Approaching Cacique Mabó, Junior extended a firm handshake, his other hand passing over a weathered canvas bag. "As promised," he said, his voice warm with respect.

Mabó opened the bag, his eyes scanning its contents—six stones with Taíno etchings, entrusted to Junior for safekeeping. He nodded, a faint smile breaking through his stoic expression. "Gracias." The words carried the weight of a father's gratitude, not just for the bag but for the journey that had shaped his son. The dock creaked softly under their feet, and the distant hum of Fajardo's evening life mingled with the lapping waves, grounding the moment in the vibrant pulse of Puerto Rico's coast.

Junior held Mabó's hand a moment longer, placing his free hand on the bohitiu's arm, a gesture of camaraderie. "We couldn't have done it without him. He was a little green at first, getting his sea legs, but he's become quite a sailor. He'll make an amazing Taíno bohitiu, like you." Junior's words were deliberate, knowing their weight to a father. "He's a good man." He wasn't sure if he was understood, but when he saw Mabó's eyes soften, the pride of a father and a spiritual leader shining through, he knew, because what he was conveying was beyond language; it was a fatherly bond. Behind them, Dream Maker swayed gently at anchor, her sails furled but her presence a testament to the journey's trials—storms faced, dangers outmaneuvered, and bonds forged. The Caribbean sky stretched wide above, its hues of orange and purple a silent blessing over the reunion, as the legacy of the Taíno and the spirit of the sea intertwined on the dock.

When Guey came down the ladder, Junior stepped aside to let father embrace son. But instead, Guey rushed to him, giving him a firm embrace. He whispered in Junior's ear, "Gracias, Amigo. We'll keep in touch."

Guey broke the embrace, grabbed his father's hand, and they walked away.

Junior stood on the dock and watched the two leave, as Faidh stepped to his side, slipping her hand into his, her eyes shining with tears. Her voice was thick with emotion. "He didn't say Good-bye, just Thank You."

Junior turned toward her, a tear welling in his own eye. His voice was gentle, a rough edge of emotion coloring his words. "It's ok. He did the same thing to me."

"Do you think we'll ever see him again?" She looked at him with a bit of sadness in her eyes.

"Of that, I have no doubt," Junior said thoughtfully.

As twilight draped Fajardo in a soft purple glow, Junior prepared a romantic dinner for Faidh aboard Dream Maker, the boat gently swaying in the calm waters of Puerto del Rey Marina. The scent of sizzling filet medallions on the grill, their surfaces seared to a perfect medium-rare, was drizzled with a rich mushroom balsamic reduction that simmered with earthy warmth. Beside it, sautéed garlic spinach glistened, its vibrant green a nod to the lush Puerto Rican hills visible through the open portholes. Junior uncorked a bottle of Argentinian Malbec, its deep ruby hues catching the candlelight as he poured two glasses. They sat close at the table behind the cockpit, the warm breeze carrying the faint hum of Fajardo's evening life, their plates balanced on a small table adorned with a single hibiscus flower. Each bite and sip was savored slowly, the meal a quiet celebration of their shared journey, their eyes often meeting with unspoken affection.

Over dinner, Junior and Faidh spoke of their future, their voices soft against the backdrop of lapping waves and the distant call of coquí frogs. They dreamed of new horizons—sailing to distant islands, building a life intertwined with the sea. The conversation flowed as easily as the Malbec, touching on memories of their adventure, from outrunning El Tiburón to the thrill of the spinnaker's pull. They discussed the next steps and decided that Faidh would meet Junior in Saint Lucia in just two weeks. He had already planned to meet his best friend and girlfriend there for a month-long sail up and down the Lesser Antilles. As the sun dipped below Puerto Rico's rolling hills, painting the sky in fiery oranges and pinks, they paused to watch, Faidh's hand resting in Junior's. The sunset felt like a promise, a moment of stillness after weeks of motion, binding them closer in the fading light. The world beyond Dream Maker seemed to dissolve, leaving only the warmth of their connection and the vast Caribbean night.

After dinner, they descended below deck, the cabin aglow with the soft flicker of a lantern. There, they made love, their movements tender and unhurried, a wordless affirmation of their bond forged through storms and open seas. Afterward, they lay entwined, Faidh's head nestled against Junior's chest, his arms wrapped protectively around her. The gentle rock of the boat lulled them, their breaths syncing with the rhythm of the sea, as they drifted into a deep, contented sleep.

She stood at the helm, the trade winds caressing her face, all the isinglass down to let the fresh breeze tangle through her hair like a lover's touch. The sky was a flawless azure, dotted with fluffy white clouds, and the sea shimmered a deep turquoise, calm and inviting under the golden sun. Dream Maker sailed under full canvas, her twin masts tall and proud, cutting through the waves with a graceful rhythm that felt like a heartbeat. To her left, Junior sat close, his laughter a rich melody as he teased her about her steady hand on the wheel, his arm brushing hers in a comforting warmth that made her heart swell. Beside them, a couple of friends whose faces glowed with joy joined in, their voices rising in playful banter about the horizon's endless promise.

The deck buzzed with life, the sails billowing perfectly, the hull slicing through the water with a satisfying hum. The couple, a man with a hearty laugh and a woman whose eyes sparkled with mischief, shared stories of past voyages, their laughter blending with the cries of the gulls overhead. Faidh felt the boat respond to her every command, the wind filling her sails as if in celebration, and she steered toward a distant island, its green hills rising like a welcoming embrace. Junior leaned in, whispering something about their future adventures, his smile lighting her world, and the couple raised glasses of rum in a toast to the sea's beauty. The moment wrapped around her like a warm blanket, a happiness she'd never known flooding her chest—love, contentment, and a sense of belonging that anchored her soul.

She glanced at Junior, his eyes reflecting the sun's glow, and felt an overwhelming peace, as if every storm they'd weathered had led to this perfect day. The couple danced a light step on the deck, their joy infectious, and Faidh joined in, laughing as the wind whipped through her hair, the boat gliding effortlessly. The sea stretched out in all directions, a vast canvas of possibility, and for the first time, she felt no fear—only the pure, radiant joy of being alive, loved, and free. Dream Maker seemed to sing beneath her, a vessel reborn not just for Junior, but for all of them; her journey was now a shared dream under a sky that promised forever.

Faidh awoke with a soft sigh, the dream's warmth lingering as the first light of dawn crept through the porthole, casting a gentle glow on Junior's sleeping form beside her. Her heart carried the echo of that happiness, a bittersweet comfort as she faced the reality of leaving him and Dream Maker behind. The trade wind's memory still danced in her hair, and she pressed a hand to her chest, holding onto the love and contentment that dream had gifted her, a treasure to carry into her next chapter. She looked at her phone; the Uber she had set up was already at the dock office. She leaned over, her lips brushing Junior's in a lingering kiss, her whisper soft in his ear: "I'll see you in Saint Lucia in two weeks." Slipping out of bed, she cast one last glance at him, the promise of their reunion already bright in her heart, as Dream Maker rested quietly under the first light of morning.

EPILOGUE

Junior woke alone on Dream Maker for the first time in over two weeks, the silence pressing in like heavy fog. Before Faidh came aboard, solitude felt right—a perfect fit. Now it left an ache, the cabin empty without her laugh. It had only been a couple of hours. Already, he missed her, her presence a ghost in the stillness. In two weeks, they'd reunite in Saint Lucia—her smile and warmth flooding back to fill the void. That promise kept him steady.

Before leaving Fajardo, Junior took the day to restock Dream Maker, first loading provisions for the next leg. Grateful for the U.S. port's ample supplies, he carried bags onto the boat and checked inventory before heading to the office. There, he settled the water and fuel bill while the clerk tapped the register. Junior then approached the Dock Master, asking if he'd heard about the stolen boat, El Tiburón, and mentioned that he had already reported it to the authorities at Palmas Del Mar.

The Dock Master leaned in closer, his voice dropping to a conspiratorial whisper, as if sharing a secret. "That boat, El Tiburón? Nearly met its end in Hurricane Wendy," he said with a sly grin, his eyes gleaming with a hint of satisfaction. "Lost all power and steering. Just drifted out there, like a ghost ship, till it ended up stranded over on Playa Blanco's windward side in Vieques." His tone seemed to relish the ship's misfortune. "They found two brothers knocked out cold on that wreck, arrested them right there. And listen to this," he added, barely containing his excitement, "they claim a third guy slipped away. Who knows where he is now—hiding out somewhere in Puerto Rico, maybe."

Junior's pulse quickened at the mention of the escapee. Somehow, deep down, he knew this third man held a key to unanswered questions, a thread that might weave into his own journey on Dream Maker. He nodded, noting the urgency this new piece added to his plans.

Junior nodded, "Do you know the name of the third guy that got away?"

"Sure don't," he added, "But you can probably find it on the internet."

"Yep, I'll have to check it out. Thanks for the hospitality and the update on El Tiburón. I guess we should all keep an eye out for the third guy, huh?"

The Dock Master just nodded.

Back on Dream Maker, Junior prepped her for departure and set a course for Culebra. He chose to anchor off Playa Carlos Rosario on the west side, avoiding Ensenada Honda this time. With all the time in the world, he decided to take it slow, at least for this first leg. He rigged only the Genoa and Main. As the sails caught a gentle breeze, promising four to five knots, he could hear the soft hiss of the reef-break in the distance. The scent of sea-grape mingled with the salt air, grounding him in the evening's serenity. He timed their arrival with the sun's fiery descent, watching the sky blush shades of coral and amber.

Sitting at the helm, the loneliness creeping in like a quiet tide, Junior decided to call his old Navy buddy, Trace. They'd flown FA-18s together in the early years—two and a half wild ones, raising hell and exploring the Western Pacific. Hong Kong, Thailand, and a massive trip to Australia, where they chased adventure as if it were a mission. Beyond catching up, Junior needed to confirm the last details for Trace joining him on Dream Maker in Saint Lucia—at the same time, Faidh would return. Trace and his girlfriend, Elle, were taking a month-long break through Christmas and New Year, eager to roam the Lesser

Antilles with him. Trace didn't pick up—he rarely did—so Junior hung up and sent a text: "Call when you can."

Junior set the autopilot. The sails held steady as he ducked below deck for a Diet Coke and the Pirate's Logbook from the treasure chest. They'd barely glanced at it before tucking it away from the BVI authorities. Back at the helm, he opened it carefully. The fragile pages crumbled like dry leaves under his fingers, each crackle a reminder of the precariousness of his own voyage. He was cautious not to worsen the damage, the ancient musty scent of the logbook mingling with the salt air, a reminder of both adventure and decay. Most of the pages were blank or smeared beyond reading, much like the blurred lines of his uncertain journey. He revisited the page that they read after opening the treasure—nothing new stood out. A few other pages contained faint Spanish scribbles, which were hard to decipher. On the last page, the ink was clearer: "Maria" emerged from the smears, followed by "hij" and a blurred letter, then "amorosa," and later "ojos oscuros." The bottom, spared by water, was a tangle of shaky handwriting—more scribble than words to his eye. He snapped a photo and texted it to Guey, asking if he could read and translate.

Guey's reply came quickly: *"Maria. Possibly loving daughter. Dark Eyes. Please take care of this treasure and ensure that whoever finds it is worthy. R.C."* A second text followed: *"There are more words on the page, but they are illegible; maybe in a different light, we could make out more."*

Junior texted back, *"Thanks. I think we got what we needed."*

Guey asked, *"What am I missing?"*

Junior replied, *"Cofres'ís daughter was named Maria, and I'm guessing she had dark eyes, like the spirit that you, Faidh, and I each saw in our dreams."*

Guey responded, *"Ah. That makes sense. We never discussed who she was or could have been. It appears that the logbook had more to offer than we initially thought. And clearly, Junior, you are worthy."*

Junior smiled, warmth spreading through him as he read the last text. He typed, *"I think we all were!"* and gazed out at the endless sea. The vastness of the ocean mirrored the vastness of his emotions, both infinite and profound. He felt a profound sense of connection to those he shared this journey with, past and present. Junior had always believed that the sea had a way of whispering secrets of the heart, and it was in moments like this that he understood why. His heart felt fuller, less isolated, wrapped in a tapestry of shared experiences and dreams. As Guey's words lingered with him, Junior embraced the overwhelming nostalgia that rushed through him — recalling the silent camaraderie of his Navy days. It was a reminder that true bonds transcended time and distance, offering a semblance of comfort and belonging even amidst the solitude of the vast blue.

Three dots came up once more on Junior's phone.

Then Guey's text popped up, *"I meant to tell you. On my drive back to Jayuya with my Dad, he said something exciting to me. He told me that Dream Maker is a very special boat. He said when he watched me step off and walk toward him, he could see an aura of powerful positive energy surrounding her."* A quiet moment enveloped the boat. The wind died briefly, causing the sails to flutter as if to breathe in sync with the revelation, enhancing the air of mystique surrounding Dream Maker. The faint rustle of the sea was the only sound, a gentle reminder of the vessel's soulful presence.

Junior responded as he looked around at Dream Maker's beauty and strength, *"I have no doubt. I have felt something special about this boat since the day I saw her."*

"Take good care of her. And she will do the same for you."

Three dots again.

"And anyone who is under her care."

314

ABOUT THE AUTHOR

J.J. Reich, a retired Navy and corporate pilot, is an adventurer and storyteller who splits his time between Boquerón, Puerto Rico, and St. Augustine, Florida, where he restores his sailboat, *Dream Maker*. Drawing inspiration from his love of the sea and a lifetime of adventures, J.J. weaves tales of high-stakes adventure and discovery, as seen in his *Sailing Dream Maker* series. Alongside his partner, Marcy, and his two children, Garret and Turner, he embraces a life of travel, from skiing in Steamboat Springs to sailing the Caribbean. His fascination with Puerto Rican culture, developed since moving there just a couple of years ago, infuses his writing with vibrant, authentic details. When not writing, J.J. is often found navigating the open waters or uncovering the next story hidden in the many places he explores.

www.ingramcontent.com/pod-product-compliance
Lightning Source LLC
Chambersburg PA
CBHW052016240626
47153CB00006B/1833